Raising Rain

DEBBIE FULLER THOMAS

Raising Rain

A NOVEL

MOODY PUBLISHERS
CHICAGO

Editor: Pam Pugh
Interior Design: Ragont Design
Cover Design: Studio Gearbox
Cover Image: Veer
Author Photo: Shirley Borba

Library of Congress Cataloging-in-Publication Data

Thomas, Debbie Fuller
Raising Rain / Debbie Fuller Thomas.
p. cm.
ISBN 978-0-8024-8734-6
1. Mothers and daughters—Fiction. 2. Terminally ill—Fiction. 3. Feminists—Fiction. 4. Female friendship—Fiction. 5. Domestic fiction. 6. Psychological fiction. I. Title.
PS3620.H6266R35 2009
813'.6—dc22
2009017395

Published in association with the Books & Such Literary Agency, 52 Mission Circle, Suite 122, PMB 170, Santa Rosa, CA 95409-5370, www.booksandsuch.biz.

Moody Publishers
820 N. LaSalle Boulevard
Chicago, IL 60610

1 3 5 7 9 10 8 6 4 2

Printed in the United States of America

To Don, Megan, and Ian for their support and encouragement, and to my mother for her loving example.

Chapter I

When Bebe heard that Jude Rasmussen didn't have long to live, she felt a curious mixture of sadness, guilt, and relief. Not exactly normal feelings for a friend of over thirty-five years, though you couldn't exactly describe their relationship as "normal"—more like a thinly veiled hostage situation.

"Her cancer is back," Rain said, gently swirling her coffee. "She didn't want sympathy, so she kept it to herself. I haven't connected with Mom in a while, so it wasn't hard to keep it a secret. William finally made her tell me."

Bebe put her hand on Rain's arm. "I'm sorry, honey. I guess the hysterectomy didn't help much. What can we do?"

Rain glanced up at the line of people snaking around their small table and leaned in toward Bebe. "Well, actually, she had her reasons for giving in to William and agreeing to tell me. I'm here on a mission." She winced.

Bebe leaned in as well. "Go ahead. What is it?"

"She wants to have a Celebration of Life before she dies. Not a memorial—a send-off, she calls it. One last chance to do something significant and she wants us all to help plan it. You, me, the old college roommates. You know Mom. It's got to be something big. I'm not exactly sure what she has in mind, but it sounds . . . complicated."

Bebe blew out a breath and sat back in her chair. "That's putting it mildly." Then she added, "Oh, I'm sorry, Rain."

"Don't worry. I know what she's like. I've been her daughter for thirty-seven years." Rain glanced at the time on her cell phone and gathered her wallet and sunglasses. "I've got to go. I can't be late again. Loren's just looking for an excuse to replace me as the lead on this Murrieta project."

Bebe gathered her purse and dug for her keys as they headed out the door into the heat of the morning. The blast of dry air baked her skin, absorbing the layer of SPF 30 she'd slathered on to prevent more freckles. They crossed the parking lot to where their cars sat side by side like a pair of mismatched shoes.

Bebe paused to give Rain a hug before she got in, and caught the unexpected scent of baby powder. "I'll call you later to see how you're doing. And of course I'll call Toni and Mare."

They got into their cars and Bebe cranked up the air conditioning. Immediately, her cell phone rang, and Rain's number displayed.

"You forget something?" Bebe asked, looking through her window into Rain's car. Rain looked back from the driver's seat, her eyes hidden behind sunglasses.

"Mom's timing couldn't have been more perfect." There was a long pause. Bebe could hear the insistent warning of an unfastened seatbelt. "Hayden and I split up."

"Oh, Rain—"

"It doesn't matter. I don't need him. I can have a baby by myself. Love you." Bebe heard Rain's cell phone snap shut and watched her glance over her shoulder and back her car into the street. Then she was gone.

❖ ❖ ❖ ❖

Bebe raced home brooding on what Rain had told her and pulled her lavender scrubs with the black pawprints from the dryer. She'd been on-call the night before, and Mr. Woofles had suffered a severe asthma attack at 1:00 a.m. She needed to get in early and work him into her packed appointment calendar.

Bebe drove across town, parked in one of the clinic's few employee-parking stalls and slipped into the staff entrance. A whiff of betadyne and the whine of pups from the kennels greeted her, and she sat down at her desk to check her e-mail. She pushed back a pile of mail from pharmaceutical companies that threatened to slide onto the floor when she jiggled her mouse. She checked the charts of two patients who'd undergone procedures the day before, but nothing demanded her immediate attention. She listened to her voice mail, deleting old reminders to pick up hair color and her prescription at the pharmacy. Leaving herself messages had become a necessity of late.

"Hey," Neil said, coming up behind her. She tilted her head back and he kissed her forehead. "I think I heard Mr. Woofles complaining in room five."

Bebe closed her e-mail, and a picture of her boys, Scott and Dylan, smiled at her from her computer desktop. Their white teeth flashed in their tanned faces against a backdrop of snow, sugar pines, and blue sky. She felt Neil's hands resting on her shoulders, and they shared a moment of appreciation for their handsome family.

"They'll be fine," he said.

She reached up and touched his hand. "I know. It's just hard that they're both leaving within a few weeks of each other."

He gave her shoulders a light squeeze and sat down behind her at his desk.

"Oh, I had coffee with Rain this morning." Bebe twisted around to face Neil, who was leafing through a file on his desk. "She had two pieces of bad news. Unfortunately, she and Hayden have called it quits, and Jude's cancer is back. I guess her prognosis isn't good."

Neil looked up. "That's too bad. Any idea what happened between her and Hayden?"

"It must have something to do with having a baby. She's determined to have one by herself." She reached behind her head with a ponytail band around her wrist, and in smooth strokes, wove her hair into a French braid. "I thought they would be moving toward marriage by this time."

Neil whistled. "I always pictured Hayden as a family guy."

"So did I. I suspect there's more to it."

"How's she taking the news about her mom?"

"She seemed to be fine, but Jude wants some kind of last hurrah before she dies, and she wants me, Mare, and Toni to help plan it. And of course, Rain."

Neil shook his head. "Always in control, right up to the end. Do you think Mare and Toni will cooperate?"

Bebe stood and draped her stethoscope around her neck. "They'll do it for Rain, if for no other reason."

Bebe stopped outside the door to room five and removed the chart from the holder, taking a quick overview of the tech's notes. She briefly knocked and opened the door, breezing in to take the small rolling seat with a greeting to Mr. Woofles's owner.

"So, Mr. Woofles, I heard you had a bad night." She let Mr. Woofles sniff her hand and reached out to scratch behind his soft, floppy ears. He moaned low in his throat. She pulled back the skin from his eyes, and then from his mouth to examine his teeth. "Looks like you're due for a cleaning. When you're feeling better."

He stood long enough for her to listen to his heart and lungs, and then sank down onto the cool linoleum with a *humpf* and the jingle of his tags hitting the floor. His lungs were free of the cackles and wheezes typically associated with asthma.

"Okay, this morning we'll do a chest X-ray to rule out the possibility of pneumonia or heart failure. If it's clear, we'll try some antihistamines. But call me if he has another severe attack because you may have to bring him in for a shot of steroids. I'd keep him inside out of the heat as much as possible. It would also help if you had a cold-mist humidifier running at night. I would remove any cleansers from his area,

and make sure no one smokes around him until we determine what triggers these attacks." His big eyes rolled up to keep an eye on her.
"Don't worry, Mr. Woofles," Bebe assured him. "We'll get this figured out."

* * * *

Rain pulled into the parking lot at Steele, VonTrapp, and Evers and squeezed her Hyundai into a narrow compact space near the front of the building. She shimmied out the door, barely grazing the Honda Civic parked beside her, and hurried into the air-conditioned lobby.

She slid into her cubicle and shoved her purse beneath her desk with her foot. Then, she quickly logged on to her computer and spread her papers around to give the impression she'd been in the middle of a project instead of arriving twelve minutes late to work. She glanced down the row and saw Lisa shaking her head in playful disbelief over the top of her cubicle.

Her morning consisted of reviewing new legislation and forwarding updated information regarding mortgage lending and foreclosures to the attorneys. She drafted letters to clients whose contracts were pending and set appointments to review the contracts of others. Twice, she visited an Internet site for discounted baby furniture.

Rain stayed inside out of the heat at lunch and bought a deli sandwich from the food cart to eat at her desk. She tilted her computer screen just enough so that passersby wouldn't get a full view as she Googled "donor catalog search." She pulled up a blank questionnaire for a sperm donor and played around at filling in the blanks. A tall Caucasian with brown hair and eyes and medium skin tone who was an athletic Stanford grad with an engineering degree would cost her just $15,000. Fifteen thousand dollars. Rain slowly chewed her sandwich. Wow. A mental calculation revealed she was two thousand dollars short in her savings. And that didn't include any fertility procedures.

She'd had no idea how much a sperm donor could cost. But until Hayden left, she'd had no reason to know. She could settle for less than the perfect donor, but would she regret it? If she spent all her savings, how would she pay for child care?

What was the perfect baby worth in terms of dollars and cents?

By rights, it shouldn't be costing her more than a room remodel to transform their extra bedroom into a nursery. *Her* empty bedroom now.

She should have seen it coming with Hayden. Over the past year she'd dropped subtle hints about wanting a baby. She dragged him to their friends' baby showers, and finally, when they were the last couple in their group to be childless, she came right out and announced that it was time. He disagreed. The more she pushed, the harder he dug in his heels and grew distant, and when she more or less gave him an ultimatum, he left. Just like that.

She couldn't understand his problem with having a baby. He'd had a normal, happy childhood, and even his mother had mentioned that she looked forward to being a grandmother. Maybe that was it. Maybe his mother's interference had tipped the scale.

Rain never would have brought up the subject of grandchildren to her own mother. Jude wasn't the maternal type. Rain had been a mistake, herself.

A baby planned and wanted isn't a mistake. Rain picked up her cell phone, scrolled down her list of contacts to the number of her ob-gyn and hit *send*.

* * * *

Bebe heated her leftover pizza in the staff kitchen microwave and sat down at her desk to leave Rain a voice mail. She was surprised when Rain answered on the first ring.

"What's up, Bebe? I can't talk long. I'm waiting for a call-back from Dr. Lazenby's office," Rain said.

"Why, are you sick?"

"No, that's my gynecologist."

Bebe took a moment to dab pizza sauce from her mouth. "Your yearly checkup?"

"Not exactly." Rain paused, and her voice level dropped dramatically. "I've been checking out this sperm donor site and I want to get things rolling."

Bebe sat back in her chair and sighed imperceptibly at Rain's doggedness.

"Maybe you could give me some advice," Rain said. "You know a lot about assisted reproduction."

"For animals, not humans. You'd better stick to your gynecologist," Bebe said. "I called to remind you about Scotty's going-away barbeque at Mom's a week from Saturday before he leaves for boot camp."

"Sure, I'll be there. But I need to go. I don't want to miss the callback from the doctor's office."

"Rain, aren't you jumping the gun a little here? How long has Hayden been gone?"

Rain was silent for a moment—a clear sign of annoyance. "Three weeks. And, no, I'm not jumping the gun. He's not interested in having kids. Period. He made that very clear. And I'm not interested in having kids with him, anyway. He's out of my life."

"But you two were together for a long time. Six—seven years? Maybe in time this will work itself out."

"He's coming by to pick up the rest of his stuff when he gets back from his vacation in Mexico." Rain paused. "He's practically allergic to tropical sunshine. I don't think it will work itself out."

Bebe hung up and sat for a moment processing everything Rain had said, and the things she had not. Clearly, Rain was not addressing the real issue. It was just like her to become immersed in something to avoid facing the truth that she loved and missed Hayden, and that there could possibly be other reasons for his leaving. Maybe even that she needed him more than she cared to admit. She remembered Rain telling her sometime in the past year that Hayden had actually brought up the idea of marriage, and that Rain had flatly told him no. When it came to marriage, she was more like her mother than she knew.

They had known Hayden for a long time. Maybe she could talk Neil into meeting him for coffee and working a little magic.

⁂ ⁂ ⁂ ⁂

Bebe woke up the next morning to an orange glow and the acrid smell of smoke. She reached over her head and slid the window shut, then rolled over and turned off the alarm before it rang. She'd caught the late news about the fires on the coast and hoped their clients would be smart enough to keep their pets inside on days like these when the smoke from the coast bumped up against the foothills and settled into the cracks.

She fed and watered Jimbo and Suzie, the two retrievers they had acquired five years before when a desperate owner tied their leashes to a light pole in front of the clinic in the dead of night and bolted. The incident had prompted Neil to install a surveillance camera on the front of their clinic. They'd tried to find someone to adopt the dogs, but ended up keeping the gentle pair after Scott and Dylan grew attached. Now the dogs were showing signs of age and she hoped that nothing would happen while Scott was away at boot camp. She let them out to do their business and put them back inside for the day. She or Neil would have to slip away at lunchtime to give them a potty break.

Her Toyota sat in the driveway lightly dusted with ash like an unexpected snowfall. She resisted the urge to look up at the vibrant sun colored neon orange by a veil of smoke and haze. She dug out her sunglasses and slipped them on.

It was her day in surgery, but she took time to check in with Mr. Woofles's owner as soon as she got to her desk. He was keeping the dog inside out of the smoke and things were going well.

After two castrations and the removal of an abdominal tumor, Bebe took a break at her desk. She called her mother to firm up the menu for the going-away barbeque and to remind her mother of her offer to contact all the family in the area, which was a task Bebe didn't have the time to do. Besides, it would give her mother the opportunity to brag on Scotty for joining the Marine Reserves. Bebe also told her about Jude's illness.

Neil had to work late again—a consequence of being one of the few large animal doctors in the area. Bebe left work and swung by the Colonel's for chicken on the way home.

Standing outside her front door with her arms full, she could hear music pounding inside and feel the door vibrating. She rang the doorbell several times with no response, and after juggling her bags, finally managed to open the door for herself. She came in, irritated, and found the boys in the family room engrossed in Rock Band. They didn't even hear her come in.

"Guys, turn it down please," she shouted, setting down a tub of fried chicken on the kitchen counter.

Dylan grabbed the remote and quickly lowered the volume. "Sorry! We didn't hear you."

Scotty's fingers flew to match the frenetic pace of the notes scrolling down on the TV screen. The guitar rested against his stomach and connected him to the TV by an umbilical cord of cable. Dylan wailed on a drum set. As the song ended, the virtual crowd cheered and their scores appeared on the screen. The room buzzed with silence.

"Why aren't you playing this downstairs in your room?" she asked, pulling cans from her grocery bag.

"This screen's bigger. The sound's better, too."

Another song began, which Bebe recognized as "Fortunate Son" by Creedence Clearwater Revival. She frowned. Turning away, she popped the lid on two cans of green beans and dumped them into a pot on the stove, splashing juice onto the burner. The words of the song were haunting and familiar, and she watched the liquid sizzle until it evaporated. She set the oven for broil and wrestled with a stubborn baking rack to position it closer to the flame. She chipped a mug unloading the dishwasher and mixed up the forks with the spoons in the drawer. By the end of the song, she found she was gritting her teeth and forced herself to relax her jaw. "Won't Get Fooled Again" by The Who started up. She pulled out a loaf of French bread and messily slathered more garlic butter onto the soft middles than was necessary. Midway through the song, Bebe turned to the boys with her hand on her hip, pointing the buttered knife at the TV.

"Don't they have anything besides this old stuff?" she said, raising her voice to be heard over the music.

Scott called over his shoulder, "Yeah, but the oldies are great. You and dad probably know them. Grateful Dead, CCR, Guess Who."

Bebe turned back to her bread and stretched her neck, side to side. She placed the loaf on a cookie sheet buttered side up and slid the pan into the oven, slamming the oven door a little too hard.

The Guess Who started playing "American Woman," and Bebe's stomach tightened. Amazing, how a song can transport you back to one distinct moment in time, to a place you don't want to be.

Scott called over his shoulder without breaking rhythm, "This was a war protest song. Did you know that, Mom?" He played a riff. "She's the Statue of Liberty."

"Yes, I heard that somewhere," she said. "Scott, shouldn't you be working out?"

"Already did," he called without looking up. "I'm up to eleven pull-ups, and I ran three miles."

When the bread and green beans were done, she set the table and they reluctantly took a break to eat.

"Do these songs bring back the good old days, Mom?" Scotty asked as he dug in the bucket for a chicken breast.

Bebe stabbed a few green beans with her fork. "I wouldn't exactly call them the good old days. And I wasn't crazy about some of the songs because I disagreed with the message."

"But this is great stuff. They're classics."

"They're classics now. You can listen to them because you like the style and the impact the era had on rock music. You can detach yourself from the lyrics. But if you liked this kind of music back then, you were pretty much aligning yourself with the artist and his message."

He shrugged. "Anyway, that was then."

After dinner, the boys picked up Rock Band where they'd left off. Neil came in at 8:30 and wolfed down his warmed dinner. He became interested in the music, and was soon planted in front of the television with them. It was still loud, but how could she complain when in just one week Scotty would go to boot camp and in four weeks Dylan would be away at college? They would both be changed, and she couldn't cheat them out of this time together.

Bebe took her cell phone into her bedroom to the relative quiet at the back of the house. She closed her bedroom door and tuned the radio on her nightstand to a classical station. Then she called Mare and Toni and broke the news about Jude. Both were sorry to hear that her cancer had returned and were concerned about Rain. Bebe didn't feel like it was her place to share Rain's bad news about Hayden, so she kept it to herself. She considered inviting them to Scott's going-away party, but decided against it. Except for Rain, who had practically been a member of the family, she couldn't very well invite one of her old roommates without inviting them all. And that would be a mistake.

They agreed to meet on the following Saturday to discuss Jude's Celebration of Life at Dulcinea's, an organic restaurant in Davis, where Mare could have something vegan and Toni could still have a mimosa.

Lastly, Bebe punched in Jude's number and waited, almost hoping she wouldn't pick up so that Bebe could just leave a message. How cowardly she felt. William answered, saying that, thank heavens, Jude was asleep.

"Please let her know that we're meeting at Dulcinea's in Davis on Saturday at noon to plan her celebration. Do you think she'll be feeling up to it?"

"She should be. She doesn't have a treatment scheduled until the following week, but she'll tire easily."

"How is she, William?"

He sighed. "Difficult. She'd probably divorce me, if we were married. But we both know that would never happen." He chuckled grimly.

"I'm sorry you're in a bad place. She can't be easy to care for."

"No, she's not. Still, as cantankerous as she is, it's hard to see her like this."

"Do you have a friend or someone to talk with about it?"

"Not unless my therapist qualifies."

Bebe was surprised at his candor and imagined how isolated he must be feeling.

"Rain just told me about it yesterday," she said. "Why didn't Jude tell anyone before this?"

"Pride. You wouldn't know now, if she hadn't thought up this Celebration of Life."

"Is there anything I can do?" Bebe offered. "I could drive over."

"That's not a good idea right now. She would probably see it as pity, since you haven't seen each other for a while. Just keep her involved in the celebration planning. She won't be satisfied unless she thinks she's in charge of the whole thing."

Bebe heard the weariness in his voice. "It sounds like you could use a day off. Would you rather that we come to your house instead? San Francisco isn't that much farther for us than Davis. You could have the morning all to yourself."

"No, I think I'll explore Davis while you're having lunch and come back when you're done. Don't worry about me."

He promised to let Jude know about the luncheon, and Bebe hung up. She imagined William sitting in their living room with every piece of artwork leveled exactly one hand-width above the furniture, his architectural magazines stacked precisely on the glass coffee table, restacking them alphabetically with his fingernails clipped to a thin moon of white. Jude was the one thing in his life he couldn't control, no matter how he tried.

The strains of "Carry On Wayward Son" filtered through the bedroom wall. She wanted to go out to the family room and spend the rest of the evening with Neil and the boys, but the music made her uncomfortable, even though she found herself tapping her foot with the beat.

She didn't want to nag them or interfere with their "guy time." Considering where they were each headed, the boys would both be exposed to much more than classic rock lyrics soon enough.

In a few weeks, there would be just her and Neil again, and, guys being guys, there weren't many ways for the boys to connect with her as it was. They'd gone out for pizza as a family every Friday night, until the boys started dating and preferred going out with friends instead.

They'd all gone to church together, until the college-aged class began meeting on Saturday nights instead of Sunday mornings. She longed for the days when they could all agree on a movie to watch and spend the evening together eating popcorn and laughing. Those days were gone. Perhaps it was the combination of the looming empty nest, the fact that Scott and Dylan were already distancing themselves, that Rain was broken and searching, or that Jude was terminally ill. Perhaps it was the music of a turbulent generation subtly underscoring everything. She suddenly felt overwhelmed and vulnerable, and got ready for bed.

But one question presented itself to Bebe in sharp relief about the celebration of Jude's life. Did she really want to celebrate the life of someone whose influence had almost caused her to lose her way?

Chapter 2

Bebe was already waiting at the table at Dulcinea's on Saturday when Toni and Mare arrived—Toni a fragrant and elegant orchid to Mare's simple sweet alyssum. They both hugged her and settled their high-backed rattan chairs closer to the table.

"So where's the guest of honor?" Toni asked, waving her manicured hand to the server. "Fashionably late again?"

"Toni, be good," Mare chided.

The server came to their table and introduced himself as "Rolf."

"Mimosa, please, Rolf," Toni said, flashing him a sly smile.

Bebe ordered iced tea and Mare ordered hot chamomile.

Toni rolled her eyes at Mare when the server left. "You're still drinking that stuff? Honey, when are you going to grow up?"

Mare looked offended. "Chamomile is very—"

"Ladies," Bebe said, "let's all play nice and this morning will move along faster."

"All right. Sorry, Mare," Toni said, air kissing her across the table. "I guess I'm a bit stressed about today."

"I think we all feel that way," Bebe said.

"So, what exactly did Rain say about her mom when you talked to her?" Mare asked.

"You can ask her yourself. Here she comes." Bebe waved to Rain who stood at the entrance scanning the tables. She headed toward them, weaving through the elephant ear palms that made each table into an island of its own. They fawned over her like she was three years old again.

Bebe pulled out a chair beside her and Rain settled into it.

"What did Mom say when you called her about today?" Rain asked her.

"She was asleep, but William said he'd make sure she got here."

Rain's countenance carried the weight of too many worries, and frown lines had already deepened between her brows. While Toni shamelessly admired the servers and Mare prompted her to act her age, Bebe took advantage of their distractedness to ask Rain how things were going.

"Hayden and I haven't spoken, if that's what you mean." She glanced nervously at the entrance. "Did you say anything?"

"I haven't said a word."

Rain frowned. "I don't care if they know Hayden moved out. They're going to find out anyway. I just don't want to discuss why yet."

Toni's voice rose. "Not only is Marin closer than San Jose, but they were doing work on the Benicia Bridge and I had to allow two hours just to get here." She immediately turned apologetic eyes to Rain. "Not that I'm complaining. You know I'd do anything for you."

Mare *hmphed* and took the teacup from the server who appeared at her elbow. Toni threw an admiring look at the young man and daintily took the champagne glass from him with her diamond rings twinkling.

"Toni, you're shameless," Mare scolded as he left. "You do realize he's young enough to be your son."

"I don't want him to marry my daughter, I just want to look." Toni took a sip of her mimosa.

"You don't have a daughter," Mare pointed out, dunking her teabag into the hot water.

"I have a stepdaughter, poor old thing. And Rolf is decidedly too good for Alfie. She wears Birkenstocks."

"Toni," Bebe warned.

Mare's jaw dropped. "There is nothing wrong with—"

"I only meant that she's . . . boring." Toni waved away the visual.

"Ladies, Mom's here," Rain broke in.

Bebe looked from Rain's solemn face to the entrance. Jude stood looking down her nose at the restaurant patrons, framed by the arched doorway with her jacket draped over her arm like a modern-day Nero scanning the restaurant for survivors.

Toni turned back to the group. "We could duck under the table. She'd never find us in this jungle."

Mare flapped her hand to shush her and Toni chuckled. "Just joking, Rain."

Bebe waved and Jude lifted her chin when she saw them. "Here she is," Bebe said under her breath. "Now behave."

Jude carefully navigated her way through the tables and they greeted her with smiles.

"We'd give you hugs, but we know you're not the huggy type," Mare explained.

"Thank you for that," Jude said.

The only open chair was across the table from Bebe. As Jude settled into it, Bebe saw her take note of Rain's close proximity to Bebe.

"Would you like to switch places with me?" Bebe offered.

"Of course not. I'm fine right where I am." Then she scrunched up her nose as though some smell offended her. "But I would prefer if Toni would switch seats with Mare. Your perfume is overwhelming."

Toni opened her mouth to protest, but checked herself and gave Jude an overly sweet smile. "And I was so frugal with it this morning."

Mare got up to switch seats. "What do you wear now? It smells nice." She lifted her nose to an invisible scent. "It's different."

"It's my own fragrance. The last time Lawrence took me to Cannes we stopped by Gasse and toured the perfume shops. He had it specially made for me, and I'm almost out. You can tell it has base notes of cinnamon." She extended her wrist to Mare, and then to Rain and Bebe. "It's obscenely expensive."

Rain said that it was sensual, and Bebe added, "We always knew when Toni was home because of the cloud of Chantilly that settled over the house."

Jude added, "We hung gas masks by the front door."

Toni shrugged, lifting her hands in surrender. "It was my signature scent, what can I say?"

"I see you're still wearing purple," Jude said to Bebe, nodding at her shirt.

Bebe glanced down at her V-necked top with the white camisole peeking from the front and didn't know how to respond. Was that supposed to be a slight? "It's not *purple*," she said, shaking the word loose. "It's a tasteful, understated . . . plum."

Jude hiked her eyebrows as though Bebe were only fooling herself.

"Bebe, you look good in shades of purple," Rain said, coming to her aid. "It complements your skin tone."

Bebe flashed Rain a discreet grin.

Rolf returned to the table to take their orders since their entire party had arrived. Jude ordered only pomegranate juice. Mare took her time ordering, asking for detailed descriptions of each entrée she was interested in. Toni thought she took way too long, and told her so when the server left.

"I care what I put into my body. What's wrong with that?" Mare answered.

"Do you really think it matters? You used to eat sugar by the spoonful. It's a bit late to start worrying now."

"It's never too late to be concerned about your . . . health." Mare's eyes slid to Jude and her voice trailed off.

Rolf refilled Bebe's iced tea and slipped away before she could get his attention. "I was going to ask him if they had any sweetener." As soon as the words left her mouth, she looked up at Mare. "Oops."

"Bebe, sweeteners are just little packets of chemicals. How many times have I told you?"

"Too many." Toni rolled her eyes and took another sip of her mimosa.

Rain nodded toward the next table. "There's organic sweetener over there. You want me to get some?"

"No, this is fine," Bebe assured her, reaching for the raw sugar. She spooned it into her tea and it sank to the bottom of her glass like tiny aquarium pebbles. "So, how's your boutique doing, Mare?"

"Very well, since we reopened last February. We have a beautiful new line of natural fiber clothing from bamboo and hemp. But we're finding that we have to be careful about our suppliers, because not all the hemp clothing we're getting is organic."

"Hemp?" Bebe repeated, stumbling over the word.

"Yes. In fact, you might be interested in a new line of hemp linen scrubs that I found recently. They're incredibly soft and easy to care for."

Toni jumped in. "And if they shrink in the wash, you can roll them up and smoke them in your pipe."

Mare dismissed her and continued. "And bamboo doesn't require fertilizers or pesticides, so it's ecofriendly. I just designed a line of gorgeous caftans in earth tones. You should visit our new website."

Toni tilted her head and waggled her champagne glass. "Mare, I hate to break it to you, but friends don't let friends wear caftans."

Mare turned to Toni. "Now, that's just your opinion."

"It was on *What Not to Wear* just last week." Toni pointed her finger at Rain. "Rain, back me up on this."

Rain lifted her hands in defense. "No comment."

"This woman had a closet full of caftans that were ugly and baggy with huge flowered prints, like these seat cushions. Very 'old lady'. They gathered them all and tossed them in the trash."

Mare shot back, "Well, you're an old lady now. Maybe I'll whip up a very special caftan for you. One with a wild tie-dyed print like that tunic you wore every single day of your freshman year."

Toni beamed with the memory. "I wore it with style, didn't I? And

I had a macramé bag with an extra-long strap that elongated my body."

Rain leaned toward Bebe and asked, "Were they always this bad?"

"Yes," Bebe answered emphatically. Both Mare and Toni stopped mid-argument and looked at her. "Can you imagine the four of us living in the same apartment house for four years? It's a wonder they didn't kill each other."

Toni lifted a penciled eyebrow and tilted her head at Rain. "You were there, too, little missy. I remember the time you stuck a fork into the electrical socket in the kitchen. Scared us crazy. It's a wonder you survived at all."

Mare added, "I remember that you were forever cutting teeth. The drool just soaked up all your little T-shirts. We knew what you'd eaten by the color of the stains. Some stains weren't identifiable, as I recall. And you absolutely refused to wear bibs."

"I wasn't merely a baby, I was a social experiment." Rain glanced up at the handsome young server as he sat her plate of tilapia and mango chutney in front of her, and she flushed pink.

Bebe had visions of two-year-old Rain in her little girl undies sitting in an inflatable kiddie pool on the sideyard of the Victorian they all shared. Drinking out of plastic butter tubs and spitting the water back into the pool. Leaves and blades of grass floating in the water that her bare feet had tracked in. Her wispy brown hair sticking to her forehead and neck. The way she folded up in your arms when you wrapped her in a towel.

"So, what are you up to, Toni?" Jude asked. "Still a kept woman?"

Toni smiled demurely as Rolf set a salad before her. She waited until he'd left to answer. "I don't *have* to work, if that's what you mean. It's not a crime to marry rich, you know."

Jude tapped her finger on the tablecloth. "Betty Friedan is spinning in her grave."

"Well, spin, spin, spin," Toni answered, drizzling dressing over her greens while giving her a playful smirk. "Betty might be surprised."

"Remind me what Lawrence does again?" Bebe asked, changing the subject.

"He gives away grant money to colleges. That's how we met."

Rain leaned forward. "Tell me about it."

Toni smiled dreamily. "He came to the journalism department where I taught and, what do you know? My department got the grant. We had a lot of competition from other departments. A lot of jealous little girls, but, I don't know, something evidently tipped the scale in my favor."

Mare muttered, "Spare us the details."

Bebe asked, "Do you still write?"

Toni looked up, surprised.

"You wrote stories when we were in school. Some of them were pretty good, as I remember. One was published in the school's journal."

Toni shrugged. "I write a little. Whenever the mood strikes."

Bebe saw Mare glance covertly at Toni. Toni asked about Neil and the clinic, and Bebe answered that everything was going fine.

Jude examined her fingernails. "If you had stayed in nursing instead of going to veterinary school, you could be my hospice nurse."

"Well, you dodged *that* bullet," Toni blurted. Everyone looked horrified at Toni, and she waved her hand. "Sorry Jude—it's the mimosa talking."

Bebe folded her arms. "I remember how enthusiastic you were when I chose this field. Back then you said nursing was for smart but unenlightened women who thought it wasn't their place to be doctors."

"And I was right. As I recall, you were one of only five women in your graduating class."

"We're back in the saddle again," Toni said, under her breath.

Mare chuckled. "Next, we'll be protesting at recruiting stations all over California."

"Well, I'm out," Bebe said, before taking a sip of her drink and avoiding eye contact with anyone.

"But it would be like old times," Mare said, teasing. "You used to drop everything for a protest."

Bebe looked at her like she had lobsters coming out of her ears. "You're delusional, Mare. I did not."

Mare glanced at the others. "Wow, that struck a nerve. Sorry, Bebe."

Toni leaned across the table toward Mare. "What planet have you been on? Scotty joined up. He's a leatherhead now."

Bebe corrected her, "Leather*neck,* Toni."

Toni shrugged. "Same thing. Different body part."

"My, my," Jude said quietly. "So our boy's gone over to the dark side."

"He's my boy," Bebe told Jude pointedly. "And he's very much not on the dark side."

"Of course he's not," Mare said, shaking her head. "But, how did it happen?"

"Neil and I came back from our vacation in Maui and he'd enlisted with a friend."

Mare reached over and squeezed Bebe's arm. "I always felt sorry for you, stuck in that house without a single female to balance all that testosterone."

"She always had Rain," Jude said. There was a long, awkward moment before Bebe answered as though she hadn't heard.

"For the time being, I have a houseful of men. But Dylan is starting school at McFarlane in a few weeks, and Scott has to report to the recruiting office a week from tomorrow."

"Isn't there anything you can do to stop him?" Mare asked.

Bebe deliberately kept her gaze steady and averted from Mare. "This is something he's always wanted to do. Neil and I have seen it coming for a long time. It's not anything we have control over. And no matter how we feel about the situation, we support him one hundred percent. At least he's in the reserves. He should be home for Christmas."

Jude sat back in her chair with a grim look on her face. "Has he seen the news clipping?"

Bebe lifted her chin. "No, he hasn't. And there's no reason to show it to him. That was more than thirty years ago and anyway, things were different then."

"I wonder if your brother feels the same way."

Toni scowled at Jude and turned to Bebe. "Tell Scotty we're proud of him, Bebe. And give me his address so I can send him something nice at boot camp."

"Sure, Bebe. Arnie and I will write, too." Mare grew thoughtful. "I don't know, Toni. Can they accept packages in boot camp? I found a recipe for high-energy granola bars that would pack well and they're so healthy. I can make some for you, too, if you like, Jude."

Jude stared down Mare, who said, "Or not."

"It must be hard to have them both leave at the same time, Bebe. That old empty nest thing," Toni said. "Not that I ever had one. Lawrence's nest was empty when I married him."

"I haven't had one either," Mare said with a sigh. "They won't leave. Autumn split with Ty and brought the kids home to live with us, just when Crystal finally got her own place with Barrett."

"So, Rain, how is your significant other?" Jude asked, swirling the ice in her glass.

Rain had been sitting back, listening to the conversation, but Jude had radar for such things. "I haven't seen Hayden lately. He, um, we decided to call it quits."

Mare crooned, "Oh honey, I'm so sorry."

Toni was assuring Rain that she would find someone better soon, when Mare broke in, "Was he cheating on you? Because there have been times over the years that Arnie cheated on me, and let me tell you, sometimes I think it would have been easier to just throw him out and start over."

Toni looked at Mare, incredulous. "He was cheating on his first wife with you when you met him in art class. With you and probably every other female student in Design."

Mare glanced at the people at the table near them and motioned for Toni to keep her voice down. "Well, that's exactly what's kept me from throwing the first stone, so to speak."

Jude said to Mare, "You should pay him back in kind. He certainly deserves it."

Mare's jaw dropped. Then she added, lowering her voice, "What would Autumn and Crystal say? Besides, it would be a sin."

"That old Catholic guilt," Jude said. "You never get away from it."

"Leave her alone, Jude," Bebe said.

Jude looked up sharply, and then her countenance relaxed. "Oh, that's right, you're religious now."

Bebe let it go. This wasn't the time or the place to continue the argument between Jude's idea of being religious and Bebe's of making peace with her Creator.

"Well, at least I married him." Mare twirled her wedding ring with her thumb. "I started going to Mass again, too."

Toni leaned in, resting her elbow on the table and her chin on her knuckles. "So tell us, Rain, did you throw Hayden out? Because if you did, I'm sure you had a very good reason, which you don't have to tell us, if you don't want to."

"No, it was nothing like that. We just had . . . differences. That's all." She folded her arms and glanced over at Bebe. "I don't feel like talking about it."

Bebe looked up to find Jude studying her.

"You don't seem surprised, Bebe. I guess you already knew."

Bebe didn't look at Rain. "Well, we have coffee together occasionally. It's hard to keep something like that a secret for long."

"And other secrets, too, perhaps." Jude slowly extricated herself from the oversized chair and excused herself to go to the restroom.

They all relaxed, exhaling.

"Wow." Mare folded her arms across her chest. "We haven't even discussed the Celebration of Life yet."

"Maybe today we can get an idea of just what she has in mind, and we can meet later to divvy up the responsibilities," said Bebe.

Mare snorted. "You think she's going to let us do that? When has she ever relinquished control of anything?"

"She doesn't look well," Toni said, then realized and reached across to gently tweak Rain's arm. "Sorry, darling."

The server refreshed their drinks and left the bill on the table. The conversation paused awkwardly when Jude came back to the table and slowly settled into her chair.

Bebe plunged in. "How are you doing, Jude?"

"Well, my oncologist says I'm dying."

Bebe saw her glance around the table, noting their reactions.

Mare's focus shifted to the centerpiece of exotic flowers in the middle of the table and Toni ran her finger around the base of her champagne glass while sneaking a look at Rain.

"But that's why we're here, isn't it?" Jude continued. "It's been years since we've all connected. I'm not surprised that it would take something this drastic to get us all back together." Jude took a sip of her pomegranate juice. "It seems appropriate that it should just be the five of us again. Just like the old days."

"Mom," Rain said, giving her a chastising look.

"Sorry, dear. This is difficult for you, isn't it?"

"Of course it is," Rain said, "but it's hard for everyone to find time when we all have busy schedules, and we live hours from each other in every direction. William had to—"

"William didn't have to 'anything.' I drove myself here."

They all looked at her. Suddenly she appeared tired and drawn, with more wrinkles than her age should have to account for.

She lifted her chin defiantly. "What?"

"You look great, Jude," Mare said. "We just want to make sure you're taking care of yourself, that's all."

"I've taken care of myself for fifty-seven years. I guess I can continue to do it."

Rain looked away, seeming frustrated.

"So, what exactly did you have in mind when you said you wanted a Celebration of Life?" Bebe asked.

Jude laced her fingers and rested her elbows on the armrests like a queen on a throne. "I want us all to go away for a weekend somewhere to plan one last contribution. One last chance to make a difference. For me, at least. You all seem to have an unlimited amount of time at your disposal."

They each sat silently brooding. Toni squinted at Jude. "When you say 'make a difference,' what exactly do you mean?"

Jude looked at her like she was dense. "What do you think I mean? I mean that we used to believe in things, we championed causes, we weren't afraid to speak out. Don't you remember the university, putting ourselves on the line for what we believed in?"

Toni lowered her voice. "That was almost forty years ago, Jude."

Mare protested, "We're too old for that stuff. I was joking about picketing the recruiters' stations. I'm a business-owner now."

Jude closed her eyes for a few moments and the others glanced at each other. Finally, she opened them and said in an overly patient voice, "It's not that we're too old for that, Mare, but there are more efficient means to use now. We need to brainstorm." She looked around at her subjects. "So, which weekend is good for all of you?"

❖ ❖ ❖ ❖

They had to settle on the second weekend in December to meet for Jude's Celebration of Life. Rain wished they didn't have to wait so long, but everyone had commitments. Mare had to prepare for a big organic textile show in Atlanta set for October, and Toni and Lawrence had scheduled a villa in Tuscany for four weeks, followed by a trip to New York. Scott would graduate from boot camp in October, followed by ten days' leave before he had to report back to Camp Pendleton. Bebe vehemently guarded that time, saying she would have almost no contact with Scott for the thirteen weeks that he would be gone. Thanksgiving came soon after. Rain told Bebe privately that her mother had treatments scheduled, too, and she wasn't sure how Jude would respond to them. They all crossed their fingers.

Toni e-mailed them all to say that a friend of Lawrence's had graciously offered his home on the coast near Carmel for their celebration weekend. It had plenty of room for them to spread out and a breathtaking ocean view that would more than make up for any unpleasantness that might occur due to excessive togetherness over the weekend.

Rain had to chuckle at the dynamics that always ignited when the former roommates got together. It was a wonder their spontaneous combustion hadn't burned down that Victorian they shared. They sometimes still treated Rain like an adolescent, but she no longer took notice. She would forever be the baby they had all helped to raise. What she had noticed was her mother's insinuation that she and Bebe were keeping secrets from her. Why, now? Why, at the end of her own life, would she suddenly want to be involved in Rain's?

She made a note on her calendar about Scott's going away party, though she wouldn't have forgotten it. She had nothing else to do. She was always included in Bebe's family events, even though she wasn't related. Bebe could use the extra support when it came to her family, and especially at this time when Scott was leaving for unknown territory.

At lunch, she narrowly missed being caught by a coworker as she cruised Craigslist for baby furniture as she ate a salad at her desk. She had already Googled baby name sites earlier in the day and added a few Gaelic names to her running list for boys. She had no problem with girls' names. If it was a girl, it would be Isabella Grace. Or Julia Danae. Something a girl could live with. Anything but Rainbow Star.

What had her mother been smoking?

She did more online research about in vitro and read an article about frozen embryos being just as healthy and weighing more at birth than fresh. Fresh or frozen. It sounded more like vegetables than babies. Not babies—embryos.

She made a mental note to stop by Whole Foods for sushi on her way home. Or for whatever she wanted. She didn't have to check with anyone else about dinner, and that was liberating. The house stayed cleaner, too, now that Hayden was gone. She had control of the remote and there were no little spikes of hair in the bathroom sink from his shaving, and only one towel hung in the bathroom. No shoes left in the living room, or coats draped over chair backs.

And no one to rehash the day with before sleep.

Sometimes she felt conspicuous in the checkout at the grocery store. She would examine her cart and realize that by the frozen entrees and single cartons of Ben and Jerry's, anyone could see she was single.

Near the end of her lunch break, she pulled up the donor catalog search information, checking boxes at whim. The donor she created was a cheaper version of Mr. Stanford Grad All-Star—a tall Caucasian with curly brown hair and hazel eyes with fair skin tone with a degree in engineering. With a start, she realized that what she ended up with was Hayden.

Chapter 3

Bebe pulled up to the Starbucks on her way to the clinic, but when she saw the long line of cars winding around to the drive-through window, she parked and went inside instead. She wore her favorite purple scrubs with the Dalmatian print that always drew attention, and the barista recognized her.

"Grande bold with room?"

Bebe said yes and handed over her Starbucks card with the hula dancer on the front.

"I love this card," the girl said. "I'm getting one when we go to Maui at Christmas."

Bebe thanked her, and when she took her coffee to the island to load it with Splenda, there, standing tall, was a young Marine in his dress blues. He politely moved aside to make room for her while he stirred his coffee. Bebe couldn't help but stare. The crisp, commanding quality of his uniform was softened by the fact that he was some mother's boy.

Bebe yearned to ask him . . . what? She turned to him, fearing he would leave before she knew what she wanted. "Can I ask you a question?" she blurted out.

He straightened taller, if that was possible. "Yes, ma'am."

She suddenly felt tongue-tied. What *did* she want to know? Everything. Can it be done? Is it as bad as I've heard? How did you make it through? Awkward seconds went by before she finally admitted, "Oh, I . . . I don't know what to ask."

He stood there, waiting respectfully, perhaps sensing the struggle inside of her.

She focused on the medal over his heart. "I see you're a sharpshooter."

"Yes, ma'am." Still, he waited.

"My son leaves for boot camp in a week."

To her chagrin, her eyes brimmed with tears. The young man inclined his head and spoke quietly between them. "You're worried about him."

She nodded with an ache in her throat.

He said, "It's hard, and it's arduous, but it's doable. He'll be fine."

She smiled up at him briefly and he purposefully met her eye. He couldn't have been more than nineteen, and he was comforting her like a sage. She murmured her thanks, and left.

Bebe sat in her car wiping away tears until her coffee cooled. She hadn't realized her feelings were so raw, so close to the surface. She said a prayer asking for strength and comfort, and realized with a start that God had sent this young man into her path to assure her that boot camp was "doable." That was the word he'd said. Doable.

God loved her that much—enough to send comfort before she even realized that she needed it.

She knew others would scoff at her simplistic belief that it had been more than just a chance meeting. But how often did one even see a Marine in his dress blues? She could have queued up with the other cars in the drive-through instead of going inside, or passed the young man without gathering her courage to speak. She could have stopped at a light and missed him altogether, or a whole list of other possibilities.

But none of those things had happened, and she didn't believe it was chance.

She always marveled at the unexpectedness of God's undeserved love. She, of all people, didn't deserve it.

She drove around for a while to gather her emotions before reporting to the clinic. Neil was reading a patient's file at his desk when she arrived and could tell that she'd been crying. She told him about her encounter and they comforted each other. The thought occurred to her of how hard it would be to go through something like this alone.

* * * *

"Mom, we're here," Bebe called as she pushed open the screen door of the farmhouse with her arms laden with bags and dishes. Scott and Dylan followed with coolers. They were soon enveloped by the ample arms of her mom and her sister-in-law, Karen, who exclaimed over how much they'd grown since the spring.

"Take the coolers out to the barbeque," Bebe told the boys, and they passed on through to the backyard to deliver them and find their cousins.

"Where's Neil? He's not working today, is he?" her mother asked while they unloaded the hot dogs into the fridge.

"No, Mom, he's outside. He wouldn't miss Scott's party. Rudy's showing off his new car."

Karen leaned over the kitchen sink to look out the window. "That Rudy. It's not ours, he borrowed it from the lot." She turned on the faucet and starting washing a colander full of purply-red tomatoes. "You know your brother. Always hoping to stir up a little business."

Bebe went on through to the backyard where she was greeted by Max, an Australian shepherd mix, and a collie named Bandit who were overjoyed to see company. She loved on them for a moment, and then she hugged her dad and told him that Neil would be out soon. She embarrassed both of her teenage nephews by planting huge kisses on their cheeks. They suckerpunched Scott in the arm and gave him grief about joining up. She noticed on her way back inside with relief that her brother Bobby wasn't among them.

Bebe picked up a gorgeous purple tomato from the windowsill, smelling the mouthwatering tang. "Did you pick these today, Mom?"

"The Cherokee Purples? Yes. And those Brandywines. You two can slice some up and put them on a plate."

Bebe washed her hands and joined Karen at the sink, pulling out her mother's cutting board and a knife. "They wanted $2.59 a pound for Heirloom tomatoes in the grocery store."

"You girls can take some home with you when you go. I've got more in the garden."

Karen lightly elbowed Bebe and gave her a wink. "Thanks, Mom," she called.

"Is Bobby coming?" Bebe asked, as nonchalantly as possible.

"He'll be here for dinner."

"Where's Paul?"

"Your brother had some business to take care of with Frank. That's our new foreman."

"Does Sal still pick for you?"

"No, he's too old now. He lives in the trailers year-round. Pilar died last winter and his kids finished school and moved away awhile ago. He still doesn't speak much English."

She handed Bebe cucumbers and green and yellow peppers to slice.

The kitchen was already heating up, and Bebe brushed back damp hair from her forehead. "The vines look great. Who do you sell to now?"

"I don't know. You'll have to ask Poppa."

Bebe and Karen sliced the vegetables and grated cheese for the salad as her mom patted out hamburger rounds. "This is the last of our beef. Poppa will have to butcher in the fall."

Bebe's maternal aunt and two uncles each trickled in with their families. Her father's family still lived in North Dakota. She hadn't seen them since she was a child. Her mother sent the men out to the backyard; the women she put to work in the kitchen. When Neil came in to see if he could help, she turned him around and shooed him out the door.

Karen and Bebe exchanged a look, and Karen said, "Come on, Mom, he's a surgeon. He's safe with a knife."

"Men don't belong in the kitchen," her mother-in-law answered as she dug in the pantry for buns.

Bebe rolled her eyes with her back to her mother and Karen quietly snickered.

Rain arrived just as they put the meat on the grill and Bebe's mom greeted her as if she were one of her own, expressing her sorrow about Jude's illness. Bebe wasn't surprised when Rain explained simply that Hayden couldn't come. She had brought a container of store-bought black bean salsa and whole-grain corn chips. Bebe gave her a hug before she went out to the backyard. Bebe grabbed a chip-and-dip serving bowl from the cupboard, as she knew her mother wouldn't want the containers on the table.

Rain was friendly to the family, but reserved, as Bebe knew she would be. Theirs was the only extended family Rain had known growing up.

Bebe went to the laundry porch for a few more tomatoes, and saw Rain lean in to give Neil a big hug. He kissed her on the cheek and Bebe smiled. She was so beautiful—like a daughter to them both. Sometimes, she had to remind herself that Rain wasn't a young girl anymore.

When Rain first moved in with Hayden, they saw less of her, partly because Hayden had some family in the area, and partly because Bebe's parents didn't approve of Rain's living arrangements, being unmarried. There had been a huge blowup between Bebe and her parents when they found out. Bebe defended Rain's right to make her own choices, even if she didn't agree, and pointed out how unchristian it would be to withdraw their love from her considering her unorthodox upbringing with Jude. In the end, at least her mother appeared to offer Rain her unconditional love.

❖ ❖ ❖ ❖

Rain was aware of the tension that infused the room when Bobby walked in. He came in just as the food was set out and shotgunned a general hello to everyone, except that he skipped right over Bebe, who managed to step out of the room for something. Karen hugged him and asked how he was doing. His mother tugged his shoulder down so she could kiss his cheek, and then scolded him for being late. After Bebe's dad said a blessing over the food, Rain watched Bobby fill his plate and head out to the backyard. She was a nonentity to him, due to some fortunate twist of fate. He was moody and pampered by his mother, even though he was older than Bebe, to whom he rarely spoke. There had been some major blowup between them in their younger years that no one ever spoke of. A little family dirty laundry, Rain guessed.

"Hey, Rain," Scott greeted her as he lined up next to her with his Chinette plate.

"Scotty, how are you doing? Are you getting nervous?" she asked, spooning macaroni salad onto her plate.

"Naw. I've been working out since February." He sounded hyper like he'd pounded an energy drink. Too much testosterone in the backyard.

He loaded two hamburgers onto his plate. "I'm up to eleven pull-ups and three miles a day." He spooned Jello salad next to his burgers. "I think I'm good."

One of the cousins behind Scott called down the table to where Bebe was setting out baked beans. "Aunt Bebe, you want to hear something funny? When I was little I thought you were a soldier like Uncle Bobby, you know, because Mom said you were a vet. Stupid, huh?" He laughed and Rain glanced up when the conversation around them skipped a beat.

"That's funny, Mike," Bebe said, forcing a smile before she turned back to the house.

Rain raised her voice. "Will they let you receive packages, Scotty?" she asked, deftly turning the attention back to him. "I'll send you some power bars, if you want."

"Don't know. I'll find out and write to mom."

"You need to do that a lot, you know? She's going to miss you."

He nodded. "Yeah, I know. She cried when I told her I signed up." He scooped up four chocolate chip cookies with his thumb and forefinger. "I gotta load up on these. It will be thirteen weeks before I get them again." Then he called, "Hey Grandma, you made kuchen, didn't you?"

"Peach and apricot. They're for later."

"Thanks, Grandma."

"And don't get into them until they're set."

Karen held up her Chinette plate. "Good for you, Mom," she said. "Make it easy."

"They're not fancy," she answered, "but it's too hot for you girls to wash so many dishes."

Rain saw Bebe and Karen exchange a look.

Everyone sat around a long table on the patio in the shade, their iced tea glasses sweating rings on the checkered tablecloth as the hot breeze swirled around them. Rain listened to the conversation and watched Neil with the boys, looking for clues that he'd left his indelible mark on their lives. Scott and Dylan were polite toward others, but together they engaged in playful and competitive banter that she'd never experienced with a sibling. Beneath their rough-and-tumble relationship she also saw compassionate young men, like the summer day when she'd stopped by the clinic to see Bebe. Scott and Dylan were working part-time there, cleaning out the cages of the boarded animals, playing with the kittens and puppies and mopping up their messes. She actually heard baby talk from Scott as he rubbed the potbelly of a beagle mix and let him chew his finger. The boys had been reliable and pleasant at the office, but argued with each other all the way out the door to Scott's car. Occasionally, when she stopped by the house to see Bebe and happened to find the boys watching the Giants with Neil, she would see an easy interaction between the three of them, as though they spoke some abbreviated language she didn't understand.

Rain watched the other men and their sons, including Bebe's dad.

Was it so important to have a father? She'd never had one. Neil had been the closest thing to a dad that she'd known. You couldn't really call William a father, joining them like he did when Rain was twelve. Jude had made it very clear that he had no business interfering with her raising of Rain and he never challenged her. Sometimes he seemed more like an older brother than a parent figure.

Here, she saw the guys naturally drawn to each other, in where they chose to sit, in their body language, and their topics of conversation. Even Neil joined them as though some division had occurred when they'd parked out front.

Neil and Bebe's dad got up from the table when they were finished eating. Rain noticed that Neil threw his trash away and Bebe's dad left his plate where he sat. They headed toward the barn, and she saw Bebe watching them go, looking almost sullen, but her expression quickly changed when she turned back to the conversation at the table.

When it was time to clear the table, Bebe said something to Scott and Dylan, and they dragged a trash can over to the table and began tossing trash into it. Their grandmother protested, but the boys insisted that they didn't mind helping. When the table was cleared, Bebe's brother Bobby started taking down the tables and Bebe slipped inside, repelling each other like the north poles of a magnet. Rain made several trips to the kitchen with dirty tableware and serving dishes, where she noticed that Bebe and Karen had taken their places again at the sink. Karen's arms were deep in suds and Bebe had a dish towel slung over her shoulder rinsing dishes.

Rain felt oddly out of place. She could have offered to help, but even though she'd spent many holidays with the family, today there seemed to be a strange undercurrent. She made some excuses, said her thanks and good-byes, and left. She had research to do.

❖ ❖ ❖ ❖

Bebe could see Scott and Dylan out the window talking with Bobby and a few other cousins headed toward the vineyard. Neil wasn't there like he'd promised he would be to monitor and diffuse any military talk. What was Bobby telling them, she wondered? Tales from Nam, probably. With Scott joining the military, this was his perfect opportunity for payback. She prayed that Scotty would know her well enough to realize this and not believe everything that Bobby told him.

When Neil returned from the barn with her father, she went outside, pulled him aside, and told him about Bobby. They stood looking down the rows of vines heavy with grapes, but saw no sign of Bobby or the boys.

She nodded over her shoulder toward the barn. "What did Dad want?"

Neil shifted his feet and shrugged. "Mazie's got some hoof problems. He just wanted me to have a look. I checked it out and told him to let the farrier handle it."

"Naturally, he didn't ask me."

Neil draped his arm around her shoulders. "He knows I do big animals at the clinic. It was nothing." He turned her around to face the barn. "But there's a litter of feral kittens out there, if you want to doctor something." He playfully pulled her toward the barn.

"More kittens? No, stop. It's too hot."

Neil stopped and together they walked back toward the vineyard.

She wove her fingers into his. "Dad would never ask me to take a look at Mazie, even if you weren't here." She kicked a rock. "We went to the same school. My GPA was even higher than yours."

"Ouch. No need to get nasty," he said. "I'm only trying to help."

"You know what I'm getting at. It's simple. He doesn't respect me as a doctor. He never asks me for any advice. He has never asked me to check out an animal."

"I think your dad's the type to compartmentalize things. He sees me as a farm animal doctor and you as a pet doctor."

"And he has no use for pets."

Bebe fell silent, tendrils of hurt wrapping her in sadness. Neil pulled her to him.

"I don't know what's wrong with me," she said into his shirt. They stood in the vast rows of green vines with the powdery dirt dusting their shoes and the bugs humming and chirping around them. "After all these years, why do I still care what he thinks?"

"Compared to his dad's generation, he's probably downright liberated."

"*He's* not from the old country. His father was."

"Well, personally, I think you're the best doctor at the clinic." He kissed her on the forehead. "But maybe this isn't only about your dad."

She shrugged. "Probably not."

"Scotty will be all right, Bebe. He's been ready for a long time."

"I know, but I just don't know what Bobby's telling him. And Dylan's leaving next month, too." Her eyes filled, standing there with his strong arms holding her tightly.

"I'll talk to Scotty," he said. "He knows about some of Bobby's problems and he loves his mom, so I don't think you have anything to worry about." He pulled back to look Bebe in the face, giving her that crooked smile that had made her fall in love with him. "Maybe we should get away somewhere after Dylan leaves for school." He leaned in and spoke into her ear. "Just the two of us. We'll go to Napa. Doctor's orders."

She smiled, wiping her eyes. "You're just what the doctor ordered."

"Really?" They turned and headed back toward the house and Neil slipped his arm around her waist. "Well, I have a plan of treatment that I think you're going to like."

❖ ❖ ❖ ❖

It was late afternoon, and the room air conditioner was blowing hard in the front parlor where the adults had gathered to enjoy their kuchen. The conversation touched on Bebe and Neil's soon-to-be empty nest, and skirted anything controversial, including Bobby's last stint in rehab. Her dad looked tired and older than his seventy-eight years. Her brother Paul talked about the consolidation of two large wine producers in the area, and how it would affect their business. Her mom pursed her lips and picked at a thread on the arm of the sofa while he talked. She got up and began collecting empty plates and forks and took them to the kitchen. Bebe gathered the dishes near her, and followed.

"You have more kittens at the barn, I see. Do you want me to take them to the rescue clinic?"

"No, they make good mousers. They'll be gone soon enough."

"The coyotes will get them, Mom."

"I know. That's a shame."

Bebe lowered her voice and asked, "How's Dad feeling? He looks tired."

"Oh, he's fine. Doctor says he needs to slow down, but you know your father."

"I thought Paul was running the farm now."

"Retirement has been hard on Poppa. He worries, you know. He can't seem to let it go."

Bebe stacked the dishes in the sink and glanced sidelong at her mother. "Scott's graduation ceremony is in October. It would be nice if you could go with us. Paul could handle everything at the vineyard. We could do some sightseeing in San Diego."

"We'll have to see." Even though it was over 100 degrees outside, her mother was putting on a pot of coffee. "It depends on the harvest."

Bebe didn't press it. She had avoided bringing up the subject of Scott's military enlistment, but now that the door was open, she plunged through.

"Bobby looks good."

Her mother nodded while she concentrated on pouring the water from the carafe into the coffeemaker. When she was done and switched it on, she said, "He's got a good job managing a car wash in Modesto. It's one of those big fancy ones."

"That's good." Bebe thought about saying she would drive down sometime to get her car washed, but they both knew it wasn't true. "Have you heard from Cynthia?"

"I saw her in Walmart last year at Christmastime. The girls were with her. Vanessa was visiting from Florida, and Breanna was starting graduate school in the fall."

Bebe watched her mother as she set out creamer and sugar on a tray with her back to her. She could just imagine how pleased her mom would be if Bobby were still married to Cynthia and those girls were his instead of a product of Cynthia's second marriage. Bebe and her brothers had only produced boys.

"We're taking Scotty down to the recruiting office tomorrow afternoon."

"How long will he be gone?"

"Thirteen weeks." Bebe focused on the undulating rows of vines through the window. They led away across the flat land into a low agricultural haze that obscured the horizon.

"He'll be a man when you see him again."

Bebe blinked back some tears and took a deep breath. "He's already on his way. He was twenty in June."

"Your brother was already a soldier by the time he was twenty."

"He wasn't even old enough to drink the wine from our grapes," Bebe said. She quickly regretted her words. She knew her mother blamed herself for Bobby's forays into alcohol dependency because they, like all the vineyards around, had had to switch from selling table grapes to wine grapes years before to survive. Earning the disapproval of certain church families at the time had only compounded her mother's guilt, though she'd had little say in the decision-making process.

Bebe edged closer to the chasm that so often separated them. "These times are different."

Her mother glanced up and then pulled open a drawer for spoons. "Will they send him overseas?"

"I don't know." Bebe added a stack of napkins to the tray. "Probably. I'm sure his unit will be deployed eventually."

Her mother arranged the spoons and napkins next to the cups on the tray with careful precision and said without looking at Bebe, "Let's hope his homecoming is different, too."

❖ ❖ ❖ ❖

August 31, 1969

Bebe lugged her suitcases up to the porch of the white Victorian and knocked on the door as her brother Bobby came up behind her with boxes from the car. The paint flaked from the doorjamb and the boards of the porch listed as though the foundation of the house was taking a corner too quickly.

A young woman came to the door with her hair tied back with a red bandanna and wearing no makeup. Her T-shirt said "Doors" and her jeans were extremely worn.

"You Roberta?" she asked.

"Bebe. This is my brother Bobby," she said as he stood behind her, balancing the stacked boxes on one knee.

The girl looked Bobby over and gave a sly smile. "Jude. Nice to meet you." Then she wheeled around and held the door open so they could carry in Bebe's things. "So the dorm's full?"

"Yeah. They lost my room assignment and the housing office was so packed that I couldn't get anybody to help me. We almost turned around and went home before I saw your flyer that you were looking for a roommate." Bebe noticed a funny odor that she couldn't identify.

"I posted that today after roommate number four dropped out. It's a good thing you called when you did. I've had five calls since then," she said, leading them down a hall to a bedroom. "Where's home?"

"Lodi."

"So," she said, addressing Bobby, "do you need a place to crash?"

"He's not staying," Bebe replied. They set the suitcases and boxes on the empty bed.

Jude smiled up at him until he blushed. "Pity. You'll have to come up and spend some weekends with us."

"Who sleeps there?" Bebe asked, gesturing toward the other side of the room with an unmade bed, stacks of drinking glasses, and an oversized movie poster of *Romeo and Juliet* over the bed.

"Oh, that's Toni." She gestured in disgust at the poster. "Can you believe that?"

"Tony?" Bobby asked, with a hint of alarm.

"Toni with an 'i,'" she said. "Short for Tonya."

"Hmph," he grunted, scanning Toni's side of the room with distaste. A giant peace symbol fashioned from a collage of what looked like magazine photos of soldiers and war hung on the wall.

"You might want to get ahead of the traffic, Bobby." Bebe took his arm and directed him back toward the front door. "Come on, I'll walk you to the car."

She walked beside him in silence, trying to read his mood. The campus and students they had met seemed very different than when she had visited the previous fall with her parents. Now it would be up to Bobby to tell her parents about the change in residence . . . if he told them.

He paused at the car door and looked back toward the house with suspicion etching his face. "Mom and Dad won't like it that you're sharing a house with strangers. I've got a bad feeling about this."

She looked up into his face and gave him a pleading look. "They don't have to know. It's just three other girls, and if things get weird, I'll move. I promise."

He looked down at her, clearly conflicted about leaving her there. She hugged his neck and said she'd be fine, and backed away from the car.

"You call me if you have any trouble. I mean it, little sis."

Tears sprang to her eyes at the endearment when she realized how much she'd miss him. He'd have to go soon or she'd change her mind. To her relief, he slowly got in, turned on the motor, and pulled away from the curb. Only when he was out of sight, did she turn and head back up the broken walkway to the porch. An unexpected mixture of relief, exhilaration, and homesickness swept over her. For the first time in her life, she was completely free of brothers, fathers, mothers, and the expectations of friends and extended family. The possibilities were endless, unpredictable, and completely foreign. She looked up at the

Victorian to find Jude watching her through the screen door.

"Smooth," Jude said. "In another minute, he would have dragged you back to Hicksville with him." She held the door open for her, and Bebe walked in. "Come on, I'll show you around."

Bebe followed her through the house to see the layout. Off of the small kitchen was a back door.

"Be careful," Jude said, pointing out that the door only hung on by one rusty hinge. "It's gonna break soon and I don't want the landlord to charge us for it."

They peeked through the screen into a tiny yard surrounded by a paint-bare white picket fence badly in need of repair, and tufts of grass growing intermittently in clumps. A ghost of a stepping-stone walkway wound around to the side. A rickety outside staircase led to the second floor.

"What's up there?" Bebe asked.

"There's an upstairs apartment, but it's off-limits. Some of the floors are rotten, which is lucky for us because they couldn't rent it out."

Bebe turned back to the kitchen. A small, white refrigerator hummed loudly like it was striving for attention, and Jude pulled open drawers and cupboards, giving her a rundown of where everything was.

"I didn't bring any kitchen supplies with me," Bebe said. "I thought I would be buying a meal ticket."

"Don't worry, we're good for now. We can't cook much on that stove, anyway."

Bebe saw that the narrow miniature stove had only two gas burners.

"We do lots of macaroni and cheese. Julio's Market down on the corner has it four for a dollar."

Bebe had never eaten boxed macaroni and cheese. Her mother's version was an Americanized variation of her grandmother's spaetzle recipe.

"We need to get a small table that will fit in here. We should use the big table in the dining room for homework."

One of the windows in the dining room sported a piece of cardboard taped against the glass. Jude gestured toward it. "Five guys rented this place last semester," she said. "We're waiting for one more to show. Mary Kathleen Kavanagh. We'll have to wrestle her rosary away from her when she gets here."

Bebe was a little shocked by Jude's irreverence, and she obviously took note. "Just joking," Jude said with a grin, and quickly sobered. "You're not a Jesus Freak, are you?"

Bebe's growing dissatisfaction with her straitlaced Christian upbringing hardly qualified her as one. "No. I'm not a Jesus Freak."

"Good." Jude went back into the kitchen, calling over her shoulder, "Hey, you want a beer?"

"No, thanks," Bebe replied. She'd never had one in her life, and wondered how Jude managed to get it. She didn't look twenty-one. "Do you have any sodas?"

Jude looked up from digging in the fridge and gave Bebe an amused look. "Sure, help yourself."

Bebe opened a can of Fresca and took a long drink. The condiments in the refrigerator were a third empty and the mustard had crust around the lid. "How long have you been here?" she asked.

"Since June. I moved in as soon as the landlord got the place cleaned up after the frat boys vacated."

The front screen door slammed. Jude lifted her head and called, "Toni?"

The strong scent of flowers wafted in and a female voice answered from the bedrooms. "Yeah?"

A moment later Toni came out to the kitchen and Jude introduced them. Toni's long, dark hair bounced and caught the light and she wore lots of makeup, particularly white eye shadow, pale pink lipstick, and mascara so thick it clumped on the tips of her lashes. Bebe recognized her scent as Chantilly. Her shapely figure was enhanced by a knit shirt that tucked into her tightly fitting hip-huggers and was held in place by a macramé belt, the ends of which hung down past her knees.

"Hey," she said, cheerfully. "The stuff on the bed's yours?"

"Yeah, I just got here."

"Fresh off the farm," Jude told Toni with a wink.

"Vineyard, actually," Bebe said, feeling a bit defensive.

"Oh," Toni said, appreciatively. "Did you bring any to share?"

"No, we raise the grapes, but we don't crush them."

Toni shrugged. "That's a shame." She took a plastic tray from the freezer and twisted out some ice cubes into a glass. "I got here early on Monday to look for a job." She opened the freezer to return the half-empty tray, and Jude reminded her to refill it.

Toni complied, spilling water down the front of the fridge onto the floor as she slid it back into the freezer. "Oops," she said. Then she dropped a dishrag onto the wet spot on the floor, slid it around with the toe of her shoe, and put the rag back in the sink. "There," she said, popping open a can of Tab and filling the glass as she walked away.

Jude watched her go. "Bring back all the glasses you have in your room."

Toni's answer was to sip the carbonated foam from the top of her glass before it spilled over.

"I guess you know classes start Tuesday," Jude said. "What's your major?"

"I haven't declared one yet. I've thought about nursing."

"Why settle for being a nurse?" Jude asked in disdain. "Nursing is for smart women who think only men can be doctors. You should go to medical school."

Bebe sipped her Fresca and shrugged. "I don't think med school is for me."

Jude leaned back against the kitchen counter. "I'm going to law school after I graduate. I'm not going to depend on a man to take care of me." She took another long drink, and said, "Not like my mom did. They always leave you," she said, pointing her beer at Bebe. "Always. And usually with a kid."

Bebe thought of her father and brothers. "Not *everyone* leaves. My mom and dad are still married, and my brothers are okay. There are still some responsible guys out there."

Jude considered Bebe, appraising her as if for the first time. "Well, I don't know any." She pushed off from the counter and left the kitchen.

"I have to go to the clinic. I'll take you down there later. You'll want to know where it is." She looked back and said, "If Mary Kathleen shows up while I'm gone, show her the extra bed in my room."

Bebe went into her room to unpack and found Toni lounging on her bed with a glamour magazine. She acknowledged Bebe and went back to scanning the photos.

"Sorry, I needed the big dresser," she said. "I'll share, if you want."

"This one's big enough," Bebe said, gesturing to a distressed little four-drawer dresser covered with carvings and graffiti. She pulled open a drawer. "Gross."

Toni looked up over the top of her magazine. "I guess those guys were out of control last year. It smells like they tried to roast a goat in the living room."

Something on the wall caught Bebe's eye. It was a faded ghost of a design or lettering beneath the paint, and she picked at it with her fingernail. The paint flaked away to reveal wallpaper beneath.

"I wouldn't do that," Toni warned. "The landlord will take it out of our deposit."

There was a knock at the door, and they both went to answer it. A young woman with a dishwater-blonde pixie cut wearing a peasant blouse and long skirt looked at them through the screen door. She gripped the handle of an overnight case with both hands and addressed Toni.

"Hi, I'm Mare Kavanagh," she said tentatively. "Are you Jude?"

Toni snorted. "Not on your life. But you're at the right house. Come on in."

Mare pulled the door open and shuffled inside. A large suitcase, a box marked "art supplies," and an easel waited on the porch. Toni and Bebe gathered the rest of her belongings, and Toni led the way to Jude's room.

"You'll be rooming with the commandant," Toni said as she dropped the box of art supplies onto the bed. "Have a great year."

Toni went back to her room. They stood watching her go with an awkward silence between them.

"Did I say something wrong?" Mare asked.

Bebe grimaced. "Who knows? I just got here myself. Maybe she was offended when you called her Jude. Come on, I'll give you the tour."

She led her through to the kitchen and Mare followed. "Who's Jude? Is there something I should know about her?"

Bebe paused, frowning. "Um, just don't hang up any religious pictures or icons or anything."

Mare's blue eyes widened. "I didn't bring any."

She showed Mare around and offered her a drink, but she declined.

"I'll just go and unpack," Mare said, looking a little unsettled. "I need to get centered."

Bebe watched her go back toward the bedrooms and felt for her. What would life be like rooming with Jude? She went back to her own unpacking, and came out later to scrounge something to eat. She wasn't sure yet how they were handling the division of groceries, but she could surely pay someone back for a few crackers and some peanut butter. When she was done, she cleaned up her dishes and put them back in the cabinets to hide the evidence, just in case.

Jude came home later and met Mare. They ordered take-out pizza for dinner to mark their first night together and held a meeting at the dining room table to decide on the ground rules of their arrangement. It was obvious that Jude saw herself as the first in command since her name was on the lease.

"And I've invited some friends over on Friday night for a little party, so you guys can meet some really cool people."

Bebe glanced from Mare to Toni, trying to read their thoughts.

Toni said, "Fine by me." Then she added, lifting an eyebrow, "But how much is it going to cost? I don't have a job yet."

"Don't worry about it," Jude said, waving her hand, dismissively. "There'll be plenty to go around."

"What about the neighbors?" Mare asked. "Will they complain?"

"We're surrounded on all sides by other students. They'll probably drown us out." Jude popped the top on her second beer. "We need to work on finding a kitchen table and some chairs. And a TV. There's too much going on in the world right now to be out of touch. I don't suppose anybody has one to spare at home? Maybe that they could bring back after the break?"

They looked from one to the other and shook their heads. Bebe didn't even know of a family that owned more than one television.

"There's a protest rally scheduled next week," Jude said. "We should all go."

"What are they protesting?" Mare asked. "Classes haven't even started yet."

"All the more reason to start the year off right. We're fighting for change at the university. For the right as students to govern ourselves. I guess some of the professors are even talking about going on strike to support it."

Bebe wasn't too sure of this, but she was curious. Jude must have sensed the hesitation it caused in the roommates.

"You don't have to join, just check it out."

They all agreed, and so it began.

Chapter 4

Rain dreaded Sunday mornings now that Hayden was gone. Their routine for almost seven years had been to wake to the hiss and the aroma of coffee beans programmed to brew at 8:00, which they enjoyed propped up with pillows fluffed behind their backs in bed as they read the Sunday paper cover to cover. Today would have been Hayden's turn to bring in the paper and the coffee.

Rain pulled on a light robe as she went into the kitchen for her coffee. She hadn't bothered to wear one until Hayden left. Somehow she now felt exposed running around the house in her camisole and baggy shorts. As if a robe would be some kind of protection. It made no sense, and she knew it.

Noah curled around her ankle while she stood by the coffeepot, his stub of a tail twitching as he meowed. "Hungry?" she asked. "You must have really worked up an appetite last night." She shook some crunchies into his bowl. "Next time you cry at my window at 3:00 a.m., I'm dropping you back off at the clinic."

Bebe had introduced her to Noah after he was brought to the clinic by an elderly man who found him treading water in a ditch in the pouring rain. He hadn't been even three months old, and his tail was so badly infected that it had to be amputated. He wasn't feral, but he didn't have a chip and they couldn't locate his owner, so they nursed him back to health and Rain adopted him.

It occurred to her that, although he did provide some company, she'd had too many one-sided conversations with Noah in the last four weeks.

She had cancelled the Sunday paper in a burst of anger when the carrier called to renew two weeks before. When she thought about it afterward, she realized what a sensible thing it had been. It was one less thing to carry down to the Dumpster and she saved some money. She only enjoyed the front page and the entertainment section, anyway.

She settled into bed with her laptop and her coffee and read the paper online instead. She checked her e-mail, deleting miscellaneous trash and spam that had gotten through the filter. She checked her Facebook page, but there were no messages or updates. She removed some pictures she'd posted of both of them at Bodega Bay and one at his last year's birthday dinner at Luigi's. None of her friends were online, so she logged out.

She tried to connect with Lisa to catch a movie in the afternoon, but it was her mother-in-law's birthday and they had to drive to Gilroy. Her friend Sarah offered to bring her along while she shopped for wallpaper for the baby's nursery, but she begged off.

Rain showered and dressed and went to Whole Foods for some groceries. She found it challenging to plan meals for one person. She tossed a large bag of frozen prawns into the cart (Hayden hated the smell) and planned to have them twice in the same week. She bought Heirloom tomatoes for a tomato and mayonnaise sandwich on white bread, like Bebe's mom would make, and which Hayden would have frowned on. She threw in a container of pesto and whipping cream for pasta and a tub of Dreyer's Girl ScoutsThin Mint ice cream. Hayden was lactose intolerant. And because he bordered precariously on vegetarian, she bought bacon for BLTs, and a juicy, organically raised rib-eye steak with garlic butter.

She bagged up a big orange sweet potato and picked up miniature marshmallows to melt on top. She bought an aromatic plug-in scented with mango, which most certainly would have set off his allergies, and another one in vanilla for the bathroom. She found a bar of heavenly lavender soap. She even tossed in a catnip mouse for Noah. Last, she cruised the flower aisle for a small bouquet of yellow roses and baby's breath. Then she headed to the cashier, admiring all her purchases as a sort of rebellion.

The total rang up to a little more than she'd expected to pay, but she'd made her point and there was no going back. She'd never realized how much of herself she'd changed for Hayden.

❖ ❖ ❖ ❖

The boys went to church on Sunday with Bebe and Neil since Scott was leaving that afternoon. They went out to lunch together afterward and let Scott choose the restaurant.

He chose Ruby's Roadhouse where he filled up on ribs, curly fries, and cornbread, and even ordered cheesecake for dessert, like it was his last meal. He asked whether they would be able to come to the swearing-in ceremony the next morning, but they said it was a full day at the clinic and Neil had a surgery scheduled.

He spent the afternoon playing Rock Band with his brother, and all the while Bebe sensed that the time to say important things was slipping away. Thirteen weeks was a long time and a lot of change could happen. He wouldn't be the same Scott when he returned, and she was reluctant to give him up.

Scott made small talk with Dylan in the backseat on the way to the recruiting office that afternoon, and he seemed nervous when they finally arrived. He recorded an away message on his phone, telling callers that he'd be back in October. Then he shut it down and handed it over to Bebe along with his wallet.

He blew out a big breath of air. "I guess that's it."

They got out and walked up to the storefront office where they met the recruiter, who went over some brief instructions with Scott. Bebe could tell the recruiter was also sizing up Dylan and she didn't like it. Dylan wasn't the military type. The recruiter finally let them know it was time to go. He gave them some privacy, but she noticed that he kept his eye on them. He'd probably seen some pretty emotional farewells and she wondered if he would try to intervene if things began to escalate, or if they tried to talk Scotty out of it at the last minute.

They each hugged him. Bebe kept her voice as level as she could and looked him in the eye to make the most of their last few moments. "Listen," she said quietly between them, struggling not to cry, "you remember who you are. You need to find good friends and stick with them. You need to ask God for help every single day. We'll be praying for you all the time—every day. We know you're going to be all right." She pulled out a small Bible from her purse and gave it to him. "There's a letter inside for you to read on the plane." He nodded, and she felt her face crumble as she kissed him good-bye. Neil and Dylan said their good-byes, and as they left for the car, she looked back at Scott for one last glimpse.

The evening was long and hollow, and it was impossible to think of anything other than him—whether he was nervous or homesick or worried, or whether he'd already read the letter in the Bible she'd given him.

The next morning, Neil got to the clinic early. Soon after, he called Bebe to say that he'd found that his morning surgery had been rescheduled. He'd moved their appointments until later in the day so that they'd have time to go to surprise Scott at his swearing-in ceremony. Bebe felt elated. He swung by the house to pick her up, but Dylan couldn't get time off from work. Bebe felt a surge of gratefulness that she'd be able to see Scotty one more time before he left.

They checked in at MEPS, the Military Entrance Processing Station, and waited in the lobby with other parents whose young men and women were being sworn in for every branch of the service. They watched every face that appeared, hungry for some sign of him. The officers gave the recruits simple instructions that involved walking on the line leading from one location to the next, and more than one young man found out that they meant this basic command literally, and had to sheepishly retrace his steps. Finally, Scotty's unit was called and their spirits rose as they saw him go past. They were soon ushered into a formal room with flags and plaques on the walls for every branch of service and a small stage. The parents lined up around the walls and waited. The doors opened and he entered with other young men in civilian clothes. They caught his eye and his face lit up briefly before resuming his stoic demeanor.

Bebe's heart swelled with conflicting emotions when he raised his hand and pledged to serve his country. The future was such an unknown. So many things in the world were tenuous. But at this point in time, he was safe and happy and so, so proud. She fought the tears that threatened to spill over, and saw that Neil was dabbing at his eyes, too. After the swearing in, they were able to hug Scott and tell him how proud they were, pushing aside their fears for the future, which she would not allow to ruin the moment. They were able to spend five minutes with him in the lobby seating area. Before they said their goodbyes, he told them that he'd already seen a lot of idiots who couldn't follow basic instructions and others who weren't as prepared physically as he was, and assured them that he would be all right. He seemed so much more confident and relaxed than he had the night before, and it put Bebe's heart at ease.

She missed Scotty all day, wondering where he was at that moment and whether he felt any regrets. He might be exhausted and even homesick and wonder what he'd gotten himself into, especially in the first week or so, but she knew he was as ready as a young man could possibly be for the rigors of boot camp—even the longest and most grueling boot camp of any branch of the military. It would feel like an eternity before they received a letter from him. He'd said that they got one phone call when they arrived, and Bebe and Neil kept their cell phones with them, fully charged, the whole day. She tried to keep the line free, inadvertently hurting her mother's feelings when she asked her to call the house phone instead, but she would not miss an opportunity to talk to Scott.

They waited all evening, but no call came. Was something wrong, she wondered? She checked the news, but there were no plane crashes reported. She sat down and wrote him a letter, even though she didn't yet have an address where he could receive mail. By the next morning, Bebe knew that, for whatever reason, Scott hadn't been given the opportunity to call. But she knew from experience with her brother that the military did their own thing and didn't need to give explanations. She was only his parent. Scotty now belonged to the U.S. government.

She had to resist the urge to read stories about the war and the editorials that appeared in the newspaper and online. She just wasn't ready to handle that, and it did no good to brood. She remembered how her mother had watched the news reports about Vietnam on television when Bobby left, and how she would shush them all harshly, and wipe her eyes and retire to her bedroom. Bebe had been at school when Bobby left. She didn't even get to tell him good-bye.

Chapter 5

Rain got a call on Tuesday morning that Dr. Lazenby had an opening if she wanted to move up her appointment. She rearranged her work schedule and took extra time at lunch. As she sat in the waiting area of the doctor's office, she wished she had taken time to shave her legs that morning. It was something she had become lax about since Hayden left, and she considered even explaining to the doctor by way of an apology.

She watched an extremely pregnant woman try to get comfortable in a narrow armchair, twisting this way and that. Her partner read a brochure on menopause, glancing up now and then to ask if she was okay. The woman tried pacing, stopping to take breaths, with her hands on her lower back and her feet spread like the base of a trophy. The receptionist called for them, and as they disappeared behind the office door, told Rain it would only be a few more minutes.

Rain picked up a brochure about in vitro fertilization and pregnancy. Cutaway diagrams explained the procedures in more detail than necessary, stripping away the warmth and wonder involved in bringing life into the world. Rain closed the brochure and supplied her own desired results. She couldn't wait to hold her baby in her arms.

The receptionist appeared and held open the door. The pregnant couple came back, and this time the man was supporting the woman as he hurried her out the door. The receptionist turned to Rain and said that her appointment would have to be postponed. Dr. Lazenby was on her way to the hospital.

Rain wondered who would hurry her to the hospital when her time came.

* * * *

Rain got a call from William that evening asking her if she could take Jude in for her treatment. The doctor was trying an experimental drug in an attempt to improve her quality of life. He had an unavoidable business trip on the following Thursday, and Rain would need to stay until he could make it back from the airport that afternoon. Rain said she would, and asked if her mom had agreed to it. He responded that, for once, it was out of Jude's control.

Rain arranged to take the day off and drove over to the Bay Area in the wee hours on Thursday morning to avoid traffic on the bridge. Her mother was dressed and waiting, and said it really hadn't been necessary for her to interrupt her day.

Rain drove her to the oncologist's and waited in the seating area while her mother checked in at the desk. People at different stages of illness shuffled through, some sitting with family members and others waiting alone. Some wore scarves and looked extremely tired, and one man had an oxygen tank. Jude sat poised with her chin lifted, keeping her gaze on a magazine, and flipping pages occasionally. Her attention settled on an advertisement for a new diabetes drug, even though diabetes wasn't an issue for her.

The nurse called Jude back for her treatment, and Rain was surprised when it didn't take long. Jude said that it was due to the fact that she'd had a catheter embedded in her chest after her veins collapsed.

Rain suppressed a shiver as they left the office. Jude moved slowly and deliberately, speaking of other things as though her appointment was just one of many errands she had to run that day.

Rain could tell that her mother was worn out, and over her protests, she supported Jude's elbow as she made her way up the stairs to her bedroom. The bedroom was in her signature disarray, and smelled stale and medicinal.

She offered to make Jude some lunch, and after an initial squeamish look, her mother asked her for Jello from the refrigerator.

Rain headed down to the kitchen, remembering back to the luncheon when Jude had driven herself. She must have been on the point of exhaustion when she returned that day. Rain felt mildly irritated with William for not insisting on driving her.

Rain opened the immaculately clean refrigerator and took out the container of Jello. She scooped the wobbling mass of orange Jello into a bowl and wiped down the sides before returning the container to the refrigerator shelf. She set it on a tray along with a glass of ice water and climbed back up the stairs.

"Since when do you eat Jello, Mom?" she asked.

"It's basically flavored sugar water. At this point, I need all the fluids I can get." Jude labored to sit up and prop herself against the headboard. Rain arranged the pillows behind her for support and set the tray across her mother's lap.

Rain stood gazing out the window at the busy street below while Jude ate her Jello. A messenger went by on a bike and was almost clipped by a van turning right. The day was gloomy with drifting fog and a chilly 60 degrees. What a difference from the 100 degree heat that simmered Sacramento the day before.

Rain turned at the clatter of Jude's spoon in her empty bowl. She removed the tray and left the water on the nightstand with the TV remote. "Is there anything else you need?"

Jude hesitated. She gave Rain a brief sidelong glance and said, "Well, actually, I need a new patch." Jude directed Rain to where she kept her medicines. The bathroom counter looked like a pharmacy, filled with prescription bottles, suppositories, and other supplies. Rain tried to look nonchalant when she came back in with a new patch. She peeled off the spent patch, curled the edges back until they stuck together as Jude directed, and flushed it. Then she applied the new one onto Jude's stomach and washed her hands. Her mother visibly relaxed as the medication began to kick in.

"So, what's going on between you and Hayden?" she asked, leaning back into her pillows.

"Nothing." Rain picked up the tray. "We grew apart. Normal stuff."

"Fine, keep your secrets," Jude said, closing her eyes. "I can always pump Bebe for information."

"Do you want anything else?"

Jude draped her arm across her eyes. "Just close the mini-blinds, if you don't mind. Really, you can go, if you have things to do. I'll be fine."

Rain moved to the window to shut the blinds. "I'll be here until William gets home."

"*If* he comes home, you mean. He's probably not in Chicago at all. He's probably down the coast with that Valerie woman from Marketing."

"You're just babbling."

"You don't know."

Rain started to leave, but Jude said without opening her eyes, "You don't need him, you know."

It took a moment for Rain to realize that she didn't mean William—she meant Hayden. Rain paused at the door and studied her mom. She looked frail and drawn with her arm draped over her eyes and her hair splayed against the pillow. Smaller than Rain remembered. How could her mother possibly know what she needed? Jude didn't even realize that she needed William.

"Call if you need me," Rain said, pulling the door almost shut.

Once downstairs, she put on some soft classical music and picked up a magazine. She realized that the architectural magazine was chosen for its appearance, because it obviously hadn't been read. The room was tastefully minimalistic and immaculate, but at the same time, inviting. William's influence, of course. He couldn't tolerate messes and clutter. Even his name was tidy. He was never a slovenly "Will" or "Billy." With his borderline obsessive-compulsive disorder, it was a wonder he could even tolerate Jude—the biggest mess and clutter of all.

When Jude entered a room, she claimed it with her belongings. Her room always looked as though she were in the midst of packing and could take off at any moment. Perhaps that's the way she wanted it. Noncommitment. Her clutter also clearly stated that she was no domestic goddess, and it handily drove William crazy.

Rain went into the office and sat down at her mom's computer. She checked her e-mail and found a message from her friend Lisa, asking if she wanted a ticket to see John Mayer in concert, but she declined. She couldn't afford it, even though she was tired of spending evenings at home alone. She answered back, suggesting a movie on the weekend.

She almost checked the assisted reproduction site, but realized that her mother could easily check the history and the secret would be out. She wouldn't risk that.

Rain had a devilish idea. She listened for noise from upstairs, and, hearing none, checked the computer's history and found something very interesting. An alumni site for San Angelo State University had multiple log-ins over the last few months. That was her mother's alma mater. Was her mother looking for something—or someone? She navigated to the site, but could go no further without a password.

She closed it out and ruminated as she went in search of food. With the exception of a coffee she'd grabbed when gassing up at Dixon, she hadn't eaten since she left home at four a.m. Rain opened the fridge again and marveled at it. Maybe she could get William to stop by and clean hers. The bottles and containers were lined up and sorted by size, and all the caps were clean. The glass shelves gleamed. She spooned some yogurt into a bowl, wiped the lid, and replaced it in the same spot, label facing out.

She dozed on the sofa until William returned. He said hello, placed a take-out container of sushi on the counter, and took his overnight bag to his room. He came out and gave her a hug, looking her in the eye.

"How are you, Rainy day girl? I brought you sushi." He lowered his voice and nodded up toward Jude's bedroom. "Did she give you any trouble?"

"No, she was good," Rain answered, getting out two square plates from the cabinet. "She tried to get me to leave, but I kept my post."

"Good for you." He went over to the staircase, tilted his ear up to listen, and returned to the kitchen. "Sounds like she's sleeping. Was she in a lot of pain?"

"She was grumpy, but I changed her patch." Rain suddenly looked up at him. "That was all right, wasn't it? She's not getting dependent or confused about her medications, is she?"

"No, she's as lucid as ever," he said, getting out black lacquered chopsticks from the drawer. "Maybe more so, if that's possible. I think the pain might be giving her an added edge."

He opened the refrigerator, took out a bottle of Sierra Nevada Pale Ale and held it up questioningly to Rain, but she shook her head. "I can heat up some sake, if you prefer."

She scrunched up her face. "No thanks. I'll stick to tea."

"Suit yourself. Tea's in the cupboard." He poured the ale into a glass, making sure it didn't foam while she chose a White Pear infuser bag and plugged in the teakettle. He arranged the California rolls and sashimi on a rectangular black serving plate.

"I picked this up from Hanami on the way home," he said. "It's criminal the way the airlines refuse to feed you more than peanuts when you're crossing three time zones and have to sprint to catch your connecting flight." He took the plate to the table along with two dipping bowls. "Now, sit down. I got a Tiger Roll just for you. No roe."

She smiled. "Twist my arm," she said.

"If you leave now, you'll just get stuck in traffic anyway."

Rain slid into a chair across the table from William and placed the cloth napkin in her lap. "So what did you do in Chicago?"

"Detroit." He shrugged. "It was training for union negotiations. Very boring stuff. I changed planes in Chicago."

"That's too bad. Did you have to travel alone?"

He paused and pointed a chopstick at her, looking conspiratorial. "Your mother's been filling your head with stories. Valerie Young didn't go—it's not her department."

"It's none of my business, but why does she get like this?"

"I don't have a clue. Maybe she's looking for an excuse to cut me out of her will."

Rain paused with a bite of sushi poised. He looked more sober than sarcastic. "You're serious."

"She did mention it, as a matter of fact."

The teakettle screamed, and Rain considered his answer as she put her tea bag to steep. Her mother was fully capable of being vindictive. "What would that mean if she did?"

"Well, the house belonged to her when I moved in, and I haven't sunk a dime into it. So I guess I'm out. But that's not the real issue, is it?"

She studied his face as he concentrated on lifting the last bit of sashimi to his mouth. His face was lined and pudgy in the folds, like a quilt whose stuffing had lost its shape. He'd put up with so much from her mother, and stayed so even-keeled. He didn't react to her, but responded with a certain inner calm that Rain had often mistaken for compliance. It was an excellent trait for union negotiations, or hostage situations.

"Why do you put up with her, William? She's treated you so badly for such a long time."

"In sickness and in health, Rain."

"She can't hold you to that. You're not legally married."

"In some states we would be by now. No, we've had some good years together and she doesn't deserve to be abandoned now." He waved his chopsticks at her, and said confidentially, "Besides, whether she realizes it or not, she needs me."

Rain smiled at him. "You're a good man, Charlie Brown."

"You're a good girl, Rainbow Brite."

William set his plate off to the side, placed his chopsticks diagonally across one corner, and brushed an imaginary crumb from the table. "So, I understand that you and Hayden have called it quits."

Rain sat back in her chair and cradled her teacup in both hands. How much should she really disclose to William? She was pretty certain that he would keep her confidence, but her mother was just upstairs, and sound traveled. For all she knew, Jude could be listening in.

"We had some disagreements and he moved out."

"Ah." William rubbed his chin, looking thoughtful. "Is there any chance you could work it out? Sometimes things seem less important when it comes down to losing someone you care for."

When she didn't answer, he lowered his voice and leaned in. "It wouldn't have anything to do with starting a family, would it?"

Rain started to say no, but didn't want to lie to him. She nodded instead, while gently swirling her tea. The dregs lifted, floated, and settled back on the bottom.

"You know, I really don't want to talk about it. I'm not sure what I'm going to do yet." She looked up, hesitating, and whispered, "I'm thinking of having a baby by myself."

His eyebrows lifted in surprise and his mouth made an O. "You're very brave," he whispered back. "Would that make me a grandfather?"

He hadn't argued with her or told her she was out of her mind, bless him. Rain reached across the table and put her hand on his, smiling. "You'll make a wonderful grandfather someday."

He squeezed her hand and silently signed with the other, "I love you."

"I love you back," she said.

Rain stood and carried the containers to the counter where she transferred the few leftovers into separate plastic tubs. She wiped the edges and placed them on a shelf in the fridge. She almost closed the door, but quickly counted the containers and moved one down to the lower shelf, making the condiments and containers come out even. William took the plates to the sink and rinsed them, refusing her help and saying it would give him something to do for the evening.

"Well, if you won't let me help, then I need to say good-bye to Mom and head back."

Rain went up and pushed open the door to her mother's room, tiptoeing quietly to her bedside. Her mother's face sagged in sleep, with her mouth open slightly and her eyes moving rapidly beneath her closed eyelids. Rain could see white roots in her thinning hair. It had been a defiance of cancer to keep as much hair as she had. Jude's arm lay on top of the blanket, and Rain placed her hand on it. Her skin felt dry and thin, without a cushion of fat beneath to soften it. Her mother startled awake when she spoke her name.

"William is back, Mom. I'm leaving now."

Her mother closed her eyes and said a dreamy good-bye. Rain kissed her cheek and left.

How would her mother react to discovering that she could be a grandmother? Would she feel aged and resentful, or would it be a joy that Rain would cheat her from if she kept the knowledge to herself? It was just one more uncertainty for Rain to ponder on her long drive back through the traffic to Sacramento.

Chapter 6

Bebe carried the laundry basket of folded towels and linens to Dylan's car and wedged it between his stereo and his suitcase in the backseat. She mused that at least if he had an accident, flying glass would be minimal since most of his windows were blocked.

"Is this legal? You can't even see out of the back window."

"I have the side mirrors," he said, mashing down the blankets in the passenger seat to give him a clearer view.

"Are you sure you don't need some help moving in?" she asked. "We could drive over with you. How in the world are you going to move all of this up to your room?"

"Mom, I'll be fine. There's an elevator in the parking garage. These go up front," he said, tossing his CD case onto the dash. "Traveling music."

"There's something I forgot," Bebe said, going back inside the house to retrieve an index card from the kitchen table. She hurried back to his car and showed it to Dylan. "This has emergency contact information in case you . . . well, just in case. In case someone needs to reach us."

"Don't open the passenger door," he said. "You'll cause an avalanche."

Bebe went around and slid into the driver's seat. She reached over and slipped the index card into the strap of the sun visor of the passenger side.

"Mom, I'm a good driver—"

"Other drivers aren't."

"I'm not going to have an accident."

"I know. It's just in case."

Neil came out, surveyed the vehicle, and handed Dylan a credit card. "Here's a gas card. Don't let your friends use it."

"Thanks. I won't," he said, pulling out his wallet and sliding the card in front of his driver's license.

"You shouldn't have to use it much since you're living on campus. It's for when you get a job and for coming home. When do you think you'll be back?"

"I'll try to come back for Labor Day. There aren't any classes on Monday. Unless I get a job and I can't get off."

"That's only a few weeks. Why don't you just plan to look for a job after Labor Day?" Bebe said.

"I'll run out of money before then." He gave her his sweet, manipulative smile. "Unless you and Dad want to give me some cash."

Neil laughed and said, "Just try to get time off, okay?"

"We'll send your brother's address when we hear from him. Make sure you write to him. You'd better take one last look around," Bebe said. Then she followed him inside. She found his toothbrush in the stand and handed it to him as he scanned his room.

Finally, the time came to say good-bye. Bebe hugged him and made him promise to find good friends and remember who he was, just as she'd said to Scott. She encouraged him to check into the different ministries on campus and get plugged in somewhere. He promised to take it slow and to let them know when he got there safely. Although they would see him soon, it was still hard to say good-bye. It was more than going to college—it was the close of a chapter in his life, and of an era for them all.

Dylan waved as he pulled away, and they stood arm-in-arm in the empty driveway watching his car disappear in the distance, brushing away tears. They made their way back inside the quiet house, reassuring each other that they could call him and also keep in touch by e-mail. He would be home in four weeks, full of excitement about college life.

"The game's on," Neil said, taking a soda from the refrigerator and heading for the couch. He looked up expectantly while he changed channels with the remote, but she said she needed to clean up Dylan's room. Baseball had never been her thing.

Bebe stood in the doorway to his room and surveyed the damage. True to his nature, he'd waited to pack until the last minute and didn't have time to clean up before he left. She stuffed dirty laundry into his hamper and scooped up clean clothes that he'd decided not to take or had forgotten to take, and placed them neatly in his dresser. She made his bed and sat on the edge of it. Long ago, he had put away his baseball trophies and replaced his major league posters with legends of rock. Jimi Hendrix, Jim Morrison, and The Who gazed down on her from the walls. She prayed that they wouldn't mean for Dylan what they had meant for her.

She suddenly felt overwhelmed by her now-empty nest. The distant ballgame roared from the family room, and she thought of Neil sitting out there watching it alone, without Dylan or Scott to enjoy it with him. He was a good husband and father, and she didn't deserve him.

She knew that this was a time when many couples split up, as though their children's leaving pulled the single thread that held them together, and their marriages unraveled at the seams. As her eyes filled again she tried to tell herself that she was being foolish. It wouldn't happen to them.

But why should their marriage be immune? She'd even seen it happen to couples in church—people who'd seemed happy enough. She felt vulnerable, and dropped her head back, studying the curls in the plaster, boring a hole through the ceiling to heaven. She sensed Jimi

Hendrix gazing down on her, accusing. She had some bad stuff in her past that wouldn't let her go, even though she'd asked for forgiveness. Asked many times. She didn't rate any special favors from God.

"Hey," Neil said, suddenly there in the doorway.

She quickly looked away and wiped her eyes. He sat down beside her on the bed and pulled her to his side. The warm scent of buttered popcorn clung to him.

"Dylan will be fine, honey. He'll be home before we know it."

She nodded. When she trusted herself to speak, she ventured, "Maybe we should have gone away somewhere after all. Just the two of us."

"We can still do that. Pick a weekend and we'll blow this Popsicle stand."

She smiled and laced her fingers through his. "I'll check it out tomorrow."

A distant roar from the television piqued Neil's interest and she said, "I'm okay. Go on back to the game."

"Come out and watch it with me," he said. Then he tempted her, saying, "I have contraband. Extra butter."

Bebe followed Neil out to the living room and plopped down on the couch in front of the TV. He filled a glass with ice and presented it to her, along with a can of Diet Pepsi. A bowl of buttered popcorn sat on the coffee table.

"Such service," she said in appreciation.

"We aim to please."

He sat down beside her and she took in his rapt expression when the camera cut away to show Giants pitchers warming up in the bullpen.

It looked like a beautiful day in San Francisco, with the breathtaking views of the city against a hologram of blue sky, and the little boats poised to chase home runs that sailed into McCovey Cove.

"We could spend the weekend in San Francisco," she ventured. "Maybe catch a Giants game."

He glanced at her in mild surprise. "It won't be hard to get tickets.

They're having a lousy season." He patted her knee. "I like the way you think."

Later in the evening, Dylan called to say that he'd arrived safely and had moved his stuff in. It was all in a big pile in his room and he was going out with his new roommates for pizza. He thanked Bebe for the stash of snacks that she'd hidden in his laundry basket when he wasn't looking, and for the forty dollars that Neil had slipped into his pocket when he hugged him good-bye.

After the game, she wrote to both boys, telling them both how proud she was and how much she believed in them and prayed for them. Each had his own challenges to face, and she had no choice but to leave them in God's hands.

❖ ❖ ❖ ❖

May 14, 1972

"Can you watch her for me?" Jude asked. Without waiting for an answer, she hefted the eighteen-month-old Rain into Bebe's arms. "I'm going to a rally downtown and then I have to close the Women's Center tonight."

Rain patted Bebe's cheeks and blew raspberries, expecting them in return. Bebe puckered and imitated Rain, and was rewarded with a shower of bubbles and baby spit.

"The rally's today? It's Mother's Day," Bebe stated.

"Yeah, so?" Jude pulled her hair back two-handed and twisted it into a knot before pinning it onto the back of her head.

"An abortion rally on Mother's Day?" Bebe was incredulous.

Jude slipped the long strap of her bag over her head. "You know a better day?" she answered as she breezed out the door.

Rain didn't even notice that her mother had gone. Bebe had a project due, but she was the only one there to take care of her. Mare had gone home to visit her mother for the weekend and Toni was on a date. As usual. Bebe decided to take Rain to the park and play mommy for a while, happy to have her all to herself for the day.

Bebe could have gone home to visit her own mother, but ever since her family had seen the newspaper photo, she'd kept her visits few and brief. The clipping was pretty self-explanatory, if not misleading, and her first phone conversation with her mom after they saw it let her know they weren't interested in her reasoning. She missed them, but she wasn't up to the firestorm she could trigger just by showing up.

Even before her photo appeared in the papers, Bebe had no longer fit in at home. All through high school she'd been the good daughter, but as she became more aware of some of the issues swirling around her, she found herself resenting her father's traditional attitude toward women. Eventually, she equated his outlook with what she assumed was also God's, and by her senior year, felt as bleak and as pruned to the quick as their vineyard in January.

Her mother became critical of her appearance and her father barely spoke to her, probably because, for the first time in her life, she argued with him. She no longer wore makeup, and let her hair follow its natural frizz. She didn't bother to shave. Her younger brothers, Paul and Rudy, were outwardly disapproving like her parents, but privately they wanted to listen to her music and asked her what marijuana was like, assuming she would know. She'd never realized what a buffer and confidant she'd had in Bobby as her older brother until he was no longer speaking to her.

Bebe packed a little bag so that she and Rain could enjoy a snack in the park, and tossed in extra diapers and Rain's blanket in case she got tired and fussy. It would be a nice little diversion from studying.

School would be out in two and a half weeks, but Bebe was staying on campus to work and take summer classes instead. Mare would go home for a long visit, but probably end up coming back early because of her art teacher. Toni would go home for the summer and Jude would have to deprogram her all over again when she came back looking too girlie and glamorous. Toni enjoyed sharpening her feminine wiles on the boys back home.

Bebe and Jude would have to arrange their summer classes and work schedules around taking care of Rain without the help of Mare and Toni. Bebe considered offering to come home for a week later in the summer to help her mother with the canning. If Mare came back in time to relieve her, she would go, if her mother wanted her.

Rain fussed a bit when Bebe strapped her into her green umbrella stroller, which enveloped her like a canvas pea pod. "Sorry, babe," Bebe said. "When I get old, you can strap me in and push me around."

Bebe took the route to the park that passed by a thrift store where she'd had luck before. She was surprised to find it open even though it was Sunday and a holiday, and she steered Rain inside. The place smelled musty and she felt the breeze of a fan whirring in the back, blowing around the dust.

Rain was growing out of her clothes at an alarming rate, and it fell to Bebe to find clothes cheaply or to somehow improvise. Jude didn't even notice that her little shirts had grown tight beneath the arms and that her elastic waistbands were leaving zigzag marks on her tummy. Bebe could take apart some of her own T-shirts and cut them down to fit Rain as a last resort, and Rain's cords could be cut off at the knees for shorts if she snipped the elastic.

"Let me know if I can help you," a voice called from the back.

"Okay," she answered, without looking up. She pushed Rain over to the baby clothes and found three little shirts that weren't too stained or frayed. She could only afford two, so she chose the lavender one over the yellow one, in addition to the T-shirt with small purple flowers. Then she pushed Rain up to the cash register and dug out her money.

A nice, athletic-looking guy with a crooked smile rang up her purchase. "That'll be one dollar."

She looked at the money in her hand. Athletic-looking, maybe, but not a math genius. "Don't you mean a dollar fifty?"

"There's a special sale going on today," he said, pointing to a sign on the counter. It said, "Sale on Red Dot Items."

She smiled uncertainly. "Those aren't Red Dot Items."

He leaned over the counter and made a silly face at Rain. "Red dots or babies. It's Mother's Day."

Rain blew raspberries and stuck out her bottom teeth at him, bouncing her feet in the air. Bebe placed her dollar on the counter and pocketed the other fifty cents. "Thanks."

"No problem-o." He stuck out his hand. "I'm Neil."

She shook his hand, noticing deep scratches on his wrist and forearm. She looked up at him, suddenly wary.

He waved it off, seeming embarrassed. "They're cat scratches. I earned them volunteering down at the SPCA on Fargo." He gestured grandly at the surroundings. "When I'm not selling upscale merchandise to discerning clientele."

"Or going to class," Bebe added.

He cocked his head, puzzled. "Right."

"You're wearing an SASU shirt." She pointed to his T-shirt with the San Angelo State University logo. "Unless you shop here, too."

He chuckled and opened the cash register, depositing her dollar in the drawer. "Well, we do have a vast assortment of SASU T's. But I bought this one at the bookstore." He gestured to a stain on his front. "Looks like I'll have to buy a new wardrobe. This one will never last for four more years of veterinary school."

Bebe looked him over with renewed interest. "I'm applying for the veterinary program, too."

"No kidding?" He leaned against the counter and considered her. "That's great. There aren't many women in the field." He pointed down at Rain. "Won't it be hard juggling . . . everything?"

She looked down at Rain, who had pulled off her shoe and tossed it, watching it bounce across the worn carpet. "Oh, she's not mine. I'm just watching her. For her mom. My roommate." For some reason, she felt she was betraying Rain.

"Well, that should make it easier."

He gave her his crooked smile and she found herself wondering if he was seeing anyone. Rain let out a howl and arched against her seat strap in frustration.

"Well, we're off to the park. Thanks for the discount." She grabbed Rain's shoe and screwed it back onto her foot.

"See you around campus," he said, looking pleased.

Bebe left thinking that even if he didn't, she knew where to find him.

❖ ❖ ❖ ❖

Rain updated Bebe on her mother's condition when they met for coffee on Friday morning. Bebe seemed to be a little down, and Rain remembered that Dylan and Scott had both left.

"So, are you and Neil getting away to someplace special, now that the boys are gone?" Rain asked.

Bebe removed the lid from her coffee to let it cool and shrugged. "We're trying. But it's the end of the summer and we have staff vacations already scheduled. We'll see."

After an awkward silence, Bebe asked, "Have you heard from Hayden?"

"He sent me an e-mail saying that he wanted to come by on Sunday to get the rest of his stuff."

"Are you going to be okay with that?"

"What choice do I have? I just hope he doesn't bring somebody with him."

Bebe frowned. "He doesn't seem that insensitive. But maybe you should have a friend with you, just in case."

Rain sighed. "Well, that's another problem." She glanced over at the table to their right where a young couple sat close together. Rain lowered her voice. "How often do you see Toni and Mare?"

"Not very often, why?"

"Well, do you have any friends that you get together with—without Neil?"

Bebe thought for a moment. "Not on a regular basis." Then she added, smiling, "Just you."

"Ever since Hayden left, I've tried to connect with my old friends, but they're all preoccupied. Lisa from my office is married and their families monopolize her time, and Sarah is *very* pregnant and only cares about baby stuff, which would be great if I were pregnant, too. Kim works seventy hours a week at her travel agency when she's not leading a tour with her boyfriend, Mark. It seems like we all cut our ties when we found guys. We all isolated ourselves—except that they haven't realized it yet because I'm the only one who is unattached at the moment."

"I see what you mean."

"It's so June Cleaver."

"Have you mentioned it to any of them?"

"They don't want to hear it." Rain's attention caught on an attractive young barista behind the counter, but he was too young. She needed someone with a steady job and a future, not a college boy. "Sometimes I feel like they see me as a threat."

"A threat?"

"That it could happen to them." Rain had never put the feeling into words before, and now that it was out, she felt betrayed. "Do you ever worry about that?"

Bebe smiled into her cup and swirled her coffee. "Well, no. Neil and I have been together for over thirty years." She chuckled. "That really makes us sound ancient. I suppose it could happen to anyone at any stage of life."

Rain didn't want to cause Bebe concern, but she needed to ask. "Isn't this the time when a lot of married couples split up, after the kids go away for college? Aren't you worried about that?"

Bebe paused for a moment. "When the boys first left it felt a little odd, but we're finding it's kind of fun being alone again. We work with each other every day and we go to church together, so we haven't really grown apart much. I pray for our marriage, you know, and not just when we have challenges to face. It's important to find common interests and to do things together—even small things. But even that's no guarantee of security."

Rain ran her hand through her hair. "Relationships are so complicated. I mean, look at William and Mom. She treats him like dirt and he doesn't say a thing. I feel so sorry for him."

Bebe dipped her head. "You never know what goes on between two people. He must have a reason, or he wouldn't stay."

"Maybe change is just hard."

"And maybe he loves her. When you love someone enough, you can let them be who they are and not demand that they change for you."

Rain remembered the last conversation she and Hayden had before he left. She had given him an ultimatum. Maybe she loved the idea of having a baby more than she loved him.

❖ ❖ ❖ ❖

Bebe carried in the mail and dumped it on the kitchen table along with the grocery bag containing fixings for a quick dinner. Peeking out from the stack of bills was the corner of a white envelope with an eagle, globe, and anchor and Scott's crooked handwriting. She didn't even bother to find a letter opener, but peeled open the top of the envelope and pulled out a sheet of lined notepaper dated August 3rd addressed to "Mom and Dad." She groped behind her for a kitchen stool, not taking her eyes from the letter, but hungrily devouring this evidence of her son's well-being—this look into his present life of which she had no part. The letter was brief, and he sounded exhilarated and tired at the same time. The days were going fast and the training was challenging. He wished he had pushed himself harder to prepare, but he was doing better than some. He missed them and he included his mailing address. He couldn't wait to get a letter from home. He had gone to religious services with the other recruits, and he knew he couldn't do this on his own. "Funny how God works," he'd written. Her son was maturing before her eyes and she felt her heart swell within her just knowing that God was answering prayer in his life.

She called Neil, who was on his way home, and read him the letter. When he walked in the door, he read it for himself. Bebe posted it on the refrigerator with a magnet and they paused to read it several times during the evening. They each wrote letters to Scotty while they relaxed watching the Giants game and folded laundry on the couch. Bebe called Dylan to see how he was doing and found that he had also received a letter from Scott. He said it was basically the same, but she wondered what details Scott may have included in his brother's letter that he didn't share with them.

Dylan's classes were going well and he had an interview for a job at an off-campus bookstore, but he would insist on having Labor Day weekend off if they offered him the job. He sounded like the same old Dylan, but with an added dimension that they weren't part of. In the background, they heard guys calling for him to hurry up because they were leaving for McDonalds.

She handed the phone to Neil who spoke briefly to Dylan and hung up.

"Fries are calling," he said, then went back to watching the game.

⁂

On the Sunday that Hayden had arranged to stop by, Rain found herself cleaning up the house and applying makeup. She wasn't sure when or if Hayden would actually come by, but she didn't want to look pathetic if he did—especially if he brought along a "friend."

They had bought the house together without even the suggestion of marriage. Hayden knew how Rain felt about it, and the subject was never raised. He'd moved in with his clothes and books, which was basically what he left with. The only mutual purchase that he took was the flatscreen TV, which she wasn't upset about. He didn't take furniture or kitchen appliances, and it seemed so easy that she wondered whether he had another place waiting for him. Another home she didn't know about.

While she waited, she called her mother to see how she was feeling. William answered, saying that Jude had had another treatment that week and asked if she wanted to speak to her. Rain heard another female voice in the room, and she would have thought it was the television, if she hadn't heard William answer before handing the phone to Jude. Her mother was coherent, but groggy, and determined to return to work the next day.

During the whole phone conversation, Rain kept a lookout for

Hayden's car. She decided to wait to go to Whole Foods until after he came by because she was impatient to get his things out of the house. The afternoon wore on and she began to regret giving up a whole Sunday to wait around for him, but by then, it was really too late to leave. If she missed him now, he would just have to reschedule. She grew tired of Noah begging for food, so she opened the back door and shooed him outside. Then she heard Hayden's car pull into the driveway.

She peeked out the window and stepped back to watch him without being seen through the miniblinds. The driver's door of the Expedition opened and Hayden stepped out. She felt relieved that he was alone. He shut the door and shook the wrinkles from his khakis. The first thing she noticed was his tan and his hair curling long in the front where he needed a haircut. He wore a collared polo shirt in that soft shade of green that looked great with his eyes. She wondered where he was going, all dressed up.

When he came up to the door, she jumped back to the hallway to give the illusion that she was coming from a distant room instead of watching for his car. She let him knock twice before she called "Coming," counted to five, and opened the door.

They both said hello and she stepped aside to let him in. Strange, that he needed permission to enter the place he'd called home for seven years. He still had a key, and she wondered whether he ever secretly stopped by when she was at work. She never saw signs of intrusion.

She offered him a seat on the sofa that they had bought together the weekend after they'd moved in. He sat on the edge of the leather cushion and looked around.

"Where's Noah?"

"I just let him out. I can call him." She started to get up but Hayden quickly answered, "No, that's not necessary. Thanks."

He sniffed. "Is that mango?"

She remembered her plug-in air freshener. "Yes."

A long period of silence ensued while they both cast around for something to latch on to, some common, neutral ground without buried landmines just waiting for them to detonate.

Finally, Hayden asked, "How is your mother?"

Rain wondered how he knew, but she couldn't read his face. "She has good days and bad days. They're trying out an experimental drug, but if it doesn't work, there's not much else they can do for her."

His eyebrows lifted in surprise. "Sorry to hear that."

"She wants to have a Celebration of Life before she dies. One last chance to make her mark. She wants me and the old roommates involved in the planning of it."

"Knowing your mother, it sounds complicated."

"That's exactly what I said. But Bebe's unofficially in charge. Maybe she can satisfy Mom."

"How are Bebe and Neil?"

"They're fine." She gestured to his face. "I see you got some sun."

He raised his hand to the bridge of his nose. "I overdid it a bit. I was sick for two days."

She noticed that his hand was healing from a bad scrape. "What happened?" she asked, motioning to his hand.

He turned it over to look at the back, and then curled it into a fist and covered it with his other hand. "It's nothing. I was . . . just helping out a friend."

An awkward silence descended. He didn't elaborate on his vacation. Finally, he said, "Well, I don't want to keep you. I'd better get my things."

He stood up and went back toward the bedrooms. Rain remained on the couch with her hands in her lap, listening to the sounds of another human being in her home. For a moment, the sounds were so normal and natural and she sighed deeply. She wavered. Was their life so empty, their home so lacking in love that a child was needed to fill it? Was that part of her that yearned for motherhood not to be denied without eternal consequences?

Eventually, Hayden came out of the extra bedroom—the future nursery—with a box of winter clothing and his ski pants. He stacked them by the door and went to the stereo. He shuffled through the rack of CDs, pulling out some of her favorites, because they were also his.

He stood up and asked, "Do you mind?"

She shook her head. "No, go ahead. They're on my iPod."

He smiled nervously and something stirred within her. She pushed it down, turned to the kitchen and poured herself a glass of water.

She heard him go out the front door, and for a moment she thought he'd left without saying good-bye, but the stack was still sitting by the door. She heard the garage door open and he brought out his skis and placed them in the back of the Expedition, and then he loaded the box and CDs.

She was standing in the kitchen drinking her water with the island counter between them when he came in to say he was leaving. He hesitated at the door and looked back, and then said good-bye and closed the door behind him.

Rain heard his car drive away, and she went to the back door to call Noah. He was waiting on the step. Perhaps he'd heard Hayden's car and had wanted to come inside.

She opened a can of tuna and poured half of it into Noah's bowl as a peace offering. Then she wandered from room to room, seeing what was missing, and finally went out to the garage. She flipped on the dim light switch, and saw her skis hanging on the wall with a bare spot beside them. She turned the light off and went back inside.

Rain took off her makeup and changed into her comfy clothes. She took the whole container of Dreyer's Girl Scouts Thin Mint ice cream to the couch with a big spoon and sat with her feet crisscrossed in front of her. She clicked on the small television she had brought in from the bedroom to replace the monstrosity that Hayden had taken away, and watched reruns of *Project Runway*.

It was perfectly natural to feel lousy after all that had happened, she reasoned. But she had to move ahead. A baby was something she wanted so badly, and she had to stay focused or her window of opportunity would close forever.

Noah jumped up on the couch, licking his lips and breathing his tuna breath in her face. He curled up by her side and gave his paws a thorough cleaning.

She wondered whether Hayden was happy to have that bit of business over and done with. Their meeting had reminded her of the striking figure he made, tall and self-possessed as though he'd stepped from a Jane Austen novel. Did he regret moving out? Did he ever have second thoughts about having a baby? Was he simply glad to get away?

Something her mother had said in her drug-induced haze came back to Rain, and Rain wondered at the answer.

She realized she still wanted Hayden. But did she need him?

Chapter 7

Monday morning offered the favorite part of Bebe's job—giving a wellness checkup to an eight-week-old kitten.

"Our neighbor's cat had kittens in our attic, so we got to pick," said the kitten's ten-year-old mommy, Dakota. "We named her Rogue because of the white fur on her forehead. You know, Rogue from the *X-Men*? She has a piece of hair that went white after she died."

"Oh, I see," said Bebe as she took the kitten's temperature.

"There were five kittens and we could see them playing on the roof," said Dakota's mom. "We had a hard time catching them all when the mother cat finally brought them down. They were absolutely wild."

"Well, you've done a fine job of domesticating Rogue." Bebe made a notation on Rogue's chart that her temperature was normal and she checked her ears. The kitten gripped Bebe's hand and dug in her claws playfully. She tried to sink her baby teeth into Bebe's finger, but didn't like the taste of Bebe's antiseptic soap. "She appears to be very healthy for a roof-cat. Are we vaccinating her today?"

"Yes, please, and we want to check into having her spayed."

"We don't want any more kittens on our roof," said Dakota.

"That's what I would recommend. But we usually spay at about five months. You can schedule the procedure with Georgeann when you stop by the front desk to arrange for her boosters in four weeks. And you should have a talk with your neighbor." Bebe smoothed the fur on Rogue's neck and the kitten relaxed in her lap. The kitten's eyes rolled back while they talked, and she soon fell asleep. Bebe administered the shots, which drew little response from Rogue and her eyes soon closed again.

She handed the kitten back to Dakota and made a note in the file. Rogue stirred briefly and then lay completely limp on her back in Dakota's arms with her paws dangling. Bebe reached over and gently rubbed her tummy. "Do you have any questions for me?"

"We were interested in getting a chip, in case she gets lost."

"That's a great idea, even if Rogue is mainly a housecat."

"How much does it cost?"

"I think it's forty dollars to inject the device and eighteen to have her registered in the database. You might want to confirm that at the front desk."

"Oh, I see," said the mom. "Maybe we'll do that when we come back for her boosters."

"We also have brochures available," said Bebe. "Just make sure you update your contact information yearly, or any time that you move."

Bebe smoothed the feathery fur beneath Rogue's chin by way of saying good-bye and walked them to the front desk where she slid the kitten's file into a plastic holder on the wall. She said that the staff would be right with them to set up a follow-up appointment for Rogue.

Bebe washed her hands and headed into Room 4, pulling the patient's file from the slot on the door and perusing it briefly before knocking and entering. Scout, an Aussie-German Shepherd mix, needed a foxtail removed from his ear. Later in the morning, a teeth cleaning was scheduled for a fox terrier named Jerome, and a parakeet named Chipper was seen for loss of feathers around his eyes. Bebe told Chipper's owner that she wasn't an avian veterinarian, but suspected that the condition was due to a sinus infection. The bird left a spot on Bebe's scrubs, which she tried to remove before seeing her next patient.

On her lunch break, she called Mare to set up another meeting in late September to finalize plans for the Celebration of Life. She caught Toni clothes shopping for their vacation in Tuscany, but she took time to put it on her calendar. Bebe waited until the end of the day to confirm with Jude. Secretly, she hoped to catch William after he got home from work.

They hadn't talked since the lunch at Dulcinea's, and she felt some guilt about it. Jude wasn't the kind of person to ask for help, but she probably needed it, all the same. Bebe didn't know William extremely well, but he seemed like the kind of person who would be there for Jude in her illness, even though Jude never spoke very highly of him. She never spoke highly of anyone except Rain, and never to her face.

Bebe knew that Jude had always been a bit jealous over her relationship with Rain, and perhaps that was another reason that kept her from calling. Jude had hinted at the luncheon that she knew how close the two were, and Bebe didn't want to inadvertently add to a sick woman's pain.

❖ ❖ ❖ ❖

October 2, 1975

The kindergarten classroom teemed with children and parents milling around between small tables and chairs, play centers and displays. Rain held tightly to Bebe's hand and pulled her directly to the table with her name tag. Neil followed, ducking his head around low-hanging mobiles and simply worded signs, such as Blocks and Housekeeping.

"This is my table," she said, plopping down into her small chair and grinning up at Bebe and Neil.

Her work folder was there, and Bebe and Neil took time to peruse it, ooing and ahhing over her accomplishments.

After examining every page, Rain tugged Bebe toward Mrs. Waters and Neil followed. Her teacher wore her long hair loose and she pulled it to one side when she bent down to speak to a child. Her silky hair told a younger story than her skin. Bebe was surprised to see faint crow's-feet fanning from her eyes. The hem of her long skirt grazed the top of her ballet flats. She ended a conversation with a parent and turned to Rain, who beamed at her while swinging Bebe's hand.

"Hello, Rain, is this your mother?"

Bebe caught her breath. If Rain said yes, it wouldn't be the first time she'd made the mistake. On top of her nontraditional upbringing, she had just gotten in under the age cutoff for kindergarten and wouldn't turn five until the following month. Bebe had argued that she was too young to start school, but Jude had insisted that she get a jump on the competition.

Instead, Rain answered, "No, it's Bebe!" as though the teacher were being silly.

Bebe stuck out her hand. "Hello, I'm Bebe Hoffman. We met at the orientation. Her mother will be here soon. I'm her mom's roommate. And this is Neil St. Clair."

"Oh, yes, I remember." She shook hands with them and turned to Rain. "Is Mommy working late?"

Rain looked up at Bebe, confused.

"Mommy is in law school," Bebe explained. "She has a class tonight, but she promised to leave early so she can make it over here."

Rain squeezed in between Bebe and Neil and took both their hands, swinging them like a jump rope. Her teacher considered the trio for a moment, and slowly smiled. "I understand," she said. "Rain, why don't you show Bebe and Neil your artwork while you wait for your mother?"

Rain nodded animatedly and tugged them both to the art bulletin board where self-portraits of all the children were displayed. Some had huge heads or hands with splayed fingers. There were drawings of pets with very pointy ears and lopsided houses. Rain pointed at hers. Her name was printed in uneven letters at the bottom. She rocked on her heels, tongue curled to the roof of her mouth.

"Oh, my, Rain," Bebe gushed. "It's very good. You're quite an artist."

Rain had painted herself as a large figure in the forefront with a head of dark hair, large ears, large eyes, and a small mouth. She had two round pink spots for cheeks and an upside-down V for a nose. She held hands with a curly-haired girl with large glasses and a boy with a mustache. Bebe looked closer. A boy with a mustache?

Rain dropped hands with Neil and pointed at the girl and boy. "That's you and that's Neil," she said proudly, taking Neil's hand again. "We're going to Happy Hollow for a picnic."

In the background, a train engine with smoke curling from its stack idled on a set of railroad tracks and a dragon sat in the far corner by the tree. A smaller stick figure stood apart from the others, with a straight line for a mouth, an oversized head, short arms, and long legs.

Bebe glanced down at her. "Who is that, Rain?"

"That's Mommy," she said, bouncing. "She's scared of the dragon."

"Well, at least it's anatomically correct," said a voice behind them.

Bebe looked up to see that Jude had arrived and now stood behind them. Bebe dropped Rain's hand and moved aside to make room for her in front of the display, feeling awkward in light of Rain's obvious view of their relationships.

"Have you seen Mrs. Waters yet?" Bebe asked. "She wants to meet Rain's mother."

"I'll meet her." Jude didn't take her eyes from the painting, but stood with her arms crossed.

To Rain, she said, "You're so big. Right in the middle of the picture. Good girl."

Jude uncrossed her arms and said, "Okay, where's this teacher?"

* * * *

Rain had rescheduled her appointment with Dr. Lazenby for the end of August, which disappointed her a little because that much more time would pass before she made real progress toward having a baby.

Money was a concern. She had a good job as a paralegal with benefits and a 401K, but she and Hayden each had their own checking accounts and they'd split up the household bills for years. The house payment came out of her account, and Hayden paid the rest. She realized that she'd resisted making any official changes, just in case their separation was temporary, but his visit on Sunday had finalized things between them. She needed to make some big decisions and move on.

After work, she ate a Lean Cuisine dinner at the computer while she did more baby research. She came across a blog by Seekergirl, who was the product of artificial insemination with a sperm donor. Seekergirl was in her early twenties and venting about growing up without a dad and how she grew up wondering if she shared the same DNA with every man she saw. When she was old enough to notice boys, it had occurred to her that she could be dating her half brother without even knowing it. She wanted a face to hold on to. Who gave her mother the right to choose a fatherless existence for her?

Rain sat back in her chair with her cannelloni turning cold on her plate. She was unexpectedly flooded with memories. Memories of her first awareness of Father's Day and the fact that she lacked something other kids naturally had, along with the ensuing confusion about who Neil was in relationship to her. Memories of her mom sitting alone in the stands approving as Rain hit a line drive to centerfield between the legs of the two nine-year-old boys in the outfield who were so sure Rain could never hit the ball past the pitcher's mound. Rain had wondered if her father played in the major leagues then, until the boys matured and easily surpassed her skill level so that she could no longer compete. She was decent on the clarinet in middle school, and wondered if her father was a musician and whether her genes would kick into gear so she would astound her fellow band members, but that never happened, either.

Years later, Jude met William, but it was too late to fix her lack of a dad. She could never think of him as a father, anyway.

Seekergirl had inadvertently struck a chord with being fatherless, and Rain wasn't even a donor baby. What would that mean to her own child?

❖ ❖ ❖ ❖

Bebe made her callbacks in the morning and then checked on Webster, the rottie, who had undergone a castration the day before. She had advised Webster's elderly owner to let him stay overnight because she didn't feel that he would be able to manage the dog's care alone. Webster's coloring made it look as though he had a smile on his face when she checked his kennel and he seemed to be recovering fine. When Webster's owner came to pick him up, Bebe told him to make sure Webster continued to wear his E-collar at all times to control excessive licking at the surgical site, and to keep his activities limited. Due to Webster's age, it would take a month or two before he would tone down his aggressive behavior toward other dogs. She rubbed behind his ears and let him lick her cheek. "Be nice to your friends, Webster," she told him.

Later in the day, Michelle, their technician, received a needle stick when the Chihuahua to whom she was giving a shot squirmed and managed to avoid it altogether. Michelle was upset because she was four months pregnant and worried about her baby, so they sent her to their worker's compensation doctor to be checked out.

The day went by quickly, and Bebe realized that Michelle hadn't returned to work. Bebe wasn't worried about the baby—there were no hormones in the shot. Bebe had been stuck before, and it wasn't fun, but no medicine ever actually got into her bloodstream. Georgeann, the office manager, said the doctor wanted Michelle to stay off of her feet for the rest of the day, but she could return to work the next if she had no problems. Michelle had worked at the clinic for about a year, and Bebe was fairly sure she wouldn't try to take advantage of the incident, but one never knew.

Bebe dreamed that night of Chihuahuas with sharp teeth. She was standing in front of her old college library looking for something she had lost, but couldn't remember what, and trying to avoid the Chihuahuas. Whatever she had lost filled her with sadness and the oppressive feeling stayed with her into the morning.

Michelle came back to work that day and Bebe breathed a sigh of relief. The dream had put her on edge and she chastised herself for being silly.

When she finally got home, she changed out of her scrubs, plopped down on the family room couch, and announced to Neil that she wasn't cooking. She wasn't going anywhere, and what did he want to do about dinner? He opted to have a pizza delivered—half pepperoni, half veggie, along with breadsticks.

She wrote a letter to Scotty while they were waiting for the pizza to arrive. In his last letter to them, he had said how great it was to get so much mail, because some of the guys didn't get any. She felt so bad for those recruits who didn't have families to care enough about them to write. They had started martial arts training and everyone was getting sick with colds and flu, but he had stayed healthy.

The pizza arrived and they ate too much of it. She fell asleep on the couch during her favorite show, which she had looked forward to watching ever since she recorded it on the DVR two nights before. That was one thing that Bebe really hated about being fifty-seven—the fact that if she sat down and stopped moving in the evening, she simply fell asleep. She'd gotten into the habit of removing her makeup and brushing her teeth before she settled down with a good book or in front of a movie, and she always changed into something she could wear to bed—just in case.

She and Neil both had the weekend off, and they spent Saturday cleaning together, which took hardly any time since the two of them didn't make much of a mess. The long, hot afternoon lay before them, and Bebe suggested that they go to Lowe's for some mums and marigolds to replace their spent flower bowls. Neil was always up for a trip to Lowe's, and they spent the late afternoon working in the yard after the heat of the day began to cool. They fired up the grill and ate their steaks outside on the deck with soft jazz playing in the background of their conversation and in stretches of pleasant silence.

Their time alone together was good. She still thought of the boys often and prayed for them frequently, but she felt at peace. Life was back to the way it was before they had a family, and she allowed herself a tentative feeling of satisfaction.

❖ ❖ ❖ ❖

Rain returned from faxing contracts to the corporate office, and Craig, one of the new attorneys, stopped by her desk. She wondered if he would ask for her help with another contract negotiation. He made twice as much as she did, and she would love to just say no, even though she couldn't. He glanced nervously over his shoulder, cleared his throat, and tapped his fingers on the top of her cubicle divider. She waited.

"I have two tickets to see Journey at the Sleep Train Amphitheater this Saturday night, and I wondered if you wanted to go," he blurted. "They're decent seats—at least they're not lawn seats." When she didn't respond right away, he continued, "They do a great live concert. I think they're with Heart and Cheap Trick."

Rain couldn't answer immediately. Her first thought was how he even knew she was available, and her second was why he waited so late in the week to ask her. Had his first choice changed her mind?

But the thing that really threw her was the fact that her first date with Hayden had been a Journey concert, too.

"I've seen Journey in concert." She had to fill the dead space with words and no fresh ones came. Wasn't he younger than she? She glanced over at Lisa's cubicle. "This Saturday?"

"Yeah. I mean, if you've got something going on, I completely understand." He squirmed a bit. "I know it's kind of late."

"*This* Saturday." She hadn't been on a date with someone other than Hayden for seven years. And she loved Journey. She took a breath, overriding her initial flight response. "Sure. What time?"

He smiled, looking relieved, and she noticed that he had a dimple in his chin.

"The doors open at 6:30. I should probably pick you up about 5:30 so we have plenty of time." He tapped the top of her cubicle once more. "See you Saturday." He pushed off and looked back at her as he headed toward the elevators.

Rain saw Lisa peek over her cubicle and dive back until Craig had passed. Then she popped her head up and grinned at Rain. Rain narrowed her eyes. So that's how he knew she was available.

Rain dug some change from her desk drawer and went to the vending machines. Lisa followed and leaned against the Coke machine while Rain fed it with quarters. "So what's up?" Lisa asked, looking happily guilty.

"As if you don't know already." She popped the top of her Diet Coke and took a drink, feeling flushed. "I'm going to see Journey on Saturday with . . . him." She pointed her Coke can in the direction Craig had gone and headed back to her desk. Lisa followed.

"No, I did not already know. I just happened to overhear that a certain someone was interested and I tossed him a bone. It was all perfectly legal." She sighed. "I wish Lyle would take me to a concert."

In spite of herself, Rain felt a bit of excitement about hearing Journey live again. "Maybe I should dig out my leg warmers and cut my hair in a mullet," Rain joked, and then quickly sobered. "What if Hayden's there? He loves Journey. He's probably already got tickets." She sat down heavily at her desk, her shoulders sagging.

"So what?" Lisa said, cocking her head with her hand on her hip. "You're not in high school anymore. He'll see you didn't wait around for him," she said, going back to her desk.

Rain swiveled her chair around to face her computer, jiggled her mouse, and the screen pulled up the last site she'd been on—the sperm donor site.

A wave of embarrassment broke over Rain. Had that site been displayed the whole time Craig was asking her out? What must he think?

Chapter 8

Bebe was putting in a load of laundry one evening when the phone rang. She almost let the answering machine pick up, but finally grabbed it on the fourth ring.

"Mom! Hey, it's Scott."

Bebe felt a thrill go through her, and as she greeted him, she frantically motioned to Neil who was on the couch. She pointed at the bedroom. "It's Scotty!" she said. Neil jogged into the back room and picked up the phone.

"Hi, son, how are you?" she heard him say from the extension.

"I'm good. I only have a couple of minutes. My unit earned a phone call today because we did so well on drills. I didn't get to call when we first got here because one of the guys ruined it for us all."

Briefly, and with the guarded words of one alert, he told them he was doing okay and couldn't wait for graduation. He had made some buddies and said he appreciated receiving letters. They chatted for only a minute or two and they heard a voice speak in the background.

"I have to go. I love you guys and I miss you."

They said their good-byes and he hung up. Neil came out from the bedroom and they looked at each other in wonder that they had at last spoken to Scotty and he sounded fine. They were grateful that they had both been home and that Bebe had answered the phone. Bebe said she would put another letter in the mail the next day.

She called Dylan to tell him that Scotty had called. He said classes were going well for him, but the job at the bookstore didn't turn out and his car's brakes were getting mushy. He said he would be home a week from Friday for Labor Day.

Before she went to bed, Bebe called Rain and arranged to meet for coffee the next morning. She thought she detected a certain lilt to her voice when she agreed.

❖ ❖ ❖ ❖

Rain picked up her coffee and snagged two cushy chairs, placing her purse in one to save for Bebe. Rain and Hayden used to frequent this Starbucks together, and she always scanned the faces of the other patrons when she came in. Of course, he might not even live in the area now—it could be completely out of his way. She thought again how odd it was that he'd left all their furniture and taken only his clothes.

Lately, she'd begun to wonder if he had commitment issues. All she had wanted to do was to move them to the next level, and certainly a baby would add a deeper dimension to a couple's relationship.

Bebe came in wearing scrubs with patterns of playful kittens on them. Bebe's cheerful smile always managed to lift Rain's spirits, no matter what was going on in her life. The smile made Bebe's eyes sparkle and called attention to her freckles, which were still plentiful, even at her age. You couldn't really call Bebe beautiful by today's standards. She wore hardly any makeup now and did little with her hair other than occasionally putting it in a French braid, but she still looked youthful and vibrant—more than Rain was feeling at the moment. Bebe paid for her coffee and grabbed the chair that Rain had saved for her.

"Hey, how's it going?" she asked Rain. "What's up?"

"Well, I have a date. At least, something like a date. I'm not really sure. A 'not-date.'"

Bebe forced a smile. "Oh, a 'not-date.' Who with?"

"Craig, one of the attorneys in the office. We're going to see Journey in concert tomorrow night."

Bebe made another effort to brighten her face, but the effect fell short. "That sounds like fun. How do you feel about it? I imagine the first date with someone new might be a little strange."

Rain shrugged. "It's flattering to be asked, but I don't really know him very well. It's only a concert. It's just that . . ."

Bebe waited. "Just what?"

"It's just that Hayden and I met singing 'Don't Stop Believing' at a karaoke night and our first date was a Journey concert. So I'm not crazy about the possibility of running into him there." She shook her head. "Thousands of people will be at the concert. What are the odds that I would even run into him?"

"Oh, I see." Bebe carefully popped the lid from her coffee and sipped lightly. "How did it go when he came by for his things?"

"It was fine. He came alone. He looked like he was on his way somewhere, though. He's officially moved out now."

Rain kept her eyes lowered and tried to look casual, but she felt Bebe's eyes on her.

"How's your mom?"

"She's still working half-days when she's not recovering from her treatments. I don't know how much longer she'll be able to keep it up. It will be hard for her to let it go when the time comes. She thinks the firm needs her. She says she brings 'balance to the force.'"

"That doesn't surprise me."

Rain studied her. "She must have been a real pain when she was young. I don't know how the three of you put up with her for so long."

Bebe chuckled. "All the dorms were full that first year, and the lease was in her name. After that, we just kind of settled into a routine." She grew thoughtful. "The truth is that we were clay in her hands. She had so much more experience with life than we did. I was a farm girl just off the vineyard. Mare was fresh out of Catholic school, and Toni still spoke Polish to her grandmother. Although Toni definitely gave Jude a run for her money. Jude was so charismatic and together." She gave a rueful smile. "We were primed, what can I say?"

"She must have been more fun back then."

"Did you know she was in Haight-Ashbury during the Summer of Love? She met the bass player with Jefferson Airplane—at least, that's who he told her he was. She was young. But she's told you this stuff already, hasn't she?"

"She told me more than any adolescent girl should know about her mother." A question formed, and she asked it even though she wasn't sure she was prepared to hear the answer. "Do you know who my dad was?"

Bebe took a long sip of her coffee and frowned like she was thinking. Then, she shook her head. "No. There were a couple of guys Jude hung out with, but nobody special. Hasn't she ever talked to you about it?"

"Mom never talks about it. She said she didn't need a man."

Rain remembered her own words to Bebe that she didn't need Hayden to have a baby. Would her own child resent her years from now?

"You have to realize that times were different then. A lot of people embraced the idea of 'free love.' There were no curfews or dorm mothers monitoring coeds by then, and we were off campus in our own little world. So much changed so fast, that no one knew where the boundaries were. It was heady stuff."

Rain sat back and crossed her arms. "Are you saying that my mother was typical?"

"No, Jude worked very hard not to be. Back then, women were just beginning to realize that they had choices. Jude arrived fully loaded with the opinion that women should have control of their own bodies and take charge of their own sexuality. And guys were only too eager to agree." Bebe pinched the rim of her coffee cup. "Some of us found that that type of freedom wasn't all it was cracked up to be."

Bebe's cell phone buzzed, and she pulled it out of her pocket and turned off the alarm. "I'm scheduled for surgery this morning. Oh, here." She dug deeper in her pocket and produced a slip of paper. "It's Scott's address. Sorry I didn't get it to you sooner. He called us last Sunday." She gathered her purse and they headed for the door as she filled Rain in on the phone call. "He sounded good, but of course, moms never stop worrying."

Outside, Rain gave Bebe a hug before she left. "You're a good mom."

Bebe hugged her back. "I try to be. Love you."

"Love you, too," Rain answered.

As she drove to work, Rain felt warmed by Bebe's motherly affection. She wondered what it was that kept Jude from being the mother Rain had always wanted and needed her to be, and which one she would naturally emulate—Bebe or Jude—if given the chance to mother a child.

* * * *

Bebe talked to Neil that night about connecting with Hayden to encourage him not to give up on the relationship. She had hoped Hayden would change his mind himself, but when she heard that he had officially moved out, she became disheartened. Neil wasn't sure it would make any difference, or that Hayden would even agree to meet with him, but he promised to try.

Bebe checked the mailbox on Thursday, hoping to find their weekly letter from Scott. Inside, among the bills and junk mail, was a white envelope with the eagle, globe, and anchor in the corner and Scott's handwriting. He had established a schedule of writing on Sundays, which was his only day off, and mailing his letters in time to arrive on Thursdays. It gave her a thrill to hold this paper that Scott had held and written his thoughts on, and she grinned like silly, smitten woman.

She opened the envelope, slid out the single lined sheet, and began reading on her way back to the house. "Dear Mom and Dad," it began.

What followed was a brief rundown of his normal day-to-day activities and comments that he'd lost weight and wasn't getting enough sleep. He sounded distracted and perfunctory, and she thought he was just tired until she got to the end. He said that Uncle Bobby had sent him a letter and given him some things to think about.

❖ ❖ ❖ ❖

Rain laid two complete outfits on her bed and stood back with her arms crossed. Which one should she wear on a first date? She considered the blousy babydoll-peasant top, but decided that it might not be a good choice if Craig had gotten a good look at the donor site on her computer. Her indigo jeans would work if the temperature dropped when the sun went down, but by then, she could have a very embarrassing heat rash going on. She knew it was an open-air concert and that the weather could stay sultry, or drop from blazing hot to a chilly 60 degrees in the space of a few hours.

She had to admit that she was also worried about what to wear in case she ran into Hayden. What would she have worn if it were Hayden instead of Craig who was picking her up? A screen-printed T-shirt and capris with sandals and a lightweight zippered sweatshirt for the evening. Rain and Hayden no longer felt the need to impress each other. It wasn't a bad thing—it was just familiar. Comfortable.

She decided to go for comfort and dressed up her simple T-shirt and capris with dangly earrings and a necklace. As it turned out, Craig dressed for comfort too, and she pocketed the earrings when she saw him come up the driveway.

At the amphitheater, she scanned the crowd to the point of distraction and finally quit after Craig asked her who she was looking for. She never saw Hayden. They had a nice time, but Rain established a comfortable distance between them from the start and he didn't even try to hold her hand. He must have known about Hayden and was smart enough to figure out that she wasn't ready for a new relationship yet. She wouldn't even let him walk her to her door, but insisted that she could just hop out. She gave a wave as she went in and closed the door behind her.

She dropped her purse on the counter, kicked off her shoes, and set out some catfood for Noah. He preened as she put a dollop of mashed salmon into his bowl. She reached down and stroked him as he dove into it. "Well, *that's* over," she said.

Would it get easier to be with other guys that she really didn't have a "thing" for, or should she wait until she found someone who made her feel the way she did with Hayden? Did lightning ever strike twice?

If she wanted a baby, she decided, she may have to settle for making lightning of her own.

❖ ❖ ❖ ❖

Rain breathed a sigh of relief to find that this time the waiting room at Dr. Lazenby's office was devoid of women in their third trimesters. She explained to the doctor about her desire for a child, her recent change to single status, and lack of candidates for fatherhood. Since it was determined that she would need a sperm donor and artificial insemination, the doctor recommended a fertility clinic that she knew had good results. Dr. Lazenby gave her a physical exam to rule out obvious reasons why she wouldn't be able to conceive and carry a child to full term. She told her to begin charting her ovulating cycles by taking her basal temperature each morning before she got out of bed. In conjunction with that, she suggested that Rain buy ovulation predictor kits (OVPs) that tested the levels of luteinizing hormone in her urine and were more accurate than taking her temperature alone. She gave Rain a lab slip for a complete blood workup and said she would forward the results to whatever clinic Rain decided to use.

Gathering this information in advance would help her to expedite things. Dr. Lazenby gave her some literature to read and told her to go ahead and call for an appointment with a fertility clinic, since there could be a waiting list.

Rain left the doctor's office feeling a mixture of excitement and frustration. At last she was making progress on having a baby, but if it took months just to get an appointment at the fertility clinic, taking her body temperature would be like slogging through wet cement, and she felt that time was not on her side.

She stopped at a drugstore on her way to work where she didn't normally shop to purchase a basal thermometer and an ovulation kit. She placed the kit on the floor of her backseat and covered the bag with a blanket she pulled from the trunk. Later, on her lunch hour, she checked out the clinic Dr. Lazenby had suggested and was encouraged by their success rates, although their prices were a shock. She set up an appointment for mid-October, which fortunately, was a cancellation that had occurred just that morning. Rain wondered whether the cancellation had been the result of a successful pregnancy, or of a woman accepting defeat.

Rain found herself making mental notes about the guys she saw at work. It was always possible that she could save some money by getting one of them to agree to be a donor instead of paying lots of money to the cryobank. She tried to stay open-minded about which ones had the potential to be a good donor. There was Luke from Accounting, who was attractive and smart and moving to the top of her list, until she cruised by his cubicle to find him playing Warcraft online during his lunch hour. David was a junior attorney and his stock was rising within the firm, from what she'd overheard, but then she saw him with a Spice-girl-type stick in three-inch heels and decided he probably wasn't the right type. Kyle, the FedEx delivery guy, was a hunk and obviously spent a lot of time at the gym, but he had the imprint of an absent wedding band on his left hand and a roving eye. He was either freshly caught-and-released, or was a shark cruising shallow waters.

There was also Craig. He was sweet, and she'd had a nice time at the concert. He wasn't on the "no" list, and she couldn't really find any objections to him except for the fact that he was boring. On a color scale, he was a gray winter's day. He told her about his Saturday fly tying class and his favorites, the woolly bugger and the Montana nymph. They worked best for trout, pike, and walleyes. At Starbucks, he preferred frou-frou macchiato drinks to a good cup of Kona or a strong Caffe Verona, and he bought his clothes online because he couldn't stand to shop at the Galleria. Ever. The worst part was that she sensed that he was interested in her. He would interpret being approached as a donor to be an overture for a relationship. If he agreed, he would want contact with the baby, she was sure. She wasn't in it for the relationship—she was in it for the baby. Plain and simple.

She stopped by the mall on her way home from work and looked at the new fall fashions at Macy's. Soon the weather would be turning cool again, and she saw some things she liked, but reasoned that she shouldn't spend the money in light of her tenuous financial situation.

She wandered down to the baby department to see what was new. She found an adorable pink sweater in a delicate knit with rosebuds, and a matching hat. She ran her hand over the soft weave and breathed in its scent. She could imagine baby powder and saltines. Maybe Cheerios. She took it to the counter and charged it to her Visa card. The clerk exclaimed that it was the prettiest sweater they had, and she carefully wrapped it in tissue before bagging it up. She asked Rain if it was for her, and she answered that it was for a friend.

When she got home, she went into the spare bedroom and opened the dresser. In the top drawer, neatly folded, lay pale yellow baby blankets, onesies with ducks and bunnies, and dresses with tiny collars. Soft terrycloth toys, designer baby shoes in supple pink leather, and a Hello Kitty pacifier were tucked in between the stacks. She pulled the new sweater from the Macy's bag and pulled away the tissue paper. She refolded it gently so that the tiny buttons would show in the front and carefully placed it in the stack. Reverently, she closed the drawer.

❖ ❖ ❖ ❖

It had only been a little over three weeks since Dylan left for college, but Bebe felt a surge of joy at the prospect of having one of her boys at home again. The Friday afternoon before Labor Day was slow, so she left work early. Next Tuesday morning, the fun would begin.

Someone's pet always ended up with allergy issues, foxtails, or injuries after a long weekend of fun.

When Dylan's car pulled into the driveway, Bebe was taking a pan of brownies out of the oven. They were his favorites, and made the house smell wonderful.

She went out to help him carry in his stuff, and hugged him hard, planting a kiss on his cheek. He hugged back one-armed and popped open his trunk. Inside were two baskets full of dirty laundry. He deposited them in the laundry room before following the scent of chocolate into the kitchen where the brownies sat cooling on the counter.

He poured a glass of milk, positioned himself at the counter in front of the plate of brownies, and complained about the traffic he'd encountered. "I think I'll wait until 8:00 to leave Monday night after the traffic has cleared out."

"That reminds me," Bebe said. "Grandma's planning a barbeque for Monday."

He winced. "I told Tyler that I'd go with him to Nicole's on Monday. Her parents are having a cookout and a pool party, and Zach and some other guys are home from school. I kind of promised to go."

"Oh, okay." Bebe was not so much disappointed that he wouldn't be going to her mom's, as the fact that she wouldn't be seeing much of him all Monday. "Don't worry about it. But you should call your grandma sometime this weekend to say hello."

He agreed, and after he had downed four brownies and the milk, he put in a load of laundry and kicked off his shoes in front of the television.

It turned out that he had plans for that night also, but they insisted that he at least have dinner with them first. He quickly agreed, especially since they were paying.

He came in late after seeing the movie with Tyler, said good night, and headed for his room. It seemed odd to Bebe how fast she and Neil had gotten used to being alone after Dylan left for school. Now his belongings were strewn between the family room, the kitchen, and his bedroom, as if he were reestablishing his territory.

The weekend passed quickly and Bebe enjoyed spending time with Dylan whenever she could. He said he was starting a new job as a bagger in a grocery store when he returned to school. Bebe encouraged him to check at the student union to find on-campus Bible studies and Christian groups to plug into, and he said that he would.

They went their separate ways on Monday; Neil and Bebe to her mom's and Dylan to his friend's pool party. She made him promise that he would come home long enough to say good-bye before he drove back on Monday night. Bebe breathed a sigh of relief when her mother said that her brother Bobby had left town for the weekend and wouldn't be there. Everyone wanted to know if she'd heard how Scott was doing. She and Neil left the cookout early so they could be home when Dylan came by to pack up his clothes and go back to school. It was still hard to say good-bye to him, and she made him promise to request time off for Scott's graduation in October. Dylan said that he had made that stipulation when they hired him, and the store was willing to let him have the time off to support his brother.

After he drove away, she straightened his room, which left her missing him more. She'd made him promise to call when he arrived, since he'd gotten a late start, and the phone startled her awake two hours later. He was safe and sound, and said he'd had a fun weekend at home. He even said, "Love you, Mom."

Later in the week, there was another brief letter from Scott, and while Bebe was happy to get it, she again sensed that he was distant. Different. He mentioned that Rain had written, and that he'd heard from Uncle Bobby again.

Bebe sank into a chair at the kitchen table with the letter in her hand and stared at the words. There were several reasons why Bobby would write to Scott, and not all of them were for encouragement and support. Some reasons were bitter and selfish. He still had ghosts following him from his tour of duty, and from his homecoming, and a grudge that he continued to nurse. Perhaps he was entitled, if it brought him some comfort. But her part in it was exaggerated, and he wouldn't let it go. It overshadowed every family gathering, whether Bobby was there or not. She wondered if he realized that his bitterness could affect Scott's morale.

Bebe had ghosts, too. Some that he and the family knew nothing about and never would. But she owed it to her son to try to exorcise this one.

She picked up her stationery and addressed the letter to Scott. She began, "I don't know if you're aware that your Uncle Bobby has suffered from post-traumatic stress disorder and that he has a problem with substance abuse. He was drafted into the army at a very difficult time in America. Please share with me what he wrote."

Chapter 9

Rain spent Saturday afternoon with Jude. She brought Thai take-out for their lunch, but the strong flavors proved to be too much for Jude's queasy stomach. It had never occurred to Rain that her mother might have a problem with her once-favorite food, and she felt like a bad daughter. She offered to pick up something else, but Jude said that she wasn't hungry.

Jude gave some vague reason for William's absence, giving Rain the impression that she either didn't believe him or was angry. She was up and around, looking thin and wan, wearing a stylish velour pantsuit, with her thinning hair tucked under a soft turban.

They watched a documentary about the effects of global warming on the penguin population and surfed the channels for news. They made small talk, and finally Rain asked her mother how she was doing. Jude settled back into the corner of the couch and dismissed the topic of her health as hardly worth mentioning.

"So," she asked Rain, "what news on the dating front?"

Rain swirled her iced tea. "Not much. I went to a concert with a coworker." She shrugged. "It was nice, but there's nothing there. We probably won't go out again."

Jude chuckled. "Since when does there have to be 'something there' to go out with a man? I certainly never made that part of the criteria."

Rain lowered her eyes and answered, "That was you, Mother. I'm more . . . discerning."

"Discerning? Why, are you looking for a husband?" Jude had obviously meant it as a joke, but it fell flat, and she said, "You *are* looking for a husband."

"No," Rain said. "I am not looking for a husband. I just meant that I don't enjoy going out with someone just to . . . to . . ." Rain realized she had to tread carefully here. "If it's not someone I really enjoy being with, I'd rather be home."

"Home with Moses, or Elijah, or whatever that vicious cat's name is."

"Noah."

"How did you ever let Bebe talk you into naming him after some dusty Bible character?"

"He came with the name. He was rescued from a drainage ditch—"

"Yes, yes, I remember. The point is, you're a beautiful, capable woman and you shouldn't be sitting at home with the cat. You should be out spreading your wings, so to speak. Taking charge of your sexuality."

"Mother." Rain looked at Jude, exasperated. "Can we change the subject, please?"

"All right, how is Hayden?"

Rain narrowed her eyes at Jude.

"Well, if you're not going to tell me anything, I have to ask." Jude ran her finger around the rim of her glass. "I'll bet Bebe knows everything."

Rain stood and held out her hand for Jude's empty glass. "No, she doesn't." It was true—she hadn't seen Bebe in days. Jude handed over the glass and she refilled it in the kitchen.

She didn't want her mother to feel slighted, so when she returned with the freshened drink, she added, "Hayden and I had a disagreement, and it's something neither one of us will give in about. And that's all I'm going to say."

Jude lifted a hand of dismissal while she took a sip. "How's your job going? This seems like the perfect time to go back to law school. You have plenty of time on your hands."

Rain shook her head and laughed. "I am perfectly satisfied being a paralegal. I have no interest in going to law school, and you know it." Rain suddenly wondered whether she had avoided law school to consciously confound her mother's plans for her, or whether she sensed that it was as close as she'd wanted to come to being like her.

"But you shouldn't settle when you have so much potential. You owe it to—"

"Don't give me your second wave feminist guilt about not reaching my potential—"

"And don't give me your third wave excuses for not properly shouldering your responsibility to society."

Rain's voice rose in frustration. "So how does it help society when you win a case for Billings & Coombe that saves pharmaceutical companies from having to pay settlements to victims who are entitled to it?"

Jude looked momentarily stunned, but quickly recovered. "Well, touché. Just don't let your employers take advantage of you, or pass you over for a promotion because you're a woman."

"Mom, gender discrimination's not legal anymore."

Jude punctuated her response with a pointed finger. "It's not legal because women fought for the passage of Title VII. You've never worked in a world where your right to equal pay for equal jobs wasn't a given."

"Yes, Mom, thank you. And I'll pass my appreciation along to Toni, Mare, and Bebe when I see them. I didn't come over here to argue, you know."

"Who's arguing?"

At that moment, the front door opened and William came in with grocery sacks.

"What's all the shouting about? Can't I leave you two alone for an hour without finding World War III going on?"

He passed by the couch and gently tapped Rain on the top of the head on his way to the kitchen.

"I was just about to tell Rain that it wasn't arguing. It was stimulating banter," Jude told him.

"Stimulating banter," he repeated dryly. He pulled cereal boxes and cans from the bag.

"Can I give you a hand?" Rain offered.

"I've got it. Thanks," he said, giving her a wink on the sly.

"I can't stay long. Mom, are you still planning to meet us two weeks from today at Dulcinea's?"

"Of course. I wouldn't miss planning my own funeral."

Rain scowled. "I wish you wouldn't talk like that."

"I'm sorry. Celebration, then. I wouldn't miss planning my own celebration."

Jude glanced over to where William was methodically filling cupboards with his purchases. "William has no objections to discussing my funeral."

Rain looked over at William. He paused momentarily with his hand on the knob of a cabinet with his back to them. "Whatever makes you happy." He pulled it open and placed a can on the shelf, label front, next to another can of the same height and straightened them both.

Jude continued to watch him with veiled eyes. She started to comment, but Rain interrupted.

"I need to be getting back," Rain said, sliding her arms into her jacket and tugging her sleeves down.

"Oh, by all means, hurry back to Noah. He's probably wondering where you are."

Rain flipped her hair out of her collar and reached down to give Jude a peck on the cheek. "I'm ignoring that. Remember, two weeks from today at Dulcinea's." Rain looked over at William.

"I'll make sure she's there," he said.

"I can get there myself, thank you," Jude said, rising unsteadily from the couch. She stood tall and braced herself on the back of the chair beside her.

Rain glanced back to wave at William. He gave her a sweet smile as she left.

❖ ❖ ❖ ❖

Janice—Dr. Owens—called in sick at the veterinary clinic on Tuesday, which was, unfortunately, her day for surgery, and Bebe switched days with her. It meant sandwiching in her own appointments that she couldn't reschedule, and she felt under the gun. She spent time briefly familiarizing herself with the files of Janice's patients before scrubbing for surgery.

Her last surgery of the day was for Dinah, a feral cat who had just weaned a litter of kittens the month before. The adoptive owners wanted to ensure she didn't have another litter, so it was imperative that the cat be spayed as soon as possible. Although they assured the staff that the cat had not been around any males and could not possibly be pregnant, they expressed a desire that any pregnancy be terminated, if found. Bebe proceeded with the surgery, only to find that the cat was, indeed, pregnant with two-week-old fetuses. Bebe paused and considered her options. She could refuse to continue the procedure, but she knew it was very possible that the owners may simply abandon Dinah and the kittens if Bebe were to leave the pregnancy intact. She proceeded with the surgery, even though she wasn't comfortable with their decision.

Bebe informed Dinah's owners that she was, indeed, pregnant at the time and that she had followed their wishes. Dinah appeared to be recovering well, but needed to stay the night. She made a note on the chart to inform Janice so she could follow up the next day.

Bebe closed down her computer and drove home, feeling angry with Dinah's owners for putting her in the position of playing God. They were adamant that Dinah hadn't been exposed to males. Bebe wondered if they had been fully aware of the possibility of her pregnancy, but didn't voice their suspicions, in case the doctor refused to perform the procedure.

Bebe shared her frustration with Neil that evening, and he sympathized because he'd been placed in a similar situation in the past. Bebe made a mental note to inform the staff in the morning of her decision to test each female prior to spaying. There were other doctors at the clinic who would oblige owners if the tests came back positive, but she would not be terminating pregnancies anymore.

Sleep eluded Bebe that night. She carried her pillow to the couch and sat in the dark, wrapped in the afghan Neil's mother had crocheted before she died.

There had been four tiny fetuses, perhaps an eighth of an inch long, but kittens, nonetheless. Evidence of life. Babies. She rubbed her eyes and tried to erase the picture from her mind. It shouldn't have been her patient at all.

The truth was that this wasn't the first time this situation had come up. She had faced it several times since she'd been in practice. Perhaps back in the early days she had been so focused on being successful as one of the few women in the field, that she'd pushed aside the question of ethics to prove that she was capable of dealing with any situation. She couldn't afford to be squeamish. She'd had to prove herself. And perhaps she was just a bit in denial of what had been required at that moment in time.

She saw it differently now, after giving birth to two sons and seeing them grow to adulthood. She now had an intimate knowledge of the God from whom she had distanced herself in her college years. Life was life.

Her guilt was ever present like the scratchy white noise of an old recording.

❖ ❖ ❖ ❖

Toni fluttered to their table at Dulcinea's where Mare, Rain, and Bebe waited for her and for Jude to arrive.

"Buon giorno!" Toni dramatically threw kisses and settled into a rattan chair. She reached over to pat Rain's cheek.

"You obviously had fun in Tuscany," Mare said with a note of sarcasm.

Toni closed her eyes, breathing deeply. She opened her eyes wide. "*Everyone* should spend a month every year in Tuscany. The world would be a much better place."

"And look at this." Toni took off her shoe and passed it around the table. "Isn't it adorable? I picked them up in one of the little shops in Cinque Terra."

"Is it leather? You should really try animal alternative shoes, Toni," Mare chided.

Toni took the shoe out of her hand. "Yes, Mare, they're leather. I gave up cardboard shoes when my family left the old country."

"Girls," Bebe warned.

Rain gestured toward the entrance. "Here come Mom and William."

They waved them over to the table and began shifting their chairs.

"We'll make room for you, William," Bebe said, moving the place settings over.

Mare's chair scraped the floor as she scooted it on the tiles. "You have to join us today, William."

"No, no, ladies. I'm not staying."

They protested, but he begged off. He said he had an appointment and that Jude would call him when she was ready to leave. He gave Rain a kiss on the cheek and they watched him go while Jude scanned her menu.

"He's such a sweet man, Jude. Tell me again how you met," Mare asked.

Jude glanced briefly over the top of her menu. "In a book club. When it was his turn to choose the next book, he chose a play—*The Women*. I was impressed initially, but then I realized that he didn't choose it for the subject matter. He chose it because it was only a hundred pages long."

"Oh, Jude, I think it's great anyway. Arnie would never have chosen that," Mare said. "I think you're perfect for each other."

"He's a quivering bundle of neuroses, and I don't resemble him in any way, shape, or form."

"Mom!" Rain demanded. "Don't talk about William like that."

Silence reigned at the table as Jude appeared to be uncharacteristically at a loss for words.

"Speaking of book clubs," Toni added, diverting attention from them, "has anyone read a good book lately?"

"I fall asleep reading veterinary journals," Bebe said, scanning the menu. "Rain, how was the tilapia last time?"

"It was good, but it was a lot of food. I think I'll try the Asian Pear Salad this time."

Toni was disappointed when their server was female and that it was Rolf's day off. She waited until Mare had picked apart every entrée and settled on a grilled portobello mushroom on foccacia without cheese. Toni ordered a hamburger, medium rare, with avocado and bacon, with sweet potato fries.

She held her hand up to Mare, who had opened her mouth to speak. "Don't even say it. I knew you when you ate icing by the spoonful."

Mare swallowed her comments. She changed the subject by inviting them all to check out her website to see the textile exhibit she'd put together for the trade show. She made a point of telling Toni not to miss her line of organic shoes that were *not* made out of cardboard, by the way.

They all asked about Scott, and Bebe was guarded in her sharing, making sure to sound positive—perhaps, more positive than she felt. Rain said she'd gotten a letter back from him and that he sounded great. Bebe deliberately avoided eye contact with Jude. She had remembered not to wear any shades of purple whatsoever to spare herself unnecessary grief, and realized then just how secure and empowered the color made her feel.

After everyone had ordered and the drinks had arrived, Bebe could see that Jude was fading, and she took it upon herself to initiate their planning. Mare asked if they could wait until after they'd eaten to discuss it, which drew a sour look from Jude.

"I think we should get started." Bebe looked over at Toni. "You said we have a place to stay in Monterey, right?"

"Yes, I've never been there, but judging by what I know of Marshall Davis, it should be fabulous."

Rain said, "I think we should make menus and divide up the shopping. Maybe everyone should take a meal."

Toni tapped her finger on the glass tabletop. "There are so many wonderful restaurants. Wouldn't it be easier to just dine out?"

"Toni, maybe you can afford to eat out every meal, but some of us aren't so fortunate," Mare said.

"It was just a suggestion." Toni sipped her mimosa. "I already have a meal in mind, actually."

Mare studied her. "I'll bring along some miso, just in case."

Toni frowned and waggled her head. "And I'll bring along a nice juicy steak, just in case."

Bebe saw Jude sigh heavily and the energy seemed to drain out of her. Bebe chided them, "This is not productive, girls. We need to move along."

They each threw her a penitent look.

"Now, assuming that we arrive on Friday afternoon and return on Monday morning, we have eight meals to plan."

"Well," Toni said, glancing over at Mare, "if no one objects, I'll pick up the tab for one of the meals. We can dine out or have it delivered—whatever everyone wants to do."

"That's very generous, Toni," Bebe said. "Just make sure we have a variety of choices available for whatever restaurant you choose."

"Of course," Toni said. "I'm easy."

Mare rolled her eyes.

The other meals were divided between the four of them and suggestions were given. Jude was conspicuously quiet, and Bebe glanced over at Rain, who caught her eye. Bebe made a mental note to ask what accommodations they should make for Jude's meals.

They moved on to an agenda for the weekend and decided that a trip to Cannery Row was in order for anyone who felt up to it. They would have to get an early start to avoid traffic and to find parking on the weekend. Afterward, they could take the 17-Mile Drive on the way back to the house.

They continued to plan when their food came, and Bebe was mindful of how subdued Jude was. She tried not to let her concern show, knowing that it would only bring a curt response. As they ate, she noticed that Jude merely picked at her food and put her fork down again. When the server asked if she wanted a to-go box, Jude shook her head and waved the food away. The others also noticed. She wondered if Jude would have the stamina to follow through with any kind of plans that they made as a result of the weekend.

Bebe thought about trying to move the date up, but remembered that everyone had a full schedule. Mare had the textile show, and she, herself, would be gone next month for Scott's graduation and then have ten days with him that she wouldn't sacrifice. Toni was accompanying Lawrence to New York while he visited universities in the state, and she doubted that Toni would give up a shopping trip to the city.

"Why don't I drive?" Mare asked.

Toni pointed her fork at Mare. "There's no way I'm riding crammed in your Prius all the way down to Monterey."

"Oh, it's not that far," Mare said indignantly.

Bebe offered her Highlander. "It has plenty of space. We could all meet at Jude's and I'll drive the rest of the way. It's not a hybrid, but it's better than each of us driving separately."

Mare agreed reluctantly.

They ordered two slices of cheesecake to share between them, along with coffee. After the plates were cleared away and leftovers boxed, they split the bill evenly and included Jude's meal. "Our treat," they told her, and for once, she didn't argue. Bebe suggested that Rain phone William while they waited for the receipt.

Later that day, Bebe gave William a call to check on Jude, and he said that she slept the afternoon away. The luncheon wore her out.

"William, tell me honestly, do you think she'll be okay for the weekend in December? Is there anything we should know?"

He hesitated. "Call me when it gets closer to that time. The stairs are getting the best of her, so I'd put her on the ground floor near a bathroom. I suspect she'll reserve all her energy for this event. But I don't think it's a good idea that she attends any more luncheons with the four of you. Too many hormones."

"The same goes for me, frankly. I don't know how we managed to live together for so long in that house without killing each other."

"Common bonds. Militant sisterhood?"

"We weren't all that militant. Some of us were just naïve and confused. But you're right about having a common bond. That was Rain."

❖ ❖ ❖ ❖

November 10, 1971

"Did you pick up the ice cream?" Bebe asked Mare as she came in and set two bags of groceries on the kitchen table. Bebe shifted Rain to her left hip and rooted around in the freezer until she found a frozen pizza.

"Rainbow sherbet." Mare handed the sherbet to Bebe who placed it in the freezer. Mare tweaked Rain's tiny nose as she gazed wide-eyed at Mare over Bebe's shoulder. "Got your nose! What a happy birthday! You have ice cream named after you."

Bebe turned the oven temperature to a mark they had scratched onto the dial that they estimated was 400 degrees. The numbers on the dial had long since been rubbed off. One mark was for pizza, another was for frozen dinners. The oven would only accommodate one pizza at a time, which was just enough for the four of them.

Rain sucked on a handful of Bebe's hair and yanked on it until Bebe dislodged the brown curls from her clenched fist and set her down on the linoleum floor.

"What about frosting?" she asked.

Mare produced the box from the grocery sack. "I got two, just in case. And candles and matches."

Bebe read the instructions on the white frosting mix. "Do we have any food coloring?"

Mare rummaged in the cupboard. "Yellow, red, and blue. No green." She opened the fridge and got out the milk and margarine. "Hand me the mixer. I'll make it."

"Just don't eat it all," Bebe said.

"I won't!" Mare ripped the top from the box of powdered icing and dumped the contents into a mixing bowl. Then she measured out the margarine, vanilla, and milk, and turned on the mixer. A fine powdered mist and a sweet aroma rose from the bowl as the beaters spun.

Rain had pulled herself up by the metal kitchen chair, and slapped the plastic chair seat, jabbering. Bebe pushed objects on the table out of her reach.

Toni came in from class and let her macramé purse slide off her shoulder onto the floor, making a beeline for Rain. She picked her up and blew raspberries on her stomach, making Rain scream with delight.

Bebe picked up Toni's purse from the floor and gave her a stern look. "Toni, you know you can't leave this where Rain can get into it," she said, over the noise of the mixer.

Toni rolled her eyes. "Yes, mother."

"You would feel really bad if she got into pills or something that made her sick—or worse."

"Uncle. You win. I'll be good next time." Toni kissed Rain on the top of her head and set her back down on the floor. Then she picked up her purse and took it to her room.

"Hang it up out of reach," Bebe called, and then said under her breath, "She's too young for birth control."

Rain crawled to the electrical outlet and patted it. Bebe scooped her back up onto her hip.

Bebe got out plates and cups and slid the pizza into the oven one-handed. The door hung open slightly, since the round pizza pan didn't quite fit. Rain leaned down and reached toward the heat. Bebe turned away from the stove. "Here," she said to Toni when she came back in, "take her."

Toni took Rain and zoomed her through the air and out of the kitchen, making airplane noises. Rain screamed and laughed.

Bebe got out four bottles of Tab, and a bottle of juice for Rain and set them on the table. Toni zoomed Rain back into the kitchen and handed her over to Bebe's empty arms. She smelled like a mixture of Chantilly and something rotten.

"I think she's got a present for you," Toni said, scrunching her nose.

Bebe peeked into Rain's diaper. "For heaven's sake, Toni, you know how to change her diaper."

Toni smiled sweetly, and picked up the receiver of the wall phone. "I've got to call Denny about tomorrow," she said, stretching the phone cord around the corner so they couldn't hear her conversation.

Mare turned off the mixer and took a spoonful to test. Then she took another. "I have to remind Arnie about tomorrow, too." She looked at Bebe. "It's okay if he comes, isn't it?"

Bebe decided to be truthful with Mare. "You know, I really don't like being your partner in crime. What if his wife finds out?"

"Oh, she doesn't care. They're getting a divorce."

Bebe hiked Rain farther up on her hip and asked as she left the kitchen, "Are you sure about that?"

"I'm sure, okay? Arnie said."

Bebe took Rain into Jude's room and waded through her dirty clothes and textbooks to change Rain's diaper on the bed. The pile of dirty clothes was disgusting, but at least it would cushion the fall if Rain rolled off the bed in the few seconds it took Bebe to rinse out the diaper.

She gave Rain the keys from her pocket to play with. Rain shook the keys and repeated, "Mma-mma-mma-mma." A small thrill went through Bebe, and she smiled and repeated "Ma-ma" with Rain, accentuating the sounds as she changed the diaper. Then she gave Rain a sloppy kiss in the crook of her neck.

Bebe twisted the small ring with an amethyst stone from her finger and slipped it into her pocket as she rinsed the dirty diaper in the toilet and deposited it into the diaper pail. She washed and dried her hands, and slid the small ring back onto her pinkie. She briefly held up the stone to catch the light, which that day shone a clear violet, and she smiled as she went back to the bedroom for Rain. The ring had been a gift from Bobby when she was in elementary school, and she could still wear it, although it now left an imprint on her finger.

She was just bringing Rain out all powdered and fresh, when Jude came home. Jude tossed her books onto a chair and took the baby out of her arms. Rain got a fistful of Jude's beads and stuck them in her mouth. "How's my little Raindrop?" Jude asked, as she nuzzled the baby's temple. Bebe watched them go, feeling dismissed.

Bebe smelled the pizza and went back to the kitchen. Mare was frosting the top of the cake and telling Toni to hurry and get off the phone to take the pizza out of the oven, so Bebe grabbed a pot holder and removed it. Mare peeled off the "Happy Birthday" sugar letters from the damp cardboard backing and lined them up on the top of the cake, adding one candle.

They all sat down together at the table and Jude fed Rain some puréed carrots and chicken before she ate some of her pizza. They took turns holding and feeding Rain on their laps while trying to keep her baby hands out of their food. Toni let Rain suck pizza sauce from her finger and laughed when she puckered her mouth, but Bebe pointed out that it was too spicy for Rain's tummy. They agreed that they would have to somehow find a high chair for her, since she was getting too big to pass around during meals.

They cleared away the dishes, piling them in the sink, and set Rain's cake in the center of the table with the ice cream and paper plates.

"Go get your camera, Bebe," said Jude. "We need to take pictures."

Bebe looked at her and said, "But you have a camera."

Jude made silly faces at Rain and bounced her on her hip without looking up. "It's out of film."

Bebe gave in and retrieved her camera from her bedroom closet. When she brought it to the kitchen, Mare, Toni, Jude, and Rain were already lined up around the cake. Bebe hesitated.

"Bebe, here," Toni said, reaching for the camera. "You get in the picture and I'll take it."

Rain squirmed in Jude's arms and started to fuss.

"Will somebody just take the picture?" Jude complained.

"No, no. It's fine," said Bebe. "Stay there."

Bebe focused the lens on the group. "Say cheese." She snapped the picture, and they all sang "Happy Birthday" and blew out the candle together.

After they had eaten cake and ice cream, and Rain was a mess, Jude handed her off to answer the phone. Bebe got a warm rag and began wiping Rain's hands and face. Toni silently got Bebe's attention, held up the camera, and motioned for her to pose with Rain beside what was left of the cake. She glanced over at Jude. She had her back to them leaning against the wall, deep in conversation. As the camera flash brightened the room, Jude turned to see what was going on. Bebe saw a fleeting look of anger cross Jude's face when she saw Rain and Bebe posed together, just before she turned back to her conversation. Toni advanced the film and handed the camera back to Bebe with a devious wink.

Chapter 10

The first thing Rain did every morning now, was to take her temperature before she moved from her bed. She charted the temperature and studied the numbers, wondering what it all meant. She couldn't tell whether she was normal or abnormal, but she knew she was getting a little closer to motherhood each morning. The chart would further define her options, regardless of the outcome, and it was a hundred times better than doing nothing at all.

To further feel like she was making progress, Rain started a journal. She wrote down physical descriptions and character traits that would make up the perfect father. The problem was that the character traits were hard to gauge. She would have to get to know a donor to truly know his character, and that wasn't part of the deal. Most of the information online was sketchy and many wanted to remain anonymous. Besides, she didn't want the mess of interpersonal relationships clouding the issue. She would be raising the baby alone, so she reasoned that, ultimately, her character was the more important factor. Nurture over nature and all that. Or was it nature over nurture? Whatever, she didn't need a dad—she needed a donor.

She stood in her extra bedroom and envisioned where a crib, dresser, and changing table would fit best. The crib should be away from the window, for obvious safety reasons. She could make curtains for the window and coordinate with a soft rug in any color or pattern she wanted to use, and no one could argue with her.

There was always the chance that she would have to sell the house. She hadn't heard from Hayden, but they would eventually have to meet to discuss what to do about it.

Hayden would have made a great dad.

She wanted a girl. She'd been around Bebe's boys when they were growing up. She had seen the division of labor at the time between Bebe and Neil, and she wondered if things had changed since the boys had left. She knew that Neil was the sports enthusiast and parent volunteer for their overnight Boy Scout events. Of course, it didn't necessarily follow that any boy Rain had would also be into sports or have outdoor interests, but at least, for Bebe's family, it was fortunate that Neil was around, she had to admit.

Rain read up on assisted reproduction technology and was initially discouraged at the success rates for women in her mid-to-late thirties category. She had a better chance of getting pregnant using someone's donor egg than using her own, but that gave her more than a 30 percent chance of having a multiple birth. What would she do with twins—or triplets? That also raised the likelihood of having low-birthweight babies and miscarriages.

If she had to use donor eggs, she would give birth to a child to whom she was not related in any way. And there was always the matter of money. It was an expensive undertaking, requiring time and money with no guarantee of success. How much would she give to have a baby of her own?

A niggling thought unsettled her. Assisted reproduction technology was simply a sign of the progress of the times available to her, wasn't it? It was her right to have a child, whether or not there was a father figure. Who knows, she could even meet someone later who was open to a relationship with a woman who had a child—the right kind of man who would love the child as his own.

That opened up all kinds of issues. Should she tell her child that she was not biologically related to either parent? There would be questions about her medical history when she became an adult. But would she want to know her "real" parents? Would she be angry? Possibly, by then it could be very commonplace to be a product of in vitro. Should she choose a donor listed as "open," just in case her child wanted to know her paternal parent, or close off the option of future contact altogether? She never knew her own father, and it hadn't made a difference.

That wasn't entirely true. To be honest with herself, she had to admit that a chunk of her life was lost because she grew up without a dad. She didn't entirely blame her mother. Somewhere out there was a man who dodged his obligations to her. But it was entirely possible that Jude never even told the guy that she was pregnant. And it was also possible that she didn't have a clue as to who he was.

Even though Rain could carefully choose the physical and genetic characteristics of a father, she still wouldn't know him, and neither would her child. Would it be enough to know that Rain made a conscious choice to have a child—that she chose having a child over having Hayden?

❖ ❖ ❖ ❖

"I don't know how Fluffy got pregnant, Dr. St. Clair. She never goes out of our yard. Never." Fluffy's mommy smoothed the white hair from the dog's eyes.

"I understand, Mrs. Lanham," Bebe said, checking Fluffy's soft underbelly. "But Fluffy couldn't get pregnant on her own. Is it possible that another dog could have gotten into your yard?"

"Oh, no. My Jojo is so protective. Why, if another dog ever came into our yard, Jojo would chase him right away."

Bebe paused and considered the woman. "Jojo?"

"Why, Jojo is my other dog. Fluffy had a litter two years ago and we decided to keep Jojo. He's been such good company for her when we're gone."

"Has Jojo been neutered?"

"No, we've been meaning to, but money's tight, you know, and we just haven't been able to afford it."

Bebe covered her mouth to hide a grin. "Mrs. Lanham, I think it's very likely that Jojo is the father of Fluffy's puppies."

The woman looked at her in distaste. "Jojo is her son," she explained delicately, smoothing Fluffy's fur. "There is just no way that he could be the father. He would never do that."

"Dogs don't think in those terms. I assure you, he's quite unaware that Fluffy is his mother. When she's in heat, she's just another dog to him, I'm afraid. And a fertile one, at that. You really should find a way to have her spayed."

The woman appeared to be processing the situation as Bebe completed the exam. Finally, she said, "This is really a bad time to have puppies. Is there any way it can be, you know, um . . . terminated? People do it all the time. And Fluffy's just a dog. She'll never know, will she?"

Bebe glanced up briefly and then focused on Fluffy's file, making notations, with silence hanging in the air between them. Bebe worded her reply carefully.

"I'm sorry, Mrs. Lanham. I don't terminate animal pregnancies unless the mother's well-being is in question."

"But you should have seen how the other litter completely wore her out. It can't be healthy for her to have more puppies."

"Fluffy is in excellent health. There is no medical reason why she should have any problems giving birth." Bebe smiled perfunctorily and closed the file. "But there are three other doctors at the clinic. I would be happy to refer you to one of them, if you'd like. They may be willing to accommodate you."

Bebe saw her out to the front desk and left the file with Georgeann. "Give her a referral if she asks," she told Georgeann quietly.

Later in the morning, Neil came up behind her and asked about

Fluffy. Mrs. Lanham had asked to set up the procedure with a different doctor, and he had an available spot in surgery. Bebe shared her conversation about Fluffy and told him of her decision.

He put his arm around her shoulder and gave it a squeeze.

She was feeling irritable, and slipped from beneath his arm. "Don't make more out of it than it is."

At home, she was happy to find a letter from Scott. He said they would qualify in the gas chamber the following week and that now they were doing their swim qualifications. That gave her the shivers. They had to jump into the pool with full packs, right themselves in the water and float, and he was surprised at how well he'd done, since swimming wasn't his strength. Some of the guys panicked and had to be pulled from the pool, but they had to do it over until they passed. There was no mention of Bobby or what he'd written to him. She hoped that he might just stop writing to Scott altogether.

Bebe waited until later in the evening when she thought that Jude was probably asleep and called William on his cell phone.

"I'm sorry to bother you so late, William, but I didn't want to wake Jude. To tell the truth, I didn't really want her to know I called at all."

"It's no problem, Bebe. She's so full of pain meds I don't think a freight train could wake her up."

"I wanted to know what food you think we should bring for Jude on our weekend trip. I mean, if there's something special we should have, in case she has trouble eating what we've planned."

"She hardly eats anything anymore. I think in addition to her illness, her medications lower her appetite."

"She didn't eat much of her meal at Dulcinea's. Just sort of pushed it around her plate. We've divided up the meals for our trip, but I'm sure there will be at least one meal she won't be able to eat."

"Bland food seems to agree with her the most. A word to the wise—some days she gets a craving for salsa, but she can't handle it. No Mexican food."

"Right. If you think of anything else specific, please call me. Or Rain. By the way, has Rain visited Jude lately?"

He sounded a bit guarded when he answered. "Occasionally. She's coming over for a few hours on Saturday while I'm out."

A plan began to form in Bebe's head. Saturday was her birthday, and she'd like nothing better than to stop by the outlet mall with Rain on their way back to celebrate. "Maybe I should come with her. The luncheons don't give us much time to talk."

"I think Rain should come alone, Bebe. You'll have plenty of time to talk later on your trip."

"Oh, yes. Of course, Rain should spend time alone with Jude. I'll see her soon."

Bebe said good-bye and hung up, smarting at the suggestion that it was best for her not to come. She knew that Rain wasn't crazy about going to Jude's, but she hadn't meant to horn in. She hoped that William didn't see it that way.

* * * *

When Rain got the call from William asking her to spend Saturday afternoon with her mother again, she considered saying she had plans, but guilt won out. She had wanted to take Bebe to lunch for her birthday, but she had to scrap that idea. There would be other birthdays, and she could always swing by with her gift on Sunday after Bebe and Neil got home from church.

For many years while she was growing up, Rain spent weekends, including Bebe's birthday, at their house. Before Scott and Dylan were born, it was just the three of them, and Rain loved it. Sometimes she'd thought of her mom spending those weekends alone, but Jude was never home when Rain called to say good night. Often Rain found her in a sour, combative mood when she returned on Sunday night, and as she got older, finally put two and two together and realized that on those weekends her mother had had dates that ended in disappointment. Occasionally, her mother was surprisingly optimistic, but it never lasted. As an adult, Rain watched her mother sabotage any relationship that showed promise and Rain didn't know why—until her mother met William. Rain had first thought him to be very brave. But she finally recognized that their relationship had settled into one of codependency. To her mother, he was simply manageable and safe.

As Rain grew older, she felt less guilty about the secrets she kept from her mother. Like the fact that she had a whole set of Barbies at Bebe's house, which she couldn't wait to get into and even dreamed about when she was back at home in the Bay Area. Or the bag of discarded makeup that Bebe let her play with, along with her old high heels and jewelry. There were only two pieces of jewelry that Bebe refused to let her play with—her grandmother's pearl necklace and a small silver ring with an amethyst stone. She said it had been a gift when she was little. Bebe had almost lost it once and didn't want to chance losing it again.

She let Rain play hairdresser and she filled Bebe's hair with barrettes. Sometimes Bebe swept Rain's hair up into a bun and she'd look like a prom queen or a movie star. Once after coming home from Bebe's when she was older, she even bought a teen magazine and hid it from her mother, but it disappeared, and the next time she asked to go to Bebe's, Jude made up a flimsy excuse to explain why she couldn't go, giving Rain a look that said the reason should be apparent.

Sometimes when Rain came home from a weekend at their house, she would line up her stuffed animals and play veterinarian. But she sensed that her mother disapproved, Jude was jealous of the time she spent with Bebe, and she kept her doctor play to Bebe's house. At Bebe's, they took her to visit the clinic on Saturdays and she got to know the other doctors and some of the staff. They suggested that she volunteer there in the summer when she was fourteen, but her mother wouldn't allow her to live with Bebe all summer.

As Rain grew up, her mother was always busy working or out supporting some cause. She specialized in cases involving sexual harassment and gender discrimination, and when Rain was a teen and Jude had explained to her the definition of a hostile work environment, Rain couldn't help but think that it would apply to William, if only he were paid for the work he did keeping house for her mother. Jude did pro bono work for a local women's shelter and actively supported high profile pro-abortion election candidates, plastering her car with bumper stickers, until she moved to a law firm whose main clients were pharmaceutical companies. She became more conservative in her activities and ceased to put stickers on her increasingly expensive vehicles. Rain figured that the pharmaceutical companies didn't like controversy. But it didn't mean that they saw more of her at home. If anything, she spent longer hours at the office.

Then Bebe got pregnant—several times—and lost the babies. Sometimes the miscarriages interfered with plans they'd made, and Rain felt like an afterthought. But eventually, when Rain was seventeen, Scott was born, and the next year they had Dylan. It marked the end of their trio, and Rain had felt a bit jealous.

When the boys were babies, she saw a side of Bebe and Neil that she'd never seen before. They became totally preoccupied with the smallest progress the boys made and used baby talk with them as they did with their puppies. Rain thought it was a bit excessive, but she watched Neil, in particular—fascinated with his transformation—remembering how his eyes shone when he held the babies.

When the boys were toddlers, Bebe and Neil started going to church. Rain had never been to church and had no religious training at all, but she'd gone with them a few times. She went mostly to help with the boys in the nursery. They would cling to her until they felt comfortable around the other children and adults, and their little hands felt warm in hers or around her neck when they cuddled in her lap. Sometimes, holding them brought tears to her eyes. Then her jealousy would dissipate and she felt like she was still part of the family. Often, she pretended they were hers.

It reminded her of the baby she'd "lost" just after she turned sixteen, the one Bebe knew nothing about, and she struggled to justify it all over again. When she first told her mother she was pregnant, Jude's anger flared and quickly burned away as she assured Rain that it was a rite of passage for a woman to have an abortion. She could choose when to have children later, after her career was established—there was no rush. Rain knew that as far as her mother was concerned, it was her only option. Jude assured her that Bebe would agree. But Bebe was struggling to carry her own pregnancy at the time, and it seemed almost cruel for Rain to tell her that she'd gotten pregnant through carelessness with a boy she didn't love. It was the only real secret she'd ever kept from her.

Rain realized that she was now at the same age as Bebe when she'd had her boys. There was hope for her, yet.

* * * *

Rain was the good daughter and drove over to stay with Jude on Saturday so that William could run errands. Her mother was asleep when she arrived, so she went to Jude's computer in the office and logged on. To her surprise, the alumni site popped up again.

What (or who) was her mother trying to find? Was she just feeling nostalgic, or was she connecting with someone? Rain wondered whether William knew.

Jude began to stir about an hour later, and Rain went up to say hello and to check on her. Jude said she was going to take a shower, and that she didn't need any help.

She slowly made her way down thirty minutes later looking totally exhausted and dropped onto the couch. Rain fixed her a glass of water, poured herself an iced tea, and sat down across from her mother.

Sensing that her mother was too exhausted to talk, she tried to find something on television that they could watch.

"Well, there's football, and there's football," she said, flipping through the stations. "Or we have a special about jungle predators—ew. Never mind." She kept scrolling, but nothing caught Jude's attention until they passed a red-faced television preacher with overly styled white hair, shouting from a grossly ornamental pulpit.

"I don't know how Bebe ever got caught up in all of that," Jude said, shaking her head in disgust. "She used to have a good head on her shoulders."

Rain clicked the guide button and continued to scroll through movie channels. "Bebe's church isn't like that, Mom. It's very simple and down-to-earth. And her pastor doesn't yell. He doesn't even wear a suit."

"So, she has you going to church with her, I see. Better hold on to your wallet."

"Oh, mom, I only go a couple times a year, and they don't beg me for money, either." Rain settled on *The Philadelphia Story*, even though it was almost over. "You like Katharine Hepburn, don't you?"

"Not in this role. She's a dizzy female who goes back to her abusive husband."

"But it's Cary Grant. Who could blame her?" She glanced over at Jude who had narrowed her eyes at her. "Just kidding."

Jude sank back into the couch, propped her feet up on the coffee table, and rested her head back against the cushion. She closed her eyes.

"Did William happen to mention where he was off to this time?" she asked.

Rain looked away from a very young, very smitten Jimmy Stewart. "No, where?"

Jude smirked, and opened her eyes long enough to say, "Groceries. Again." She closed her eyes, draping her hand across her brow.

"So, what is that supposed to mean? 'Groceries again.' You need groceries every week, don't you?"

Jude looked at her as though she were dense. "No. We don't cook. He brings home takeout every night. So why does he need to go to the store?"

"Oh, I don't know. For deodorant. Shampoo. Jack Daniels?"

Jude slowly tucked her legs beneath her and inclined her head toward Rain. "He's not at the store," she stated.

Rain tossed the remote onto the cushion between them. "Okay, I'll bite. Where is he?"

"How do I know?" she said with a shrug. "But I do know that wherever he is, Valerie is with him."

Valerie again. Rain rubbed her temple. "She's just a coworker, Mom.

What makes you think he's with another woman?"

"It's a very common occurrence when a spouse is terminally ill."

"You're worrying yourself over nothing. And you're not his spouse. If he hasn't left you by now, he's not going to."

Jude folded her arms across her chest and lifted her chin. "She's talking William into cheating you out of your inheritance. I know it. I owned the house before we met. I'm really thinking of leaving everything to you and cutting William out of my will entirely."

"Don't you dare," Rain said, pointing her finger at her mother. "He's been very good to you for a long time." Rain held up her hand when Jude tried to interrupt. "You know what? I don't want to hear anything negative you have to say about him."

Jude sat back and pouted. Finally, she said, "You don't know everything."

"Unless he's plotting your demise, I'd like to keep it that way."

After a period of silence, Jude looked at her sidelong, and asked, "Have you heard from Hayden lately?"

"He came by for the rest of his stuff. We didn't talk much. We haven't discussed the house yet, either, but I imagine we'll have to sell it."

"You were smart to stay and make him move out. It will be harder for him to get full possession."

"Who said anything about him getting full possession? We're two reasonable people and I'm sure we can both be fair."

Jude lifted her eyebrow at Katharine Hepburn's inebriated character giving a silly musical giggle. "Don't be a fool. I've seen some very reasonable people take their partners for all they're worth."

"Hayden's not like that."

Jude shook her head. "He's a man, Rain. He thinks he deserves it, and he thinks he can easily take it. You can bet his friends are giving him that advice." Jude shifted and winced briefly before continuing. "I've seen a string of men just like that over the past thirty years. Men who promise one thing and deliver another. And in every one of those relationships, the women started out with stars in their eyes."

Jude had seen too many nasty divorces, and from what Rain could gather, had too much baggage from her adolescence to see men in a positive light. Simply put, she was too jaded to give any man the benefit of the doubt. But what if she was right?

Rather than arguing with her mother, Rain considered her words. She trusted Hayden, but Jude had seen a lot of amicable divorces turn ugly. Perhaps, just as a precaution, she should go to the bank on Monday and remove his name from her account.

She looked up to find her mother watching her.

"I can help you with it, if you want," Jude said.

"With what?"

"Taking the house, of course."

"Mom! Please drop it." Rain immediately felt remorse for being harsh with her sick mother, and softened her tone. "If I need help, I'll call you, okay?"

Jude sighed heavily. "Better not wait too long."

Rain looked at her in alarm, but Jude added, clear-eyed, "You don't want him to get a jump on you."

Rain grabbed the TV remote and started flipping through the channels again. "Oh, look. *Project Runway*."

"Give it back," Jude told her. Rain passed it over and Jude began to cruise the stations, dropping the subject of Rain's house.

"Looking for anything in particular?" Rain asked.

"There was a cancer special. William didn't record it like I asked him to."

Rain knew that William was normally very conscientious, and probably had a good reason for neglecting to record it.

Rain was just irritated enough with her mother that she decided to test the paternal waters. "Mind if I check something on your computer?"

"Go ahead," Jude said, without glancing up from her search.

Rain went into the office and logged on to the computer. The browser menu pulled down to reveal the alumni website her mother had recently visited.

"Mom," Rain called from the office. "What's this alumni website? It says San Angelo State University alumni."

There was silence from the couch.

"Were you looking somebody up?" Rain continued.

The silence continued until Rain thought her mother was going to pretend she didn't hear her, even though she was only in the next room. Finally, her mother said, "No. None of your business."

Rain grinned to herself and took time to check her own e-mail since she had to pretend that she had a purpose for being on the computer. She soon emerged from the office and offered to refill her mother's glass. Jude kept her focus on the channels as she scrolled through the same shows that Rain had just perused, and said she didn't need anything.

Rain decided to take a direct approach, and see if she could read anything in Jude's body language that might connect the answer to the alumni website. She sat down and curled up on the leather sofa across from her mother, hugging a small chenille throw pillow that was lying there.

"So, Mom, there's something I've wanted to ask you about for a while."

Jude gave her a weary look. "If you waited until now to ask, it must be messy."

"Maybe not. You might not even know the answer."

"Well, that would be too easy." Jude settled on a news station and tossed the remote aside. She looked Rain in the eye. "Shoot."

Rain glanced away from her mother's direct gaze. Did she really want to know the answer?

"Well?"

Rain took a deep breath, and spit it out. "My dad. I want to know about my dad."

Jude looked incredulous. "What dad?"

"Exactly. Do I have one or not? *Did* I have one or not."

Jude rolled her eyes. "You didn't have one. You didn't need one. Toni, Mare, Bebe, and I—we were enough."

Rain was confused. "Are you saying I was a test-tube baby? Was there a guy or not?"

"Yes, of course there was a guy and no, you were not a test-tube baby. Babies were never made in test tubes."

Rain felt her irritation rise, but now that she had opened the channel, she had to keep going. "So, what happened with him? Or did you all just decide that I didn't need a father?"

Jude waved her hand dismissively. "He was nobody. *I* decided you didn't need a father. The others had nothing to do with it. It just worked out that we were able to arrange our schedules and share the duties of raising you. Sort of like a commune. Those were very popular in the early seventies."

"But did you know who my fath—my biological father—was?"

Jude drummed her finger. "Not necessarily. You were the product of an art happening and a skipped birth control pill." She frowned. "I think. There was one other guy I remember. But he wasn't important."

"An art happening?"

"An artist brought his exhibit to the school and they recruited students to pose wearing only body paint." Jude gave a small, wicked grin and quickly sobered. "But as I said, it may not have been him at all. You don't exactly ooze with artistic talent."

"Tell me it's not the same art teacher that Mare—"

Jude looked affronted. "Of course not. That man was a sleaze who used his position at the college to prey on impressionable young students."

"Oh, so this 'happening' artist wasn't a sleaze who preyed on young students. Gosh, I'm so relieved," Rain said sarcastically.

Jude sighed. "Rain, it wasn't a big deal. It was a time of great liberation and freedom. It was very commonplace, and even more so after abortion became legal." She looked pointedly at Rain. "We've had this discussion before."

Rain studied the nap on the pillow, framing her last question. Somehow, it seemed important. "Did the others know who he was?" she asked.

She shrugged. "They might have known him, but they didn't know who he was, any more than I did." Jude rubbed her eyes. Rain could tell that she was clearly tiring of the discussion. "What difference does it make? Why on earth is this so important now?" Rain could almost see the lightbulb go on. Jude's eyes grew big. "You're thinking of having a baby."

Rain put on her best disgusted face. "By myself? Am I crazy?"

Jude continued to study her, so she kept talking while squirming internally.

"Okay, so maybe Hayden and I had discussions about it, maybe even disagreements. But it's a moot point now. You can't very easily have a child without a father."

"Well, you can, but it's expensive and you never know what you're going to get."

"Exactly."

"And besides, your eggs are probably too old by now."

Rain was silent. She had tried to keep that fear at bay in the deep places of her desire for a child.

"You're what, thirty-seven? You never know. There are always donor eggs, but that, of course, is another expense. You could end up with a mutt."

Rain couldn't maintain her poker face. "But Bebe had her boys when she was my age."

"Yes. Well." Jude lifted her eyebrows, as though she were leaving things unsaid. "Anything's possible."

William came in just then, and Rain started gathering her things.

Her mother asked, "Are you sure you don't want to keep the house for yourself? The money might come in handy."

"I'll let you know." Rain noticed that William glanced over at that remark. She would have to call him later and assure him they weren't talking about Jude's house.

Bebe hugged them both and left, not even realizing until she was on the freeway heading home she hadn't gotten an answer to her alumni site question.

Chapter 11

Bebe was pleasantly surprised when Rain called late Saturday night to ask which church service they were going to attend the next morning. Bebe told her they were going to the early one, and Rain wanted to take them out for brunch afterward for Bebe's birthday.

Bebe's birthday on the day before had been quiet, since Neil got called out for a horse that slid off a trail into a ravine, and both of the boys were away. Dylan called her to say Happy Birthday, but of course, she didn't hear from Scott. Her mother sent her a check for twenty-five dollars, and Neil gave her a gift certificate to Nordstrom. Neil's heart was in the right place, but she wasn't the Nordstrom's type. She didn't have a thing to wear to even shop there.

They met up with Rain outside the church on Sunday and went in together to sit near the back. Bebe wondered what Rain thought about the music and whether the sermon on forgiveness struck a chord with her in regard to her mother. The pastor read from Psalm 147: "He heals the brokenhearted and binds up their wounds." Bebe sneaked a glance at Rain, hoping that she would seek healing for the circumstances in her life.

Halfway through the service, Neil was paged about complications with the horse and had to leave. They met him later after the service at a Mexican restaurant where Rain picked at her fish tacos and boxed up the rest to go. Bebe wondered whether the sermon had touched a need or whether something else had left Rain with little to say. She asked Bebe to meet her for coffee one morning that week.

Bebe spent the afternoon writing a letter to Scott. He'd said in his last letter that he survived the gas chamber, and was disappointed to only qualify as a rifle marksman. "I got the stupid 'pizza box,'" he wrote. The badge was shaped like a square with a target in the middle. He wanted to qualify as an expert, and he would try harder when he requalified the next year. Coming up was field week where they would sleep under the stars, hike for miles, and generally prepare for the crucible. Bebe didn't like the sound of it, but he seemed enthusiastic. He said he'd gotten another letter from Bobby, but he didn't elaborate.

In less than three weeks they would be going to his graduation, and Bebe could hardly wait to see him again. She called her parents and offered to take them along to San Diego with them, but her mother said she wasn't sure if they'd be able to go. Bebe was a little disappointed, and a bit hurt. Were they using the farm as an excuse not to go, and would they extend their lack of forgiveness to her son? Those wounds happened so long ago, but they seemed to be just below the surface in all her interactions with her parents.

She met Rain for coffee on Tuesday morning, wondering what was on her mind. Rain asked her whether she and Neil had finally managed to get away somewhere, and Bebe answered that it hadn't worked out, but they'd spent many pleasant hours watching baseball together, and would need to find a replacement activity since the season was drawing to a close. Rain expressed her surprise at Bebe's newfound interest, and then got down to business.

"I went by Mom's last Saturday. The stairs are really getting to her. And I think I might have to ask William not to bring the office home while Mom's . . . well, for now." She sipped her coffee and gathered her thoughts. "I hate to ask him. He ought to be able to rehash the day when he gets home from work, but it jump-starts Mom's imagination about this coworker of his."

"William would understand, Rain. He probably doesn't realize the impact it's having on her."

"Oh, I'm pretty sure he knows," she said ruefully. "It's not something she would keep to herself. That's why I don't want to ask him. If he knows and he's bringing it up to irritate her, I would just be meddling in their affairs."

"I think you need to be honest with him. They've been together for a long time, and it would be a shame if he had regrets later."

Rain curled a stray lock of hair behind her ear. "I guess you're right. I just need to find the right time."

"I've been meaning to ask you whether Jude's had any contact with her own mother. Whether she knows about Jude's condition."

"Shirley's got dementia. Mom sends money to a nursing home in Florida, but I don't think they've spoken since I was in high school."

"That's too bad," Bebe said, thinking *for you*.

"Frankly, after being an alcoholic for so many years, I'm surprised she's still alive."

"She must be made out of tough stuff."

Rain chewed her bottom lip. "There's something I wanted to ask you about." She glanced around at the people. "I'm just not sure this is the place to ask it."

"That sounds serious," Bebe said. "Why don't we find a table outside that's more private?"

Rain stood up and gathered her purse, and they moved outside to a secluded table. The October morning was pleasant though cool, but the metal seats were still chilled from the temperature drop during the night.

When they were settled, Rain said, "Well, there are really two things I wanted to ask you." She pinched the lip of her coffee cup and left an indent. "One is that I wondered whether you had trouble getting pregnant with the boys."

Bebe felt a bit surprised. "The hard part wasn't getting pregnant, it was carrying them. I don't know if you knew, but I had several miscarriages back when you were in high school."

"I figured it out. Did you ever find out why?"

Bebe paused to phrase her words. It wouldn't be welcome news.

"Well, yes. The truth is that it was a bit late for me to start having children naturally." Bebe glanced at Rain. "I was thirty-seven."

Bebe let the truth of it sink into Rain, whom she could tell was trying to remain unfazed. Finally, Rain asked, "But you didn't use in vitro, or anything?"

"No, we didn't. Like I said, fortunately for us, getting pregnant wasn't the hard part. We got lucky. Women are all different, and there are lots of factors that determine whether a woman can carry a healthy baby later in life." Bebe gave a grim chuckle. "Thirty-seven doesn't seem 'late in life,' does it?"

Rain shook her head.

Bebe ventured, "Have you undergone any tests?"

"I haven't gotten that far, but I have an appointment with a fertility specialist in a few weeks."

Bebe wanted to ask the obvious, which was whether or not she and Hayden had made any headway in reconciling, or what she would do for a father, but she kept it to herself.

After a period of silence, Rain changed the subject. "The other thing I wanted to ask is whether you remember my mom dating an artist in college. She said my father might have been some guy who came to the college showing an exhibit, but she was pretty vague about it."

Bebe sat back in her chair and thought. Jude had prided herself on how many guys she'd known at school, but there was only one with whom she had formed a brief attachment.

"I couldn't really say for sure," Bebe said. "There was one that your mom really liked, but that doesn't make him your father. He wasn't an artist."

Rain brightened. "Do you remember his name?"

Bebe thought hard. It seemed like such a long time ago. "Let's see. It might have started with a J. Or a G."

"Would you recognize his picture or the other guy's art if you saw it?"

"Possibly. Do you have pictures?"

"No, but I think Mom might be searching an alumni website. It was in her browser, and when I asked her about it, she got pretty touchy."

"Why do you want to know after all these years?"

Rain glanced off to the side and shrugged. "I guess I didn't care so much before. I believed her when she said I didn't need a father. At least, I wanted to. And I had William." She watched a mother and child enter the Starbucks. "But now I'm not so sure."

Bebe watched the expression play on her face. "You know, Rain, it's not easy raising a child by yourself."

Rain pursed her lips in irritation. "Women do it all the time."

"I'm not saying it can't be done. I'm saying it's hard enough at times with two parents. A single mom never gets a break."

"Are you saying you won't support me?"

Bebe gave her a gentle, chastising look. "Of course, we would. But we can't take off work when the baby is sick, or take turns walking the floor at night if he's colicky. We can't make decisions for you, and it's difficult to raise a child on one income."

"Women do it all the time."

"All right," Bebe said, sitting back and sighing. "I'll take a look at the website, if you want me to. What will you do if I find him?"

"Nothing, probably." She put the plastic lid back onto her cup. "If I did ever contact him, it wouldn't be while Mom's alive."

Bebe nodded. "You're right. It would be a good idea to wait."

Rain gathered her cell phone and keys, saying that she would be late for work. They got up and tossed their trash as they headed toward their cars.

Bebe felt an overwhelming grief for Rain and her impending loss, and she didn't want her to feel like they didn't support her. Soon she would be without a parent. Bebe worried that Rain might face rejection if her biological father was located.

"I can understand why you'd want to locate your dad, Rain. Especially since you're losing the only parent you've ever had. But just be careful. He may not want to be found."

Rain paused and hugged her neck, planting a kiss on Bebe's cheek. "Who said I'm losing the only parent I've ever had? I had four moms, and you were the best one of them all."

Bebe gave a little wave as Rain pulled away, and got into her car. She sat in silence in the parking lot with the October chill still penetrating from the long night before.

❖ ❖ ❖ ❖

Bebe left Dylan a message on his cell phone with the dates for Scott's graduation events to remind him to make arrangements with his professors. The plan was to drive down to San Diego on Wednesday afternoon, attend Family Day on Thursday, and return with Scott immediately after graduation on Friday. Even if her parents declined to go, it would be as special as they could possibly make it. She'd hinted to Scott in her last letter that Grandma and Grandpa might not be able to attend, just in case. She decided to ask Rain if she wanted to go.

Bebe called Mare to check on her progress with the meal planning for Jude's celebration, but Arnie answered and said she had already left for the show in Atlanta. Next, she called Toni, hoping to catch her between her Tuscany and New York trips, but was sent to voice mail. She felt time was slipping away from them, like the weight had shifted onto her shoulders alone, so she made her own lists for the celebration weekend. She needed to get the exact address of the loaner house from Toni to print out maps and to check out its proximity to shops, restaurants, and tourist spots. There were too many unanswered questions. Was the kitchen completely furnished? Should they bring cooking supplies, wood for the fireplace? Should they bring their own toilet paper?

More than their living accommodations, the purpose of the weekend weighed on Bebe. It would be so much easier to celebrate Jude's life if Bebe felt richer, instead of conflicted, for having known her. Bebe had often wondered how the three of them had fallen under her spell so completely.

❖ ❖ ❖ ❖

October 11, 1969

Bebe came back from studying at the library and found the Victorian once again full of students. She could hear Creedence Clearwater Revival playing "Bad Moon Rising" as she came up the walkway. She pulled open the screen door and wove her way through the people to her bedroom where she dumped her books on her bed. Then she slipped back through to scavenge food in the kitchen, hoping to remain unnoticed, as usual.

Mare acknowledged her when she came into the kitchen and then turned her full attention back to Mr. Bloom, her art professor, who insisted they call him "Arnie." The harsh ceiling light shone on the balding spot on the back of his head as he slouched against the counter and leaned in toward Mare. He was trying to look so cool with his top three shirt buttons undone revealing a nest of curly dark chest hair. He disgusted Bebe, and she couldn't figure out what Mare saw in him. Bebe noticed that some of the students were making jokes about him.

The Doors started singing "Light My Fire." She heard Jude's laughter over the music and marveled at how she could be the center of any group, even though she was just a freshman. It didn't hurt that she had already established herself deep in the inner workings of the Women's Center and had attracted the attention of one of the activist seniors. Jude's outspokenness and understated sensuality was a powerful draw, and Bebe had seen her work her wiles on guys before—albeit more subtly than Toni.

"Bebe! Over here," Jude called, and then turned to the other students. "You guys know my roommate Bebe." Bebe had no choice but to stop and acknowledge everyone. Jude waved her over and Bebe slipped between the students to where Jude stood by the couch. She draped her arm across Bebe's shoulders. Bebe noticed that she was slightly unsteady and her breath smelled like beer.

"Bebe came here straight off the farm—"

"Vineyard," Bebe corrected her.

Jude dismissed it with her other hand. "—vineyard. But don't get excited, 'cause she didn't bring anything to share."

A chorus of good-natured complaints broke out.

"Even though she might have grape juice in her veins, she's no bumpkin," she said, emphatically punctuating the last word.

She motioned to a couple entwined on the couch. "Hey, you, pay attention. This is important."

The couple laughed and gave Jude their full attention.

"Bebe is really tuned in and she's my right-hand *woman* and you all need to get to know her."

Bebe squirmed at all the eyes on her while Jude gave her the stamp of approval. Lifting her hand in a small wave, she slipped from beneath Jude's arm and drifted over to the opened front door to get some air. Soon, one of the older students sidled up beside her and struck up a conversation. He said his name was Oz, and after small talk about classes and professors, he said he was going to the peace vigil on the fifteenth because he couldn't get off from work soon enough to go to the protest at Golden Gate Park with everybody else. He asked her if she was going to the vigil, and she said that she might. When he smiled at her, she felt both flattered and panicked.

He waggled his empty bottle and left her thinking about the encounter while he went to the kitchen for a refill. She looked over to find Jude watching her, and Jude lifted her head with a satisfied smile. In spite of herself, Bebe smiled back.

❖ ❖ ❖ ❖

Rain balanced the clipboard on her knees while sitting in the waiting room of the upscale fertility clinic as she completed the medical questionnaire for her initial visit. This visit did not commit her to further expense and the cost was reasonable. If she wanted to go ahead with the procedure, then she would have to do some creative financing. She realized how healthy she was, answering no to so many questions about illnesses and diseases. She noted that her mother had cervical cancer, but she could answer no questions about her father's medical history. She returned the clipboard to the receptionist and dug out her basal temperature chart to have ready for the doctor.

Photos of families with children covered the walls. A variety of magazines on health and pregnancy, along with travel, world affairs, gourmet cooking, and fashion lay neatly stacked on the side tables. Trying to mask her anticipation and anxiety, Rain flipped through a fashion magazine that smelled heavily of perfume.

She glanced over the top of the page at the other patients. A couple looking close to her age sat without speaking, but holding hands. The man occasionally brought the woman's hand to his lips and planted a light kiss on the back. The woman looked up at him once, and Rain felt like a voyeur for the sadness she saw in the woman's face. This seemed odd to Rain, noticing the small bump on the woman's belly, and the way the woman seemed to cradle it with her other hand. She was the only obviously pregnant woman in the seating area, and Rain thought she should be happy. It appeared that she'd gotten what Rain wanted. Maybe there was something wrong.

Another woman looked to be in her forties. She was well-dressed—Ann Taylor perhaps—with manicured nails with matching purse and shoes. The only clue to her composure lay in the frown lines between her eyes, and the fluctuating tension in her jaw. Rain never saw her turn the page of her travel magazine.

How odd, Rain thought, that in this room where women waited for news of motherhood, there was no common bond, no connection between them. No recognition that they shared a common hope or experience. Each woman was alone with her own fears and the realization that they all swam in a great, shallow statistical pool that guaranteed at least one of them would end up childless.

At last they called Rain into a consultation room, and Dr. Sykes breezed in a few minutes later. He was clean-shaven, middle-aged and compact, with neatly trimmed fingernails and a buzz cut. She found his manner to be cordial, yet businesslike and competent. He briefly went over her information, the basal temperature chart, and lab work, and then asked about her reasons for coming.

"I'm single and I want to have a baby. I was in a relationship for almost eight years, but he didn't want children, so we separated. I just couldn't wait any longer."

"Unfortunately, we see this scenario often nowadays, and that's why we're here. I will say at the outset that your age may be a factor in whether or not you will be able to conceive and carry a child full-term."

Rain nodded and kept her eyes on her charts spread before him on the desk.

"The quantity and quality of a woman's eggs usually decline with age, although all women are different. We'll do an assessment of your remaining egg supply through hormone testing and do a vaginal ultrasound to measure follicle development. Unfortunately, there is no specific test available for egg quality."

"What do you mean by quality?"

"As women age, the eggs they release are less perfect, and there is a dramatic increase in chromosomal abnormalities. We recommend amniocentesis for abnormalities such as Down syndrome and cerebral palsy. There is always the option of using donor eggs."

He flipped through her chart to the results sent over by Dr. Lazenby. He pursed his lips as he read, frowning.

"Did you attempt to become pregnant with your partner?"

"Yes, for about a year."

Rain remembered the morning Hayden found her using a pregnancy test. Unfortunately, she wasn't pregnant, but he forced her to admit that she'd been off the pill for eleven months. She thought he would adjust to the idea, but it drove a wedge between them. She'd never seen him so angry.

Dr. Sykes asked about her lifestyle and family history, none of which seemed to her to give clues to her infertility.

"I see that you terminated a pregnancy at age sixteen. Were there medical issues at the time that you're aware of?"

"None that I know of."

"Based on your unexplained infertility and your age, I recommend we move ahead to intrauterine insemination. It's possible that your partner's sperm count was the factor in your infertility. If we're not successful, we'll progress to in vitro fertilization, before all fertility potential is lost."

Rain felt he draped hope in a dark blanket of chance. "What exactly does that involve?"

"You have a slightly irregular ovulation cycle, so we would prescribe a ten-day supply of Clomid and depending on the results of your day 3 FSH test, we may add a small dose of gonadotropin injections to force your body to produce multiple follicles and eggs. We remove the eggs from the ovaries and coerce fertilization in the lab. Then we culture the embryos for several days and pick the best ones for transfer to the uterine cavity."

"You do that here?"

"Yes. The egg retrieval is done by needle aspiration under local anesthesia."

"It sounds painful."

"As with any procedure, there is a certain amount of discomfort. We hope to retrieve five to seven eggs for the best results."

Rain felt bombarded by the technical information and incapable of taking it all in. "Seven eggs?"

"We'll transfer only two or three embryos, and you can choose to freeze the rest for a later transfer, if you prefer."

"So I could end up with twins or triplets."

"Multiple births are a possibility. The live birth rates for triplets and quads is low, or they are often premature, so we generally recommend fetal reduction to increase the likelihood of a live singleton birth."

Rain wasn't at all sure she heard him correctly. "Fetal reduction?"

"To reduce the number of fetuses in utero. Miscarriage rates increase with the number of fetuses. It's also in the best interest of the mother. There is much more stress placed on the body with multiples than with singletons."

The doctor continued, not noticing that Rain was stuck on the words *reduction* and *fetuses*.

"We do offer assistance with a donor service. Will you need donor sperm?"

"I've already checked that out." Rain colored. "On a donor website, I mean."

"Here is our rate sheet and consent form." He handed her a packet of information. "You can set up your next appointment as soon as those are completed and you've visited our finance office. I wouldn't wait too long, if you're interested."

Rain tried to make sense of the figures, but they were four and five number places with zeros and they blurred and scrambled. "Thank you. I'll have to take a look at this and come back."

Rain thanked him and left the clinic to sit in her car in the parking lot and comprehend the charges involved in the various procedure scenarios. Including medications, one cycle of IVF treatment without a sperm or egg donor was just under $10,000, with only a 20 percent chance of success, judging by the age chart. The two-cycle plan included assisted hatching and storage of frozen embryos, and the price went up by $4,000, but her chances also went up to 50 percent. A single cycle of IVF with an egg donor was $25,000—without including the cost of the sperm donor. As if it wasn't bad enough, the prices increased when she turned thirty-nine. Medication was estimated at $1,000 and was not included in any of the plans.

Rain clocked in at work just after lunch and e-mailed her insurance broker, briefly outlining the procedures to determine whether she qualified for any medical coverage. The agent told her that her comprehensive group policy covered the fertility meds, the actual IUI procedure, and the office visits, but not the ultrasounds. But in the case of in vitro, her insurance would only reimburse her for the office visit and part of the medication. The State of California Health and Safety and Insurance Codes required group plans to offer coverage for treatment of infertility, except for cases of in vitro fertilization.

She would follow the doctor's advice and try IUI first. She speed-dialed the fertility clinic's number to set up an appointment. She had enough in savings to cover what the insurance didn't for the first round. If that didn't work, she would have to move to Plan B.

Chapter 12

Bebe's parents decided they couldn't make the long trip to San Diego for Scott's graduation, but at least they planned a party for him at the farm on Sunday after he got back home. Paul naturally had to stay home because of the harvest, and Rudy and Karen's family had a conflict and couldn't go, either. Bebe asked Rain if she would like to go along, and to her surprise, Rain said she would love to.

Bebe contacted the travel agency that assisted parents in making hotel and other arrangements for the graduation weekend, and Neil cleared their schedules at the clinic. She checked the weather forecast and printed directions from the hotel to MCRD on Mapquest.

If she was honest with herself, she had to admit that it was both a disappointment and a relief that her parents weren't going with them. At least she didn't have to worry about them unintentionally ruining the day for Scott. They could say what they wanted to her, but things would get ugly if they carelessly said things in his hearing. She could only hope that Bobby wouldn't be there, since Scott hadn't mentioned that he would be.

Dylan drove home from college on the night before they were to leave, ate dinner, filled the washer with dirty laundry, and took off to connect with some friends. Bebe warned him to be ready to leave at 6:00 a.m., because it would be at least an eight hour drive without hitting bad traffic. The next morning, they had to drag him out of bed and wait until he got his clothes packed.

They swung by to pick up Rain, and hit Interstate 80. It was great just to get out of town, and Bebe felt euphoric, although she noticed that Rain seemed preoccupied at times. They took Highway 99 through the central valley to break up the monotony and stopped for fast food at the base of the Grapevine before they crossed. They crawled along Interstate 5 in Los Angeles, and finally came out on the other side into Orange County traffic, which lightened as they continued south toward San Diego. They knew they were getting close when they caught occasional glimpses of bright ocean.

They checked into the hotel and noticed that a majority of cars in the parking lot boasted USMC stickers. They found a place to eat and then turned in early. Bebe shared a bed with Rain, and Dylan and Neil wrestled for blankets on the other bed. Like a kid on Christmas Eve, Bebe had difficulty sleeping. Not only was she excited to see Scott, but she also harbored worry about Bobby in her mind.

The next morning, a long line of cars snaked through the gate at MCRD and they got out of the car at the checkpoint to let the MPs check over the car, including the trunk and under the hood. Other families stood around waiting for their cars to be checked: mothers, fathers, grandparents, brothers, sisters, cousins, children, and babies. Bebe began to wish that they had a better showing for Family Day and hoped that Scott wouldn't be too disappointed with just the four of them.

The day began with an orientation in the courtyard with the drill instructor. Afterward, they heard deep male voices chanting in the distance. A twitter ran through the crowd as more people recognized the sound. The officer explained that the recruits were doing a motivational run and would line up behind a rope barrier where they could find their recruit, but the recruits were not yet permitted to interact with them.

Then they would return to their squad bay to get cleaned up and the ceremony would soon follow, after which they would be able to spend the afternoon on base together.

The families hurried en masse to the roped area and waited in anticipation. Bebe heard the voices grow louder. Her heart swelled with pride and she felt tears prick her eyes at the thought of seeing Scotty again.

A blur of green T-shirts and running shorts bobbed along and stopped behind the rope directly across from the waving and yelling families. The men snapped to parade rest, standing stony-faced, with eyes focusing on a point beyond the heads of their ecstatic families, just six feet away.

Bebe scanned the faces, anxious that she would miss Scott.

"Do you see him?" Bebe yelled to Neil, who stood taller than the others in front of them.

Neil shook his head and continued to scan the crowd. It was impossible to tell one from the other, they had so assimilated with short hair and bodies tightened by being pushed to unfamiliar limits. Not one of them cracked a smile. The noise was unbelievable. Every family member shouted and waved at their recruit.

"There he is!" Neil shouted. He grabbed Bebe's arm and pushed her ahead of him through the pulsing crowd. And there he was, standing tall behind the rope, tanned and looking so much older, the muscles in his arms more defined and his face slim and etched.

She yelled and gestured along with the thousands of other family members, but Scott focused on a point where faces couldn't be discerned. It was like being on the other side of a looking glass and not being able to communicate. Soon, the drill sergeant gave them the signal to move on, and they jogged out of sight.

They looked from one to the other with shining eyes and then followed the group to the auditorium and found seats. The group was addressed by officers about the day's coming events and shown a slideshow about boot camp. Bebe was amazed at the challenging training that Scotty had experienced over the last thirteen weeks.

After what seemed like an eternity, they were told to move to the stands where the ceremony would take place. The officers stated clearly and in no uncertain terms that they were not to cross the parade deck, as it was only for Marines who had successfully completed boot camp. Bebe was amazed at how many clueless people still crossed onto the blacktop and were sternly reminded to go around. They took seats directly in front of the area where Scott's platoon would be standing to receive the eagle, globe, and anchor. The crowd reached fever pitch when they heard the first platoon enter the parade grounds. Everyone stood and craned their necks to see the lines of uniformed men marching in to stand before the crowd.

Orders were given, and far down the line, out of sight, Bebe heard the slap of each unit turning as one to face the stands. Bebe couldn't see Scott until his platoon turned with a snap. There, in front of her on the parade deck, was her son in his uniform. Neil took pictures, and then handed the camera to Bebe when she tugged at his sleeve. She fumbled with the zoom lens, and finally focused on his handsome face, resplendent in detail. He looked for all the world like a man. In spite of herself, she couldn't help thinking of Bobby in his army uniform, looking young and grim. Turmoil and regret for the way things turned out welled up inside her. She almost wished that he were there to see it, too.

It was a beautiful San Diego morning, and the sun heated up the crowds in the metal stands while they waited for each recruit in each platoon to be pinned. Finally, the staff sergeant stood before Scott and handed the pin to him. Scott removed his cover and fumbled with the back of the pin, taking long moments to get it correctly positioned. Then he stood saluting his sergeant, and they moved on to the next recruit. He was no longer a recruit, but now officially a Marine.

Then the last platoon was pinned and the men were released to be with their families. Everyone rushed down the stands and dispersed through the crowd to find their loved ones. When she caught up with Scotty, Dylan had him in a bear hug, pounding his back. He released Scott as Bebe came forward to throw her arms around him. He smelled like freshly pressed laundry and shaving cream, and he hugged her tight. Tears welled in her eyes and she was laughing in spite of it. Neil hugged him and lifted him off the ground. Rain even wiped away some tears of her own. Bebe was so glad to have her along. She really was part of their family.

They spent the day with Scotty on the base, eating lunch at the Bay View Restaurant and shopping for Marine Corps T-shirts, license plate frames, and bumper stickers. Scotty walked tall and was a perfect gentleman, giving his arm formally to Bebe, always aware of the fact that he had not yet graduated and was still under scrutiny while on base. He showed them around and talked about the guys he'd met and their experiences, especially about the crucible, that challenging two-and-a-half-day test, putting what they had learned into practice. He didn't seem overly disappointed that no other family members attended.

The time finally came to say good-bye until the next morning when they would see him graduate and take him home for ten days' liberty. They pulled away, and Bebe watched him through the window as he waved and joined some friends who were walking back to the squad bay.

The next morning, they checked out of the hotel, loaded the car, and headed over to MCRD to find a spot on the aluminum bleachers for the graduation ceremony. The color guard preceded the men on the parade deck, who marched out with perfect precision, and the band played the Marine Hymn. Bebe was moved by the music and the expansive American flag as it unfurled in the breeze over the proceedings. She silently wished that her parents were here to see him. They would have been so proud. She wondered if they'd regretted not coming, after all.

In no time, the ceremony was over and they were hugging Scott again in a crush of family members trying to locate their Marines. He grabbed his duffel bag and hoisted it over his shoulder as they headed for the car.

"Can we go to In-N-Out?" Scott asked as he buckled in beside Rain. "All the guys have been craving double-doubles for months. It was the food we talked about missing the most."

They got on the road and found the closest In-N-Out Burger, discovering that it was also the destination of other Marines and their families. Bebe had brought Scott a change of clothes because the only ones he had besides his uniforms were the jeans and T-shirt he'd worn to the recruiter's office thirteen weeks before. She handed him his old backpack with a clean pair of jeans and a T-shirt tucked inside. He changed in the restroom, and came out, glancing around self-consciously. She imagined that he felt odd since other Marines were still in their uniforms sitting with their families.

It took them nine hours to drive back home. Scott talked through the first two hours and then fell asleep. Bebe stole glimpses of him over her shoulder. His head lay back against the seat and his mouth slacked, looking like the old Scotty, except leaner and with a tan line showing through his close-cropped hair delineating where his cover had protected his white scalp from the hot San Diego sun.

Bebe felt a deep sense of well-being, with the four people she loved most in the car after an exhilarating two days. Just hearing the lilt and tenor of their voices and listening to topics of conversation she wouldn't ordinarily be part of opened windows into their everyday lives. Dylan told Scott about friends and activities on campus that only a brother would appreciate, and Scott shared some of the stupid antics of his bunk mates that almost cost their platoon a night's sleep or a phone call home. Rain teased him about changing his diapers when he was a baby, and asked him questions that Bebe hadn't, such as what movies he wanted to catch up with, and whether he'd written to any girls while he was gone.

Once at home, Bebe asked him what favorite meals he would like her to prepare, and she stocked the fridge and cupboards with things he'd missed. Scott and Dylan caught up with friends and played Rock Band late into the night. He replaced the license plate frame on his car with the one he'd bought on base and placed the shiny Marine Corps emblem with "Our son is a United States Marine" on the back of the Highlander.

Driving around town with this symbol of support for the Marine Corps on her car was something new. She wondered what Bobby would say if he saw it. He would probably call her a hypocrite. Her family might, also. But she began to notice the stickers on cars everywhere all over town, and felt like they had entered a vast brotherhood of supporters.

Her mom had everyone over for dinner on Sunday and it was Scott's time to shine. Bebe brought photos of the graduation ceremony to share. Rain was invited, of course, but begged off, saying she had plans.

Bobby stopped by briefly to eat and say hello to Scott. He certainly didn't give Bebe the time of day. She felt relieved when her mother covered two slices of apple pie with plastic wrap for him to eat later at home, and he left. She heard Scott remind him about his graduation from the School of Infantry in December and encouraged him to come down.

They returned home early after dinner because Dylan had to drive back to school that evening. Bebe wondered what Scott would do to keep busy without Dylan around until he had to return to SOI.

He came by the clinic the next day to say hello to the staff. Everyone made over him. Georgeann offered to let him have his old job back of cleaning the kennels, but he said he was busy catching up on his sleep.

Before they knew it, Scott was washing his clothes and repacking his gear. It amused her to see how serious he became with this process, double-checking again and again to make sure everything was complete.

They drove him to the airport on Monday morning, feeling much more relaxed about this leave-taking. He'd packed his cell phone and charger, and promised to call when he got there and faithfully every weekend. They reminded him to keep in touch with Dylan, too. He packed his iPod and extra clothes for weekend liberty. He said he didn't think he'd be able to come home for Thanksgiving, but unless he got sick and his training was pushed back, he should be home for Christmas. They kissed him good-bye at the curb in front of the Southwest terminal and watched him wave as he disappeared inside the building.

Bebe breathed a sigh of bittersweet relief. They'd had a great time together as a family and his SOI training was only eight weeks long. They would be able to catch up with him by phone, especially on Thanksgiving, which would help her make it through that day more easily. It would be the first time in their lives that they hadn't all been together for the holiday.

❖ ❖ ❖ ❖

Rain opened the door holding a bowl of Hershey's Kisses and DumDums. Three miniature characters looked up at her, one peering from a tricked-out stroller.

"Trick-or-treat!" they yelled in uneven cadence, producing their reflective sacks.

"Oh, my," she said. "Who do we have here?"

"I'm fairy Barbie," said a girl in a pink cloud of organza, pushing forward with her open bag. Her bitten fingernails glittered with frost and pink makeup flushed her face.

"Me! Me! I'm Buzz Lightyear." A small spaceman wiggled in beside her, knocking his soft helmet askew.

The little one in the stroller kicked her feet and pushed her Dora mask up out of her eyes. She held out her bag with the other hand until Rain dropped candy into each bag. Dora reached in to inspect what Rain had given her.

The mother prompted the children to say "thank you" and hurried everyone along as another group came up the walkway. Rain could see their fathers hanging back under the streetlights. One broke away from the group and continued to the next house with Dora, Buzz, and Barbie.

A steady stream of children came for about an hour and a half, some with adults and some unsupervised. As it grew later, they grew older. At 8:30, Rain locked up, shut off the lights, and read by a book light in her bed. She heard knocks at the door until 9:30, even with the house looking dark and deserted. She hoped whoever it was wouldn't get angry and resort to vandalism.

She tried to gather Noah beside her, but he jumped off the bed. She'd heard some horror stories from the vet clinic about pets being left outside on Halloween and she had made him stay inside all day. His stump of a tail twitched angrily in protest, and she hoped that he wouldn't retaliate with creative vandalism of his own.

Rain loved to see the little children who came to her door, all dressed up and absorbed in make-believe, but Hayden had never liked Halloween. He felt that they should give out something other than candy, like stickers or erasers, so in case a child was poisoned, they wouldn't be suspects. It had happened in a neighboring community when he was growing up, and every family where the child stopped was questioned mercilessly.

She admitted it was a good idea, and she had complied, even though it was obvious that some of the trick-or-treaters thought they were getting gypped. This year, she felt free to give the children the treats they really wanted, and she delighted in seeing their eyes shine.

One Halloween, she and Hayden had gone to a party dressed as Christine and the Phantom of the Opera. Hayden rented a tux and cape—woof. *That* was fun. They didn't try to sing together that time. Opera doesn't lend itself as easily to karaoke as Journey. But they made a great couple and they danced until she had blisters on her feet. It was one of the rare moments when he allowed himself to be lost in the moment. Perhaps the mask helped.

She had a vision of him with a child, tossing him in the air, snuggling, playing peek-a-boo. Was that why he didn't want a child? Was he afraid of being lost in the moment when he became a father?

❖ ❖ ❖ ❖

Bebe felt relieved when they received no emergency calls for the clinic on Halloween night. It was hard to deal with the aftermath of human cruelty. It usually left them with no choice but to euthanize the animal.

She'd had to lock up Suzie and Jimbo while trick-or-treaters combed their neighborhood. It was the first time that neither one of the boys was there to help her answer the door and to keep the dogs quiet. At 9:00 she let the dogs back into the house from the garage, and let them bark their heads off when someone had the nerve to ring the doorbell. Their racket never failed to discourage the teenagers who came out late.

It was their Saturday to work, and Neil had left early to make his rounds at the farms and ranches. She spied some minor damage on storefronts from pranksters as she drove to the clinic. Luckily, their building faced a busy street and wasn't an easy target, except for eggs and paintballs from drive-bys. It looked like they had been spared from a major cleanup this year.

"Where's Georgeann?" Bebe asked when she arrived at the office to find Michelle working the front counter.

Michelle looked up from the paperwork she was completing. Bebe could tell in her face that she was gaining weight with her pregnancy, and that she was tired. "She called me in early. She'll be in after she gets the TP out of her trees and replaces her front window."

"Yikes," Bebe said, flipping through an invoice for medications and initialing the top copy. "Sounds like she got hit hard." She looked up and greeted a client who was signing in. "Were they random targets?"

"No. Her daughter has enemies at school. Or rivals for Homecoming Queen. Something like that." Michelle stamped the chart and tossed it into Georgeann's in-basket. She turned to the client. "Hello Mr. Baxter. How is Romeo today?"

"Not so good," Bebe heard him answer as she ducked into the hallway.

Bebe checked in with Domino, a Dalmatian that had undergone emergency surgery for a stomach obstruction the day before. Domino raised his head when she greeted him and she reached into his E-collar to stroke his head.

"Good boy, Domino. You feel better without that chunk of Frisbee in your tummy?"

Domino's eyes rolled back in his head as she rubbed his ears. He laid his head back down and she gently examined the surgical site. It was healing nicely, and she asked one of the techs to change his dressing again.

She opened Rascal's kennel to check his stitches and found he was on schedule to be discharged. She asked Michelle to call his owner and to make a follow-up appointment. Bebe went to her office and sat down at her desk to check her e-mails. Neil came in from his rounds at the local farms, smelling ripe from the manure he'd been tromping through all morning.

"Hey," she said, scrunching her nose. "Did you change your shoes?"

"They're outside." He showed her the clean pair of jeans and shirt he had rolled beneath his arm. "I pulled a calf at Lassen's Dairy this morning. And I told him they need to assign someone to the calving pen. They're losing too many."

He slipped into the staff restroom and moments later emerged with his soiled clothes tied off in a plastic bag, which he slipped beneath his desk. Almond-scented soap now masked the faint odor of manure. "Remind me to take this home, will you?"

"You'd be better off tossing it in the trunk of the car," she said. "I have a hard time remembering my own stuff."

Bebe's day ended right after lunch, and the house phone was ringing when she unlocked the front door. Toni gushed on the other end about the fabulous shopping and the horrible gridlock in New York. When she finally wound down Bebe asked her about the place in Monterey where they would have the Celebration.

"Lawrence and I checked it out when we got back. It's a gorgeous house just outside of Carmel overlooking the ocean with private access to the beach. Marshall said there are linens and towels, and the kitchen is fully stocked, except for perishables, of course. He offered to have his cleaning service come to the house on Monday after we've left so we don't even have to strip the beds or do the dishes, if we really don't want to. There are three fireplaces, and a patio with a jacuzzi."

"Is it convenient? It's not too far out, is it?" Bebe asked.

"It's outside of town, but it's only a short drive to Carmel, and Monterey's only a mile or so farther. But it's private, just in case, you know . . . things get ugly."

"Toni, things are not going to get ugly."

"Bebe, how do you think Jude's going to react when we refuse to organize a war protest or petition to legalize pot or burn our Victoria's Secret bras? Any way you look at it, things could get dicey."

Bebe was silent for a moment. "I don't think that's what she has in mind. But we've got to be armed with some good ideas she'll be satisfied with that won't get us fired or ruin our reputations."

"Jude would consider either of those outcomes a success."

Bebe ignored her sarcasm. "For Rain's sake, we need to do this Celebration right."

"Okay, I get it," Toni said. "I think it's interesting, though. They've never been particularly close before."

"I think they might be making up for lost time. Rain's been going over on Saturdays to help William out."

"Poor William can use all the help he can get. I don't know how the man stood by her for so long."

"Maybe he loves her."

"What's to love? She belittles him in front of others and doesn't seem to appreciate anything he tries to do for her. She knows he's OCD and she purposely drives him crazy by keeping her stuff a mess. And besides, she's vindictive enough to cut him out of her will."

Bebe frowned. "Yes, that bothers me. He did mention that to Rain."

"I'm not surprised. She could do it, too."

"I know."

Toni hung up, promising to be more available. Bebe called Mare next, and asked how her textile show went.

"It was such a success, Bebe. I wish I had gotten back into it sooner. I don't really know what stopped me. Arnie, I guess. He was so needy and demanding, until I caught him with that nude model from his figure drawing class. Now he knows better than to cross me." Her voice dropped a little. "Sometimes I think God is giving me a taste of my own medicine." There was the sound of shifting the phone to her other ear. "Anyway, I handed out a ton of business cards and brochures, and I generated a lot of interest in my designs. I actually found a great nail polish that's water-based and nontoxic. Did you realize that traditional nail polishes have formaldehyde? All those toxins are absorbed directly into your skin."

"I never seem to have time for any of that," Bebe said.

"I know you go natural, but Toni should know about it. Maybe I'll bring a few sample colors to the Celebration."

"Please don't antagonize her, Mare. It will only make for a long weekend."

"Don't worry, I'll be good. You should have seen the eco haute couture that Freda Jiff made from recyclables. They were incredible. And the natural dyes that are coming out are just beautiful. Most people don't realize that the dyes in their clothes contain dioxin, formaldehyde, and carcinogens. And poor little kids and babies absorb those toxic chemicals right into the bloodstream because their little bodies run so hot and their pores are open. I found a line of organic children's and infants' clothing that's safe to wear."

"I'll keep that in mind if I ever have a baby to buy for. Have you had a chance to work on your menu, by the way?"

"Yes, and I've meant to ask whether we'll have access to a grill at the house."

"There probably is, but the weather might not cooperate. You'd have to call Toni to be sure. What did you have in mind?"

"Fish. Tilapia or freshwater salmon. We can always bake it, if there's no grill. It will be so healthy for Jude, full of omega-3 fatty acids, and very low in mercury."

"I would check with her first. I imagine that certain odors might be difficult for her to handle with her treatments."

"Yes, I guess you're right. I just thought fish might appeal to everyone."

"I thought you were vegan."

"I am, mostly. It's hard to travel and remain strictly vegan." Then she added, with all sincerity, "But it's always humanely raised, and I never eat red meat."

"Of course not." Bebe filled her in about the house and said she was planning for them to make some forays to Cannery Row and perhaps to Point Lobos, if she felt it would be accessible for Jude. "We'll have to play it by ear. A lot can happen in a month."

"Yes, poor thing. Well, I need to do some shopping. Arnie filled up on fast food while I was gone and he needs to detox."

They said good-bye, and Bebe put a roast in the slow cooker and added a few onions before getting back to investigating activities for the Celebration. She was worried about getting everyone together for an entire weekend with empty stretches of time and nothing to do.

She checked into the Monterey Aquarium and decided that it would involve a lot of walking and standing, and they could go only if Jude agreed to use a wheelchair. Point Lobos State Reserve would be a beautiful distraction. She checked online and found that Sea Lion Point Trail was visible from the parking lot and wheelchair accessible, so Jude should be able to navigate it without being too worn out to enjoy the beauty once she got there. It was thirty minutes round trip, and they could take lawn chairs if there weren't benches available.

The website photos stirred Bebe's desire to return to Point Lobos. It was at this dramatic, virile coastline where they took the boys when they were very young, that she had felt an overwhelming sense of peace and a tugging of her heart back toward the God of her childhood. No, not the God of her childhood—the God who knew the woman she had become. The God who could help her make sense of her life and confront the fallout of her choices.

It would be wonderful if Jude could gain some sense of peace at the end of her life, make some connection with her Creator to help her cope. Bebe could just imagine what that conversation would be like, and although she knew God could handle it, she wouldn't want to be in Jude's shoes.

Chapter 13

January 12, 1971

"Where have you been?" Bebe demanded over Rain's angry cries as Jude came in, chilling the house with a blast of cold air. Rain had turned a bright shade of red from crying and her tiny hands were clenched into fists. "She's been screaming for an hour," Bebe shouted, bouncing the infant in an attempt to quiet her. "We're completely out of formula."

"Aw, sweet baby," Jude said, cooing and smiling, and shrugging out of her coat. She scooped Rain from Bebe's arms and handed Bebe a grocery sack, saying, "Here." Jude cuddled the baby and rubbed her nose against Rain's cheek. The fretful baby quieted to a whimper at her mother's voice and rooted toward Jude's face, but immediately gained a second wind.

Bebe took the sack into the kitchen and prepared the formula while Rain cried, and Jude sang to her. When Bebe finally had the bottle of formula ready, Rain hungrily gulped it, alternately hiccupping and sucking.

"Where were you, Jude?" Bebe asked again. "If you knew we were out of formula, there's no excuse for coming back so late."

"I had a little errand to run," she said, rubbing Rain's tiny fingers that grasped her large one. "Something big. And I know I was a bad mother, but you'll understand when you hear about it."

"So what was more important than a hungry baby? Mare and Toni are gone, and I couldn't very well push the stroller down to Julio's in the dark with Rain screaming the whole way."

"Can't tell you." Her green eyes flashed and she grinned. "You'll hear soon enough."

"I hope it was worth it to poor Rain." Bebe huffed and went to her room. She wanted to slam the door, but it might have disturbed the baby, so she put on her Abbey Road album and plopped down on her bed with her economics book. The class syllabus said they were having a quiz the next day, and she had lost an hour of study trying to soothe Rain. As she began reviewing her notes, she heard a commotion outside in the streets. A fire truck raced by, rattling the windows, startling Rain into crying again.

Bebe went out to the front room and found Jude standing by the picture window rocking side-to-side with Rain contentedly draining her bottle. Jude's attention was not on the baby, but what was happening outside. Students ran past and turned the corner at San Rey, but Jude watched, detached, as though she was not surprised or alarmed, or even curious.

Bebe grabbed her coat and slid her arms into it. "What's going on?" she asked, flipping her long hair out of her collar. Something between excitement and fear flickered in Jude's face before she turned her back to the window, rubbing her cheek against Rain's head.

"Don't know. Maybe somebody pulled the fire alarm," Jude said casually.

Bebe went out into the street and headed toward the Commons with a group of students that grew like a spreading stain onto the campus. Bebe caught up with Kevin from her biology class. A plume of dark smoke rose from one of the buildings.

"It's the ROTC building again," he said. "They just moved in after the last building got toasted."

They continued on and stopped across the street from the burning building, keeping a safe distance from the rock-throwing crowd and the police. By then, the building was totally engulfed, reaching blazing white-hot fingers toward the darkening sky. Firemen channeled a torrent of water into the broken windows and onto the rooftop. The roiling ball of flame threw its energy across the street to sear their faces and blind them with its intensity.

Bebe looked back over her shoulder in the direction of the Victorian with a sense of foreboding. Was this what Jude had been doing? Was she involved in this?

The mob of students began to chant antiwar slogans, and the words throbbed like a collective pulse. Signs appeared. "Get US out of Vietnam." "Give peace a chance." As the firemen faced the blaze, the police turned to address the eye of the storm. Bebe and Kevin stepped backward onto the grass, but other students crushed in, getting into the faces of the police. Two students slipped through the police line and attacked the firemen before being dragged away by officers. The chant grew to a deafening roar as police in riot gear arrived. Bebe recognized a friend of Jude's in the front line angrily making his point until a policeman shoved him back with his riot baton. He came back again, and the policeman shoved him harder, knocking him to the ground and raising his baton high. Bebe quickly looked away.

From out of nowhere, a canister of tear gas lobbed into the crowd and students scattered in every direction, knocking Bebe to the ground. Kevin grabbed her by the arm, pulling her to her feet, and together they ran back toward the apartments away from the crowd. Bebe's eyes burned and her lungs congested as the gas wafted across their path. When they were safely out of range, they sat down on the curb, coughing and wiping their eyes.

Bebe had never experienced tear gas before, nor had she witnessed the type of mob mentality that suddenly combusted like opposing elements. She shivered with the sheer proximity she'd had to the violence, feeling unfairly victimized. She pulled her coat tighter across her chest against the gathering chill.

"You okay?" Kevin asked. She nodded and he continued, "Then we'd better get off the streets in case they come looking for somebody to blame this on."

She thanked him for helping her, and turned down 37th Street toward the house while he continued on toward Market Street. When she got to the Victorian, she looked up to see Jude watching from the window with her arms crossed and back lit by a lamp. Bebe felt her anger grow as she came up the steps to the door. Jude turned away from the window and went into the kitchen as Bebe came in and tossed her coat onto the worn sofa.

"What's happening?" Jude casually asked, popping the bottle top on a beer.

Bebe considered her coolly. "Someone set fire to the ROTC building. It's the second time in two weeks."

Jude sat down at the table and crossed her legs at the ankle, sipping from the amber bottle. "You'd think they would take the hint and close up shop." She wiggled the beer. "Want one?"

"No." Bebe pulled out a chair at the table and sat down across from her. "You were part of this, weren't you? I saw that guy . . . Jerry. Jerry Sandusky. Arguing with the police. You hang out with him."

Jude shrugged and hiked her eyebrows. "That doesn't mean I had anything to do with it."

"The police were getting pretty rough with him just before the tear gas. With a riot baton."

Jude's demeanor sagged minutely, and she licked her lips. Bebe continued. "I wouldn't be surprised if he was arrested, maybe even beaten. Things heated up really fast."

"He's a big guy. I'm sure he can take care of himself." Then she added thoughtfully, "We need to get out of Nam."

Bebe stared at Jude until she looked back. Jude met her gaze unflinchingly, and challenged, "What?"

Bebe answered, in a barely controlled voice, "How can you risk losing Rain over something as stupid as this?"

"So you think it's stupid to protest sending a half a million guys to risk their lives in Viet Nam? To come back maimed, or in a body bag. Your brother is one of them. Don't you care about him?"

"Of course I do," Bebe spit out. "But you're responsible for Rain now. You need to think about what's best for her. I love Bobby, but it was his choice to go, and I would never break the law and take a chance on losing Rain." Bebe shifted her gaze away from Jude's. "I mean, *you* shouldn't take the chance."

Jude studied her with hooded eyes. "That won't happen. If the police come, you're my alibi."

"Don't count on it." Bebe stormed off.

"Don't worry," Jude called after her. "If I do get caught for anything I'll tell the police that you had nothing to do with it."

That night, there was a knock at the door and when Bebe looked up from her book, she saw a uniformed police officer through the sheer curtains. She glanced up at Jude, who had come out from the kitchen where she was feeding Rain. Jude tried to look unconcerned, but the set of her mouth and the slight frown between her eyebrows told Bebe that she was not. Jude stepped back into the kitchen, leaving Bebe to answer the third knock.

The officer greeted Bebe through the screen door and asked her name and whether she'd been home all day. She answered that she'd been home since ten o'clock that morning. Then he asked if it was the residence of Judith Rasmussen. Bebe heard Rain begin to cry in the kitchen and Bebe answered, "Yes."

A feeling of sickly cold gripped her when he asked if she was on the premises. Jude stepped out of the kitchen with Rain over her shoulder, patting her back to shush her. Bebe had to admire her composure as Jude came to the door, giving the policeman her poker face.

He asked Jude about her day's activities and she lied that she'd missed class all day because Rain was colicky. The policeman turned to Bebe and asked her to confirm it.

Bebe met Jude's gaze and recognized the predicament she was in.

Lie for Jude or take the chance of losing Rain. Bebe was no relation to Rain. If Jude was arrested, what would happen to the baby? Jude's mother was an alcoholic and there weren't any relatives close by. They would probably put Rain in foster care and she could get lost in the system. Suddenly, Rain let out a wail that almost broke Bebe's heart.

Bebe turned a calm face to the policeman. "Yeah, the baby's been like this all day and she had to stay home with her. Is there a problem?"

He considered the three of them. Bebe irrationally felt as though he were reading her mind. He thanked them and left, and Bebe watched him all the way to his car. She sensed Jude watching her, and looked over. Jude smirked as she turned away and kissed Rain's little fist.

"See, baby, I'm never going to lose you."

Bebe's mouth went dry at the sway Jude now held over her.

◆ ◆ ◆ ◆

The first workday after the time change always unnerved Rain. She sensed the shadows lengthening outside on the fringe of windows surrounding their work space, and the darkness silently sneaking up on them. She wandered over to the bank of windows. Lisa joined her with what was probably her fifth Diet Pepsi of the day. It was only 5:00, and the cars in the streets below had already turned on their headlights.

"I hate this," Lisa said, shaking her head. "I wish I could hibernate until April."

"But you'd miss Thanksgiving. And Christmas." Rain noticed how the succession of streetlights in the intersections resembled a string of decorations.

"Holidays in our families are always a nightmare. Last year we went to five places on Thanksgiving, and then we spent Christmas alone in Kauai and made everyone mad."

"Five places?"

"Both of our parents are divorced and remarried, and Lyle's mom is on her third."

Rain looked back out the window at the string of streetlights.

"Sounds like you got off easy for Christmas."

"Some of them aren't speaking to us yet."

With a start, Rain remembered that Hayden had purchased tickets for them to see the Trans-Siberian Orchestra at Arco Arena in November. She wondered if he still had the tickets, or if they were at the house. She would dearly love to see the show, but how would she go about asking him for them? What if he'd already arranged to take someone else?

Rain realized that her holidays were now uncertain. Who would she spend time with? Would she be alone? For the last seven years, they had split their time between Hayden's family and Bebe's. Her mother and William didn't celebrate the holidays at all, so that was a relief. Jude said the holidays were too commercialized, but Rain knew it was just an excuse so she didn't have to deal with them. For all she knew, the holidays could hold bad memories for her mother. Rain didn't really know how William felt about them, and she hoped that after speaking with him the night before about not mentioning Valerie again and keeping the house an office-free zone, she would still be welcome at whatever they did.

"Hey, girlfriend," Lisa said, giving her a side-bump with her bony hip. "We need to celebrate your birthday."

Rain frowned through the darkening window. She felt a mixture of anxiety and elation about her impending appointment at the fertility clinic, complicated by the fact that she was one year older on the baby-scale.

Rain sighed and let the muscles in her face slack like a slipping mask. Had she been keeping it up all day? "Maybe I'll just forget about it this year."

"Hey, snap out of it," Lisa ordered. "Be thinking about what you want to do, okay? No excuses."

Rain mimicked Lisa affectionately, and Lisa went back to her desk. In less than two weeks, on November 10, Rain would turn thirty-eight. Not a reason to celebrate. Time was slipping away from her, diminishing her chances of becoming a mother.

Rain went back to her desk and cruised Internet sites for baby clothes until 5:30, when she could officially clock out. She hated coming home in the dark. Even when Hayden was expected to come home any minute, she never liked walking into a dark house. She hadn't thought to leave a light on when she'd left that morning, not realizing until she'd gotten to work that it would be dark and chilly in the house at 6:00 when she got home.

She pulled the car into her garage and did a visual scan of the interior before she closed the automatic door, unlocked the car door, and got out. The timed light went out before she could gather her things and get to the door that led into the kitchen. For several uncomfortable moments, she groped in the dark for the light switch, tripping on the bottom step that led to the kitchen door. When she was safely inside the kitchen with the lights on, she made sure the door was locked behind her. As she stripped off her coat and draped it over a chair, she heard Noah crying at the front of the house. She turned lights on as she went into the living room. He raced inside and she securely locked it after him.

"You didn't expect this early night either, did you, Noah?" she asked, shaking out crunchies into his bowl. "Better get used to it."

She turned on the television for noise and headed back to her bedroom, flicking on light switches as she went. It was ridiculous, being creeped out like this for no reason. She turned on the bedroom overhead light and went to her dresser. As she unhooked her earrings, she looked down to the plush carpet and froze when she saw a trail of deep footprints.

Rain blinked and her skin tingled with a heightened sense of fear as she glanced around the room, pushing down a rising sense of panic. Nothing looked out of place. She forced herself to take a deep breath. They could be her footprints, she reasoned. She placed her foot beside one of the impressions. It dwarfed her small shoe.

She groped behind her to the baseball bat that she kept propped in the corner by her bed for security. She hefted the cold metal and wrapped both fists around the base of the bat in a tight grip. She crept silently to the bathroom and quickly pushed the door open with the bat. Nothing looked different from when she'd left that morning. She glanced into the shower, but saw that it was empty and she pivoted to turn back to the bedroom. The only sound she heard was the distant voices from a television commercial.

She went to the phone, thinking to call the police. But what would she say—that there were footprints in her carpet? She silently crept down the hall, kicked open the spare bedroom door, and flipped on the light switch, like an action hero. She sidled in and did a visual scan, opening the closet and sweeping beneath the bed with the bat. Next, she crept up on the guest bathroom, stepped in, flipped on the light, and whacked the closed shower curtain with the bat. The bat hit air and shower curtain, and she jumped when the shampoo fell down from the corner rack and rattled in the tub.

She checked every door and window for signs of entry, but found none. Why would someone enter her house and leave without disturbing anything? There was one solution—it could have been Hayden. He had a key, but there was no other sign that he'd been there.

Feeling satisfied that she was alone, she wandered back into her bedroom and checked all her secret hiding places, which she knew were not secrets to real thieves. She checked a locked box in the bottom drawer of her dresser. Both his birth certificate and his Social Security card were missing.

She sat there looking at the contents feeling stupid and incoherent. Why did Hayden come and go, using his key to get these documents, thinking she would never know? Maybe he didn't want to see her again. Maybe he just wanted to avoid her.

She locked up the box and went back out to the kitchen, picking up her cell phone. She punched in his number, but when she heard his voice, she fumbled for words.

"Hayden. Hi. Did you . . . were you over here today?"

"Rain? Hold on." He turned away from the phone and said something to someone. Did she hear a female voice?

"Uh, why?" he asked, his voice a little too perky.

"Just wondering. It looked like someone had come while I was gone."

He cleared his throat. "Well, I did actually, when you were at work. I hope it didn't alarm you."

"No problem. I can take care of myself. I mean, it could have been someone else." She winced. Shut up, she told herself.

"Sure."

"Did you find what you were looking for?"

"Yes, I think I have everything now," he said. "In fact, I left the house key on the counter by the coffeepot."

Rain looked up to see the small silver key lying by the sugar bowl on the beige tile.

"Okay, well, I need to go," she said. "If you think of anything else, call me."

He hesitated for a moment. "I will," he said. And she hung up.

She went around methodically turning off excess lights and curled up on the couch with Noah, who wouldn't stay to be petted for long. He jumped down and left her alone to stare at the key from across the room.

She hugged a throw pillow to her chest. The thought occurred to her that he may have remembered the tickets to the Trans-Siberian Orchestra and come for them at a time when there would be no argument over them.

Why did it have to be like this? She hadn't stopped loving Hayden, she just wanted a baby. She just didn't want to kick herself years from now because she hadn't tried hard enough.

She knew she would be a better parent than her mother had been to her. She wasn't afraid to show affection or to risk being vulnerable with someone, or to put the child's best interests before her own. She had loved watching Scott and Dylan grow and being part of the process. Hearing their little voices, their fresh logic and never-ending questions. She remembered Scott beaming when he finally rode his bike without training wheels. Dylan always made pictures for her to take home with his name printed in wavering letters. He would climb up beside her on the couch to read a picture book and then correct her if she skipped any words. She was lucky that she'd had great examples of the parent she would be in Bebe, Neil, and William.

She wondered again what her biological father was like. Would her childhood have been dramatically different if she'd had a dad around? Perhaps Jude would have been a better mom with someone else around to share the load. Even someone to love her. Or maybe they would have fought. Probably, they would have fought. Maybe Jude had been lonely or scared and all her harshness was only bluster.

When Rain looked at the way her mom raised a child on her own, what made her think she would be any different? As she'd heard Bebe's mom say before, the acorn doesn't fall far from the tree.

⁂ ⁂ ⁂ ⁂

Neil tossed the morning paper onto the kitchen table in front of Bebe and poured himself a cup of coffee. "There's enough for one more cup," he said.

"No, thanks, I've had enough," she answered. She scanned the headlines while she ate her blueberry yogurt. The aftertaste of the coffee lent it an unpleasant tang. Almost every day, somewhere in the world there was a car bombing or an assassination or a government being overthrown. Her attention focused on a story about the probability of sending more troops into Afghanistan. She spread out the paper on the table, folding it back to read the article.

Neil sat down across from her and pulled out the sports section. He glanced up to see what she was reading. "You shouldn't dwell on that." He opened the paper to the second page and folded it back. "This isn't Vietnam."

Bebe swirled her yogurt with her spoon. "I just don't want Scotty to go through what happened to Bobby."

He looked up from the football stats. "You're not responsible for that," Neil said. "Scotty knows he has our support. We can't answer for the others."

"I know, but it's my job to worry." She got up and tossed her empty yogurt container, rinsing her spoon and coffee mug in the sink. "Come to think of it, he didn't call last weekend. I wonder what he's doing."

"I think it's the three-day war. He said it's a simulation training."

She slipped into her coat. "I'll feel better when we hear from him. Are you watching the time?"

He looked up from the paper and glanced at the wall clock. "I've got to swing by The Lone Star Ranch before I go in." He got up, leaving the paper in a heap on the kitchen table. "Come with me."

She grabbed her purse. "I have appointments this morning."

He wrapped his arms around her waist and pulled her to him. "Come on. Let Janice cover for you. She needs the practice."

"You're bad. But you're cute." She kissed him and playfully pushed him away. "See you at the office," she said, as she went out the door.

Bebe had a long morning of consultations and follow-up appointments that went right through the lunch hour. Even though the office was closed from noon to one thirty, she had paperwork and e-mails to catch up on. Neil brought them back some lunch when he returned from a ranch visit, and they ate it at their desks, sitting back-to-back.

One of the perks of going into veterinary medicine was having classes with Neil. He immediately recognized her from the thrift store the first year, and sat beside her in molecular biology. He moved in with her and Jude the next. Of course, her family never knew. By then, Toni was in grad school in Los Angeles, and Mare had moved in with Arnie. It left just the three of them and Rain.

Rain was a great buffer. She called Neil "Daddy" until Jude nipped it. Mare married Arnie when she was seven months pregnant with Autumn. Once again they had parties, except that the parties were now for birthdays and involved balloons and cake. Jude moved out in June when she finished law school, taking Rain with her. Rain had just completed first grade, and Bebe and Neil both mourned for months.

They got married that September, having graduated from veterinary school, and moved to the foothills above Sacramento to enter a practice. They hated moving that far from Rain, but they arranged for her to spend weekends with them as often as Jude and their schedules would allow. Bebe agonized over whether Rain understood that it wasn't always their choice whether or not they got to see her.

The fact that she married Neil actually elevated her in her parents' esteem. He was a doctor, never mind that she was a doctor, too. She'd married well, and that helped to erase some of her stigma. Some, but never all.

They were married in her small church in the Central Valley on a Saturday afternoon with a few close friends and members of church who had watched her grow up since she'd been a baby in the nursery. The only thing she truly hated about the wedding was that the pastor refused to call her "Bebe," but insisted on addressing her as Roberta. She had specifically asked him before the ceremony not to use her given name, and when he said, "Do you, Roberta, take this man," she almost stopped and corrected him. But she knew that she was treading on thinly veiled ice with her parents, and for her mom's sake, she swallowed her pride.

Her name wouldn't have been so bad, except that she was named after her father, as was Bobby. She had secretly railed against it growing up. How self-absorbed could a man be to name two children after himself? She felt thankful to Bobby for her nickname. It was his childish attempts at saying her name that produced "Bebe." And much to her father's dismay, it had stuck.

Chapter 14

Bebe chuckled when she saw the chart in the door pocket of room six. Margo and Gigi Weinbrenner. Margo was an overweight silver tabby that reminded her of an aging bon-bon eating secretary of the forties with markings like rhinestone glasses and nails like stilettos. Gigi was a Siamese mix with the sleek furtiveness of a French resistance fighter, who only preened when she had an agenda, like food or freedom. They were here for boosters and to have Margo's nails clipped. Bebe knocked on the door briefly and entered the examining room, greeting their "mommy" over the howls emanating from the cat carriers. She noted that Mrs. Weinbrenner had deep scratches on both arms.

"Did you get those from Gigi?"

"Yes. She didn't mean it, did you, sweetie?" the woman said, reaching a finger through the metal door to rub beneath Gigi's neck. Gigi hissed and moved to the back of the carrier. "You didn't want to go into your nasty cat carrier, did you," Gigi's mommy baby-talked.

Bebe briefly examined the red welting scratches. Faint white scars crisscrossed beneath the fresh ones. "I hope you treated those."

"I always do," she said, smiling.

"Okay, let's start with Gigi," Bebe said.

Mrs. Weinbrenner looked at her, expectant. Then she said, "Oh, should *I* get her out?"

Bebe nodded and the woman hesitantly reached for the door latch. "Nice Gigi," she crooned, "Mommy's going to let you out now."

When she opened the carrier door Gigi darted, but Bebe grabbed the cat by the scruff of the neck and she went limp.

"I don't know how you manage to do that," Mrs. Weinbrenner said. "All I get are bites and scratches for my trouble."

"It takes practice. I sometimes get those, too," Bebe answered, examining Gigi for ear mites and checking her gums. "Does she have trouble with fleas?"

"I would never allow fleas in my house."

Satisfied with Gigi's overall condition, she gave the howling cat her boosters and tucked her back inside the carrier. Margo was surprisingly more compliant, and purred when Bebe scratched behind her ears. They were soon finished and Mrs. Weinbrenner was on her way. Bebe wondered if she would practice picking Gigi up by the scruff of her neck.

Later, she called Rain about setting up a date to take her to lunch for her birthday, and to ask her what she would like. The answers were "next Saturday" and "a perfect life," which Bebe chuckled at, and said she would come up with something more practical.

Before Saturday, Bebe went shopping at Dress Barn and found a pretty sweater in autumn colors that would enhance Rain's skin tone perfectly. She wanted Rain to feel pampered a little, and she knew that considering Jude's state, William may or may not remember to even send her a gift certificate.

They met at the Olive Garden for lunch on Saturday and she made Rain open the gift before they ordered their food. A slow smile lifted Rain's face.

"Bebe, this is beautiful. You didn't have to."

"Of course, I did. I wanted you to have a nice birthday. There's a gift receipt in case you don't like the color or it doesn't fit."

"No, I love the color. And it should fit fine. Thank you."

"Do you have any plans to celebrate?"

"Lisa from work wants to take me out. If I don't come up with something, she'll want to go clubbing."

"Aren't you two a little old for that? Oops! Sorry, I didn't mean to—"

"Well, I am. She's younger than me, but she's been married for three years. I don't know how she gets past Lyle."

"Isn't the point of clubbing to meet guys?"

"Yes. Twenty-something guys. Guys who are definitely not interested in having kids." Rain dug in her purse, produced a vibrating cell phone, and took note of the number. "It's her," she said, without answering it. "I'll have to come up with something soon. I think she sees it as her duty to get me hooked up with someone else. She already tried to play Cupid at work."

They spent a nice lunch together and Bebe invited her to join them at her parents' house for Thanksgiving, if she didn't have plans to visit her mother. Rain said she would let her know.

Bebe didn't bring up Hayden, and neither did Rain. In fact, Rain didn't have much to say at all. Bebe wondered if she had some depression going on. It would only be natural, considering all that was happening. The holidays were coming and her outlook had the potential to worsen. She gave her a big hug and a kiss when they parted at their cars, and prayed for her as she pulled away.

Bebe wondered how things would have turned out differently for Rain, if she had been her mother instead of Jude.

❖ ❖ ❖ ❖

Rain looked around at home for the tickets, but came up empty-handed. She finally screwed up her courage and left a voice mail on Hayden's cell phone, asking if he had picked them up when he came by the house that day. She didn't know if he would remember about her birthday, and she could have played that card, but when he called, he was gracious about the tickets, and there was no mention made of her birthday. He said they were in the second drawer of the file cabinet. She wondered if he even remembered they had purchased them, or if he was sorry he hadn't thought of them first.

The next day, Rain caught up with Lisa on the way into the office from the parking lot.

"The Trans-Siberian Orchestra?" Lisa repeated to Rain when she told her of her birthday plans. "Are you serious?"

"Yes, I'm serious. I have tickets for two great seats. Have you ever seen them in concert?"

Lisa scrunched her forehead. "No, Lyle's more into Rush."

"They put on a great show, with pyrotechnics and lasers and . . . well, you just have to see it. It's incredible."

"I was hoping for something more—"

"I'm not interested in clubbing, Lisa." Rain held the door open for her. "This is what I want to do. It's next weekend. Are you in or out?"

"I'm in. Of course, I'm in. Whatever you want." She said over her shoulder as she turned down the aisle to her cubicle, "It'll be fun."

They had a great time at the Trans-Siberian concert, once it got under way. Rain felt some melancholy going in, but the feeling dissipated with the visual spectacle and the dramatic music filling her senses. Lisa was impressed from the opening number and Rain knew the group had made a new fan.

At intermission, Rain's heart skipped when she thought she saw Hayden with a woman. It was the gray Burberry sports coat that he wore on special occasions, and the same unruly curls around his ears, but it turned out not to be him, after all. Regardless, the melancholy descended once more. Just last year, Hayden had been seated beside her, holding her hand. She suddenly missed the safe feeling of his hand dwarfing hers, his arm around her shoulder, the lingering scent of his aftershave. Her eyes unexpectedly filled and she quickly looked away so Lisa wouldn't see and feel like she had to fix it. It couldn't be fixed—this missing of Hayden and the way she'd felt contented only with him before she felt the loss of a baby.

❖ ❖ ❖ ❖

Rain felt more relaxed and optimistic on this second visit to the fertility clinic. She went early to make arrangements through their financial office, and proceeded to her appointment.

Dr. Sykes gave Rain an exam and an ultrasound. Soon she was dressed and sitting in his office, discussing the results.

"No abnormalities were detected in the uterus, the fallopian tubes, or the ovaries. Nor did the ultrasound show any pelvic scarring, which we sometimes see. Your antral follicle count is in the intermediate range."

"What does that mean?" she asked.

"The follicle is the housing for the egg. The higher the count, the more eggs you have remaining. As I said, it gives us an estimate to work with. The intermediate range means that treatment could go either way. We could get a very low or a good response. But the pregnancy rates are pretty good overall in this group."

Rain felt the tension drain away from her and realized she'd been clenching her jaw all morning.

Dr. Sykes prescribed a medication to initiate day-3 FSH testing, and Rain left the office encouraged. She followed through with the medication and had blood tests done on the third and tenth days.

She went back for her follow-up visit fearing, yet yearning, to embrace her future. If the news was bad, she would know she had lost Hayden for nothing.

Dr. Sykes reviewed her lab tests. Her FSH level was a 12, borderline between fair and reduced ovarian reserve, and he prescribed gonadotropins by injection, which she would have to give herself nightly. The mere suggestion of shots made her light-headed. She heard him tell her through a distant tunnel about the headaches, abdominal pain, and increased risk of miscarriage that were typical side effects. He asked the nurse to explain how to administer the shots.

That night, Rain sat in the middle of her bed, drying her sweating palms on the comforter. She flicked the vial and depressed the plunger to dispel the air bubbles like the nurse had demonstrated, and stuck the needle into her thigh. She sucked air at the initial pain and tried not to succumb to the roaring in her ears. At least if she passed out, as she usually did with needles, she wouldn't fall and break the needle off in her leg.

If this didn't prove her devotion to having a baby, nothing did.

⁂ ⁂ ⁂ ⁂

Bebe was pleasantly surprised that Rain agreed to stop by her parents' house for Thanksgiving dinner. She sounded upbeat on the phone. Bebe didn't ask for any details, but she could tell that Rain felt better than she had at her birthday lunch.

Dylan drove home after his morning class on the day before Thanksgiving, dropped off his stuff at the house, and swung by the clinic to surprise them. Bebe was just finishing up a suture removal when she heard his voice out in the seating area. By the time she was done with the patient, he had caught up with the office staff. She hugged him and they talked briefly before her next appointment. Neil was out on another farm call. She pulled out a twenty and asked Dylan to run by the grocery store for some evaporated milk and a can of pumpkin. She reminded him to drop off the ingredients at the house before he went off with his friends. She didn't want to have to wait to bake her pumpkin pie at midnight, in case he came back late.

The next morning, Bebe watched the Thanksgiving Day Parade while she chopped vegetables for Rain's favorite salad. Her mother's cooking generally included cream and butter and lots of eggs, and she knew Rain didn't eat much dairy—except for ice cream, for which she had a definite weakness. She kept her cell phone in her pocket in case they got a call from Scotty. He had written that he'd requested to be adopted by a family in the area around the base for Thanksgiving dinner, and that he would call sometime that day, but didn't know when.

They spent an enjoyable day with her family, though she was always mindful that Scotty was missing from their celebration. She felt a guilty relief that Bobby was not among them, until Karen asked where he was.

"He's in San Diego," her mother said. "He has some business down there, and he said he might try to visit Scotty."

Bebe glanced from her mother to Neil. He shook his head almost imperceptibly, cautioning her not to overreact. She determined that she would call Scotty later, if she didn't hear from him.

Neil insisted on helping to clear the table and taking out the trash. He wouldn't allow Dylan and his cousins to watch the Seattle Seahawks play the Dallas Cowboys until they helped to take down the extra table and chairs and carry them to the garage. Bebe noticed that Rain watched the interaction between them, and she wondered if Rain missed having a father, or was taking stock of what made a good dad.

Later that evening, Bebe phoned Scotty but was disappointed when she was sent to voice mail. She left a Thanksgiving greeting, and several minutes later, he called back.

"Hi, Mom. I saw that you called me, but there's only one spot in the squad bay that gets good reception, so I had to call you back."

"We missed you at Grandma's today, Scotty. Did you get to have dinner with a family?"

"Yeah, I was paired up with my buddy Stockman, and we ate dinner with a family in Oceanside. But she wasn't as good a cook as you."

Bebe glowed at his praise, in spite of herself. "It's all in what you're used to. Her family probably thinks she's a good cook. Did you just get back?"

"No, I got back around five, but Bobby came by and picked me up. Did you know he was down here?"

Bebe felt her mouth go dry. "I just found out today. What did you do?"

"We went to McDonalds. It was the only place open. He bought me a Coke and we just caught up."

Bebe was slightly relieved that Bobby hadn't contacted Scott until the end of his day, which meant he probably did have business in San Diego and the purpose of his visit wasn't to see Scott.

"How is he doing?" she asked.

"He's good. He came down yesterday to apply for a job at the airport and he stayed over. I think he might have a girlfriend down here."

"A girlfriend?"

"Don't mention it to Grandma. He didn't really say she was his girlfriend."

For Bobby to mention having any friends at all was a major step, and Bebe felt encouraged. But it didn't allay all her fears about the time he'd spent alone with Scott.

"So, did you have a nice visit?"

"Yeah, it was good to see some family. He asked me about my SOI training. You know, he was army, so his was different."

"Yes, I remember."

There was a blip of silence, and then Scott said, "Things were pretty crazy back then."

Bebe didn't know what to say. She didn't want to have this conversation over the phone on Thanksgiving Day.

"Things happened pretty fast." She motioned for Neil and said to Scott, "Here, say hi to your dad."

She handed the phone to Neil, who turned the conversation in the direction of the Dallas game. "Don't hang up," she mouthed silently to him. Then, she stuck her head into Dylan's room and told him that his brother was on the phone.

It was good to hear Scott's voice and to know that he'd weathered the first major holiday away from his family. He would be home for Christmas this year, and who knew what lay ahead for the next. She had to find some way to communicate her absolute support for his choice, in spite of whatever doubts her brother had planted in his head and no matter how much she worried for his future.

Chapter 15

Rain logged on to the sperm donor site and plugged her choices into the search window: brown hair, hazel eyes, English ethnicity. Seven donors matched the description. Donor YEJ29L was still listed. She scrolled down and clicked on his donor profile. Wavy brown hair, hazel eyes, Caucasian, born in Santa Barbara to English/German parents, medium body frame, 165 pounds, height—six feet, complexion medium. Blood type A+. He described himself as extroverted, kind, athletic, musically inclined, and he enjoyed comedies. A normal male, age thirty-two, with no medical issues in his family history. And he was listed as Open ID. That was worth more than a Stanford grad.

Yes, he could be the one. Rain paid $40 with her Paypal to get his baby picture and a more complete profile from the website. For another $100, she could obtain his personality profile, an audio recording, and a current photo, after she signed privacy agreements and releases. They also offered genetic consultations and photo matching.

The basic cost for the service started at $500. Then there were tank rental fees, late tank return fees, and restocking fees, just as if she were renting a movie from Blockbuster. Handling charges, vial fees, and courier services rounded out the charges.

She wasn't disappointed with the baby picture. It was plain to see that he'd been an adorable baby. She printed the photo along with a copy of his profile. When the time came and she had the money, she hoped YEJ29L would still be available to become a daddy.

She wondered how many babies he had already fathered. There was a ten family maximum allowed, but there would be no babies that would match their exact biological combination. Somewhere in the world, her baby would have half-siblings and deserved to know the truth one day. Since the donor had agreed to be listed under Open ID, he was giving permission for the child to contact him when he or she turned eighteen. If he or she chose to. In the meantime, she knew of a donor sibling registry where a child could connect with other half-siblings, even if they never knew who the donor was. If she was open to it.

Her thoughts went to Seekergirl, and Rain logged on to her blog. Seekergirl had posted the day before and there were two comments from mothers who were defending their choices to use donors. They described their children as happy and well-adjusted, living in one-parent or same-sex parent families, where the sperm donor was referred to as "Birth Other" or "Donor" but never as "Dad." "Dad" set the child up for disappointment and abandonment issues. Rain could agree with the reasoning in that. One mother insisted that her child accepted and embraced their family as whole without a father. A father was expendable.

Rain knew what that was like, and she knew it was possible to do, but it had taken her whole childhood and adolescence to accept. She wasn't at all convinced that she could—or should—be enough parent for any child, just herself, by her own making.

Rain rubbed her thigh on the spot where she'd given herself a shot the night before. Every morning she woke to bluish bruises over her greenish bruises. A veritable Van Gogh of gonadotropin. Her side effects had been mild, as her womb cramped to produce a nugget of viable life.

Wasn't she proving she was committed, trying to make up for past mistakes? Wasn't she already trying her hardest to be a good mom?

It was more than her own mother had done.

❖ ❖ ❖ ❖

Neil pulled the boxes of Christmas decorations down from the rafters in the garage and Bebe helped him carry them into the kitchen. This Christmas, decorating would be an act of love, more than any other. Both of her boys would be home in a few weeks, and Bebe wanted pleasant memories to assault them the moment they stepped through the front door.

By lunchtime, the Christmas tree was assembled. The tub that held the tree decorations was like opening a treasure box, with the special ornaments of the boys' childhood and from Bebe's and Neil's early years tucked inside tissue paper flecked with sparkles. She sat back on the couch to enjoy the vision of the perfect Christmas tree while she ate her sandwich. By evening, the entire house would be ready.

On impulse, she called to check on Jude. William answered, saying that she was resting and growing weaker by the day. She spent days in her bathrobe, never leaving their house. He sounded tired. Bebe remembered that he was working from home now, and offered to give him a break. He said it wasn't worth the aftermath of Jude's suspicion. She was getting a bit irrational, and accused him of being unfaithful if he even left to take the trash out to the curb. Besides, Rain was coming on Saturday and that would distract Jude for a while so he could run errands in peace. Or Rain could chaperone him at the store, if Jude felt it necessary.

She saw the mail truck go past and walked down to the mailbox. She was happy to find a letter from Scotty among their bills and magazines. He had taken to calling them rather than writing, now that he had liberty every weekend. She plucked the letter from the mail when she got back to the house and dropped the rest onto the counter. She ran a knife through the fold in the envelope and slid the letter out—a one-page sheet of white paper with blue lines. When she opened it, a faded, yellowed news clipping fell onto the counter.

Bebe stared at the clipping, not touching it. She knew what it was. The letter was addressed to her alone and was composed of two sentences. "Hi Mom, Bobby gave me this when he was here. He said a lot of stuff, but I'd rather hear about it from you." He simply signed it *Scott.*

Bebe unfolded the clipping as if it held the power of a black hole, able to suck her into its bottomless depth of confusion and passion and regrets. She smoothed it carefully out on the counter. There she was in her peasant shirt and her hair down past her shoulder blades, her frayed bell-bottoms dragging the ground. The sign she held read "PEACE NOW" but her countenance was anything but peaceful. The camera had caught her midstep, three feet away from a policeman in full riot gear, with wild hate twisting her young features into the mask of a shrew.

❖ ❖ ❖ ❖

April 24, 1971

Bebe returned from the Women's Resource Center and grabbed her sign before heading over to the administration building with the gathering throng of students. She reflected on how much had changed in the past three months since she first suspected that Jude had had something to do with the bombing of the ROTC building.

Bobby's letters had all but stopped. He'd never said much in them anyway, but at least she'd known he was alive as she pored over them to glean some hidden message. Now, she wasn't so sure.

In his last letter, he said that word had reached his unit about the reception committees awaiting returning soldiers in Oakland. The hateful jeers and taunts. Murderers. Babykillers. Being spit on. He sounded bitter, but still proud of what he was doing. She knew him well enough to know there was more he wanted to say, but couldn't. He told her to take care of their mom, because he knew she worried. That stirred a hot spark in Bebe that fanned into flame when she visited her parents and saw how haggard and preoccupied her mother had become.

Bebe had pointed out that it wasn't healthy to watch news reports on the war, but she was shushed angrily, as though she were a stranger coming between a mother bear and her cub.

Bebe worried about Bobby and what would happen to her parents if he didn't come back. She grew angry and disillusioned with the promises and lies told by the government, and could no longer sit by. On this very day, thousands of people, including veterans, would be demonstrating in front of the nation's capitol, and here she was, marching with a modern day Continental army standing up against the injustices inflicted on them without their consent.

The crowd grew in number and pulsed with a chant as they neared the Commons in front of the administration building. The words raced through their collective veins, a great artery pumping the pure lifeblood of nascent change. A powerful cocktail of adrenaline and fear caused Bebe's heart to race. She knew that what she was doing that day was more important than anything she had done in her life so far. This day was significant. It would stand out in her personal history as the day she took a stand for her brother and for what was right.

The crowd surged, raising their signs and shouting a mixture of angry words and obscenities toward the faculty who looked down from the windows. She noticed Jude standing off to the side of the crowd with her fist punching toward the sky and her other arm supporting the baby sling that held Rain across her chest. Bebe hoped she would have the sense to remain alert and stay clear of the pulsing crowd.

Soon the police arrived, along with news vans filled with reporters. Bebe raised her sign and shouted its slogan: "Peace Now! Peace Now!" The crowd edged closer, and Bebe was pushed from behind to the front of the police line. She screwed up her courage and raised her sign high, finding her words and nailing them down with the weight of her convictions. The expression of the policeman before her was hidden in a gas mask, making him look inhuman and menacing. She hesitated, and reminded herself that she was doing this for Bobby, and her parents, and herself, because no one should be pushed to these limits by their government.

The shouting drummed in her ears, but its cadence was suddenly shattered by screams and a rush of people backing away from the building as a cloud of tear gas wafted through the crowd. Bebe had no choice but to push away from the cloud as the police line advanced toward them. The crowd evolved into an animal fearing for its life, as the students pushed and shoved each other, knocking some to the ground. The students who fell were yanked up by angry police and dragged away. Those who struggled were beaten with riot batons. When the crowd thinned enough for her to find an exit, Bebe threw down her sign and ran until she got to the corner of her quiet street with the campus out of view. She coughed until she vomited by the curb, shaking with the trauma of all she had experienced and seen.

She walked the rest of the way to the Victorian and pushed open the door. She headed straight into the shower and stripped off her clothes into a pile where she stood under the hot water, rinsing away the smell of tear gas and trying to get her breathing to return to normal. When the water ran cold, she crawled into bed with her hair wet and smelling of strawberries, and slept the afternoon away into morning.

The phone woke her at 5:00 a.m., and she went out to answer it in the kitchen before it woke Rain. It was her brother Rudy, and her heart stopped as she feared the worst.

Instead, he asked, "Have you seen the *Guardian* today?" His words made no sense, couched in anger and disgust.

She rubbed her eyes to clear her head. They were still crusty from tear gas residue. "Rudy? No—no. What's wrong?"

"Just pick one up. They're teaching you some great stuff at that school." He hung up.

Bebe shook her head in confusion, but she went into her room and pulled on some jeans and a sweatshirt. She pocketed Toni's change from the dresser and walked down to Julio's Market. She approached the bank of newspaper machines on the sidewalk and her heart began to fail her as she saw the front page of the *Guardian* through the scratched plexiglass. She put the change into the slot. Slowly she opened the display and lifted out a paper. The door slammed shut and she jumped at the noise of metal on metal.

There, on the front page, was a clear picture of Bebe with her sign held high, screaming into the face of riot police, looking for all the world like a photo she'd seen of protestors meeting the trains of returning servicemen at the Oakland Army Terminal.

She never received another letter from Bobby for the duration of his tour in Vietnam.

⁂ ⁂ ⁂ ⁂

Neil found her crying on the couch in front of the Christmas tree with Scotty's letter in her lap and the news clipping balled in her fist. He understood as soon as he saw the yellowed newsprint and wrapped his arms around her. Then he took the short letter and the clipping from her to assess the damage.

"Not your best side, but I always thought that shirt showed off your best assets."

She frowned at him and he grew serious. "Scotty's not stupid, Bebe. He recognizes that Bobby's got some personal problems, so he wants you to be the one to explain it. It's your chance to set the story straight, and defuse anything Bobby might have gotten wrong." He lifted her hand to his mouth and planted a kiss on the back of it. "Just tell him the truth."

Bebe started a first draft of her letter to Scott that evening. She knew that it would be difficult to explain her reasoning for her actions and about the times in general. She wasn't even sure she completely understood the times herself, even though she'd lived through them.

She struggled with it for a long time, and put it aside. She went into her bedroom and dug in her jewelry box for the small amethyst ring. She slipped it onto her pinky as far as it would go, but it wedged above her knuckle. She held it to the light but the stone failed to sparkle, and was instead the color of deep cabernet. She removed the ring and briefly curled her fist around it. Then she put it back amid the bracelets and earrings and closed the lid.

The next time she sat down with her notepad, the words finally came.

Dear Scotty,

First of all, I want you to know how very proud I am of you and your decision to serve your country in these uncertain times. You have my full and complete support, and that will never change.

I'm not exactly sure what your uncle Bobby has told you, but when you're home, we can sit down face-to-face and talk about it. Bobby was wounded in many ways by Vietnam, and I unintentionally inflicted one of those wounds on him myself.

The newspaper photo is not what it seems. I always loved Bobby, and it was the war and the government I was protesting, never him or the other soldiers or their service to our country. Most of all, I protested because I loved him so much and I was afraid for him. The government lied to us, and we realized it could no longer be trusted, and things were spiraling out of control over there. There were photos of massacres in the news and stories about POWs and soldiers fragging their officers. Things were so crazy. I was always proud of him, and it hurt when he thought he no longer had my support. Someone in the family must have told him about the photo, or sent it to him, because when he came back, he wouldn't even speak to me. He never gave me a chance to explain.

He was pretty messed up when he came back, and I became the focal point of all that was wrong with America. To him, I represented all the hippies who spit on the wounded soldiers at the Oakland train depot, and the druggies who tuned out to their responsibilities, and the feminists who destroyed the American family. Maybe I even got blamed for his post-traumatic stress syndrome. Unfortunately, some of that rubbed off on your grandparents, and for a while I avoided going home at all. I don't blame them. I understand now that they had to show their complete and utter support for Bobby in the only way they knew how. That's what he needed at the time, and things have gotten better with your grandparents since then.

So, I say all of this to assure you that what I did was solely because I loved him so much and I felt like I was fighting for him, not against him. He just never gave me a chance to put it that way. Maybe one day he will.

As a mom, I have to admit that I sometimes have the same fears for you, but I'm hoping it will be different because you chose this yourself, whereas Bobby was drafted. His only other choice was to run. He was never cut out to be a soldier, so it was very brave of him to stay.

I think times are different now. The world is changing, and hopefully we're not quite so easily lied to. People are more aware and as a result, I believe, are forcing the government to be more accountable. At any rate, history will not repeat itself with me. Even if I disagree with the turn of events, I will always support you and your desire to serve your country.

Love, Mom

Bebe sealed and addressed the envelope before she had a chance to rewrite it. This was how she truly felt—like the lancing of a wound. She wiped away a few tears as she walked to the mailbox in the dark and lifted the flag for the mail carrier to see that she had a letter for her son who was a United States Marine.

Chapter 16

Rain pulled up in front of her mom's house on Saturday and sat in the car for a few minutes to focus. Her mom's condition had deteriorated the last time she'd visited, and she wanted to prepare herself for a change so she wouldn't react. She also wanted to put on a mask of normalcy. She didn't want to let on about the fertility shots or her hope for a child. She didn't want to hear any negative comments about her personal life at all.

Rain glanced up at her mother's bedroom window and saw her standing there with the curtain pushed aside. How long had she been watching Rain and her reluctance to enter? Nothing like dishing up a little guilt for her mother to use when she first walked through the door. Rain got out, climbed the steps to the house, and opened the front door.

"So I see you decided to come in," Jude said, as she carefully made her way down the staircase.

Rain ignored her comment and stood at the bottom of the stairs in case her mother stumbled. "Maybe you should move your bedroom down to the office. I could help William move the furniture."

"It's quiet up there, and I only come down when William isn't here."

"That doesn't exactly make me feel any better. He could come home one night to find you in a pile at the bottom."

"That should make him happy." Jude sank into an overstuffed chair and said, "Hand me that afghan, will you?"

Rain spread the blanket over Jude and went to the fridge. "Do you want anything?"

Her mother shook her head with her eyes closed.

Rain poured herself a glass of ice water and sat on the couch. "Do you need me to throw some laundry in or fix you some lunch? Anything?"

"No. Update me on the Celebration."

"Okay. Well, I know that Toni finalized the house arrangements, and Mare's working on the menu, and Bebe is investigating some distractions to keep everyone from strangling each other over the three days. She asked if I thought you would agree to use a wheelchair so we can all go to the aquarium together."

Jude frowned without opening her eyes. "Why does she think I'd need a wheelchair?"

"It's a long day of standing and walking. But from what I hear, it's pretty amazing."

Jude considered her. "I'll think about it."

"She has to buy tickets, so let me know soon."

"I assume they're also working on ideas for a group project. Something to raise awareness or a cause to commit to?"

"Oh, I think that goes without saying."

Jude opened her eyes and looked at Rain. "What is that supposed to mean?"

Rain gestured with her hands. "It means I have no idea. I haven't seen Mare or Toni since Dulcinea's and I've spent practically every Saturday over here."

"Are you complaining?"

"No." Rain gave Jude an overly sweet smile. "I'm really not."

Jude couldn't hide a small smile before she closed her eyes and settled back into the cushions.

Rain flicked on the television and turned down the volume in case her mother wanted to talk. Rain watched Jude breathing with the afghan pulled up beneath her chin like a child, and felt a softening toward her that she hadn't felt in a long time. Suddenly, she wanted to fill in the gaps about her mother. Why should she care to know a father who wasn't even there, if she didn't really know her mother who was?

Rain wanted to know what Jude was like growing up, and as a college coed in a time of turmoil. What had made her so self-reliant and so hard? Why had she written her own rules to live by at such a young age? Jude rarely spoke of her own mother, and perhaps Jude was a better mother than Shirley had been to her. What had made her so antagonistic toward men and tradition and, well, God?

Jude must have sensed her watching, because she opened her eyes and asked, "What?"

It startled Rain, and she had trouble denying that there wasn't something. When Jude pressed her, she said, "I was just wondering what you were like when you were young, that's all."

"That's all?" Jude answered, without opening her eyes.

"So, dish. 'Enquiring minds want to know.'"

Jude opened her eyes a slit, considered Rain for a moment, and closed them again. "I was a scrappy little baby who grew into a scrappy little girl from the wrong side of the tracks."

Rain balked. "You did not. You grew up in a very nice neighborhood with a pony. I've seen pictures."

"Tom Tom wasn't a pony, he was a mastiff."

"Still, he was huge and you were riding him."

"The first thing every newly poor family does is to buy a pet that they can't afford. It's a form of denial. Even at that age, when my father came home with him, I knew."

"But the house?"

"We lost it. My father gambled and was in terrible debt. My mother couldn't hold a job because of her drinking. He left us, and we moved to the Heights. If you don't mind, I'd really rather not discuss it."

Rain was just wondering how far she could push her mom about it when Jude shifted beneath the afghan, and asked, "Would you mind making me a cup of tea? It's in the cupboard, arranged alphabetically, I'm sure."

Rain made them each a cup of White Pear, and asked, "How is your mom doing?"

"Considering her condition, Shirley's probably better off than I am," she said, adding under her breath, "At least, she doesn't know what's happening to her."

"You mean her dementia?"

"I mean her physical state. Her march toward eternity. The inevitable reality."

Rain set Jude's cup on a coaster on the end table within her reach. Jude sipped her tea delicately. "William always buys cheap tea," she said, grimacing.

"It is not. I used the White Pear tea with the pyramid infuser bags. It even has antioxidants. William only buys the good stuff for you, and you know it."

Jude cradled the teacup between her palms. "It hasn't always been that way."

Rain watched her mother for a while without responding. Maybe Rain had opened a can of worms asking about her past, and by subtly chastising her about her treatment of her own mother and William. She didn't really know what went on between them.

"It might not have always been that way, Mom. But people change."

Jude sized her up as she took a sip of her tea. "By the way, have you reconsidered the house? It may be easier than you think. And you can use the money for whatever you need, down the road." She returned the teacup to the end table and snuggled beneath the afghan.

Rain wondered whether she, herself, had changed enough to treat Hayden as unfairly as her mother treated William. She had realized that every payment made on the house, every repair had come from her account alone. Since he was also listed as a buyer, it wouldn't be enough to take the house from him without giving him some kind of compensation in return, but the threat of a messy court case might be enough to intimidate the normally nonconfrontational Hayden into seeking an easy solution. But could she do that to him?

Rain sighed and reached for the remote. "Let's see what's on television," she said. As the channels clicked by, she reflected on the limited time they had left together, and wondered whether she would ever really know what made her mother tick.

After she got home that evening, Jude called her to say to go ahead and buy the aquarium tickets.

❖ ❖ ❖ ❖

Rain got a call from Hayden saying that they needed to make some financial decisions for tax purposes since the year was drawing to a close. They planned to meet for dinner downtown after work. Rain didn't want to come unprepared, so she spent her lunch looking up comps in her neighborhood. The average single-family dwelling on her street was worth $425,000, but theirs had added amenities that could increase the value, if they could find a buyer. Three houses on her street were listed, and one was a foreclosure.

Rain was late to the restaurant and found that Hayden had already been seated. From the hostess station, she saw him watching the Kings game on a television mounted above the bar, and she slid into the seat across from him before he realized she was there. He greeted her and called over the server by name. The server took Rain's drink order and handed her a menu.

Next, he turned to Hayden. "Bacon cheeseburger, medium, with mayo on the side, and seasoned fries?" Hayden glanced up, looking a bit chagrined, and answered that he would like to see a menu, also.

Rain was shocked at this drift from his near-vegetarian state, and at how the server knew his "usual."

"I come once a week or so," he said, reading her mind. "It's on the way home."

They made small talk, only briefly making eye contact like they were on a blind date. How often did he frequent this place? she wondered. Maybe this had become his second home. Rain didn't know whether she felt relieved that he was still a creature of habit with his wings clipped, eating at the same place every night, or to feel sad that he knew these people so well and preferred not to eat alone. Or maybe not. As the night went on, Rain noticed a female server with a bobbing ponytail discreetly glancing at them every time she passed by.

Hayden asked about her mother and she told him about the Celebration weekend coming in a week. She told him about Scott's graduation from boot camp, and he told her that his father had retired from his medical practice. They were having a retirement party for him after the holidays. When he said the word "holidays," the conversation took a quiet, even more awkward tone.

She noticed that he was putting on a little weight, probably from too many hamburgers, but it softened his face in a pleasing way. A few gray hairs dusted his temple, which she'd never noticed before. He'd only been gone a few months—had they always been there? He wore a new polo shirt in a soft shade of apricot and jeans with a sharp crease down the legs. He must be taking them to the dry cleaners, she thought. His favorite leather jacket hung on the back of his chair, looking supple and probably smelling of his aftershave.

As they finished eating, Hayden opened the conversation about their financial situation and suggested they use the same tax preparer. Rain saw the wisdom in continuing with the same person who had done their taxes for years, since he would be familiar with their situation and they trusted him. There were a few bills that still needed to be divided up. He offered to take the Lowe's account, but Rain insisted on paying it herself, secretly wanting to keep the repairs coming from her account, just in case. They argued over it for a while, but she had her way in the end. He had dropped his membership to the fitness center, since he'd moved too far for it to be convenient any longer. It was up to her to renegotiate her own membership, if she wanted to keep it. He would pay off the Expedition with the next payment. Her Hyundai had been paid off the year before. At last, the only thing of importance left was the house.

"We should just sell it," Rain stated, "and get out from under the mortgage." She glanced away and tried to sound casual. "Unless you want to buy me out."

"That would be easier to do if the real estate market was moving right now, or if I had money that wasn't already tied up."

"I don't see that we have any choice but to try to sell it. Comps in the neighborhood are around four twenty-five."

He rubbed his chin. "Just two years ago it was worth six."

She played with the toothpick from her sandwich. "And its worth is dropping as we speak."

She remembered walking through the empty shell of house just seven years ago as they watched the progress on this new home they planned on sharing together. They had chosen the kitchen tile and the carpet and the placement of the appliances. Even the fixtures in the bathrooms. She'd insisted on granite countertops, which could only increase the value now. Of course, they haggled over the colors of the walls, but Hayden admitted that it was perfect when they were done.

"Maybe we should hang on to it for a while longer," he suggested. "Split the payment to see if the prices come up and sell it when the market improves. It would be a shame to lose all that equity if we didn't have to."

Rain pressed her lips together, considering. Then she said, "I need the money now."

"For what?"

Rain glanced over the heads of the people at the nearby table, and then plunged in. "I need it to pay the clinic."

He looked confused for a moment, but then she saw the light come on. "The clinic."

"Yes," she said, pointedly. She crossed her arms and lowered her eyes. "It's expensive. There are all kinds of costs, depending on the treatment, and then, sometimes, it doesn't work the first time and treatments have to be repeated—"

"Is that normal?" he asked, interrupting.

She looked him in the eye. "No. Normal is two people loving each other and having a baby naturally. But that's not an option right now."

He motioned with his hands to keep her voice down, and it annoyed her. After all, she thought, these people were getting to know him. Maybe Ponytail should know up front about his aversion to babies.

"Let's at least wait until after the holidays are over. And after your mom . . . you're going to have a lot on your plate soon enough."

Rain reluctantly agreed. Her insurance would help with the IUI, and time would tell whether she needed in vitro. Then she would need the money in hand, and she just might try to take the house if Hayden was difficult and didn't want to sell.

When they were finished, he walked her down the dark street to her car, and asked her what kind of progress she'd made on having a baby. It caught her off-guard. He must have made peace with it, and accepted that she was going her own way. Perhaps he'd wanted to ask under shadow of darkness so she couldn't read his expression. She grew a little irritated, when she realized that if he hadn't been so difficult, he would be sharing this with her instead of going it alone.

"I'm getting there," she said. "I'm on some medications and shots to help things along."

They paused by her car as she dug for her keys, and he asked, "You're taking shots?"

"Yes, daily shots. I've gotten pretty good at it. But my thighs are a beautiful shade of eggplant like our . . . like the guest bathroom. The doctor is hopeful that I'll be pregnant in a few weeks." She tried to fit the key into the lock of her car, but his shadow blocked the streetlight.

"You're giving *yourself* the shots?"

She looked up at him and in the dim light, saw something like wonder and respect register on his face. "You want it that badly?" he asked.

"Yes. I want it that badly." At that moment she felt there was so much left unsaid between them. "It could have been easier, you know, if . . ."

He waited without responding.

"Nothing," she said. "Forget it."

He said good-bye, and brushed an awkward kiss on her temple. He started to walk away, but the endearment softened her, and she called after him. "Hayden, what are you afraid of? Really?"

He stopped and turned back to her.

"Pregnancy? Family?" She crossed her arms against the cold. "What is it about having a baby that scares you so much that you would walk away from seven years together?"

He walked back to her car with his head down and his hands jammed into his pockets. "You really want to know?"

Something about the way he said it made her hesitate, but she answered that she did. He looked her in the eye for several moments, and took a deep breath.

"I'm not afraid of changing diapers or losing a lifestyle or postpartum blues, if that's what you think. I'm not terrified of being a father. In fact, I'm looking forward to it." He looked down at his shoes for a moment, and then lifted his head to her. "The thing I'm really afraid of is how much you're becoming like your mother. And I don't want to bring a child into that."

His words were like icy water and the shock of them squeezed the breath from her. "How can you say that?"

"Do you know how many times over the years you have manipulated me to get your own way?" he asked, his emotions rising. "Moving out of the Bay Area. Buying the house in a bad market. Choosing where to go on vacation. Even minor things like what color to paint the bathroom and what movie to go to. I put up with it because I cared about you and I told myself that those things didn't matter. But secretly trying to get pregnant was the last straw."

"But time was running out, and you didn't care that I wanted a baby."

"That's not true. I had concerns that you didn't want to hear, or you didn't think were important, and it became a battleground. That's just the tip of the iceberg, Rain." He rubbed the back of his neck. "You know that I think selling the house right now in this market is a bad idea. But you want the money so badly for something that may not even work, that you're willing to take a chance on throwing away our investment."

She turned away from him, trying to get a handle on his words and clenching her teeth against the impulse to cry. The neon Budweiser sign in the window across the street flickered with uneven pulse. A noisy, laughing group spilled out the doorway of Ninja Sushi across the street and called to each other as they dispersed to their cars.

She heard him exhale heavily. Then, he briefly touched her elbow. "I'm sorry, Rain," he said. "Look, I'm sure there's no reason why you can't have a baby. You usually find a way to do whatever you set your mind to."

When she didn't respond, he said, "I have to go." She glanced over to see him turn up his collar against the cold. His voice was almost kind as he added, "I hope you get what you want," and then walked away. Hot tears blurred her eyes so that she could hardly see the key going into the door lock, even after his leaving had lit the way.

She got into her car and locked herself in, trembling from anger and hurt. What a horrible thing to say to her, that she was becoming like Jude. He, of all people, knew exactly how she felt about her mother. Was she really that person?

Maybe it was just an excuse. He needed a reason to mask his own fears and blamed her for becoming like her mother. It distracted her from the real issue of having a baby.

His voice rang in her ears as she drove away from the downtown district, the temperature dropping. By the time she got home, she realized the implications of his words. If he'd truly felt that way for a long time, he'd been a walking time bomb. He said he put up with it because he'd cared about her. He didn't have that reason now. He would have left her eventually anyway, with or without her ultimatum about having a baby. If not a baby, it would have been something else that pushed him over the edge.

She'd been deluding herself. She wasn't the one who broke it off. She merely provided him with the excuse he needed to leave.

Wasn't that exactly what her mother was doing with William?

Chapter 17

Christmas was just under three weeks away, and all Bebe could think about was Jude's Celebration on the coming weekend, and the fact that she hadn't heard from Scotty since she'd answered his letter about the news clipping. Every time the phone rang or the mailbox came up empty, she feared the worst—alienation from her firstborn.

She hoped to hear from him before they flew down for his graduation from the School of Infantry. Once he graduated, he would be free to come home. He would get a job and spend only one weekend away each month until his unit was deployed. It would be a long plane ride and a long holiday, if things were awkward between them. He might even move out.

She tried to occupy her mind with final preparations for the Celebration, printing information and maps from the Internet, including directions to the closest hospital, just in case they needed it. Mare had her menus finalized, and Bebe felt that she provided a balance of choices for them all. Toni had the key to the house, the key code for the alarm, and final instructions from the owner. The only real variable now was Jude.

It was decided that Bebe and Rain would pick up Toni on their way through San Jose, and that Mare would pick up Jude on her way from Marin. Bebe hoped that Mare and Jude would still be speaking to each other by the time they all met up in Monterey.

Bebe began to get headaches and didn't sleep well during the next week. Too much pressure around the holidays, she assumed. And she dreamed. Not pleasant dreams, but jumbles and snatches of people and places and conversations.

It didn't take a Freud to figure out what was going on. Rich emotional baggage lay just below the surface like an archaeological dig layered with dysfunctional relationships, mistakes from the past, and guilt. Sunken memories rose to the surface as she lowered her defenses in sleep. They left her feeling unsettled when she awoke, which was usually before her alarm rang, and she got up early to avoid falling back into that dream state.

She truly dreaded the coming weekend. If it weren't for Rain, she would cancel.

* * * *

Each of the women sitting in the lobby of the fertility clinic fell into either one of two categories—those who looked anxious with an edge, and those who looked anxious with a glow. It wasn't hard to tell the pregnant ones from the hopefuls. Rain knew she exuded "anxious with an edge." She couldn't help it. She tried hard to mask her anxiety, but it was beyond her, sitting there alone without a loved one to hold her hand and tell her it would be okay.

When her name was called, she undressed in a cubicle and went in for an ultrasound. The nurse kept a poker face as she moved the wand over Rain's body and studied the image on the screen. She remained noncommittal when Rain asked her point-blank if she thought her body was responding to the shots, but she encouraged Rain to just continue with her treatments. After the ultrasound, Rain dressed and stopped at the front desk where she got an appointment to see Dr. Sykes later in the week. She went home feeling like she was in limbo.

A sense of heaviness hovered over her as the weekend loomed ahead, realizing the potential for disaster and the fact that it was her mother's Celebration of Life. Her mother's pre-funeral.

She checked the weather forecast online and packed accordingly. She also called William to make sure he was overseeing Jude's packing. He told her he was already on top of it and nursing injuries from it.

Jude was in "rare form," he said. He would make sure all her prescriptions were refilled, and even offered to throw in a bit extra in case she grew intolerable. Then he apologized to Rain. He said that two of Jude's colleagues had stopped by to see her, and she hadn't seemed surprised, so she must have arranged it. He didn't know why and she wouldn't tell him anything. He joked that perhaps he should start packing up. Rain wondered if he would secretly be relieved when Jude was gone.

On her last day at work before the Celebration weekend, Rain's department manager, Latoya, asked her to stop by her office after lunch. Rain hoped it wasn't about more special projects. Perhaps she'd gotten wind that Rain had time on her hands, now that Hayden had moved out. It was a relatively small office.

Latoya asked her to shut the door and motioned for Rain to take the chair on the other side of her desk. "How's it going?"

"Fine." Rain crossed her legs at the ankle and folded her hands in her lap.

"Well, I asked you to come by because I just heard about an opening for a senior paralegal for one of the attorneys, Jacob Barbera. It's a fabulous opportunity, and I think you would be a great choice for the job. Gerald does, too. He said you should apply right away before they look outside."

Rain was stunned. "What exactly are the duties?"

"Basically keeping him abreast of changes in legislation, overseeing interrogatories. Taking depositions. A large part involves interfacing with clients. There is also a certain amount of travel that goes with the position. Chicago, Atlanta, and Dallas, I think. Maybe San Diego. The company needs someone of your caliber to troubleshoot potentially volatile clients and situations." She tapped her pen on the desk and eyed Rain with satisfaction. "You are perfect for this."

"Thank you. What makes you think so?"

Latoya clasped her hands on the desk, leaning in toward Rain. "You have a sort of low-key passive-aggressiveness that people naturally respond to."

Rain balled her fists in her lap. "I'm passive-aggressive?"

"In a good way. Just enough that people end up doing what you want without ever realizing what's happening. I've seen it in your projects. You're completely nonthreatening, but you get it done your way. That's the type of person they're looking for."

Rain felt the tension travel up her back through her shoulders and neck. This only confirmed what Hayden had told her. But what about a baby?

"How much travel? How often?" she asked.

Her supervisor shrugged a shoulder. "It depends on the situation, but I would guess probably twice a month. Maybe more. It comes with a pay raise, profit sharing, and a company vehicle."

More money *and* a company vehicle. That would certainly help with the cost of infertility treatments. Rain knew she should jump at the chance; after all, this was the kind of position she'd been working toward. But she felt ambivalent. The truth was that her job—any job—simply didn't satisfy like she'd expected it to.

"Thanks for letting me know. I'll have to think about it," Rain said, without enthusiasm.

Latoya frowned. "Well, don't think about it too long. They'll be posting it January 1st. If you need to talk to Gerald about it, I can give him a call."

Rain rose and thanked her again and returned to her desk. She thought about the job opportunity, and the fact that a VP had suggested her for the position, but it only raised more questions.

How would she manage a pregnancy and a baby with traveling several times a month? And if she passed on the job and wasn't able to get pregnant, then she'd be left with nothing. And she was passive-aggressive —in a good way? She sat shell-shocked, unable to focus.

Someone passed by her cubicle, and she picked up her pen and doodled on a company notepad to look busy so they wouldn't stop to make small talk. She thought again about her mother's suggestion that she take the house from Hayden. At first, she had recoiled from the idea. It was so like Jude to casually mention taking advantage of someone for personal gain. But if Rain didn't take this job and if the fertility shots didn't work, getting the house for herself might be the only way she could afford in vitro. At this point, he might roll over and let her have it. If she was a nice person and split the house fairly with Hayden or if it didn't sell, she would have to take the promotion and be an absentee mother. And either way, she could spend a lot of money on treatments and end up just like she was.

She glanced down at her doodling. "Steele, VonTrapp, and Evers" stood bold at the top, and with a few quick strokes she changed it to "Steel trap 4 Ever." She ripped off the note and stuck it in her shredder.

Perhaps she should get a phone number for one of her mother's colleagues this weekend, just in case.

* * * *

Rain sat in the waiting room at the clinic, making mental lists of things she needed to do to finish packing before she left for her mother's Celebration that afternoon with Bebe. It would be hard to keep the excitement to herself if she received good news from the doctor, and she might even make an announcement if everything was a go.

She was secretly dreading the weekend, for many reasons. She liked getting together with the women, but the dynamics could be exhausting. Sometimes they bickered like high schoolers. If Jude slept a lot, it could be a relaxing time for them, but it would mean her mother was declining. Rain felt helpless when she saw her mother's physical appearance worsen with each visit, and she wondered if this weekend would prove too much for her.

Rain was called into Dr. Sykes's office and he breezed in a moment later. He greeted her and scanned her file, frowning as he flipped pages. Then, he closed her file and steepled his fingers.

"Unfortunately, it doesn't appear that we're having a good response to the drugs. At this point, I would recommend that you move to in vitro fertilization."

"In vitro." It wasn't working. Rain felt the ground shifting beneath her.

"You'll continue with your shots. But this time, the eggs will be surgically removed before the hormones cause your ovaries to ovulate, and we'll fertilize them through IVF. The best embryos will be transferred, and we'll do an ultrasound at eight weeks to see how things are progressing."

"What are my chances of getting pregnant?"

"Roughly one-third of IVF procedures work. But there's no evidence of polycystic ovarian syndrome. I see no reason why it shouldn't work for you."

"But . . . but if it doesn't. What then?"

"If the problem lies with the eggs, donor eggs are always an option. Or if it's a matter of implantation failure, we would do a laparoscopy to test for pelvic scarring or endometriosis."

Rain felt suddenly that she couldn't handle the looming possibility of failure and the realization of the cost—both mentally and financially—on top of the uncertain weekend that lay ahead. She felt an overwhelming need to have Hayden beside her, and tears welled in her eyes, threatening to spill over. She gathered her purse and stood blindly, murmuring a thank-you, and almost knocked over her chair. She left the office, swiping at tears on her way out the door, and wondered grimly if the other patients breathed easier now that she was the designated statistical failure in the room.

She drove home in a fog and packed her suitcase indiscriminately. As she scooped her cosmetics from the counter into her bag, she glanced up at her reflection in the mirror. Her skin was blotchy and her eyes red-rimmed, the makeup washed away to reveal her age and small wrinkles around her eyes. Her lips were chapped and puffed up with crying. She couldn't help feeling disgust for herself, and for the body that had betrayed her.

Chapter 18

Bebe pulled into Rain's driveway and beeped once. Just as Bebe jumped out to go inside, Rain came out dragging her suitcase and paused to lock the dead bolt behind her.

Bebe helped her load her suitcase into the back. "Sorry if the car smells like Jimbo. We got him groomed yesterday." They settled into the front seats and Bebe asked, "Are you ready for this?"

"As ready as I'll ever be," Rain answered, stuffing her purse on the floor at her feet.

Bebe put the car in reverse and backed out, glancing over at Rain who stared out the passenger window.

"Are you feeling okay?" Bebe asked.

Rain turned to face her and said evenly that she was fine, and looked out the window again. Bebe knew something was wrong, but wasn't about to push it.

She tuned the radio to smooth jazz on the ride over to Toni's house in San Jose. It took several hours, and even though she called Toni when they were half an hour away, Toni still wasn't ready when they arrived.

Rain stayed in the car while Bebe went in to help Toni drag her suitcases to the car and load them.

"You do know this is only a four day trip?" Bebe said. "I don't think it's a good idea for Mare and Jude to be waiting on the front lawn for us."

"It's just a few things. I like to have choices when I travel, and you can never tell when a storm will blow in." She said privately to Bebe, "Chance of storm 100 percent."

Toni filled in the silence with chatter for the next forty-five minutes. Of course, Mare's Prius was parked outside the gated entrance of the house when they arrived. The "Coexist" bumper sticker written in various religious symbols on the back of her car stood out in sharp relief to Bebe when she remembered the round Marines emblem on the back of her Highlander.

Toni jumped out and punched in the entry code, and Mare drove on through without a greeting. Toni scrunched up her face at Bebe when she got back in the car and asked, "What's eating her?"

They pulled through the gate and followed Mare along the circular driveway to the garage, where they parked and unloaded the suitcases. They greeted each other and dragged their suitcases inside. Bebe went back for Jude's. Rain caught up with her and wanted to make sure her mother got a ground-floor room. Bebe said she'd take care of it discreetly so Jude wouldn't think it was patronizing.

The house was fabulous: expansive and white, with bare windows overlooking the ocean and private suites for each of them. The kitchen and dining room alone were larger than Bebe's house. She tried not to gawk.

Jude went straight to her room to rest. Mare came out to the kitchen where Bebe was checking out the contents of the cabinets and breathed a sigh of relief. She chastised Toni when she discovered it was her fault they were late.

"We weren't *that* late," Toni shot back, investigating the wine rack. "Oh, look," she said, pulling a bottle from the rack. "A 2005 Old Ghost Old Vine Zin. Marshall said we can help ourselves to anything in the rack, but his wine cellar downstairs is off-limits." She carefully replaced the bottle. "I wonder what he has down there."

Mare would not be distracted. "Jude was just exhausted, and you know how irritable she gets. I think she was uncomfortable, too, like her meds were wearing off."

Rain came into the kitchen carrying grocery sacks.

"Rain, do you know anything about your mother's medications?" Mare asked. "Would she tell us if she needed anything?"

Rain stopped and glanced in the direction of her mother's room. "She might not. Maybe her patch needs to be replaced." She set the bags down on the counter and headed down the hall.

Bebe watched her go, wondering when Rain had become so attuned to Jude's needs. Toni and Mare began to unload the contents of the cooler into the giant side-by-side refrigerator.

Toni lifted a container from the cooler and brandished it at Mare. "Tofu? I will not eat tofu!"

Mare yanked it out of her hands. "It's not for you, it's for me." Mare bent down to retrieve more items, and muttered, "I wouldn't waste it on you."

Toni made a snotty face over her head and Bebe gave her a chastising look. Toni winked at Bebe playfully, and immediately turned a straight face to Mare when she looked up.

Rain came back out to the kitchen a few minutes later and said her mom was resting with a new patch. She would probably sleep for hours. She was going to rest awhile, herself.

She turned and went down the hall to her room, and closed the door behind her. The three women looked at each other.

"She's unusually quiet," Toni observed.

Mare's eyes widened. "Could she be pregnant?"

Bebe knew that Rain would have difficulty containing her joy, if that were the case. Her melancholy fit the possibility of bad news, but Bebe didn't want to give anything away. "I don't think so. Consider why we're here, ladies. It's only natural that she should be depressed."

They seemed satisfied with her answer. They got the kitchen squared away, oohed and aahed over the appliances, and familiarized themselves with where everything was. Toni pointed out where the kitchen laptop was stored. It was used mostly as a virtual cookbook, but they could log on as guests and use it whenever they wanted. When they were done, they took their beverages of choice out to the sunporch and watched the wispy fog roll in. Toni opened a window to hear the roar of the ocean below. The sun bedded down in lavender gauze and fog eventually encased the house, extinguishing even the floodlight on the path down to the beach.

Toni rattled the ice in her empty glass. "Well, what's for dinner, Mare? I'm getting hungry."

"Shrimp fettuccini. I stopped by a bakery in Monterey for some rosemary bread to go with it."

"Mmm," Toni murmured. "Sounds good. When do we eat?"

Mare looked over at Toni, exasperated. "When you decide to get up and do something about it."

Toni's eyebrows shot up. "Meow. Draw in your claws."

"Well, I'm sorry, but I only agreed to make the menu, not cook every meal."

Bebe went over to the freezer and pulled out a bag of frozen shrimp. She took a shiny colander from the hanging rack overhead, dumped the shrimp into it, and turned on the cold water.

Toni continued to bait Mare. "I thought you were vegan. So you make an exception for shellfish?"

"Only when they're wild-caught in traps and they're sustainably harvested."

"These are huge, Mare," Bebe observed when the running water thawed them apart. "You couldn't exactly call them shrimp."

"They're prawns. Same thing, just bigger."

"How much are we paying for these things, anyway?" Toni asked.

"What do you care, Miss 'My Perfume Is Obscenely Expensive'? If you wanted farm-raised shrimp from China full of antibiotics and growth hormones, or trawled in Thailand where they're destroying the environment, you should have said something."

"Geez," Toni said. "I was only asking."

Toni brought her glass to the sink and gave an exaggerated shrug to Bebe. Bebe discreetly nodded her head in Mare's direction. "It was a long afternoon," she said quietly, willing Toni to consider what the trip down had been like for Mare.

Toni pursed her lips briefly, and said lightly, "I'll put the water on for the pasta."

They let Mare relax on the sunporch while they cooked. Toni even went to refill Mare's glass, but found her asleep on the chaise lounge.

When the meal was ready, they called Rain and checked in on Jude, who said she would come out later. They woke Mare and gathered at the long table to eat. The sleep had done both Mare and Rain some good, and when they were finished eating, they discussed their plans for the next morning.

"I thought we might do some shopping tomorrow and visit Point Lobos on Saturday afternoon. We have aquarium tickets for Sunday," Bebe said.

"Mmm," Mare said, reaching for a leftover slice of rosemary bread. "We should start with breakfast at Toasties in Pacific Grove in the morning."

Toni pulled the bread basket out of Mare's reach. "Good idea. As I recall, they have blintzes." Toni licked her fork. "We should shop in Carmel."

"You're the only one of us who can afford to shop there, Toni," Mare said.

"Traffic's bad on the weekends, and there's usually a problem finding parking," Bebe said. "I was thinking more of Cannery Row."

"But there's a jewelry store I wanted to stop at, and we could have tea at the Tuck Box in the afternoon," Toni persisted.

"Maybe you and Lawrence could come back together sometime."

"I think we should play it by ear," Rain said. "We don't want Mom getting too worn out."

"Don't worry about me," Jude said from the doorway, wrapped in her plush robe, looking haggard. "If I can't keep up, you can just leave me behind."

"Are you hungry?" Rain asked, ignoring her remarks.

Jude waved her off and shook her head. "Tea would be nice."

Rain filled a teacup with scalding water from the hot faucet and pulled out the teabags. "Where do you want it?"

Jude glanced over her shoulder. "Is there a couch somewhere? The smell of that shrimp is making me nauseated."

"Follow me." Rain led Jude into the family room.

Mare lowered her voice. "When are we going to, you know, address the reason we're here?"

"Sunday," Bebe said. "Evening. We'll have some fun first."

Rain came back in and Mare started stacking dishes. "I'll rinse if you'll fill the dishwasher," she said.

Rain agreed, and everyone carried their plates to the sink. Toni and Bebe joined Jude in the family room. They turned on the gas fireplace and found a channel on the flatscreen TV that had local news.

Soon they heard popcorn popping in the microwave. They smelled the buttery scent long before Rain and Mare joined them with brimming bowls. They perused the movies in the entertainment center and agreed on *While You Were Sleeping*. Jude dozed, waking long enough to snort at Sandra Bullock slipping all over the ice with Bill Pullman, and say, "Ridiculous. Contrived."

Toni shushed her sternly. "It's romance, Jude. You remember what that is."

Mare made a face at Toni, who playfully stuck out her tongue in reply.

At the end of the movie, Toni stretched and grinned broadly. "I'm glad they went to Florence for their honeymoon. That's so romantic."

"I don't remember you being particularly romantic in school," Bebe said. "Lawrence must have really pushed your buttons."

"That he did, girlfriend," she said, grinning.

"So what made you decide to give up teaching at the university?" Bebe asked. "Did Lawrence give you an offer you couldn't refuse?"

Toni grew uncharacteristically quiet and chewed her popcorn thoughtfully. "Not exactly."

They waited for her to elaborate. Finally, Mare said, "Well, what happened?"

Toni briefly hiked her eyebrows and then shrugged. "They wanted me to teach online journalism."

"What's wrong with that?" Bebe asked.

"I know absolutely nothing about online journalism." She shifted and tucked her bare feet beneath her. "And they knew that I didn't."

Mare made a little O with her mouth, and Rain dropped her gaze from Toni.

"They knew I wasn't comfortable with it. Curation? Flash? I'd be starting out all over again."

"I get little Sammy to help me with the DVD player," Mare admitted. "He's four years old and he can play Thomas the Train with no help at all."

"They offered me early retirement as my only other choice."

"That's too bad, Toni," Bebe said. "Were you upset about it?"

She twirled the diamond rings on her left hand. "I got over it when Lawrence suggested going to Tahiti on our honeymoon."

"That would've helped me get over a few things, too." Mare's words dripped with sarcasm.

"I'm still keeping my hand in, just in case," Toni said.

"In case of what?" Bebe asked.

"In case I need to support myself again."

Jude stirred. "I knew you were a kept woman."

They all exchanged glances and wondered how much of their conversation she'd heard.

"I enjoy every minute of it," Toni said.

Mare eyed her suspiciously, chewing her popcorn. She leaned in toward Toni's face. "If I didn't know better, I'd say you've had a face-lift."

Toni smiled, self-satisfied. "Last spring, when we were in Los Angeles."

Suddenly, the difference was apparent to Bebe. "You know, I hadn't seen you in so long, I guess I didn't notice."

"You look nice, Toni," Rain said.

"Altering your body that way to please a man," Jude said. "Every time you went home for semester break, I had to reprogram you all over again." She said to Bebe, "Not unlike the way I had to reprogram Rain after she spent weekends with you and Neil."

An awkward silence fell as all eyes went to Rain.

"Poor Rain," Mare said. "You must have been seriously confused growing up."

Bebe stood. "It's getting late. We should call it a night so we can get to Toasties before it gets crowded tomorrow." She began to gather empty popcorn bowls.

When all the bowls with stray popcorn kernels and empty glasses were stacked on the kitchen counter, they all said good night and headed for their rooms. Before Bebe went to sleep, she called Neil to check in and ask if he'd heard from Scotty. He hadn't, but he reminded her that this was probably field week, and he probably didn't have much time to himself. Not to worry. She blew him a kiss and said good night.

Chapter 19

The next morning as they went out to load into the car, Mare saw the Marine emblem on the back of Bebe's Highlander and paused. She stood frowning, and Bebe could see the wheels turning in her head.

"Get in, Mare," Bebe told her. "There's no way we'll all fit into your Prius. Think of it as supporting Scotty."

Mare gave an exaggerated sigh and piled into the car. They managed to snag a table at Toasties during a lull in the Saturday morning rush, and were out sightseeing an hour later. Jude seemed to be holding up well, but she chose to rest in the car when they went into some shops on Cannery Row. They offered to drop her back at the house, or to have someone stay with her, but she refused. She reclined her seat back and relaxed in the sun-warmed interior.

The sun bounced brilliantly off the water, and the boats left their signatures on the bay in white trails of foam. The street performers played exotic instruments and the seagulls cried as they dove for fish on the water and for stray food by the restaurant tables. Kelp swayed and danced in the current with an occasional sea otter breaking the surface to crack a clam on its belly.

It was a glorious day, and Bebe wished they were there under different circumstances. Some of the shops were decorated for Christmas and were playing carols. She dropped back behind Mare and Toni to walk with Rain, who tended to lag behind. Bebe noticed that her face appeared strained, and she wondered if Rain worried about her mother waiting alone in the car. Even though she'd insisted that they go on without her, it wouldn't stop them from feeling guilty for having fun.

They dropped in at the Ghirardelli shop for dark chocolate to enjoy after dinner that night. Toni bought a bottle of port to go with it, and also picked up a golf shirt for Lawrence at the Pebble Beach Shop. Mare bought aromatherapy candles and handmade soap, and Bebe chose a Christmas ornament. Rain was the only one who came back empty-handed.

They spent time browsing in a bookstore until Rain said she wanted to go. Bebe went looking for Toni. Oddly, she found her turning a stack of books face-front on the display in the romance section, and muttering to herself. Bebe watched her tap them neatly into place and step back with her hands on her hips, smiling to herself. Bebe asked her what she was doing and Toni seemed startled and a bit embarrassed. Bebe shook her head and motioned for her to hurry up.

On their way back to the car, Mare paused outside of a shop window displaying exquisite infant's and children's clothes. "That would look adorable on Sammy," she said, going into the store. Toni pointed out an adorable layette in the window, and Bebe looked over to find Rain standing in front of the jewelry store next door, turned with her back to them.

A moment later, Mare was out on the sidewalk again. "Sixty dollars for a sundress. It's not even organic!" she said with disgust.

They found Jude asleep in the front seat of the car, and she startled awake when Bebe unlocked the doors. She looked so vulnerable and fearful at that moment, that Bebe felt an unexpected sadness. She'd rarely seen Jude with her defenses down. When she thought of it, there had really only been one other time.

❖ ❖ ❖ ❖

February 1, 1970

The phone rang again, but this time it jangled until Bebe slammed her biology book shut and came out of her bedroom to answer it. Who keeps calling, she wondered?

Jude grabbed the phone from the wall, just as Bebe came up behind her.

"Listen," Jude spit out angrily to the caller. "I said don't call me anymore. Just leave me alone. I can't help you."

Bebe circled around to read Jude's face. Whatever was said next made Jude blanch. Her face melted into fear and despair and tears welled in her eyes. "Leave me alone," without much resolve.

"Hang up," Bebe whispered fiercely. Jude stood pale and appeared unable to disconnect from the conversation. Bebe took the phone out of her hands and hung it up.

"Who was that, Jude?" Bebe asked. "Why didn't you just hang up?"

Jude looked at her as though seeing her for the first time. She wiped away tears without meeting Bebe's eyes and grabbed her coat. The phone rang again, and Jude said, "Don't answer it." The front door slammed behind her on the third ring, and Bebe answered.

"Who is this?" she demanded.

"Lemme ta . . . talk to Judy," the woman slurred. Bebe could almost smell the liquor through the phone lines.

"She's not here."

"Judy Rasssmusss. Rassmuss . . . My Judy. Lil' slut hung up on me. Sshe can't hang up on her m . . . mother."

"She's gone now. She just left."

The woman swore. "Tell her . . . you tell her I'm coming ov . . . over right now to pick'er up. You, you t . . . tell her sshe can't run away. She's jus' like me. I know what she's doin'. Sshe's no good and sshe's gonna turn out jus' like m . . . me."

Bebe said "Good-bye," cutting off the woman mid-slur, and hung up the phone.

They never spoke of the incident, and Jude never knew that Bebe talked to her mother. Jude acted as though it never happened. She didn't even come home that night, but called and told Mare, that she was staying with a friend.

Bebe noticed that after that phone call, she only threw herself harder into volunteering at the Women's Center and stepped up the number of rallies she attended until Bebe wondered whether it was affecting her grades. She began hanging out with older, more activist students, and one in particular, who sometimes made Bebe uncomfortable in her own house. It was no surprise that Jude got in over her head.

❖ ❖ ❖ ❖

On their way back to the house, they took the 17-Mile Drive and ogled the views and expensive estates. At home, they prepared an oriental salad for lunch, and then reclined in the sunroom. The sunshine warmed them through the glass, and the pounding of the surf below made Bebe's eyes droopy. Jude retired to her room, and Rain went to check on her.

"I was thinking of taking a walk down to the beach," Mare said, "but I don't think I'd make it back up the stairs. I might find a movie to watch and fall asleep on the couch."

Toni stretched and yawned on the chaise lounge, kicking off her shoes. "I'm not moving from here." Then she added dreamily as she curled up, "Don't think I could if I had to."

Bebe fell asleep in the other chaise lounge, and woke later to a silent, darkening house. Her watch said four o'clock, and the sun was sinking fast. The pounding of the surf on the rocks below sounded amplified in the quiet, and she stepped to the glass to enjoy the view. A thin line of light hovered above the distant horizon. A movement on the beach below in the dusk drew her attention.

A lone woman walked along with her hands in her pockets. After a moment, she stopped and turned to face the surf, with her shoulder-length hair blowing wildly around her face. She crossed her arms, hugging her middle, bending slightly as though she were ill. Bebe thought she recognized Rain's sweater, but it could be someone from one of the other homes nearby, and she was too far away to be certain. As she watched, the woman sat heavily onto the sand and laid her head on her arms across her knees. Then, she curled her arms protectively over her head, as though expecting a blow. She sat for so long, mindless of the surf that climbed the rocks or the tide that rose higher and grabbed at the sand at her feet, that Bebe felt a sense of urgency.

Just as Bebe was stepping outside on the patio to shout to her, the woman stood and headed back toward the stairs. Bebe saw clearly that it was Rain. Rain wiped her eyes on the inside of her sweater, climbing the steps slowly. Bebe stepped back out of view and watched her. Her heart broke for her, but she felt that Rain had deliberately distanced herself from them this weekend, and didn't know whether she should speak to her. Was she grieving for her mother, or was there something else? For Hayden, perhaps, and the way life used to be? Then she recalled how Rain turned away from them in front of the baby shop. Could it be that she'd gotten bad news from the doctor?

❖ ❖ ❖ ❖

Rain lay in bed and wondered how she would go about the rest of her life. Far below, the surf pounded against the rocks like fate relentlessly trampling the best-laid plans.

Babies were everywhere. There was no avoiding them. All morning, strollers bumped her on the sidewalk. Babies cried in the restaurant. Couples handed their offspring to grandparents happy to share the load, and grateful for a chance just to hold them. Their smiling reflections taunted her in the shop windows when she turned away searching for distraction.

She heard the others out in the kitchen cleaning up after dinner. No one commented when she said she was turning in early, although she was aware that they discreetly exchanged glances. Perhaps they thought she was mourning for her mother, and that was part of it.

Rain dug in her suitcase for a syringe and rolled up the leg of her pajamas. Her mother was fading. Just as things were getting better between them, she was losing her. Rain took the cap off the needle, flicked the vial, and depressed the plunger to dispense an air bubble. Maybe that was the catalyst—knowing they didn't have much time left together made them stop pushing against each other. Wincing, she injected the drug and rubbed the spot with her thumb.

She got up and tiptoed down the hall to her mother's room, quietly pushing open the door. Jude lay on her side, breathing steadily. The skin on her face sagged in sleep against her bones. She little resembled the parent of Rain's youth, and perhaps that was a good thing. Rain closed the door again and went back to her room.

It was comforting to know that she was still there.

❖ ❖ ❖ ❖

After a leisurely breakfast the next morning, they packed a picnic lunch, loaded everything into Bebe's vehicle, and headed down Highway 1 to Point Lobos State Reserve. They parked and made their way down the Sand Hill Trail and the Sea Lion Point Trail paths and found places to best enjoy the scenery. Jude kept up with them for a while, and they found an empty bench for her when she grew tired.

The day was clear and the ocean view breathtaking. Sea lions on the rocks just offshore barked incessantly, changing cadence just to resume it again. Rain stayed behind with her mother, and the others walked farther on toward Sea Lion Point. Bebe pulled out her field glasses and located some sea otters floating in the kelp, and harbor seals basking on the low rocks. Gulls and cormorants dove for fish. The Devil's Cauldron petulantly tossed foam high into the air with the sound of a jetliner crashing.

Bebe walked farther on, apart from the others. The sun beat down on her, but the chilly breeze whipped her jacket and stung her cheeks, and she sat on a rock to breathe in the cleansing ocean air.

She glanced back at Jude and Rain sitting side-by-side on the bench. Jude said something to Rain, who answered with her sad smile. A low, smoldering ember began to flicker inside of Bebe. Rain leaned over and said something in confidence to Jude, and suddenly the glowing traces of rejection and betrayal inside of Bebe burst into flame. Bebe got to her feet and went further along the path out of sight of them.

It was a good thing for Rain to have some closure with her mother. Bebe acknowledged this. It would never cover the multitude of sins Jude had committed against her, but it would be a comfort to Rain, and Bebe wouldn't begrudge her that. But for Jude to think she could make up for everything at the end of her life, angered Bebe.

Bebe remembered the time when Rain wanted Neil to come to her Parent Day party in her kindergarten class. Jude told Rain gently but firmly that he was not her daddy and that, furthermore, she did not need one. Rain said the others had daddies, and Jude said that they didn't *all* have them, and the ones who did might be better off without them because their daddies would leave them anyway.

Then in elementary school, Rain wanted to join Girl Scouts and Jude said that the troop leaders were all simpering moms who baked cookies and did crafts and taught them compliance instead of free-thinking, and she would not have them as Rain's role models. Bebe knew that Rain had trouble making friends in school because of Jude, and that usually their first visit to her home was their last. Anything and everything that followed a traditional line of thought was eschewed by Jude. In high school, Jude went a step further, telling her the same thing she'd told Bebe that first year in college, that she was in charge of her own body and had every right to do whatever she wanted to with anyone, and no one could tell her not to. Not even Jude.

Over the years, Bebe had tried to repair some of the damage done by Jude, but all she could really do was to love Rain, pray for her, and try to give her advice as long as she would listen. In some ways, she felt like a failure.

Bebe surveyed the surf, desperate to connect with God, but for the first time, its primitive, unrelenting beauty failed to move her. Memories and regrets loomed large inside her and blocked the very light to her soul.

Bebe heard someone call, "There you are." It was Toni, coming down the path toward her. "Some of us are getting hungry and we need to find a place to eat." When she got closer, she took a good look at Bebe. "You okay?"

"Yes, I'm fine." Bebe tried to shake it off. "There are picnic tables at the Piney Woods parking area." Together they walked back up the path and found the others waiting by the car.

They loaded up, drove the short distance to the picnic tables, and set out their lunches. Bebe remained subdued, feeling wounded and not trusting her emotions.

As they ate, Mare read sections of the park brochure. "It says not to turn your back on the ocean. That would have been good to know before we went down there."

Toni rolled her eyes. "Everybody knows that, Mare. That's just common sense."

"But don't you think those pathways are far enough away from danger? Why would they put the trails so close to the ocean, if there was a chance of a wave taking you off?"

Jude spoke, her voiced edged with bitterness. "Because nature is unpredictable and ruthless, but, unfortunately, it's part of life and you'd better not turn your back on it."

They paused awkwardly for a moment. Then Toni quietly asked Bebe to pass the salad, and they resumed their conversations.

"Where to next?" Mare said, bending over her brochure.

Bebe started closing up containers and collecting utensils. "China Beach and Whaler's Cove are two areas we haven't seen yet, but they're not easily accessible . . . for everyone. Well, they're accessible, but it's a little distance and it takes some time to get there and back. And I'm not sure how much time we have." A breeze kicked up and Bebe shivered.

Mare opened the brochure to the picture of Whaler's Cove. "But there's a lot of history there. It used to be a whaling station, and it has a cabin and a museum. What a beautiful walk." She looked up and took in their lack of enthusiasm. "Oh, come on."

"I'll stay with Mom in the car," Rain said. "It's getting chilly, anyway."

"No, you will not," Jude began.

"Well, if we're not all going," Toni interrupted, "we may as well go back to the house."

"We came all this way, and you're ready to go back?" Mare asked, exasperated.

"I thought you wanted to grill fish tonight," Bebe said, packing away the remains of the lunch. "We can't grill in the dark. We'll take the scenic drive back and stop by the grocery store for dessert on the way. We'll look for tiramisu." She bagged up the trash and handed it to Toni.

"I'm not grilling the tilapia, I'm baking it," Mare said.

"Fish again? I don't suppose you know how to make sushi?" Toni asked.

Mare threw up her hands. "No sushi! And when we're at the aquarium, I'm getting you a copy of the Seafood Watch Sushi Guide."

They got home just before dusk and Mare pulled Bebe, Toni, and Rain into the kitchen to help her with dinner. She set Bebe chopping garlic, Rain slicing onions, and sent Toni for a bottle of sauvignon blanc to bake the fish in. Then she put Toni to work chopping fresh herbs while she assembled the dish. She also fixed some tofu for herself. As the tilapia baked, the kitchen filled with a heavenly aroma that masked the smell of fish. Mare trimmed a bunch of asparagus and briefly steamed it. At the last minute, she mixed two tablespoons of crème fraiche into the thickened sauce of the tilapia and served them all. Toni selected a Merryvale Chardonnay to go with it. Surprisingly, Jude joined them at the table.

When they were finished, Bebe made a fresh pot of coffee. Mare brought the tiramisu to the table along with dessert plates and forks. Jude passed on dessert, saying that it was one of her good days and she didn't want to push it. The others all served themselves generous portions.

Toni finished her dessert and leaned back in her chair, kicking off her shoes under the table. "That was good. And I must admit your cooking has improved since college, Mare."

Mare licked her fork. "Thank you, I think."

"You've turned into the little domestic goddess, cooking, sewing, birthing babies. How did Arnie do it?" Toni teased.

Mare gave a contented smile. "There's nothing you can say to get under my skin, Toni. I am who I am because of *my* choices, not Arnie's."

"I would venture to say that her mother had more to do with it than her husband," said Jude. "She's probably the spitting image."

"Well, I guess in some ways, I am. She's a nurturer, but I stopped at two kids and she had eight. And she put up with my dad's carousing for all those years. You know, sometimes I think she was relieved to let someone else be on the receiving end of his affections for a while."

"You've probably got half brothers and sisters running around out there," Bebe observed.

Mare laughed. "Oh, I'm sure of it. The Catholic Church was against contraception, but Dad viewed it as a build-your-own religion. He picked and chose what he wanted to observe."

"Aren't we all like our mothers in some way, at least physically?" Toni said, "I've tried to deny it, believe me, but I look in the mirror and pull my hair back into a bun, and there she is." She pulled her hair back into a knot and looked at each one. "See, it's Irena." Then she let her hair fall back and tousled it.

"Your hair used to be really long. You put it up in those orange juice cans before you went to bed, remember?" Mare said with a grimace. "The tub and the sink were always clogged with long, dark hair. It was everywhere."

"Unfortunately for me, I don't have that problem anymore." She added, frowning, "Thinning hair is something else I got from my mother."

"Didn't she want you to be a movie star, or an ice skater?" Bebe asked.

"The ice skater was my idea. I was dying to have a sequined costume.

From the day I was born my mother wanted me to be in the soaps. She watched one right after another, all afternoon. *The Guiding Light, General Hospital,* even *Dark Shadows*. I'd come home from school, and she'd say, 'Tonya, you're more beautiful than Josette, and so glamorous. You should be a TV star!'"

Jude said something unintelligible under her breath.

"I told her I wanted to go out to California for school, and she never could get it straight that Hollywood wasn't anywhere near San Francisco. She always wrote to me, 'Did you see any TV stars? When are you going to be in the soaps?'"

"But the soaps are filmed in New York," Rain said.

"Exactly," Toni said, gesturing with her hands. "*This*, I know." She put her hands in her lap. "Sheesh, I'm starting to talk like her."

"What about you, Bebe?" Mare asked. "How are you like your mother?"

Bebe thought for a moment. "I think we're aging the same way. At least, when I see myself in photographs, I see her mouth and her sagging jawline." She patted beneath her chin with the back of her hand. "And I think we're both shrinking."

"Maybe your boys are just shooting up taller than you expected," Toni said.

"From all those growth hormones in their food over the years," Mare added. Toni threw her cloth napkin at her across the table.

Bebe noticed that Rain looked almost distressed, and Jude's arms were crossed against her chest. Neither one invited a comparison between the two.

Jude shifted in her seat. "All this navel-gazing is well and good, but when do you want to address the real reason for our little weekend?"

"Oh, Jude, why spoil the fun?" Toni leaned back in her chair. "We have all day tomorrow."

"What's on the agenda?" Jude asked.

"The Monterey Bay Aquarium. It's open between ten and six." Bebe started stacking dishes. "We can do breakfast or lunch. Whatever."

"Let's do lunch. I'll buy," Toni offered.

Mare looked wary. "Who's choosing?"

"There are plenty of restaurants down the block from the aquarium. We'll look at the menus and decide on a place together," Bebe said. "If we're getting lunch, we'll need to go into the aquarium at ten when it opens. It takes a few hours to see everything. We'll have plenty of time in the afternoon and evening."

As they cleared the table, Toni announced with relish that they needed music and wandered off. Soon, they heard the strains of "Me and Bobby McGee" coming from a speaker above their heads and Toni waltzed in crooning the lyrics off-pitch. Mare joined her and together they gave their best Janis Joplin imitations. Mare loosened her graying blonde hair and shook into a wild frenzy, singing into a wooden spoon matching Janis note for raspy note, tossing her head back with attitude at the end.

They all howled with laughter until they wiped away tears.

"Gosh, Mare," Toni said when she caught her breath. "All you need are a huge pair of glasses and some underarm hair, and you could be her twin."

Mare fastened her hair back again with a clip as "Love Her Madly" started up. Bebe and Rain went back to the sink full of dishes, washing pots and loading the dishwasher as they sang along to the music. Mare wiped down the counters and Toni dried the pans as Bebe handed them over, dancing as she hung them back on the ceiling rack. Carole King started "It's Too Late" and Bebe found herself singing along, finding it ironically pleasant that just a few months ago the music could have tripped her up and laid her out flat. Somehow, being with these wonderful women took the edge off of the past.

When they were done, they moved into the family room and pulled out board games from the cupboard. Rain seemed to deflate and had trouble keeping her mind on things. She bowed out after the first round of Scrabble. Bebe thought it rather odd that Toni discreetly watched Rain peruse the books on the wall of shelves behind the leather couch. Rain ran her finger along the spines of hardbacks lined up in their dust jackets, tilting her head sideways to read the titles. Bebe saw Toni bite her lower lip and pause in arranging her Scrabble tiles. Rain moved down to the end of the shelves, pulled out a paperback and settled back in her chair. Only then did Toni turn her full attention back to the game.

Jude went to her room early and they all breathed easier. Bebe wasn't sure just why. Jude hadn't been particularly difficult. If anything, she was less vocal and acerbic, and they had seen a bit of her old self emerge. Perhaps it was just the fact that they were always aware of her condition, and of its inevitable outcome. But more than likely, it was that she represented the task looming ahead.

Rain also called it a night, and the three of them got comfortable on the couch with their mugs while Mare channel surfed.

"So, what are we going to do?" Toni asked.

Mare flipped the channel to a *M*A*S*H* rerun and glanced over at her. "About what?" she asked.

"About tomorrow. About the real reason for our little weekend."

"Keep your voice down," Bebe reminded her.

Toni kicked off her shoes and curled her feet beneath her on the couch. "Our best defense is to come up with our own ideas."

Bebe rubbed her forehead. "I'm not sure what she's looking for."

"I'm afraid of what she's looking for," Mare said. "You don't think she'll want to picket or do something illegal, do you?"

"I can't guarantee that, but we always have the power of veto," Bebe said.

Mare flipped the channel to late news. "Or get involved in raising money for abortion clinics. I just can't get on board with that anymore. Not after having kids." She sipped her coffee thoughtfully. "Sometimes I think, what if I had aborted Autumn? She was definitely a surprise. Or if she had decided to abort Sammy, or little Wesley? What a tragedy that would have been."

Images of a battle somewhere in the Middle East filled the TV screen, and Bebe grabbed the remote. She scrolled through the options and settled on the cooking channel. "I've been thinking. What about donating toward animal rescue?"

Toni laughed. "She doesn't care that much about animals, Bebe."

Bebe was about to defend Jude, since she couldn't imagine a person who didn't have a heart for helpless animals, when Toni continued.

"Remember that little gray cat that hung around the apartment at school? Remember how it just disappeared one day and never came back?"

Bebe said a slow "Yes."

"What do you think happened to it?"

"I assumed it found its way home."

Toni grimaced. "He didn't get so lucky. Jude had that guy, Terry . . . Jerry, whatever, take it out and dump it in the mountains. He did it when you were in class because she knew you'd throw a fit about it."

Bebe was speechless. After a moment, she said, "I'm not surprised."

"Besides," Toni said, "I'm not sure animal rescue is big enough for what Jude has in mind. I think she wants to go out with a bang. And what's more, I don't think she has time to pull it off and she knows it."

Mare and Bebe both grew thoughtful.

"Well, look at her," Toni continued. "She tires out so easily, and did you see her color yesterday? Positively gray, like her veins had collapsed. And she hardly eats anything."

The three of them silently contemplated Jude's condition while nursing their coffees.

"Well, it's inevitable, you know," Bebe said. "But we owe it to her to try to fulfill her wishes."

Toni looked puzzled. "We 'owe it to her'? I don't see that, Bebe. What do we owe her?"

"She's a friend, for one, and she's dying. She wants to accomplish something significant with the time she has left. You can understand that."

"You know, I only went along with this because of our friendship. And for Rain, of course," Toni said. "I think Jude's terrified that her life has counted for nothing. She wants something for people to remember her by, whether she deserves it or not."

"Now, you're being too hard on her, Toni," Mare said. "She was sincere in college, there's no reason to think she doesn't still have a heart for change."

"Are you so naïve? It's all about her, Mare."

Again, Bebe glanced down the hall and motioned for them to keep their voices down.

Bebe remembered the look of fear on Jude's face when she woke up in the car when they shopped on Cannery Row and the phone call from her drunken mother many years before. "There's something to what Toni says, Mare. She has a deep need to prove something about herself."

Toni studied Bebe over her coffee mug. "You know something," she said, leaning toward Bebe. "Out with it."

Bebe tried to make her face a blank slate. "It's nothing. Just something that happened a long time ago at school. I can't go into it."

Toni sat back, looking disgusted. "Why are you so indebted to her? As far as I can see, she did her best to try to control your life."

"She tried to control us all, from the day we arrived at school," Bebe said.

Mare looked up, surprised. "I never let her control me."

"You were never around. You spent so much time in the art building with Arnie trying to stay away from Jude and her groupies," Toni observed. "And look what happened."

Instead of being angry, Mare admitted, "True enough. You weren't around much, either. But she didn't pursue me like she did Bebe. Either one of us, for that matter. I was never sure why she focused on Bebe."

"Neither was I," Bebe answered. She got up and gathered her cup. "Good night, ladies."

Chapter 20

November 30, 1969

The air surrounding the ground floor apartment pulsed before they even reached the door, which pushed open to Jude's brief knock. The music exploded. Jimi Hendrix wailed, and the notes of his guitar climbed Bebe's vertebrae. She followed Jude inside, lowering her eyes and trying for a coolness she didn't feel. Students sat entwined on the couches and in corners stuffed with pillows. The light from the overhead bulb was dimmed by lacy smoke, thick and sickly sweet. Somebody shouted her name and she glanced to a girl named Erica she recognized from psychology who raised her beer and grinned with a guy hanging on to her neck like a leech.

Jude led her through the crowd to the kitchenette where an assortment of beer and hard liquor covered the counters. Jude reached up and briefly kissed one of the guys on the mouth. He said hello to Bebe and bent to kiss her, but she turned her face at the last moment and he grazed her cheek instead. He smelled like liquor and might have fallen over on her if she hadn't planted her hand firmly on his chest.

Jude handed Bebe a filled cup and shouted over the music, "Come on." Bebe followed her out the back door onto the crowded rectangle of patio where the music was muted somewhat and she was introduced.

"You remember Oz," Jude said, and Bebe recognized him as the guy who'd asked her if she was going to the peace vigil. She hadn't made it there. She acknowledged him and he made a move like he was trying to get up, but she raised her cup to him and crossed her arms across her chest the best that she could to discourage him.

Just that afternoon, Bobby had taken her back to school after her Thanksgiving break, and she missed him already—especially in times like these. She had been so excited to go home for the long weekend and to see everyone, but once she got there, things were awkward. It was clear that her family still saw her as a child rather than a young woman, and expected her to fit back into her same role. To keep the peace, she'd played the part and said little of her school experiences. They hadn't seemed particularly interested, anyway. When Bobby pulled up to drop her off in the front of the Victorian, she was relieved that there wasn't a houseful of visitors at the time. She gave Bobby a hug good-bye, jumped out, and grabbed her suitcase from the backseat. She waved as he drove away and watched until his car was out of sight. She didn't like keeping secrets from him, but they were necessary. If Bobby could see her now, she knew he would freak out.

One of the guys at the party reminded her of someone from high school. He was clean-shaven and his hair curled around his collar. He gave her a rueful smile and lifted his eyebrows, like he wasn't as wasted as some of them. He introduced himself as Dave. She leaned back against the glass patio door trying to be inconspicuous. Bebe didn't know anyone, but that didn't seem to matter, because just being Jude's friend seemed to be enough for people. She watched the behavior of the others. One couple was making out on the couch, and when the guy got up and then returned with a refill, someone had taken his place. Bebe tried to hide her disgust. Did the girl even notice the difference?

Jude hooked up with an older guy Bebe recognized as Jerry, and wandered off. Bebe overheard them making plans to protest the first draft lottery that was happening the next day. Bebe was left alone to entertain, or defend, herself.

Bebe's cup never got below half empty before someone refilled it. Between the drinks and the haze of pot, she was definitely feeling a buzz. She found a place to sit on the floor against the wall. She noticed that there was a room down the hall that had a lot of activity going on inside. She wondered what would happen if the cops came or whether they were as tolerant as the campus police. She sat for a long time, sipping her drink and not really talking to anyone, wondering if she could find her way home walking alone and whether it was safe. She could feel the alcohol unraveling her from the inside. The walls now pounded with "American Woman." She personally wasn't crazy about The Guess Who, but for some reason tonight the notes bounced around inside her, knocking loose her inhibitions.

Dave, from the patio, came over and she made room for him beside her on the floor. His drink sloshed a little when he sat down and he apologized, sounding very sober.

He pointed upward, indicating the music, and said in her ear, "You like them?"

She shook her head. "Not especially."

"But you were singing along."

Bebe hadn't realized it. She felt herself flush, if it was possible to be more flushed than the alcohol had made her feel already. "It's compelling, you know?"

Dave turned out to be visiting from UC Santa Cruz. They talked for a while about his major and his professors. He reminded her of one of the Cartwrights, the younger one, and she could feel herself warming to him by the minute. She ran her tongue around her lips and they felt numb. They sat with shoulders touching and she slowly rolled her head from side to side against the wall, enjoying the sensation of her hair sliding against the bumpy, crimped plaster.

She closed her eyes and breathed deeply. Someone offered them a joint, but she said no and Dave passed on it. She felt elated and calm at the same time—a pleasant and strange combination. Dave was saying something to her and she turned dreamily to look at him. He smiled and got to his feet, taking her cup from her and pointing at his vacant spot beside her. She nodded, understanding. It seemed like a split-second later that he was sitting beside her again and she thought she must have blanked out. All she could think about was how handsome he was and how there were only the two of them connecting in this room full of strangers and how his cheeks had stubble. She reached her hand to his face and caressed it. She bent his head to her and kissed him deeply.

They kissed awhile sitting on the floor, and drank. He tasted good, and Bebe had no idea how much time passed. Then he was helping her to her feet, and she felt the world spin around her. She leaned against his chest and a button on his shirt scratched her cheek. She felt his heart beating beneath it. Her stomach felt unstable. She carefully put one foot before the other, opened her eyes, and found they were walking down the hallway. She opened her eyes again and they were on a strange bed, with the sheets tangled in disarray. The sounds of the party were muffled and distant. Her head rolled side to side with the room spinning around her, and she tried to protest. When she opened her eyes again, she found the crumpled sheet pulled up to her bare shoulders, and he was gone.

* * * *

The next morning the fog rolled in, shrouding them in gray dampness and chilling them all to the bone. Bebe sipped her coffee by the windows, looking out into nothingness. The ocean sounded so much closer, so much deeper when you couldn't see it, but you were at its mercy. Bebe turned away and asked Jude if she wanted to stay back when they went to the aquarium. She wouldn't hear of it.

They ate breakfast and dressed in layers for the morning's activities.

"You aren't wearing those shoes, are you?" Mare asked Toni when she came out to join them in the kitchen.

Toni turned her foot to the side and glanced at them. "Why not?

What's wrong with them?" Toni slathered on hand lotion from her purse and rubbed it in. The scent of spiced ginger filled the air.

"They're so impractical. You're going to spend hours in those heels at the aquarium?"

"I went all over Rome in these. I'm a pro."

Bebe felt a squall coming on. "Let's go, girls. Move out." She ushered them toward the door.

Mare didn't take the hint. "You really should check into vegan fashion, Toni."

Toni swung her huge, studded leather bag over her shoulder and cruised past her. "Mare, 'vegan fashion' is an oxymoron."

They loaded up Bebe's car and drove slowly through the fog to Cannery Row. Bebe dropped Jude, Rain, and Toni off at the curb in front of the aquarium and Mare went with her to park the car. They avoided the line to purchase tickets that curled around the outside of the aquarium, and presented their tickets at the entrance.

Mare picked up a brochure and perused the map as they walked along. "There's a sea otter feeding at 10:30," she said. "And another feeding at the kelp forest at 11:30." She fell naturally into being their tour guide, leading them from exhibit to kelp forest to touch pool. A galaxy of sparkling anchovies spun silver over their heads in the Outer Bay. Bat rays glided over the bottom of the pool at the Sandy Shore, and jellies mesmerized them with their graceful, deadly dances. They spent hours enjoying the incredible, dangerous beauty, and dodging baby strollers and munchkins.

Toni stopped to read about seahorses, and commented, "Look, I found the perfect male. He mates for life and gets pregnant instead of the female."

"I think you were a seahorse in another life," Mare answered.

Rain came over to Bebe and touched her elbow. "Mom's spent," she said quietly. "Why don't you all go ahead. I'll stay back with her and catch up later."

Bebe glanced over to a bench where Jude sat with her eyes closed, looking drained. "I hate to leave you behind," Bebe told Rain. "I'll get a wheelchair."

From the bench, Jude said, "I never agreed to a wheelchair."

Rain gave Bebe a meaningful look. "Well, her hearing's not gone."

Bebe lowered her voice. "I thought she agreed to a wheelchair. I would've booked something else if I'd known."

"Give me a moment and I'll be good as new," they heard Jude say weakly.

Rain rolled her eyes. She seemed annoyed and a bit drained herself.

Bebe gave her an affectionate look. "You're tired. Go on by yourself for a while. I'll stay."

Rain looked over her shoulder at Jude, hesitating.

"Shoo," Bebe ordered, and turned to join Jude at the bench without giving Rain a chance to argue. Bebe slipped in quietly beside Jude and sat watching people go by. They sat in comfortable silence until Bebe wondered if Jude had fallen asleep, or if she even realized that Bebe was there. Jude sighed deeply and spoke.

"I know why you brought me here. You're not fooling anyone, you know."

Bebe sensed she was being set up. "What are you talking about?"

"Do you really think your God created all of this? You think there was intelligent design behind these creatures, especially that one with the three-inch teeth and lights on its head? What's the point?"

"Yes, I do believe God created this," she said, wondering where Jude was going with it. "And while I don't get the point, I see the logic behind the light-thingy on its head. It lives in the dark. I think having a light-thingy would come in handy." Then she added under her breath, "Most of my life has been spent in the dark."

Jude looked over and frowned at her. "I remember having this discussion over twenty years ago. You haven't grown up yet?"

"Over thirty years ago," Bebe corrected her. "And if you call growing 'up' growing 'cynical,' then, no, I haven't."

"I'm amazed that you're still as naïve as you were back then." Jude sank back against the wall and closed her eyes again.

Bebe chuckled grimly. "You couldn't exactly call me naïve after living with you for four years."

"Six years," Jude corrected her, hiking her eyebrows without opening her eyes. "Well, I did something right, then."

Bebe watched a child go by hugging a stuffed otter, talking to a woman who appeared to be her grandmother. This stage was next on the horizon for her and Neil, and even though Jude wasn't the grandmotherly type, she would be cheated of the opportunity.

Jude continued with her eyes closed. "I suppose religion could come in handy. Some women would enjoy having the handy excuse of being under a man's thumb. A sort of divine 'get out of jail free' card."

"Jude, God is the most equality-minded person I know. He has always held me fully accountable for my own actions. Luckily, He's also a very forgiving type."

"If you've been so enlightened since college, how can you still believe the same way about God?"

Bebe considered. "I wouldn't say I believe exactly the same way as I did then. I think I had a basic understanding about God back then, but I didn't have a mature one."

"So what's mature about believing that there's intelligence in the universe?"

"Believing in a Creator makes more sense than believing it was a random act, or just dumb luck that everything fits together so well."

Jude's eyes flew open. "War, poverty, violence. Things have definitely not fit together well so far."

"In all fairness, those things have been man's doing. Why blame Him?"

Jude said with quiet ferocity, "Because *She* could fix it, if She wanted to."

It dawned on Bebe that Jude was referring to her illness, and Bebe had no easy answers. She felt an overwhelming sadness. The fact that Jude mentioned God at all revealed that she was thinking in spiritual terms, perhaps wrestling with long-held doubts and grasping for meaning in her life.

Jude continued. "We work hard. We strive for sixty, seventy years, and then what? We get slapped down. Our bodies fail us. That's not intelligence, that's waste. It's cruelty."

Her words fell heavily upon them and they sank under the weight of them. The urge to encourage Jude came naturally, but Bebe didn't truly know what Jude was going through and didn't want to insult her with trite, pat answers.

All she could do was to be honest with her. "I don't understand it all either, Jude," she said. "But I do know there is truth that I don't understand, and that I still believe."

Jude turned to look directly at her. "Such as?"

Bebe decided to be transparent. "Sometimes God lets us go through heartbreaking stuff, but He goes through it with us to make it bearable. And sometimes He even heals." She braced herself for Jude's cynicism.

"You know so much about heartbreak and healing," Jude said, her words dripping with sarcasm.

Bebe felt anger smolder inside her and she fought it. Looking Jude in the eye, she said, pointedly but without malice, "You have no idea what I've lived with over the last thirty years. Sometimes the healing isn't physical."

"Listen, my girl. Your wounds are positively oozing."

* * * *

January 13, 1970

"Here's the number." Jude shoved a piece of notebook paper at her. "He's down on Washington. Just don't tell anybody you got it from me."

Bebe looked at the phone number. "What's his name?"

"Don't know. It's safer that way."

"But how much does it cost?"

Jude tilted her head, thinking. "About two hundred dollars, I think. You'll have to ask."

Bebe sat down heavily on the kitchen chair.

"You have the money, don't you?"

Bebe had it tucked away in savings to pay for expenses for the semester. She would have to ask for more hours at the alumni office where she worked between classes. "Yeah, I can swing it. I'll have to."

Jude tucked her shirt down into her tight hip-huggers. Bebe noticed Jude's smooth, flat belly, suddenly felt aware of her own small bulge that would soon dictate the need for looser blouses, if she didn't call the number. She had to swallow down the nausea that began every morning when she woke up and stayed with her until she crawled into bed at night.

"But how safe is it?" Bebe asked. "I'm . . . I'm just not sure."

"It's safe. Miranda had one and was back in class the next day. Nothing to it. It's every woman's right of passage to have an abortion. Joan and Suzanne were pretty impressed when I told them you wanted the number." Jude paused and lifted her head. "It wasn't your fault, you know."

Bebe looked away. "But maybe if I hadn't, you know, had so much to drink—"

"That guy purely took advantage of you."

Bebe wondered at this turnabout. At any other time, Jude would have said Bebe was free to make her own choices about sexuality, but now that there were consequences, she conveniently blamed it all on him. Clearly, taking advantage of her was wrong, but Bebe owed it to herself to keep from ending up in a vulnerable position. She rubbed her forehead and pressed her fingers into her temple.

Bebe thought about the Women's Center. She had gone to a meeting there once. A consciousness-raising session. There was no facilitator. The students sat around, braless and barefoot, bashing men or sharing their experiences of sexual abuses. Many of them had been abandoned by dads and it appeared that talking about the past was cathartic. But some weren't satisfied with being considered equal to men, and it was obvious from their comments that they felt women were superior. Bebe hadn't fit into any of those categories, and never went back.

Joan and Suzanne at the Women's Center were adamant that she had every right to make decisions about her body. It wasn't a baby, they said, it was a fetus, one pushed on her against her will. Although she knew she wasn't ready to be a mother, something inside her whispered that it was wrong. But if her parents found out about the pregnancy, they might disown her, or force her to come home in disgrace and give up college altogether. If she took care of the problem here, there was no reason for them to ever know and they wouldn't be hurt. She could take the rest of her life to deal with it herself.

Jude paused from gathering her papers and books, and looked at Bebe. "What, are you chickening out? You want to go back to Podunk and be Suzy Homemaker for the rest of your life? Give up college? Become your mother?"

"No." Bebe shook her head. "I can't."

Jude shrugged like it was no big deal. "So, call him."

"Jude, have you . . ."

Jude dug in her purse for her keys. "Have I what?"

Bebe held up the phone number. "Ever called him?"

Jude slipped her purse over her shoulder, and Bebe saw fading hickeys on her neck when she pulled her hair clear of the strap. "I never let myself get that wasted."

When Bebe called for an appointment, the doctor wanted to know who referred her. She told him the Women's Center without giving him Joan's or Suzanne's names. He seemed satisfied. His instructions were to show up at 8:00 a.m. on Monday morning and not to eat anything after midnight, just in case. She didn't ask, "in case of what?" She could bring someone with her, if she wanted.

Bebe wrote down the information and shoved it into her pocket. She broke out in a sweat every time she thought about going through with it.

Would it be so bad to have a child? Other girls did it. Then she thought of her parents, and knew she couldn't face them, or her brother Bobby, pregnant. And what about Paul and Rudy? They still looked up to her. Maybe Bobby'd been right to question leaving her there in August. Maybe he should have stuffed her back into the car and driven home, reporting that she wasn't equipped to make choices of her own.

In a few short months, she had become a different person, if only in action and not philosophy. She hadn't had time to develop her own philosophy. She had Jude's, and that of an emerging generation of young women heady with freedom. In so short a time, she had come to value Jude's assessment of her like a mooring, because otherwise, she was cast out in the wide world adrift with more questions than answers.

She loved her parents, but she was too changed to return home to her mother's submissiveness and her father's patriarchy. She would find a middle ground somewhere. She would have to make her own way in the world, somehow.

Three days before her appointment, she was no closer to deciding whether to go through with it, but instead, distracted herself from thinking about it altogether. Jude bragged to her friends about Bebe's newfound liberation, which made her feel secure and progressive, but Jude secretly watched her and demanded to know if she was going to back out, and whether she should start looking for a new roommate to take Bebe's place when she was forced to go home. Instead of arranging for Jude to accompany her, Bebe assured her that she had asked a friend from class to go along with her. Jude seemed a little jealous and suspicious, but didn't press her for a name.

As the appointment drew closer, Bebe skipped classes and drank whatever was in the cupboards or fridge. Her morning sickness increased and she couldn't eat. She ignored Mare when she tried to talk to her about her drinking, and Toni, when she wanted to know if Bebe was throwing up so badly because she had the flu. On Friday night, when the house throbbed with Hendrix and unidentified bodies, she accepted a joint that was passed around, and then something stronger that made her skin crawl and left her hugging the toilet with dry heaves. On Sunday night, when she sobered up, she realized that her stomach cramped for a different reason. She found that she was spotting heavily.

As the night wore on, her cramps increased until she rocked on the bathroom floor, hugging a pillow to her stomach and biting the cotton pillowcase to keep quiet. The cramps threatened to split her gut in two. In the early morning hours, frightened and exhausted, she passed large blood clots and considered going to emergency. Afterward, the cramps began to ease, and she crawled into bed, so weak and pale she could hardly stand.

Jude stuck her head in her bedroom door at seven o'clock and asked her if she needed a ride to her appointment. Something kept Bebe from telling her about the night before, and she reminded Jude that she had a ride. Jude left for class, followed by Toni. Mare almost didn't accept her answer that she was okay, and said she would check on her later. Bebe listened, frightened, to the quiet house when Mare slammed the door, and wondered if she would die alone in her bed.

During the morning, she passed more heavy clots, and Mare came home early from class to find her shivering and crying on the bathroom floor. Mare turned white at the sight of the blood, and Bebe confessed what had happened. Mare forced her to eat some dry toast, which stayed down for the first time in days. Bebe bathed briefly and dressed, which exhausted her, and when Mare tried to insist that she go to emergency, Bebe said that she was afraid they would call her parents. Mare found a free women's clinic in the phone directory instead. Armed with the address, Mare dug in Toni's drawer for cash, leaving an IOU, and called a cab.

They examined her at the clinic and said she had miscarried. It appeared to be clean, and she would heal naturally. They asked her questions about her pregnancy and whether anything had happened that may have caused the miscarriage. She thought of the days of bingeing, but knew they were looking for something more deliberate, and answered no. They gave her a prescription and told her to call them if the spotting didn't dissipate, or if she developed a fever. They told her to go immediately to emergency if she had uncontrollable bleeding, and they repeated it to Mare and cautioned her that Bebe shouldn't be left alone for the next twenty-four hours. They wanted to see Bebe in a week. Mare got another cab to take them home, where she put Bebe to bed.

Jude checked in on her when she got home late that afternoon. Bebe faked sleep and postponed an actual conversation until the following morning. Mare insisted on taking her temperature, and Bebe didn't argue. It was normal, which was a relief. No infection there.

Mare turned to go, and Bebe asked her not to tell Jude what really happened.

"Don't worry. I get it," Mare said. "Jude's easier to live with if she gets what she wants. And for some reason she wanted you to go through with it."

Bebe thought it was a sign of the times that Jude treated her with a new level of respect after that. She tried to play it down, feeling like a fraud in front of Mare, who pretended not to notice. Eventually Bebe came to realize that Toni knew, also.

"I had to explain the IOU," Mare said. "She's cool with it. Don't worry. She won't say anything."

For weeks, Bebe alternated between privately mourning for her loss and feeling euphoric with relief. She always wondered what she would have chosen, if the decision hadn't been taken out of her hands.

Jude tried to get Bebe to share about her abortion with a group at the women's clinic on campus, but she refused. Eventually, Jude let it go.

In the weeks that followed, Jude began to show signs of morning sickness herself. Bebe feared that she would ask her to go with her to the abortion, but weeks went by, and Jude never mentioned it. Mare and Toni asked Bebe if she knew what was up with Jude. Jude overheard them discussing her and came out to the kitchen, looking pale but defiant. That's when she announced that she was indeed pregnant and she had made a momentous decision. Instead of getting an abortion, she would have the baby and raise her to be a new woman.

None of them asked the obvious. What if it was a boy? Jude would will the baby's gender to be female.

She was due in November, and anyone who was still a roomie by then would have to pitch in to help. If they wanted out, they could move at the end of the semester.

A heavy, impenetrable veil fell between Bebe and Jude at that moment. Bebe drew it aside on the day that Jude came home from the hospital and she took Rain from her arms.

Chapter 21

Mare, Toni, and Rain found Bebe and Jude sitting silently beside each other on the bench in front of the kelp forest. Bebe saw them pass a look between them.

"Anyone hungry?" Toni asked. "It's almost one o'clock. Maybe we should find a place for lunch."

Mare looked back over her shoulder. "I need to pick up sea otters for Sammy and Wesley at the gift shop before we go."

Bebe stood and said, "I'll get the car if you want to meet me out front in ten minutes or so." She dug out her keys as she turned, and Toni caught up with her as she headed toward the exit.

"I'll try to hurry, but the gift shop looks pretty crowded," Mare called.

When they were out on the street, Toni asked, "So, how was it babysitting Jude?"

"Just . . . think of a place to eat," Bebe said, irritably.

Toni dropped back a stride behind her, and Bebe led the way up to the parking lot.

Twenty minutes later, they had loaded up the car and were heading down Cannery Row.

"So tell me where I'm going," Bebe said, glancing at the dark clouds lining up on the horizon.

"What about Gianni's?" Mare offered.

"Pizza?" Toni chuckled. "I'm buying, Mare."

"Well, the pizza's excellent," Mare said, sounding offended.

"Yes, it is. But I want something special." Toni thought and then said, "Turn us around, Bebe. Go back. Take Lighthouse to Pacific Grove."

"Not Toasties again," Mare said.

"No, Mare," Toni said, settling into her seat with a satisfied smile. "Tarantella's."

"What do they serve?" Rain asked.

"Pasta, salads, sandwiches, escargot. It's good. Even you'll find something you like, Mare."

"What's that supposed to mean?" Mare answered.

Toni dismissed her with a wave of her hand. "I mean something . . . vegan."

The food at Tarantella's was excellent. Toni was in high spirits—she was definitely in her element—but even though she managed not to antagonize Mare even once, a mood had settled on everyone. Bebe avoided looking at Jude, feeling conflicted about their conversation, and not wanting it continued in front of the others. Rain seemed preoccupied and said little, pushing her salad around on her plate. Mare got a look at the bill before Toni scooped it up and calculated the tip, but Toni refused to let anyone chip in.

By the time they drove back to the house, the storm clouds that had gathered offshore were driven in by the wind. Raindrops had begun to pelt the ground. They locked all the windows up tight and changed into comfortable clothes.

Rain followed Jude to her room to help her get situated. Then she came out and closed the door firmly behind her. She joined the others in the kitchen, waiting for the pot of coffee to finish brewing, and sat at a stool by the counter to check her e-mail. The aroma of fresh coffee was warm and comforting.

She had an e-mail from the planning committee of her high school asking for help with the next reunion, which she deleted. There was no one from high school she cared to ever see again. She deleted another message that was clearly spam, which seemed to sneak through every filter.

"Here, Rain," Mare said, handing her a steaming mug. "You want sugar or cream?"

"Black's good," she answered. She saw a familiar e-mail address that made her stop and turn the laptop screen out of view of the others. It was a message from Hayden to his entire address book, advising them of his new address and phone number, and that he had posted photos of his Mexico trip on Facebook. Her e-mail address was lumped alphabetically in the list with all the family, friends, and casual acquaintances he knew. His message was perfunctory and general, saying that life was good and inviting contact from anyone on the list. At least he hadn't deleted her. She wondered what he would do if she showed up on his doorstep. She examined the addresses more closely, and found some names that were unknown to her. He must have added them since he'd moved out. Rain hadn't added a name to her address book in a year or more.

Her curiosity got the best of her, and she logged on to Facebook and navigated to his page. At least he hadn't blocked her there, either. His profile picture had changed. It was a silhouette of his smiling, sunburned face against a background of blazing blue sky, striking and handsome, taken at an angle that would have been impossible to do on his own.

She saw that he had posted new pictures, and she hesitated before clicking on them. Did she really want to see if he was happy, or if he was with someone else?

She held her breath and clicked on an album labeled "Mexico." When it opened, she didn't know what to think. These were no pictures of resort beaches, snorkeling expeditions, and beautiful bodies.

They were photos of a half-completed cinder block and wood building in a remote location and people she didn't know. Hayden wore old jeans and a sweat-stained T-shirt and sported a bandanna rolled up and tied around his forehead. He appeared rumpled, filthy, and very happy. He posed with a group of adults with their arms draped over each other's shoulders, surrounded by a band of barefoot, smiling children. Rain bit her bottom lip at the blonde standing wedged between Hayden and another man. She was pleasantly browned with a glistening smile. The last photo showed Hayden with a Hispanic man who wore a sparkling white button-down shirt and clutched a Bible. They stood before the completed building where a cross hung above the door.

Rain felt at a loss to explain it. She did not recognize anyone in the pictures and had never heard Hayden mention a desire to join a work party in Mexico. She remembered his sunburned nose and the scrapes on his hand when he came to pick up his belongings months before. So he hadn't been girl-watching on the beach after all. He'd been doing manual labor building a church. What had prompted him to do this, and how had she not known this side of him?

The folder labeled "Thanksgiving" contained pictures of his family at dinner. She smiled when she saw one of Hayden and his parents together. He had his dad's build and his mother's coloring and facial features. There were other photos of nephews, nieces, sisters, and brothers. She caught her breath at one of Hayden holding a sleeping infant—probably his sister's new baby. He looked a bit nervous but natural at the same time.

It reminded her that he was gone, not because he didn't want children, but that he didn't want her. She was becoming like Jude and she didn't know how to stop it.

He seemed so happy with his family, so contented. She felt bitter that he could find contentment so quickly without her. Suddenly bereft, and sinking fast in front of Bebe, Mare, and Toni, she closed out her e-mail and shut down the computer. In a blur of tears, she quickly hopped down from the stool and clipped the top of her thigh on the edge of the counter. She cried out and doubled over in pain, grasping her bruised thigh where the injections had made the skin tender and sore.

Bebe was the first one to her side, helping her to sit down in a chair. Mare and Toni put down their mugs and came over.

"It's nothing," Rain said, massaging her thigh and fighting back tears.

"Come on, let's have a look," Bebe said, tugging at her pants leg.

Rain pulled away from Bebe more roughly than she intended. "It's nothing," she said, feeling like a petulant five-year-old. The look of hurt on Bebe's face made her feel even worse.

Bebe gave her some space, and asked calmly, "Can you walk on it?"

"I'll be fine," she said, and rose to her feet to prove it.

"Be careful, Rain," Mare said. "You don't want to get a blood clot or anything."

Toni said, "For crying out loud, Mare."

Rain limped away toward her bedroom, refusing help, and got halfway down the hall before she regretted leaving her coffee mug behind. She pushed open the door of her room and sank down carefully onto the bed. She gingerly rolled up her pants leg to examine the bruises. A red gash crossed a particularly greenish-purple bruise.

She heard a gasp and looked up. Bebe stood in her opened door with a look of horror on her face, holding Rain's mug at an angle that threatened to spill black coffee onto the white carpet.

Rain nodded at the mug. "Be careful."

Bebe righted it but stood bewildered in the doorway.

"You'd better come in," Rain said, sighing. "And close the door behind you."

* * * *

Bebe listened to Rain's account of her final trip to see Dr. Sykes and sat on the edge of her bed for a long time not knowing what to say. Poor Rain had carried this disappointment along with so many others, and not shared it with a soul all weekend. After promising not to tell the others, Bebe went out to the kitchen for an ice pack and some aspirin. Rain said she wanted to sleep and Bebe went back out to the family room, to find Mare and Toni waiting expectantly.

"Is she all right?" Mare asked.

Bebe noticed that they had the fireplace going as she plopped down on the couch. "She's only bruised."

"Body and soul, you mean," Toni said, choosing a magazine from the coffee table. She tucked her feet beneath her on the couch. "That takes a lot longer to heal."

Bebe quickly looked up. "You didn't hear that from me."

"We didn't need to. Rain's an open book. She's miserable without Hayden and she may even be mourning for her mom." Toni shrugged one shoulder. "Okay, she probably is mourning."

Mare tsked and looked like she might cry. "How can we help her, Bebe?"

"We can't," she said, thinking of Rain's baby woes. "When she makes up her mind about something, she's the only one who can change it."

Mare smiled dreamily. "She was always stubborn like that. Remember when she went through that period when she refused to wear clothes?"

Toni looked up from the magazine. "She had the cutest little toddler tush. I hated to cover it with clothes, myself."

Mare twirled a lock of her hair. "Remember when she insisted on joining a Little League team instead of girls' softball?"

"That wasn't her idea. That was Jude's," Bebe said.

Mare stopped midtwirl. "But she was so proud of it. She was their best hitter."

"She did it to please her mom, and she just happened to be more coordinated than boys at that age."

"Hate to say it, but it makes me glad I never had kids," Toni admitted.

Mare rolled her eyes. "For their sake, I have to agree. You would've enrolled them in beauty pageants, and had them in makeup and heels at five years old."

Toni looked up with a tilt of her head, considering. "You're right. If I didn't, my mother would have." She grinned lazily. "My kids would have been beautiful, and we would've added on another room just for the trophies and costumes."

Mare dropped her head back against the cushions. "I give up," she said to the ceiling. "You are hopeless."

Bebe listened to the fretful sound of the wind and rain against the house, and her thoughts returned to the conversation that she had with Jude at the aquarium. Were her wounds still "oozing" as Jude had suggested? And was it evident to everyone but her?

She thought about the coming evening when they would have to make some decisions. There was no seeking distraction away from the house that night. They were in it for the long haul.

"I don't suppose either of you has any ideas to offer for tonight," she said.

Mare covered her face with a throw pillow like she was trying to suffocate herself. Toni stretched out on her end of the sofa and crossed her arms over her eyes. "I'll think about it tomorrow," she said with a southern drawl. Mare tossed the pillow at her, and she threw it back.

"We have to have some ideas of our own," Bebe insisted.

After a long moment of silence, Toni asked, "Okay, so what's the worst that can happen? If we can't agree on something that we're all willing to do that doesn't cause our families to disown us or career suicide, Jude takes her marbles and goes home."

Mare huffed. "Very constructive, Toni."

"She's right, to some extent," Bebe said. They both looked at her in surprise. "Jude will go home angry and hurt and feel alienated, and probably die alone with only Rain and possibly William at her side. Probably William. But our relationship with Rain will be hurt beyond repair, and I'm just not willing to go there."

Toni leaned up on one elbow. "But Rain is smart, Bebe. She knows we can't take those risks this late in life."

"I agree. And she's probably thinking about her own career and how much she's willing to risk, herself. But the bottom line is that this is her mother's choice in lieu of a funeral. If we disrespect this, we leave Rain to do it alone."

Mare hugged the pillow to her chest. "She would do it, too."

"Yes, she would." Bebe chewed her bottom lip. Then, she added, lowering her voice, "You know, Jude's not all bad."

Toni's voice came from a dream state. "In what way? You mean in the way that the Chicago Seven weren't all bad?"

Bebe ignored her comment. "She had her issues in college, but we had some fun times, too."

"Such as?"

Silence descended while they each tried to think of something.

"Oh, I know," Mare said. "That time Jude got us free tickets to see Crosby, Stills, Nash and Young at the Fillmore. That was fun."

Toni twisted to relieve the tension in her shoulders. "Right. I wonder how the first half of the concert went."

"So, I didn't know my way around San Francisco. It's not my fault I was the only one of us who could drive a stick," Mare said.

Bebe smiled, remembering that night, which was only funny now, years later. "She shouted directions at you the whole way and you kept popping the clutch on those steep hills."

Mare said, "You know, I almost parked it in the street and walked away."

"Too bad we didn't have GPS back then," Toni said.

Then a pleasant memory came to Bebe. "When we first moved in and it was just the four of us, we ate frozen pizza and watched old movies on that fuzzy black-and-white TV that Jude scrounged from somewhere."

Mare said, "That was before Jude got involved with that radical student group."

"Okay, that counts," Toni said. She sat up in a lotus position. "I remember the old Victorian. It had such a wonderful, creepy-cozy feeling to it."

"Creepy-cozy? Okay," Mare agreed. "It was creepy because the plumbing was ancient and the toilet kept overflowing."

"And we had to take turns plugging in our electric curlers or a fuse would blow."

"That was you and Bebe," Mare said. "I went for a less structured look.

"So that's what they called it?" Toni chuckled. "Less structured."

Mare playfully stuck out her tongue at Toni, who replied in kind.

Bebe suddenly felt a rush of memories. "I remember when Rain took her first step."

Mare smiled. "She walked straight to you."

"As I recall, it didn't make Jude very happy," Toni added. "And Rain called you Momma. That didn't sit well with her, either."

"She called us all Momma until she could keep us straight," Bebe reminded her.

Bebe smiled to herself. She could almost feel Rain's soft little body clinging to her, with her pudgy arms around her neck and a sticky cheek pressed against hers. The mixture of baby powder and Ivory Snow became Bebe's signature scent.

And now it looked as if Rain might never know that feeling for herself. Bebe felt an overwhelming sadness for this young woman and wondered whether they had all done her an injustice.

Chapter 22

Bebe woke up to a darkened room and checked her watch. It was only five o'clock—just two hours since Mare and Toni had fallen asleep in the family room watching *Out of Africa* and Bebe had had the good sense to climb into her own bed.

She washed her face and came out to the kitchen where Mare was in the midst of dinner preparations. A delicious-smelling pot of broth bubbled on the stove.

"Mind peeling these?" Mare asked, handing her a vegetable peeler and three large potatoes. "Vegetable soup is on the menu for tonight."

Bebe washed the potatoes and started peeling the skins into the garbage disposal. Toni waltzed into the kitchen from the family room where the movie still played.

"That movie isn't over yet?" Bebe asked.

"No, it's a long one," Toni said. "I just love to listen to the soundtrack. It's so inspiring."

Toni sat down on a stool at the counter and Mare handed her two large yellow onions and a cutting board. "Here, get inspired with this," she said.

Toni grunted at the onions in response. Bebe waved a potato at her. "You snooze, you lose, my friend."

Toni's eye makeup was running by the time she had the onion sliced up. She scraped the onion into the pot of soup with the knife and rinsed off the cutting board. She wandered back toward her bedroom.

Rain came out moments later, yawning. She went to a dark window in the sunroom and looked out at the storm. "It's really coming down hard. If we weren't so high up, I'd be worried," she said, coming back to the counter.

"It would take a tsunami to reach us up here," Mare said, handing her a zucchini, a cutting board, and a knife. "Chunks, please, not slices."

Rain got to work cutting the zucchini, making each chunk exactly the same size. When Bebe was finished peeling and cutting up the potatoes, Mare handed her three large carrots.

"Where did Toni skip off to?" Bebe asked. A second later, Toni returned with her makeup freshened.

"For crying out loud, Toni. It's just us," Mare said. "We've seen your naked face before."

Toni refused to answer, but sat down at the counter and Mare handed her a loaf of bread to spread with butter.

"This isn't soy butter is it?" Toni asked, checking the label.

Mare answered curtly, "You wouldn't be able to tell the difference if it was."

They continued bickering until the soup was ready as though they'd awakened on the wrong side of the couch. Bebe set out the dishes buffet style and Rain went to wake Jude. Mare ladled out bowls of rich soup with tender-crisp veggies and filled a lined basket with slices of soft, buttered sourdough.

The mood was somber around the table, with the four cooks bending their concentration toward the hot soup. Jude was the only one who seemed energized, as though she anticipated the coming evening.

Jude and Rain retired to the family room when they were finished. Bebe, Mare, and Toni took great care in cleaning up after dinner until every plate and utensil rested neatly in its assigned place and every surface sparkled. Finally, they shared a brief look of silent solidarity, and joined the others in the family room.

Jude sat in the recliner like an aging queen at the end of her reign.

"So here we are again. Next August marks forty years since we moved in together on 37th Street, and unfortunately, I won't be around to share it with you."

A small movement made Bebe glance over at Toni. She had folded her arms across her chest with a bored look on her face. Bebe hoped Toni would keep a lid on her sarcasm.

"So we'll just have to pretend that it's August and plan something significant that you all can carry on when I'm gone. I've brought some suggestions, but let's hear some of yours first."

An awkward silence descended on them. Finally, Jude said, "Well, come on. This was homework."

Rain looked up at Bebe, silently urging her to speak. Bebe could only come up with the one idea that was close to her heart.

"What about setting up a pet rescue foundation for natural disaster areas to help people find their displaced pets? We could go in and set up a temporary command base where people can drop off stray pets, and maybe even join rescue crews to search for them."

Silence followed, leaving Bebe feeling exposed.

Finally, Mare stirred. "I'm allergic to cats."

Toni added, "I can't wear that fluorescent safety-green color."

"Okay, then," Bebe said, gesturing with her open hand, "it's your turn."

After more silence, Jude began, "Well, if—"

"I know," Mare jumped in. "What if we started a line of ecofriendly baby blankets and distributed them to homeless shelters? We could put together a website for monetary donations, and maybe post photos of some of the mothers and their babies who receive blankets."

Bebe glanced at Rain who had turned her head away from Mare.

Toni asked, "Start a line, as in, sew?"

"Sure. We could pull some money together for a couple of quilting sewing machines. If you didn't want to sew, you could work on distribution."

Toni yawned and covered her mouth with the back of her hand.

A stony silence met Mare's suggestion, and Bebe began to get worried that they'd run out of ideas, until Toni said, "What if we raised money to provide books for women in poor or rural communities? I've read that publishers and authors will sometimes donate books for publicity. Maybe we could eventually provide a traveling library."

Jude warmed to the idea. "Hmm. Enlightened books to rattle submissive cages."

"Fiction," Toni clarified. "Not feminist literature."

Jude thought for a moment and shook her head. "Fiction is frivolous. We should provide education, not entertainment."

Rain said, "What about providing laptops for inner-city kids? My company has a foundation that we could plug into. They always need help with fund-raising and distribution."

"That's a good idea, Rain," Mare said. "A lot of schools today can't even afford books and pencils."

"I like it," Bebe said.

"I like Rain's idea of plugging into an existing group rather than reinventing the wheel. Like breast cancer awareness, for example," Toni suggested.

"That's been over-done," Jude said.

"How can it be over-done?" Mare asked, exasperated. "It's not overdone until there's a cure."

"You know what I mean. Pink is everywhere. There are groups doing a satisfactory job already." Jude shifted in her seat and said, impatiently, "Can we think about the bigger picture? We need something with a big impact on society. Something to really shake people up."

It was clear to Bebe that Jude had obviously made up her mind before they started, and wasn't honestly considering any of their suggestions. Bebe felt anger gathering inside her like a squall. "I don't know of any ROTC buildings nearby that we could bomb, if that's what you have in mind."

Mare and Toni turned wide eyes to her.

"Too bad, isn't it?" Jude said. "Perhaps you could suggest a better target."

Jude and Bebe locked gazes for a moment.

Rain frowned, obviously puzzled. "What's going on?"

Jude answered, "Bebe's just reminiscing about the good old days."

"I had no part in it," Bebe said, folding her arms and settling farther into the cushions.

"You were an accessory after the fact, my dear. The perfect alibi."

Silence filled the room, but the storm was heard raging outside like a dissonant soundtrack.

Rain looked from Bebe to Jude. "Are you saying you bombed the ROTC building and Bebe was your alibi?"

Sadness and a suffocating fear began to grip Bebe. "Not by my choice."

Rain looked shocked. "What do you mean, not by your choice? Everybody has a choice."

Bebe licked her lips. Her mouth felt like cotton. Just as she began to speak, Jude broke in.

"After the bombing, the police came to the house to question me. Bebe lied and said that I was there all day because she was afraid they would take you away and put you in foster care."

Rain looked to Bebe for confirmation, but Bebe dropped her eyes.

"Oh don't look so surprised," Jude said. "It just took a little nudge to push Bebe into the dark side. She became quite the little radical after that. I lost my babysitter when she started joining protests, and I had to take you along in a backpack. But it was gratifying to see her break out of that shell, and to have had something to do with her metamorphosis."

"Don't take so much credit, Jude. Everybody was protesting after Kent State," Bebe said. "And I only broke the law that one . . . time."

"But you were the lucky one whose photo was sent along on the AP wire."

"Was anybody hurt in the bombing?" Rain asked.

"No, the building was empty at the time," Jude answered, with a tinge of regret.

An uncomfortable silence filled the room again, and Jude demanded, "Mare, shouldn't you be taking notes?"

Mare looked indignant. "If anyone should be taking notes, it's Toni." Toni shot her a look of warning.

Jude sighed. Bebe noticed that she was appearing to tire. "All right. Let's stay on track, shall we? We still need to come up with an idea, and since you have come up empty, it's my turn."

Bebe glanced discreetly at Rain, but she sat chewing her bottom lip, deep in thought.

Jude sat up higher.

"We could spread the word regarding stem cell research with donated embryos."

Mare shook her head. "The Church is very much against embryonic stem cell research."

"I have a problem with it, too," said Bebe.

"I'm out," Rain said, looking stormy.

"Very well," Jude said, folding her hands in front of her.

"Oh!" Mare said. "We could organize a watch group to protect kids against tobacco ads." She waved her hand dismissively at Jude. "I know, it's been done. But the truth is that the tobacco companies spend their advertising money on new smokers—the younger the better—because they know they have a customer for life."

Bebe and Rain murmured their agreement, but Toni raised her hand.

"As much as I'd love to keep youngsters smokefree, particularly in light of how long it took me to quit, I can't participate. It presents a conflict of interest with a little side job I've had over the years."

Bebe said, "Don't be so mysterious, Toni. What are you talking about?"

The confusion on Mare's face dissolved into understanding. "Oh, I think I see."

Jude grew impatient. "Someone enlighten me."

Toni looked at each one in turn.

"For heaven's sake, Toni, just show them," Mare said.

Toni went over to the bookcase behind the couch and pulled out a book on the shelf about halfway up to the ceiling. Then she tossed it onto the coffee table between them.

"It's mine. I started writing romances to supplement my income from the university about ten years ago. Of course, I had to write under a pen name. Rachelle DuPree," she said, with a dreamy smile. "I'm pretty good at it, too, if I do say so myself."

Bebe picked it up and flipped it to the backside. Toni's likeness was altered by a pair of glasses and a very different hairstyle. "You knew about this, Mare?"

"Well, it so happens that I sometimes pick up a romance for light reading—"

Jude groaned.

"And I got a used copy of it at a bookstore." She glanced over at Toni. "The author was the spitting image of Toni, and when I showed it to her she denied it, but I could tell she was lying."

Bebe handed the book to Rain, who said, "I still don't see the connection with smoking."

"Look at the publisher. They're owned by a company who also has lots and lots of women's magazines that sell tons of cigarette ads. They practically sleep with the tobacco companies."

Rain handed the book to Jude, who handled it like it was toxic.

"I could get you a bio suit, if you'd feel better about it," Toni told Jude.

Jude examined it, raised her eyebrows, and tossed it back onto the table, dusting her hands. "How can you waste time writing this drivel?" Jude asked.

"That drivel paid for my Lexus. Be nice, or you'll end up as one of my characters."

Jude narrowed her eyes. "How do I know you haven't already done that?"

"You don't. Anyway, I really have to be careful with controversial issues or my publisher will drop me. And by the way, is there something we could do that doesn't require marching in Manolos?"

Jude sighed, appearing to mentally regroup. "Since Toni isn't up to the rigors of a physical demonstration, mass communication might be the way to go. I have another idea. January 22 is the anniversary of Roe v. Wade, and the antichoice crowd plans to march in Washington that day. For around $15,000 we can purchase pro-choice advertising to run on the city buses for about four weeks or so."

They shifted in their seats without making eye contact with her.

"Even if we did agree, which I don't, we could never throw that kind of thing together in a month," Mare said.

"I'm not suggesting that. They do it every year. We would set the ball rolling for the next year, and make it a yearly event, as long as necessary."

"When you're not around to enjoy the fallout?" Toni said.

Jude glared at her.

"Oops, did I say that out loud?"

"I'm out," Mare said.

"Ditto for me," Toni added.

"I'm out, too," Bebe said. "I won't even do pet abortions."

Jude considered each of them disapprovingly. "My, my, how times have changed."

"Not as much as you might think," Toni said, raising an eyebrow.

"And what's that supposed to mean?" Jude asked.

Toni glanced at Mare, who frowned at her and then met Bebe's look of hesitation. Toni raised both hands as if she were backing away from the situation.

"Out with it," Jude commanded.

"I never had an abortion, Jude," Bebe said. "I miscarried before my appointment with that 'doctor' you set me up with."

Rain looked at her with an odd mixture of anger and disbelief on her face.

"Miscarried?" Jude said. "Now, wasn't that convenient."

"It's not as though I planned it. I guess I partied too much because

I was having trouble forcing myself to go through with it. That whole weekend was lost to me."

Jude smirked. "It was obvious at the time that you were conflicted about it. I mistakenly believed that you'd broken free from that antiquated belief system you brought to school with you."

"Well, I was young. That's why I didn't tell you. In some twisted way, I knew it elevated me in your eyes."

"Twisted? That wasn't your attitude when you came crying to me about being pregnant and not wanting your family to know and wanting to stay in school."

"I didn't fully understand the consequences at the time."

"Well, it didn't take much to convince you," Jude shot back.

"I was only eighteen, Jude. And I was compliant in those days."

Jude spread her arms dramatically. "Exactly! That's exactly my point. I was trying to help you shake off your compliant upbringing."

"By forcing me to comply with *your* ideas? How does that make me noncompliant?"

"I never forced you into anything you didn't agree to. I simply helped you see new possibilities and to escape that narrow mind-set you came with." She shifted and put her feet up on the ottoman. "Take that brother of yours, for instance."

Bebe felt suddenly defensive of him. "What about Bobby?"

"He brought you to the house, posturing like some knight in shining armor, checking the situation over. He tried to get you to leave with him—I heard you talking. He said mommy and daddy wouldn't like it if you stayed, and you begged him not to tell."

Bebe fumed. "The campus was very different from the time we first checked it out."

"My point is that you didn't stand up to him. You didn't tell him that you were doing things your way. I thought I was going to have to drag you inside by your hair." Jude's face twisted into a sneer. "You talked him down off the ledge, instead of pushing him off with both hands."

Bebe shook her head. "What are you talking about?"

"You begged him not to tell. You manipulated him like some pathetic housewife begging her husband for a little more grocery money. You couldn't even stand up for yourself. Has he always been your savior?"

"Mom," Rain interrupted, "that's enough."

A memory flashed in Bebe's mind. She was in the vineyard and Bobby was running toward her and frantically shouting her name. She wondered what he might have saved her from, if she'd allowed him to take her back home with him, and she felt an unwarranted anger that maybe he hadn't tried hard enough.

"You sugarcoated everything you said to him," Jude continued, "like you needed permission to blossom into the woman you were becoming." She looked at Mare and Toni. "Each of you needed me."

Mare's and Toni's jaws dropped.

Finally, Toni found her voice. "I was doing fine on my own, thank you very much."

"Oh, really," Jude said, turning her attention to Toni. "You were so caught up in putting on a glamorous face, catering to a man's idea of beautiful, that you were never honest. You didn't think I knew that you put your makeup on in the bathroom at school like a thirteen-year-old."

Toni looked irritated. "I started wearing makeup at twelve." She added under her breath, "If I'd wanted to live with my father, I would have stayed home."

Jude ignored her comment. "Just as you found your natural, true self, you would leave on break and return as some wannabe fashion model. I had to straighten you out all over again."

Toni folded her arms. "Including ruining my relationships."

Jude wore a self-satisfied look.

"Do you know what she did?" Toni said, glancing at Bebe and Mare. "She knew I was still seeing my boyfriend back in Philadelphia. So one time he calls when I'm gone, and she tells him that I'm going on a date with Jerome after his Black Panther meeting."

"Interracial dating was very enlightened."

"Not in my hometown in 1969. Besides, Jerome wasn't a Black Panther and we weren't even dating. We were working on a class project."

"My misunderstanding," Jude said, by way of apology. "But you wasted no time finding another to take his place."

Toni looked as close to crying as Bebe had ever seen her.

"If you'd really wanted him, you'd have gotten yourself pregnant the next time you went home, and trapped him into marrying you, like Mare did with that art teacher."

Mare's mouth dropped. "I did not trap Arnie into marrying me. That was our plan all along."

Jude raised her eyebrows. "Your plan, or his, I wonder?"

Bebe looked at Rain, wondering what she thought of this revealing look at her mother in her college years.

Then out of the blue Rain asked, "Do any of you know who my father is?"

Blank looks and silence hung in the air. A small smile curled on Toni's lips.

Bebe would have enjoyed seeing Jude on the hot seat for a change, except that it involved Rain.

Jude picked at a piece of lint on her slacks, and Bebe silently willed her to say the right thing.

"We've had this discussion before, Rain," Jude said, patronizingly. "I don't know who it was. You didn't need a controlling father, any more than I needed a domineering husband."

Bebe couldn't stand the look of resignation and disappointment on Rain's face. It was a time for honesty, and Jude let it pass by.

"You're right, Jude," Bebe said, rising from her seat to leave. "Who needed a controlling father or a domineering husband, when we all had you?"

Chapter 23

Bebe went into her room and shut the door to gather her composure. After all these years, Jude could still push her buttons, and she was angry at herself for allowing it to happen again.

Underlying all the anger she felt toward Jude were the raw feelings their confrontations had exposed within her. And it galled her to realize that Jude had seen through to the truth that, for all her spiritual understanding, Bebe hadn't allowed healing to take place.

She heard the others talking in the kitchen. She considered staying in her room and calling it a night, but she feared what would be planned in her absence. They weren't finished yet, no matter how much Bebe wished it to be over.

She sat in the quiet of her bedroom until she smelled coffee brewing. Then she gathered her resolve and joined the others in the kitchen.

Jude had retired to her room, but it was too much to hope that she would go to bed and forget about it. Bebe figured Rain must be helping her.

"I guess that's the end of Round One," Toni said quietly as Bebe pulled out a stool and sat down with a fresh cup.

Bebe considered her. "Why didn't you tell me about your books? Are they smutty?"

Toni looked offended. "No, they're not smutty! Believe it or not, I write for the Sweet and Light imprint, and they're stories of monogamous heterosexuals. They allow petting, but the characters have to wait until marriage to take the plunge."

Bebe blew on her coffee. "I would have thought that would bore you to tears."

"Yeah, you seem like more of a bodice-ripper type," Mare added.

Toni grinned mysteriously. "Sometimes it's like restraining a racehorse."

Bebe snickered and Mare gave Toni a playful shove. "You're bad," she said.

Rain came into the kitchen with her fists shoved deeply into her sweater pockets. Mare poured her a cup of coffee and drew her to a stool at the counter with them, asking, "So . . . how's your mom doing?"

She shrugged without meeting their eyes. "About the same."

"Were we too hard on her?" Toni asked. "I guess it bordered on a bloodletting, considering her condition."

"Sounds like she got what she deserved." She lifted her eyes briefly to each one of them. "I've always wondered why you all stayed friends with her after you left. It would have been so easy to just lose contact."

Bebe leaned across the counter and squeezed Rain's arm. "It was all because of you, honey."

Toni added, "We knew you'd need help. Or intensive psychotherapy."

Bebe felt worried. "You know, that whole thing with the ROTC building . . . I wasn't as bad as that."

"I know." A tiny smile tugged at the corners of Rain's mouth, and dissolved again. "At least you were worried about me. I guess I took second place in Mom's life from the very start."

She traced the pattern on the mug with her thumbnail and the three of them glanced at each other.

"That's not true, Rain," Mare said. "She was fiercely possessive of you. You were so cute in your little onesies, and we hardly got to hold you at all."

"Unless you had a poopy diaper, and then you were up for grabs," Toni teased, refilling her cup. "Mare, do we have any more cream?"

Mare looked at her in disbelief. "You're standing right beside the fridge. Open it and look."

Toni opened the refrigerator and squinted. "Not that soy stuff—"

"There's regular cream on the second shelf. You're worse than Arnie."

Toni poured cream into her cup and swirled it with her spoon. "As I was saying, Jude had an aversion to dirty diapers, so she handed you off to us when your diapers were positively bulging."

"What's this 'us'? You never changed her diapers," Bebe said.

"Well, I did at least once. I remember I was making chocolate chip cookies and I stopped to change her. I had on those Lee press-on nails, and after I washed my hands, I thought I still had cookie dough under my fingernails, but . . . it . . . wasn't."

"Ugh," Mare said. "You licked your finger?"

Toni looked rueful. "Only that once."

Rain laughed, and it was a beautiful sound.

"Bebe used to make you little shirts and sundresses out of any material she could find," Mare said. "Especially purple."

"College couture." Looking at Bebe, Toni said, "Remember when you found those old curtains in the trash next door and scrounged them for a dress?" She turned to Rain. "You should have seen the looks we got from the neighbors when they realized you were wearing their old curtains."

"But you had new things, too," Bebe assured her. "Once in a while. We were just poor college students, you know."

Rain smiled to herself. "I remember going to a zoo or a playland with a dragon. Was it Sleepy Hollow?"

Mare said, "Happy Hollow in San Jose. You're thinking of a kiddie ride—Danny the Dragon. We took Autumn and Crystal, too. They had a zoo with rides and a picnic area."

"The dragon used to scare me. I dreamed about it."

"Well, you were little then. I think they're in the midst of a remodel now."

"I remember going down a huge slide on Neil's lap. It seemed like it was high. How old was I?"

"I think you were two and a half the first time. You were six the last time we went, just before your mom moved out with you." Bebe remembered those trips fondly because Jude was so wrapped up in finishing her law degree that she was happy to let them entertain her. Even though Bebe and Neil were in veterinary school, they managed to carve out time for Rain. She completed their little family. Tears suddenly welled in Bebe's eyes. "It was hard to let you go."

Rain leaned over and hugged Bebe's neck. "I missed you all so much when we moved." She looked at Mare and Toni. "My childhood memories are kind of dull after that."

She sobered. "One thing I don't understand is why she had me in the first place? If she was so intent that you should have an abortion, why didn't she have one? Life would have been easier for her if she had."

"We all asked her that at the time," Toni said. "She wanted to raise you to be a 'new woman.' You said yourself one time that you felt like a social experiment." Toni lifted her eyebrows knowingly. "But if you ask me, I think she was in love with your father."

Mare made a face at Toni. "You would be a romantic about it."

Bebe said, "I think she was just plain lonely. Her own moth—"

"Shouldn't I be in on this conversation?" They looked up to see Jude standing in the doorway. For a moment, none of them spoke.

Bebe felt chagrined that she had once again caught them discussing her.

"After all, if you're going to pass judgment on me, I should get to have my say."

Rain jumped up, but Jude waved her away and headed for the bank of windows overlooking blackness. They guiltily exchanged looks, and finally joined her in the sunroom.

When she was settled in a chaise lounge, she began. "What I think

Bebe was about to say, was that my mother was a pathetic, self-absorbed toad of a woman who didn't know how to love another human being properly. She fell in love with my father, who turned out to be a philandering gambler. Mare, you should identify with that."

"Arnie's not that bad," Mare said, indignantly.

"My mother also defended my father's pursuits up until the time he left us for good when I was thirteen. At that point, I became particularly adept at ridding the house of some of the losers she hung out with by using the term 'jail bait'." She shifted in her chair as though in pain. "I'll spare you the sordid details of my junior high and high school years. Needless to say, I wasn't invited to many pajama parties. So you'll forgive me if I tried to distance myself from the suburban housewife stereotype and empower myself and a few friends along the way."

Bebe finally found her voice. "Your experience growing up wasn't everyone's, Jude."

"Thank you, Bebe, for stating the obvious. But if your experience wasn't so bad, why were you so determined not to repeat it? From what I gather, you had an intact nuclear family with economic security and a home-cooked meal every night. There must be some reason why you agreed to have an abortion."

"I never completely agreed to it. I might not have kept that appointment."

"You made that decision when you decided to party. And you influenced another, along the way, I might add."

Bebe looked at her. "What do you mean?"

Jude looked at Rain. "Did you know that Rain had the unfortunate experience of getting pregnant when she was in high school? You were one of the reasons she agreed to have an abortion."

Bebe looked in horror at Rain, who finally met her eyes. "But . . . I didn't . . ."

"Yes, well," Jude said, "I was under the impression that you had. And since you seemed to be Rain's hero, it wasn't hard to convince her that she wasn't ready to be a mother at sixteen if you weren't ready at eighteen."

The full impact of her deception caught Bebe like a blow. Now Rain was trying to have a child, and she'd terminated one, just because she thought she was following Bebe's example.

"Oh, for heaven's sake, it's not a big deal. It's every woman's prerogative to terminate a pregnancy," Jude stated.

"Having a legal right to an abortion doesn't make it morally right," Mare said.

Toni added, "I think it's interesting that the two people who have had experience with it have reservations, and Jude, who never had one, is pushing it and doesn't see a problem. I, personally, think they are the ones who have earned the right to have an opinion on the subject, and not you."

Jude turned cold eyes on Toni.

"I . . . I didn't know," Bebe stammered to Rain.

Rain hesitated. "I didn't say anything because you'd been trying to have a baby for a long time, and then you had a miscarriage. I didn't want you to know that I'd . . . that I'd gotten rid of what you wanted so badly." Her chin trembled. "And then you started going to church and you seemed to be changing, and I was afraid to tell you. I didn't want you to hate me. I thought it was something I could just forget about and pretend never happened, but I can't." Her voice caught, and Bebe wanted to go to her, but she continued, "So now that I want a child, I can't have one."

She turned to her mother, suddenly angry. "You're no better than Shirley."

"Rain, no," Bebe said. Jude looked momentarily stricken, but Rain continued.

"You didn't have me because you loved me, you had me for selfish reasons, to prove something to yourself. To make a point. Do you have any idea how ridiculous 'Rainbow Star' looks on a résumé? You told me to put my career first, like you did. But you were always going off to some political fund-raiser or a demonstration, and I was left to fend for myself."

"I always provided for you."

"Not in the ways I needed."

"We were fighting for your rights. Making sacrifices. If it hadn't been for socially minded women, you'd be making coffee for your boss and picking up his dry cleaning and putting up with his advances just to keep your job. And you wouldn't be enjoying the limitless opportunities that Title VII opened up for you. For that matter, Bebe might not have gotten into veterinary school without the passage of Title IX."

Bebe nodded. "Yes, that's true. I certainly didn't get any support from my family." She thought for a moment and looked at them, puzzled. "Wouldn't you think that just once in thirty years my father would have asked for medical advice on something? He never has. Sometimes I wonder whether I went to veterinary school to prove something to him or to impress him."

"Look, I appreciate the sacrifices," Rain said. "But I don't want to be told what to think. You fought for me to be able to make my own choices, and then you took it away and dictated what was best for me. You told me that I was all I needed in life. You told me it was best for me to have an abortion at sixteen. You said I didn't need a man *or* a child. You said I had all the time in the world to have both. Well, guess what? I don't. While I was putting my career first, and proving to Hayden that I didn't need him, my time was running out. If I really want a baby now, I'll probably have to use some stranger's eggs, and a stranger's sperm, and deal with choices I don't want to make alone."

She paused, gathering herself. "And you know what? I do need Hayden." Her voice trembled, and she looked up at them with tears in her eyes. "We were making a life together and now part of me is gone, and I miss him." Her face crumpled and tears spilled over. No one moved. She looked at Jude and said through her tears, "You know why he left? It wasn't about having a baby at all. He said he was leaving because I was becoming just like you." She sniffed and wiped her eyes. "But I'm not going to become like you. I'm not going to try to cheat Hayden out of the house for the money."

Jude said in a very controlled voice, "You won't have to. I made a new will and I'm leaving you mine. You can evict William."

Rain blanched. "Mom, no!"

"It's already done. One of the partners came to the house and it's in their hands now. Do with it what you like before I change my mind and leave it all to some charity."

Rain turned abruptly and stumbled in her haste to leave. She went down the hall and they heard her door quietly close.

❖ ❖ ❖ ❖

Bebe gave Rain an hour alone and then gently knocked on her door. Rain reluctantly let her in and told her to shut the door. When she asked Rain how she was feeling, she just curled into her afghan like a little child.

"Rain," Bebe began, not knowing exactly what to say, "I'm sorry you thought I had an abortion. I wish you had told me."

"What good would it have done?"

Bebe rubbed her temple. "I don't know. Maybe none. But who knows?"

Rain spoke into her pillow with her face turned away from Bebe. "They tell you that it's not a baby, it's just a procedure. They expect you to get over it and move on, and you believe it because you want to, but . . . later it comes back to you. What you did."

Bebe smoothed Rain's dark hair away from her face. "I know. That's the reason I kept the miscarriage from your mom. I just wanted to forget about it and pretend it never happened. But I never could. The choices I made had the same result as if I had gone through with it." Feelings of loss sprang to her, sharp and lucid. "I'll never really know if I would have gone through with it or not."

Bebe felt that her past was a ribbon of old highway, broken and rutted by the heavy load she carried, slowing her progress, the journey shaking her to her very core.

Rain lay very still. "Bebe?"

"Yes?"

"Is this God's way of punishing me? Maybe I don't deserve to have a baby."

Bebe's throat ached. "He doesn't do that, Rain. He cries with us. Did you know that?" She swallowed hard and rushed ahead before she had a chance to think. "I felt the same way when I had those miscarriages. I worried if they happened because of the things I had done. But the truth is, I think I'm the only one who hasn't forgiven me yet."

Silence fell between them, and Rain reached over and took Bebe's hand. "I shouldn't have told Mom what Hayden said. I shouldn't have said half the things I did."

Bebe sighed. "Maybe it needed to be said, Rain. It might help you both find some closure before . . . while she's still able. Maybe you can even find a way to forgive her."

Rain turned her head away and let go of Bebe's hand without responding. Finally, she said, "Somebody needs to check on her. It's been three days. She might need a new patch."

"Don't worry. We'll take care of it." Bebe moved to the door and paused. "We'll leave as soon as we can get everyone moving in the morning."

Rain didn't answer, and Bebe shut the door behind her. She stood in the hallway down from Jude's room, debating with herself. It was no use. Toni wasn't the nursing type, and Mare would get eaten alive. Bebe knew she would have to be the one to help Jude.

She knocked briefly and went inside, closing the door behind her. Jude lay on her side looking frail and haggard, and with her face drawn in pain. Bebe wasn't even sure if she was awake, until she spoke.

"So she sent in the reinforcements."

"She's gone to bed. I came to see if you needed anything."

Jude closed her eyes and sighed. "I need help changing my patch. There's one in my case in the bathroom."

Bebe retrieved the patch among the medication bottles and followed Jude's directions, flushing the old one when she was done. She washed her hands and came out, drying them on a hand towel.

Jude breathed deeply, relaxing with the medication. Bebe was just slipping out, and she paused when Jude spoke.

"You could have kept the baby, if you'd wanted to. I kept Rain, and we survived."

Chapter 24

The mood was somber as they packed up the cars the next morning, keenly aware of the fact that they had made no plans.

Bebe found Jude gazing out the sunroom windows at the horizon and the ocean below, and came to stand beside her.

"When we get back, I'm making arrangements for a cremation. When the time comes, I want you all to scatter my ashes."

Bebe watched a gull dive out of sight below and rise again. "If that's what you want. Any preference where?"

"San Francisco Bay. It just seems like a natural thing to do."

Bebe felt sadness at the thought of Jude's death. What must it feel like to be at the end of one's life, and be confronted with so many mistakes and bad choices? Would they overshadow the good? Would Jude remember the single moms for whom she helped to find housing or jobs, or to escape from domestic violence, or would she dwell on her past mistakes?

"We're all packed," Toni called from the kitchen. "I left a nice tip on the counter for the cleaning service people."

They loaded up the cars and headed out, locking the gate behind them. Before they left town, Bebe pulled over for gas and they waved as Mare and Jude passed them by.

Once on the freeway, Bebe found a radio station to fill the quiet. Toni sat in the front passenger seat, and Bebe resisted the urge to glance back at Rain in the passenger seat behind her. They dropped Toni off at her house and continued on in silence.

Bebe and Rain stopped in Stockton for lunch and got home in the early afternoon. She didn't ask about Jude or comment on anything that took place over the weekend. Bebe hated to leave her alone at her house without giving her a chance to debrief.

When she got home, Bebe called Neil at the clinic and told him she'd gotten back safely. He asked how the weekend went, and she said it went about as expected.

Neil was late getting home again. They had advertised for another large animal veterinarian to share the load but the field wasn't quite as lucrative as it was for small animal vets, and they'd had no response.

They caught up over Chinese takeout that evening, and Neil's only comment was that he was glad he hadn't been invited. He told her that he'd been able to meet with Hayden for coffee while they were gone, and he agreed that Hayden's reasons for leaving were complicated. His decision to move out hadn't been an easy one, and Neil felt it would take divine intervention to change Hayden's mind. One ray of hope, however, was that Hayden mentioned that he'd started occasionally attending his brother's church.

He also said that he'd spoken to Scott about the graduation on Friday.

"We'll just fly down and back the same day. Apparently the ceremony is not quite the production as the first one. I don't know if he'll be able to catch the same flight back with us or not."

"Did he have anything else to say?" she asked.

"He's ready to come home. It doesn't seem like the Christmas season to him."

"He didn't mention the clipping?"

"Nope. Honey, I wouldn't worry about it."

Bebe unpacked and climbed into bed with a book to unwind, but found it impossible to focus on the story. The weekend had been mentally and emotionally exhausting, and portions of it played over and over in her mind, refusing to let her go.

The worst of it had been in finding that Rain had had an abortion because of her example. Bebe's silence had done that. All those years she'd prided herself on being a better mother to Rain than Jude had been, but that lie, that omission, that untruth had caused Rain to make a choice that led to guilt and pain. Bebe had ultimately failed her.

In some ways, the weekend had been doomed from the start. At the best of times, the dynamics between the roommates had been unpredictable—a tangle of personalities and problems, expectations and disappointments—with Jude at the core.

Bebe wondered if Jude was truly unaware of the stress she'd caused Bebe and Neil over the years as they walked a tightrope strung across Rain's childhood and adolescence, trying to plant themselves firmly in Rain's life while avoiding anything that would offend Jude and cause her to deny them contact. It was tricky, sometimes boggy ground to cross, and Bebe sensed that Jude enjoyed watching them try to navigate it. Bebe felt that, to a lesser degree, the same went for Mare and Toni. If it hadn't been for Rain, they all might have given up contact with Jude years before.

When Bebe reflected on the weekend, she wondered if Jude had been fully aware of the potential for turmoil and had set herself up. Perhaps she wanted to feel something—anything—at the end of her life.

The things Jude had said about Bobby, were they true? Bebe couldn't deny that she had depended on him growing up, even deferred to him at times. And then, suddenly, he wasn't there anymore. Did she move away, or did he?

On impulse, Rain pulled back the covers and went to the jewelry box on her dresser. She dug around amid her earrings and bracelets until she found her silver chain with the cross that Neil had given to her when Scotty was born. She dug further beneath her grandmother's pearl necklace and found the small ring with the amethyst stone. It caught the light and splintered into shades of purple. Sometimes it was the color of table grapes—sometimes the color of the sun through a bottle of merlot.

She had removed it from her finger on the day that her brother Rudy called to tell her that Bobby had come home to the Oakland Terminal to a crowd of bloodthirsty protestors and that he didn't want to see her. But she was his sister, and Rudy thought she deserved to know that Bobby had gotten home safely, and was being discharged from the army.

She unfastened the clasp on the necklace and threaded the chain through the ring. Then she slipped the chain over her head and tucked the cross and ring into the front of her nightgown. She crawled into bed and fell into an exhausted sleep.

❖ ❖ ❖ ❖

Dylan had to work over the weekend, and would drive home for Christmas break on Monday. She had time to throw together some of their favorite Christmas goodies before then.

On Friday, she and Neil flew down early to San Diego and rented a car to drive to Camp Pendleton. She was torn between wanting to see Scotty so badly, and fearing that he might act differently toward her. The ceremony was inspiring, but more abbreviated than the one in October with fewer attendees, and they were only able to speak briefly with him before he had to rejoin his platoon. He looked so handsome in his service bravos. He hugged her tightly and on the surface seemed to be his old self, except that he hesitated to meet her eyes. He said his flight wasn't leaving until early evening and would get in about ten o'clock. They took down his flight information and said they would meet him in Sacramento.

They flew home, did some Christmas shopping, and had dinner before going back to the airport to wait for his flight. He arrived hungry, so they picked up his gear and ran through a fast-food restaurant on the way home.

He said the house and the Christmas tree looked great, and dropped off his bag in his room. He came out to the living room and slouched in the recliner as though he'd only been gone for an afternoon, slipping off his shoes and grabbing the remote. Bebe felt like she was walking on eggshells, but she decided to give him some time to come around on his own.

They went to church together on Sunday. Bebe was hoping that Rain would go along, but she declined. Bebe invited her to come with them to her parents' house as usual for Christmas dinner, but Rain surprised her by saying that William had invited her over for dinner, and she thought she should go.

"Does he know how the weekend went?" Bebe asked her.

"As much as Mom would tell him. He wants me to fill him in sometime."

"Have you spoken to her yet?"

"No, and I have no doubt that it will be awkward." She hesitated. "I don't think he knows about the house, either. She's probably leaving it up to me to tell him."

The sadness and hurt in Rain's voice was palpable. "Are you doing okay?" Bebe asked.

"It's the holidays and Hayden's gone and I'm not pregnant and my mother is dying. I don't think I'm okay."

Bebe felt stung, and realized how insensitive her question had been. "I'm sorry, Rain. I just don't know what else to say, except that I love you and I want you to be happy again."

She was silent for a moment. "I'm sorry. None of it's your fault."

Bebe was about to say good-bye, when Rain asked, "Did I tell you I was offered a job promotion?"

"That's good news," Bebe said.

"It was offered to me because I'm passive-aggressive, but in a good way. They want me to bully people to do what they want, because I'm good at it."

"That's not true, Rain. Surely they didn't mean it that way."

"That's my paraphrase, but that was the feeling I got."

"Are you going to take it?"

"I don't know yet. It involves longer hours and travel twice a month. That doesn't exactly work in with my plans—if my plans even have a chance." She cleared her throat and rushed ahead. "I have to go. I promised Lisa I'd go Christmas shopping with her. She thinks I need some cheering up."

"How much does she know?"

"She knows Hayden's gone, and she knows about Mom. That's all."

They both signed off and Bebe went back to her holiday preparations. She couldn't shake off the feeling of disappointment about the past weekend, and the fact that it was a failure, as far as Jude was concerned. She called Toni and expressed her concerns.

"I think we did what she asked," Toni said, raising her voice to be heard over background noise. "We tried to agree on something, but it just didn't work."

"I wish we could leave it at that, Toni, but you know we can't. For Rain's sake. And the truth is that I don't want Jude to leave this world feeling unloved and unappreciated."

The noise level on Toni's end droned on, but she didn't respond.

"Where are you?" Bebe shouted.

"Tahoe. Right now, I'm in the lounge waiting for Lawrence. I promised to let him play in the casino for a while after we shopped."

"So, what can we do?"

"I'm really drawing a blank, Bebe, but maybe something will come to me."

Bebe frowned. "Call me after Christmas. I don't think we have much time left."

Next she called Mare, who was taking care of her grandchildren.

"I know, the weekend was a total fiasco," Mare said. "Jude was a bear on the way back."

"I felt bad that you got stuck taking her home. But I didn't feel like the weekend was a total waste."

Bebe could hear the smile in Mare's voice. "No, it was fun. At least the parts when Jude stayed in her room."

"We have to do something, and I feel like time is running out. Will you promise to think about it?"

"Sure. I'll call you after Christmas when Autumn's kids have a week with their dad."

Bebe prayed about what to do for Jude, but her own problems kept interfering. She ruminated on them when she wrapped gifts, and when she shopped for her Christmas dinner contributions, and when she wrote Christmas cards.

She resolved to let it go until after the holidays, and they all sat down one night to watch a Christmas movie together. In the middle of the movie, she heard a beep, and Scott checked his cell phone.

"Who is it?" Dylan asked.

"Uncle Bobby. He's coming Thursday." He texted back. "He's bringing Angie."

"From San Diego?" Dylan asked, with his mouth full of popcorn.

"Yeah," Scotty answered, slipping his phone back into his pocket.

She stole glances at Scotty during the movie. He looked so grown up with his face etched and his hair in its military high and tight buzz. She yearned to know what his response was to her letter, but loathed ruining Christmas if his answer was not what she wanted to hear. Now, she had the additional worry about Bobby showing up at her mom's on Christmas Day.

She had taken the week off from the clinic to bake and shop and relax, which was impossible, and before she knew it, Christmas Eve had arrived. She had tried to meet Rain for coffee, but she begged off, which wasn't like her. She left a message for her to come over on Christmas Eve, but got no response. Bebe wondered if Rain had done some thinking about the weekend and was disappointed in them all.

On Christmas morning, they finally had to force the boys out of bed at nine to open gifts and get going for the day. What a change from the 4:00 a.m. wake-up calls the boys used to give them when they were little, Bebe thought.

Neil read the nativity story from the Bible and they opened their gifts. It was a pleasant morning, and it seemed almost normal to Bebe. They got ready and packed up the dessert and squash casserole she'd made, and headed out.

Her parents' house smelled like turkey and buzzed with activity and people. After hugging her mom, she headed to the kitchen where Karen peeled potatoes at the sink.

"It's about time you showed up," she said, giving Bebe an affectionate hug without touching her with her wet hands. "The work's almost done."

"We had trouble getting the boys up."

"Tell me about it," she said. "We almost left without Brandon and Eric."

Her mother bustled in and adjusted the temperature on the oven. To Bebe, she said, "Help me get the turkey out of the oven."

Bebe grabbed a pot holder and together they lifted the huge turkey onto hot pads placed on the countertop. It looked perfectly browned and relaxed, with its legs and wings slack like it had been given an epidural. Overcooked, as usual. Steam curled from the dressing-filled cavity.

"We'll let it sit for a while, and then you can make the gravy. Put in that pan of rolls behind you."

Bebe slid the rolls into the oven and set the timer for twenty-five minutes, and then followed her mother into the dining room to help her set the table. She was setting out her best set of china with the fading platinum ring around the edge and her grandmother's crystal goblets, which usually only went to the adults. Bebe wondered what she would do now that all of the cousins were grown and there weren't enough to go around. Bebe followed her around the table, setting out the silver and the napkins on either side of the plates. After setting out the last plate, her mother came along behind her, straightening each utensil and napkin that Bebe laid out. Bebe felt a bit irritated, until she realized that this was her mother's tangible way of showing love to her family. She was never happier than when she was in charge of the kitchen cooking her best dishes or making an occasion special for them all.

"Get out those candlesticks, the ones on the top shelf," she directed Bebe. "The candles are in the top drawer."

The crystal candlesticks had also been handed down from her grandmother, and the German crystal was probably worth more than her mother realized. Her mother set them in the center, positioned the candles in firmly, and stepped back to admire them.

"Those serving dishes on the second shelf are for the potato salad and the beans," she told her. Bebe took them from the hutch and followed her back into the kitchen. "I need you girls to chop onions and cook up some bacon for the potato salad."

Bebe was grateful to be among family and to keep her mind off of her problems, but every time the door opened, she glanced up to see if it was Bobby. At last, she heard the front door open and someone greeted him and his guest. Bebe felt her pulse skip. She hoped that his friend would keep him occupied for the day.

She heard them making their way through the house and her chest tightened. She tried to be nonchalant, but knew that her smile looked forced when he introduced Angie to them. Angie seemed like a nice woman and greeted everyone with a smile, but Bebe wondered how much she knew.

The dinner was finally on the table and eaten too quickly to do justice to the amount of time and preparation that had gone into preparing it. The food in Bebe's stomach turned leaden from the anxiety she felt, with Scotty beside her talking to Bobby directly across from her. They sat around talking for only a few moments before her mother started gathering dirty plates. Karen looked resignedly at Bebe, and they got up to help. Bebe heard the conversation veer toward Scott's recent graduation, and she was glad to be busy in the kitchen again.

The day turned out to be beautifully sunny and a warm 65 degrees, and the family drifted outside after dinner. Bebe washed dishes while Karen dried, and half-listened to her talk about their recent cruise to Ensenada. She had so much on her mind, but the most pressing problem was her relationship with Bobby and Scott.

Watching Bobby head back through the vineyard with Angie, she realized that Jude had been right about one thing. She had looked up to Bobby as her protector during her childhood. After all, it was what her father expected of him in his position as the oldest son in the family, and he'd taken it seriously. There was nothing so wrong with that. The world was a dangerous place, and the vineyard was expansive and alluring to a young child. A memory tickled in the back of her mind, an uncomfortable one that pricked, and she pushed it aside without considering.

"Some of the vines still have their leaves," she said, pulling aside the curtain.

"We haven't had a hard frost yet, like we usually do," her mother answered from the dining room where she replaced her china in the hutch. "It's been this way for the last few years."

The back door opened and Angie came into the kitchen, offering to help. Bebe's mom tried to get her to sit and visit while they worked, but she wouldn't hear of it. She grabbed a dish towel and helped Karen with the turkey roaster. Karen turned to Bebe and gave her a secret thumbs-up.

Angie seemed to be a likeable, ordinary person, but Bebe kept her remarks vague when the conversation drifted to her boys. Her mom asked about Jude and Rain, and she said very little about their situations. Bebe didn't like to seem evasive, but it was necessary.

When the last pot was washed and the counters wiped down, Bebe went outside to greet Max and Bandit. They followed her as she walked out into the vineyard, and then raced ahead to investigate some movement in the grass. Clover grew mingled with the ankle-high grass between the rows of spent vines, and the younger vines still grasped yellowed leaves. The pruning would begin after the holidays, when the workers returned from Mexico. Then the clover would be disked under to replenish the soil with nutrients, and the growth cycle would begin again. The vines would unfold into a chaos of leaves and tendrils and grapes, creating a place in which Bebe had always loved to spend time, even though her father had cautioned her about the dangers.

She heard voices and laughter coming from the house and looked back. Scott had overthrown a football and Dylan jogged toward it. His cousins were giving him a hard time about losing his touch while he was away.

She had an odd feeling of déjà vu. She tried again to shake it off, but that niggling memory forced its way to the front, and she could almost feel the heat rising from lush vines and hear insects buzzing around her as they would on a hot August day of her childhood.

Once again, she was eight years old and playing at the edge of the vineyard within earshot of the house in case her mother called her. It was a sultry, slow-moving kind of day that allowed for hours of freedom and make-believe. She had taken a spoon from the wooden box lined with dark purple felt in her mother's hutch and used it to dig her riverbed deep. Her village grew on either side of the riverbank. When she was finished, she would fill it with a pail of water from the garden hose.

The silence was broken by Bobby shouting her name. She didn't want her mother to know she had taken the spoon, so she ignored him, but his voice pitched, growing breathy and frantic. She stood up, and as she did, a movement nearby startled her, and she jumped. A man stood not far down the row from her, looking disheveled with a scruffy blond beard and dirty clothes and hands, and a look in his eyes that made her squirm. For a moment, she stood transfixed, unable to move. She heard Bobby shout for her to run. The man took his eyes from her to glance briefly at Bobby. Bobby shouted again, and the man took a step toward her. She spun on her heels and darted, clutching the spoon and scattering the small houses she had built with sticks in the black soil at her feet. She barreled down the straight row without stopping until she ran full bore into Bobby. He grabbed her by the hand and half-dragged her back to the house with their legs pumping and aching, Bobby pulling her up when she stumbled and stealing anxious glances over his shoulder.

They burst into the house and collapsed. Bobby clutched her until her mother came and pried her out of his arms, demanding to know what was wrong. Bebe saw him turn away and wipe his eyes. She'd never seen him cry before. And although she didn't completely understand the danger at the time, she knew how the man had made her feel, and the fear it had struck in her family. And she felt beyond a doubt the depth of Bobby's love for her. She realized now that the anger her father displayed when he found out wasn't directed at her as she'd thought at the time, but was simply his reaction to fear. Somehow, her guilt over taking the spoon had blended into accepting a childish responsibility for the turmoil and the unspoken implications of the man's intentions.

Bebe gazed back toward the house at the boys tossing the football. Bobby had joined them, and the sun was beginning to dull and fade in the mauve horizon. The temperature dipped and the air grew chilly, just as it had always been out on the periphery of her family where she had lived most of her life.

She felt acutely her need for reconciliation—to prune the regret from her life, and to disk the undergrowth of guilt into the nourishing soil of forgiveness. Did she truly believe that God could heal her broken heart and that He wanted to dress her wounds? She'd held this healing at arm's length for too long, knowing she was forgiven, but refusing to allow Him access to her pain. It would feel so nice to let it go.

She slipped into the house to grab a jacket and came back out to where they were playing. Bobby noticed her standing on the sidelines, and surprisingly, gave her a small nod. After a few more passes, he excused himself from the game and came over to her. They stood looking directly at each other for the first time in years.

Chapter 25

"Can we talk, Bobby?" she asked.

He considered her for a moment, and then nodded toward the vineyard without malice or insolence. They walked down one of the rows with the silence surrounding them as they moved farther from the house. Bebe toyed with the ring on her necklace as they walked, and she saw the recognition in Bobby's eyes.

"I was remembering that time when I was playing out here and you saved me from the transient."

He walked with his head down, watching his steps.

"Thank you." She looked over at him and he looked back, nodding without answering. "I remember you went back and found my ring in the dirt when we were sure he was gone."

He looked down to the end of the row. "Mom wasn't too happy about her spoon."

"When she figured out I was okay, she paddled me good."

"You couldn't have taken just any old spoon out of the kitchen drawer."

Bebe chuckled grimly. "No, I had to use Oma's silver."

Bebe felt encouraged that they were actually carrying on a normal conversation for the first time since she was in college. She plunged ahead.

"I owe you several apologies," she said. "And I just realized the connection between them."

She cleared her throat. "I think that, over the years, I've blamed you for some unfortunate choices that I made. Some situations I found myself in. They weren't your fault," she hurried to say, "and I wasn't even aware at the time that I was doing it, but I guess I have been."

He continued to walk, and she caught the small edge in his voice. "Like what?"

She took a deep breath. "Like leaving me at college. Realizing that I wasn't equipped to face the situation I was in, and not stopping me."

His countenance grew dark, and he stopped. "I tried to make you go home with me, do you remember? What was I supposed to do, pick you up and throw you into the car?"

She raised her hands. "I know, I know. It wasn't your fault. That's what I'm saying. It was totally my choice. All of it. You did the right thing by leaving it up to me." She folded her arms across her chest and continued to walk. He walked beside her.

"The things that happened, the choices that I made . . . they weren't all bad. Some of them really helped me to grow, although I wouldn't recommend them to anyone else. I think that for a long time, I saw you as my savior, and when you weren't there anymore, I lashed out."

"Just how did you lash out?"

She stopped and plunged her hands into her pockets, screwing up her courage. She spoke to the ground at their feet.

"I was really angry at you for leaving and going to Vietnam." She looked him in the face. "It doesn't make sense. You didn't have a choice. You just weren't there anymore. I was nineteen. I was in over my head with some things and I had no one I could trust to talk to about it. I was angry at the government. I was angry at Mom and Dad for not stopping you—I was angry at everybody. I didn't care about Vietnam. I only wanted you to be safe again. We heard so many horrible stories, and I was afraid that you wouldn't come back, and that somehow God would punish you for the things that I did."

He slowly began to walk again, and she kept pace with him.

"So I decided to protest the war, force them to bring the troops home. Make a difference. Except it was never about politics, it was about frustration. All it did was get my picture in the paper. That picture ruined everything." She briefly closed her eyes, and when she opened them, she saw it all again. "It was like a switch was thrown. Like gasoline to a flame. It made me feel like I was really accomplishing something, and people rallied around like I was some kind of celebrity."

"And then you stopped writing to me. At first, I thought you'd been wounded or . . . worse. But Rudy told me that you knew about the picture, and I figured I'd never hear from you again. I didn't blame you. It looked so bad and it was manipulated in a lot of ways that weren't true. And the protests in the news got worse and more violent. They turned into bombings, and Mom and Dad just assumed I was a part of all that, and they acted like I was dead to them for a long time. I didn't even know you were home from Nam until Rudy finally called me."

Bobby was quiet for so long that Bebe wondered if he had moved beyond her reach. Finally, he spoke.

"We heard things were bad here. Crazy bad. When we got back to Oakland we were told to remove our uniforms and put on civilian clothes, and then told exactly what we could expect to find out there. But I just wasn't prepared. It couldn't be fixed. *I* couldn't be fixed. None of us deserved it." He looked up at the sky and cleared his throat. "Neither did Cynthia."

His brow furrowed and he cleared his throat again like he was struggling for control. They walked in silence.

He kicked a small stone. "And then, Scotty joins up."

"Yes. Scotty, who knows nothing about any of this until he gets a copy of the clipping. I wrote him a letter, trying to explain it all. How the times were different then. But I still don't know how he feels about it."

Bobby stopped and looked at her. She didn't know what he was going to say, or how he felt, or whether any of it had made sense or just sounded like an excuse. She just knew that she'd had to say it. She needed the closure, one way or another. She needed for the healing to begin.

He reached into his back pocket and pulled out his wallet. Opening it to the billfold, he pulled out the envelope she sent to Scotty with the letter explaining about the clipping.

"Scotty sent this to me and asked me to read it. Took me about a month before I could. Angie convinced me to read it." His features softened into a gentle smile. "She's quite a woman. She said that she understood where you were coming from, because her ex was a Marine. You might have even bumped into her at a protest."

He offered it to her, but she couldn't speak and just shook her head. He folded it back up and stuck it in his wallet. He stood looking at the purpling horizon and Bebe could see a bit of the younger Bobby that she used to know.

"She sounds like a good friend to have around."

"She's helping me deal with some things." He sniffed. "I sometimes blamed myself for what happened," he said. "You know, I thought about going back for you that day. I almost turned around at Fairfield. I never told Mom and Dad. Things might have turned out different if I had. I was pretty mad at the both of us."

"I couldn't have gone back home, Bobby. I needed to make my own decisions. Times were changing. Like I said, you weren't my savior. If I had, I wouldn't have married Neil, or had Scotty and Dylan and a job that I love. And I wouldn't have Rain."

They turned around and headed back toward the house. The sun was almost gone and the air carried the scent of wood smoke.

"I always wondered about Rain. I figured she was yours, and you were just keeping it a secret from the family."

She chuckled. "No. Jude is her real mother, although I loved her like my own."

He scratched his head. "I gotta tell you, I could never see her as a mother."

"She wasn't a very good one, but she didn't have a very good example, either."

They got to the end of the row and paused, turning to face each other and considering all that had gone on between them. She hoped he wouldn't reconsider later. Over thirty-five years of anger doesn't dissolve in one conversation.

"So, what do you think?" she asked him, feeling vulnerable and thin as tissue. "Can we call it a truce?"

He looked down on her, and a small smile softened his face. "Truce, little sis."

* * * *

Rain had gone to Lisa's house for Christmas Eve, simply because she couldn't come up with a plausible excuse at the time when Lisa had invited her. It turned out that it was a setup with her cousin who was divorced and had custody of his two kids. When the evening finally ended, after the twin boys knocked over a pedestal by running through the house in a frenzy and almost set fire to her carpet, Lisa apologized to her and said it would never happen again.

Rain spent Christmas Day with her mother and William, but drove home on Christmas night over the protests of William who offered to let her stay in his room. She couldn't stay in the house any longer, and she needed to go to work the next day. It had been awkward between herself and Jude, and disappointing since they didn't celebrate the holiday, even though William made a fabulous pork tenderloin and tried to make the dinner special. Her mother had slept most of the day, and suffered from nausea, so Rain and William ate alone. Her medications weren't quite enough anymore to take the edge off of her pain.

She wished now that her mother had never had the idea about the Celebration and had been content to just enjoy the rest of her time. Now their tenuous relationship was strained again, and they were back to square one.

Rain pulled into her garage and let Noah inside. She breathed a sigh of relief that the holiday was finally over, but what a horrible way to think about Christmas. Would it be like this every year, she wondered? She hadn't spent the holiday alone for eight years, and she didn't like it very much.

She noticed that her answering machine light was blinking, and she pushed Play. She recognized Hayden's voice immediately.

"Hello. Rain. I tried your cell phone, but didn't have any luck reaching you. You must be out. Just wanted to wish you a merry Christmas and . . . well . . . Merry Christmas.'Bye."

She grabbed her cell phone and saw that she had missed a call, but he hadn't left a message. She played the answering machine again, dissecting the message for any nuance of hidden meaning.

Should she call him back, she wondered? It was eleven o'clock. Would she seem desperate if she called him back so late? She decided to send him an e-mail instead. She thanked him for calling and said she had been at her mom's.

Could it be that he missed her, too?

* * * *

Bebe discovered that Scott had seemed uncomfortable around her because he was afraid she would be angry that he passed her letter along to Bobby. He'd avoided discussing it with her for that very reason. She hugged him and thanked him for following his intuition, and he said that he never doubted her support, but joked that if she joined another protest, he would track her down.

Once she felt better about Bobby and Scott, ideas to fix Jude's botched Celebration came more easily. She arranged to have a conference call with Mare and Toni and discussed several ideas with them. They finally reached an agreement on one idea in particular and decided to follow through, with or without Jude's blessing. Bebe agreed to be the one to tell Jude. She called William and arranged a time on Saturday when she could come by. He said Jude really wasn't up to visitors, and it had to be brief.

Bebe didn't ask Rain if she wanted to go along. There were some things she felt she needed to say to Jude alone. She pulled up to the house and said a prayer before going in. William met her at the door, speaking quietly, and cautioning her that Jude was failing.

They had made arrangements with a hospice nurse. Against Jude's wishes, the hospice nurse had advised William to move Jude to a bedroom downstairs so that he could keep a constant watch on her and hear if she needed anything at night.

He told Bebe that he'd recently administered one of her strong medications and that her conversation might not make sense when it completely kicked in. He pushed the door open and let Jude know that Bebe was there.

The room smelled strongly of urine and medications, and medical equipment waited in the corner of the room. Bebe was surprised at how quickly Jude had declined in two weeks, as though she'd gone home from the Celebration weekend and given up. Her facial skin now stretched over her bones, thin and transparent. Bebe tried to keep her countenance in check, but Jude's mind was sharper than her body.

"It must be bad," she said, taking shallow breaths. "William took the mirror away."

Bebe pulled up a chair beside the bed. "I'm sorry about the weekend, Jude. Things got kind of crazy. It must have been disappointing for you."

Jude managed a brief, sad smile. "Like old times."

Bebe smiled back, in spite of herself. "It came pretty close."

"It wasn't all bad, was it?" Jude asked.

"The weekend? No."

Jude shook her head minutely. "The Victorian."

"Oh." Memories of a young, vivacious Jude came to her mind. "No, there were some good times. There was Rain. I'm thankful for that." Bebe hesitated, and then added, "Jude, I've been thinking about our conversation at the aquarium."

The frown lines on Jude's forehead deepened. "Don't want any sermons."

"I'm not going to preach any. But I'm open for conversation."

"Already had one with your God." Jude licked her lips. "Intend to finish it in person."

Surprised by her admission, Bebe started to speak but Jude added firmly, punctuating each word, "End of discussion." Jude took a deeper breath and licked her parched lips. "Ice, please."

Bebe took the cup of crushed ice from her nightstand and spooned some into her mouth. Jude sucked on it.

"I came to tell you about the cause we decided on," Bebe said.

Jude raised her eyebrows.

"You know Toni's husband, Lawrence, gets grant money for colleges. Well, he's going to help us set up an endowment in your name to help young women have money for college. The principal is never spent, so each year the interest is given out as scholarship money. We'll figure out ways to add to the principal each year so it will grow, and we need to discuss the criteria for selecting recipients."

Jude's brows knitted together. "Only for women's studies."

"We'll consider it. But young women need to be able to make their own choices. You leave that up to us. We'll pull Rain in on it, too."

Jude ran her tongue over her lips. "I hurt a woman once."

"Jude, how did you hurt a woman?"

"Won a case. Denied her settlement. She had a child." Her face twisted briefly until she struggled and won composure. "It was wrong."

Bebe was touched by another breach in Jude's vulnerability and sensed that this was her last opportunity to speak frankly with Jude in private.

"Jude, I need to apologize to you," she began, finding it more difficult than she'd expected, yet sensing the urgency. "Back when Rain was born, I felt so guilty and so responsible for losing the baby, that I wanted Rain for my own, like a surrogate. But that was no way to make it right. Sometimes I stole the affection she should have given to you. I tried to be her mother, for all the wrong reasons."

Jude closed her eyes momentarily and Bebe could see her medication was taking effect. Then her face drew up as if in pain, and Bebe almost called for William, but she spoke again with effort. "He said to do what I wanted (breath) with the baby." Tears ran from the corners of her eyes.

Bebe cast about for the meaning to her words, fearing the tenuous opening into her feelings would close. "You mean Rain's father?"

She nodded lazily.

"Who was it, Jude?"

She barely shook her head against the pillow. "He was no good father."

Bebe understood. Jude didn't want Rain to know who her father was because he wasn't a good father. She thought it was better not to know, than to burden Rain with that image of being unwanted.

"We had the right to decide." She took several breaths. "About our bodies."

Bebe waited.

"Mine betrayed me."

Then Jude drifted off to sleep, her breath fluttering. Bebe sat for a long time in the silence, listening to her shallow breathing, asking for mercy for this woman who birthed the daughter they shared. How different their lives would have been if Rain's father had loved her mother.

Bebe laid her hand gently on top of Jude's in farewell. As she was leaving, she noticed a small booklet with a pastoral scene on the cover lying on Jude's nightstand. Bebe glanced at Jude, then picked it up and flipped through to discover it was a collection of devotions from Scripture for people suffering with illness. It was slightly frayed and dog-eared. Jude's comments came back to her about the conversation she'd had with God, and Bebe hoped it meant she had found her peace.

She came out wiping her eyes and William put his hand on her shoulder. "It's hard," he said, pulling out his handkerchief.

"Do you think she'll remember when she wakes up?"

"Probably only the parts when she was most coherent."

He walked her to the door. "She wants to be cremated and her ashes scattered in the bay."

Bebe nodded. "Yes, she mentioned that."

"She's already arranged everything for a ceremony under the Golden Gate Bridge." He paused with the door open. "I don't know what went on over that Celebration weekend, but she came back and made her arrangements the very next day."

Bebe promised to keep in touch, and she left. In spite of her heavy loss, Bebe felt a lightness for having apologized to her and a freedom that Jude held no apparent grudges, which was ironic because Bebe's liberation was what Jude had fought for all along.

Chapter 26

Rain arranged for time off from work to stay with her mother. She could tell William was glad to have her help and companionship, and a chance to take a break from the situation when he needed to. Rain was even able to communicate to her mom how she wished the Celebration weekend had turned out differently, and take small steps toward mending their relationship.

On New Year's Eve, Rain watched the ball drop in New York on television and felt alone in the world. The crowd cheered and confetti snowed down on the streets. Outside the house, car horns blew and firecrackers popped. She picked up her cell phone and debated about calling Hayden. What if he wasn't alone? If he was at a party at that moment, he would never hear it ring, anyway. But he had called her on Christmas Day. He had made first contact—taken a risk. She scrolled down the contact list to his name, and pushed Send.

He didn't pick up, so she left a brief message wishing him a Happy New Year. A moment later, he called her back.

"Rain?"

"Hayden."

"Did you just call?"

"Yes, I left you a message. Just Happy New Year. That's all."

"Oh. Happy New Year."

A moment of silence followed, and she feared he would hang up. "I'm with my mom," she said.

"How is she?"

"I don't think she has much time left."

"Yes, I heard. I'm sorry."

"How did you know?"

"Neil phoned me. He's a good guy."

Silence hung like a veil between them. Rain wondered what they had talked about.

"Is there anything I can do?" he asked.

"No. But thanks. William is here. And there's a hospice nurse on call."

"Are you okay?"

If she were with him, if they were still together, she would have told him everything. "Yes, I'm okay. It's late. I should let you go."

"Thanks for calling."

"Wait—Hayden? We don't have to sell the house."

His voice was guarded. "Oh? What's happened?"

She realized he must think she didn't need it because she'd gotten pregnant. "Nothing. Nothing's happened. I . . . it's just not a good time, and it's not fair to make you sell it in a bad market."

"Well, if you're sure. If you don't need the money."

"I don't know what I need. But it's just not the time."

She gathered her courage. "One more thing." She took a deep breath. "Could you tell me . . . am I passive-aggressive?"

After a moment of silence, he stumbled. "Well, not . . ." He cleared his throat. "I . . . I guess you could say that sometimes—"

"It's okay," she interrupted. "You don't have to say any more. Latoya offered me a job promotion because of it. She thinks it's my defining characteristic."

She heard him put on his professional voice. "Passive-aggressiveness can be a valuable tool—"

"When working with attorneys?"

He gave a small chuckle. "Most definitely."

"Well, I wish I could say that's where I learned it, but we both know that's not true." She felt her inner calm slipping. "I'll let you go. I think I hear Mom."

"I wish you the best, Rain."

"Me, too."

After they hung up, she curled up on the couch with a blanket, not even bothering to go to the spare bedroom. The next morning, William woke her to say that Jude appeared to have lapsed into a coma and he'd called hospice. She lasted two more days, and on the third, Rain called Bebe at 5:00 a.m. to say that Jude was gone.

* * * *

Bebe called Toni and Mare and let them know that Jude had passed away, and that the cremation service was scheduled in two weeks in San Francisco. She warned Toni to wear flats.

Bebe stopped by Rain's unannounced to see how she was doing. She found her at the kitchen table sifting through a box of old photos. Bebe pulled out a chair.

"William found these in Mom's closet," she said. Her face was blotchy and red.

She pulled a photo out of the box and passed it to Bebe. In the picture, Rain sat on Bebe's lap with traces of icing on her face and in her hair. Jude stood in the background with her back to them. The long phone cord was wrapped around her waist and she cradled the phone at her neck.

"Your first birthday." Bebe smiled. "Toni took this one." Bebe was surprised that Jude had kept it.

"Here's another." Rain pulled out a photo of a very young Neil holding her in his arms.

"He looks so much like Dylan in this picture," Bebe said. "I never realized."

Rain passed Bebe a photo of her and Neil smiling for the camera. "Hayden called me."

Bebe looked up. "Oh?"

"On Christmas night. Just to say Merry Christmas."

"That was nice." Bebe tried to read Rain's thoughts, but Rain kept her eyes on the photograph.

"I called him on New Year's from Mom's."

"Well, that's a start."

Rain shrugged. "People get lonely around the holidays. He may be sorry we talked."

Bebe said, "I don't think so."

Rain glanced up and gave her a small smile. "You have to say that."

Rain sighed, studying the photo. "I wouldn't blame him if he was sorry. I've had such a complicated example of what two people should be like together. I've got Mom and William, and you and Neil. Mom telling me that marriage is surrender, doing everything possible to draw the line between her and William. You and Neil . . . you sort of blurred together."

"But we've each kept our own distinctiveness. We respect each other's differences and give each other space to be who we are."

"In all the years you've been together, didn't you ever want to call it quits?"

"No. Don't get me wrong, we've had our disagreements," Bebe assured her, "but nothing came up that we couldn't work out."

"Wasn't there ever a time when the two of you wanted something so opposite, that you couldn't agree? Who decided, then?"

Bebe thought about it. "That's never happened."

"Come on," Rain said, skeptical. "Someone had to give in at some point."

"Okay, I see what you mean. Basically, if it's something that Neil cares more strongly about, I don't fight it. And if it's something that I have a bigger stake in, he lets it go. Of course, that arrangement didn't come naturally. It developed over time as we learned to trust each other. Some things just aren't worth fighting over."

Bebe didn't want to alienate Rain, but she couldn't let the opportunity pass them by, so she pressed on.

"I think a marriage vow makes it a little more difficult to walk away when you disagree. You may be angry with the person, but if you hang around long enough, a solution might present itself, or you may see that it's not as big a problem as you first thought, especially if you both look to God for the answers. Of course, this is only my experience, but if Neil hadn't made a formal commitment to me, I think I might have held back a little. Maybe the intimacy and trust wouldn't quite have been there. And that would have made it easier to leave when we disagreed."

Rain looked thoughtful for a moment. "I don't know if that would have worked for us."

Bebe said, "You don't know until you try."

"Hayden brought up the subject once. We joked that if we got married and I changed my name, it would be Rain Coates." She tossed the photo back into the box and added thoughtfully, "I think he was serious about getting married, but I shut him down. I realize now I did that a lot."

She reached into the box, pulled out a picture of Jude in a pantsuit wearing aviator-style glasses and big bangs, and held it up for Bebe to see. "She would have made a horrible grandmother."

Bebe grimaced. "I have to agree with you on that." She studied Rain for a moment. "I saw a devotional pamphlet on Jude's nightstand the last time I was there."

Rain didn't look up from sifting through the photos. "The hospice nurse left it." She chuckled, with a shake of her head. "I walked in once to find Mom reading it. You would've thought I'd caught her reading someone's diary."

Bebe felt warmed by this knowledge. "Did she ever say anything about it?"

"No." Rain stacked some photos. "But she wouldn't have."

"Does Hayden know you're trying to have a baby?"

"Yes, but I've stopped taking the shots for now."

"Are you giving up?"

"It's a lot of money I don't have. And I'm tired of giving myself shots for nothing. I just have to . . . think."

Bebe tried not to let her relief show. Rain had so many other issues to figure out that rushing into raising a child alone would only multiply her problems exponentially.

Rain gathered the photos and shoved them back into the box, keeping two out. "I guess it's not just about the money. It's all part of how I was becoming like Mom. Controlling everything. Forcing my own way in situations without considering the consequences. Disregarding other people's opinions if they differed from mine. It's not right, and I need some time to take stock before I inflict any more damage." She pushed the lid onto the box. "It already cost me Hayden.

"There are just too many questions that I don't have answers for. Like, whether I have the right to deliberately choose a fatherless existence for a child. It may have been good for Mom, but it wasn't for me. And if I came up with multiples, they recommend that you do selective reduction and I don't think I could do that—not after the abortion."

She got up and placed the photo box on a high shelf, pushing it to the back. "Mom would say that I don't need Hayden. That I can make it on my own. And I could, but why would I want to if I had a choice? I mean, she may have needed to prove something, but I don't. And I don't really want to be without him."

Bebe said, "Sometimes people fight against the very thing they want or need the most. I think your mom really wanted to be loved and have security and share her life with someone. That's why she kept you. That's why she had a relationship with William. She just couldn't risk making herself vulnerable."

"Poor William. I hope he's happy now. He was gone more and more often the worse she got. I wasn't sure if he just couldn't stand being there anymore, or if he was stepping back and arranging for us to have some time for closure."

"Maybe a little of both?"

"Maybe."

"So did it help?" Bebe asked.

Rain studied the two photos she'd kept out without looking up. "Yes and no. I felt like I did everything I could to make her comfortable. I even apologized for blowing up at her, but she said it was probably all true and that was the end of it. I don't think I ever really made her happy."

"I know it seemed that way, but she was very proud of you."

Rain shrugged a shoulder noncommittally. "Did I tell you I'm signing over the house to William?"

Bebe smiled. "That's a wonderful thing to do, Rain."

"It's not my house, it belongs to him. Mom even said it was all right with her if I did." She considered, thoughtfully. "I never expected to hear her say that."

This was good news to Bebe. It was further proof that Jude's heart had softened. "Have you told Hayden about the cremation?"

Her countenance darkened. "There will be an announcement in the paper. If he wants to come, he can."

Bebe almost objected, but kept her thoughts to herself. She decided to see what Neil could do about getting him there.

Chapter 27

Bebe and Neil picked up Rain on the morning they were to scatter Jude's ashes. She looked somber, yet serenely beautiful holding Jude's ashes in her lap.

Bebe hoped that what she'd possibly set in motion wouldn't add to her discomfort or complicate the day further for her.

They drove to San Francisco, going out of the way to pick up Toni first because she hated driving in the city. She was dressed in a chic navy pantsuit with appropriate flats, and mentioned that she hoped Jude appreciated the sacrifice she was making since she'd used her last motion sickness patch on their Mediterranean cruise and was sure she would embarrass herself before the day was out if the bay was the least bit choppy.

They pulled into the parking lot of the charter company and spotted Mare's Prius. They pulled into a space beside her and got out. The others kept a lookout for William, but Bebe watched for a silver Expedition. Unfortunately, silver cars were everywhere. The day was sunny, but the wind whipped sharply, and she pulled her coat collar tight against her neck.

They walked together toward the dock and Rain checked in at the office. She said they told her everything was ready, and to let them know when her entire party had arrived. When William joined them, Rain hugged him and threaded her arm through his.

Bebe scanned the parking lot, hoping for just a few more minutes. The captain came out and asked if everyone was accounted for. Rain said they were, and Bebe frowned at Neil, who discreetly lifted his shoulders. Once more, she searched for a silver Expedition.

"Wait," Bebe said to them. "Just one more moment, please."

"Why? We're all here," Rain asked.

Then Bebe saw Rain look past her, and her countenance changed. Bebe turned to see a figure in a dark sports coat hurrying toward them. As he neared, he slowed as though he wasn't sure if his presence was expected. Rain handed Jude's ashes to William and walked out to meet him. They stood face-to-face, talking quietly, and then both walked back to the group. Bebe told the captain that they were all ready, and they boarded the boat.

The bay was choppy and ten minutes into the trip, Toni was positively green. She said it was Jude's revenge. They each said a few words in Jude's memory, and even Toni found something nice to say, although she had to swallow several times midspeech and clutched the rail tightly.

Bebe was so grateful that Neil was there, because the uncertainty of her last conversation with Jude left her feeling hopeful and remorseful at the same time. She wondered if people were ever truly at peace when they stood by the grave of a loved one. Was there something left unsaid? Was there more for which there were no words?

By the time the memorial was over, and Rain had released her mother's ashes beneath the Golden Gate Bridge, Bebe felt as bad as Toni looked. They returned to the dock and carefully disembarked.

Rain came over and hugged Bebe and Neil. "Thanks for being here with me today. I love you both." Bebe saw Neil wipe the corner of his eye.

"Hayden offered to give me a ride back, if you don't mind. We might stop for dinner."

Bebe tried to hide her satisfaction. "Sure, honey. We won't be stopping to eat, anyway." Toni looked up briefly from her seat on the curb. Her eyes were hidden behind dark sunglasses and her expression sagged in her pale face.

Everyone hugged, said good-bye, and went their separate ways.

Later that evening, Bebe left a message on William's answering machine to let him know they were thinking about him. She then checked on Toni to remind her that they were getting together on the following Saturday to work on the endowment fund. Lawrence answered and said that Toni wasn't yet among the living, and he'd pass the message along. Then he apologized that his comment had been in poor taste, but Bebe said she had spent the afternoon with Toni and that the description fit.

She called Mare next, who commented on what a beautiful day it had been and how Jude would have liked it. Bebe shared about her last conversation with Jude. She felt that Mare would understand the hope that she felt upon discovering Jude had read the devotional pamphlet, and how inadequate she had felt in the brief time she had at Jude's bedside.

"Bebe, Jude probably felt free to read it because she didn't really know the hospice nurse who gave it to her. Sometimes people will be open to a stranger before they'll listen to family," Mare pointed out. "Jude would never have admitted it to us if it had made a difference to her."

"I think, in her own way, she was trying to. She had voiced her doubts about God to me when we were at the aquarium, but she knew how to push my buttons and I let her get to me."

"I think Jude was open to the message in the pamphlet only because you sowed seeds all those years."

The Scripture verse about one man sowing and another watering came to mind, and Bebe felt comforted. "We can only hope." Bebe called Rain's house next to invite her to be a part of their project, but the phone rang until the answering machine picked up, and she smiled to herself and hung up without leaving a message.

❖ ❖ ❖ ❖

Rain felt both awkward and familiar in the passenger seat of the Expedition with Hayden at the wheel. Neither of them spoke as Hayden wound his way confidently through Bay Area traffic while they listened to smooth jazz on the radio. Rain discreetly surveyed the car's interior for signs of female occupants such as long blonde hairs, and noticed only a bit of candy wrapper in the door pocket. She resisted the urge to pluck it out and examine it for clues.

Hayden finally broke the silence. "I thought we'd head down to Half Moon Bay, if that's okay."

Rain's initial response was to ask why, but she caught herself. Did it really matter why? Instead, she answered, "Sure. That would be nice."

He glanced over at her and smiled. She smiled back, glad that she had fought the habit to challenge his plans and get started off on the wrong foot.

He listened as she reminisced about her mom, and how she felt for William. At times, the reality of the day came back sharply and her tears flowed. They spent a quiet afternoon wandering through shops and boutiques. She told him about the Celebration weekend fiasco and the fact that Jude seemed to be softening a bit toward the end of her life. He was curiously interested in the pamphlet that she'd caught Jude reading.

She noticed that he checked his watch several times, and she felt the day was slipping away from them. Was he bored or in a hurry to go back? Now that they were getting along so well, she didn't want it to end.

She glanced at their reflections in the shop window as they passed. He looked so handsome in his sports coat with his necktie casually loosened at his throat. It had been so long since they had spent more than an hour together, and Rain didn't want to be reminded of that evening that had ended so badly. She hoped this one wouldn't end in a smiliar way.

The evening fell quickly and the streetlights glowed into fullness. He checked his watch once more and finally said, "I hope you don't mind. I took the liberty of making a dinner reservation at a restaurant just down the way. Just in the event . . . just in case."

She put her hand on his arm. "It's fine. I'd love to."

They went back to the car and drove down the coast a half mile to the restaurant. Although it was dark, they could hear the waves crashing on the beach and see the ghostly white foam in the distance illuminated by the gas lamps on the patio and the bright moonlight.

They were seated at a table by the large windows with a small candle throwing intimate light into the space between them. After they perused the menu and the waiter took their orders, their conversation faltered. Rain sensed he had something on his mind, and her apprehension rose. She wondered why he had brought her there. Perhaps he had news of his own and wanted to sell the house, or buy her out. It was just like him to be kind enough to spend the day with her after her mother's funeral, and maybe he was having trouble finding the words to tell her he'd found someone else. She tried not to think of the beautifully tanned blonde from his Mexico pictures.

Twice over dinner, she looked up to find him watching her, and she would have been flattered except for the shadow of foreboding she felt.

After the waiter had cleared their plates they ordered coffee. Hayden scooted his chair closer to the table and smoothed his tie down. He cleared his throat and glanced at the people at the next table.

"Rain," he began, but the waiter appeared with two steaming cups, sugar and cream, and Hayden paused until he left again.

He continued. "There's something I want to talk to you about. A lot has happened since last July."

Rain's mouth went dry, and she spilled some sugar from the packet onto the tablecloth when she added it to her coffee.

"After I moved out, my brother let me stay with him until I could get a place of my own."

"Drake? But doesn't he live in Davis?"

"Yes. The morning commute was horrendous. Just the Yolo Causeway—" He raised his hand. "Never mind. The point is that I moved in with Drake and I went to church with him a few times. And after everything that had happened between you and me"—he flickered his eyes up at her—"I felt like I needed to get away. So I joined a work party to build a church in a little village in Mexico."

She waited, expecting the worst.

He flexed his hands and the look on his face was almost boyish. "I never knew it was such an incredible feeling to physically raise a building. And all the kids from the village came around every day trying to communicate with us. We took supplies to give out. It was a great experience. I posted some of my pictures on Facebook."

"I saw them."

Hayden looked surprised, but paused as the waiter appeared with her leftover salmon wrapped in foil in the shape of a swan, and left it, along with the bill.

"You sent me an e-mail with your new address," she explained. "Just before Christmas. You mentioned the pictures, so I took a look."

He nodded. "Oh, right. So, I've gotten to know some of the people at his church really well, and I've been going there ever since."

She waited, and when he didn't continue, she said, "That's nice," not sure where he was going with it.

He drew on the tablecloth with his fingernail, and then he studied her as he spoke. "And I started reading the Bible. I even joined a Bible study."

She blinked and dipped her head questioningly. "Are you saying you're religious now?"

"No, not religious." He glanced out the dark window where the ocean pounded the sand just yards away, appearing to search for words, and looked back at her. "It's more than that, Rain. I can't really explain it yet. I just know how I feel when I'm there and when I hear people talk about their experiences. How they feel a connection with God." He looked at her with intensity, and the expression on his face moved her. "I want that, too."

She didn't know what to say, what he was asking of her.

"And the other thing is that I don't like being apart from you, Rain. I miss you, and I was hoping we might give it another try."

Rain felt exhilaration rise within her, even though she was unsure how she felt about his new interest in church. "I've missed you, too," she said, and the thought of having him back in her life was sweet relief.

"Walking out like I did—that was no way to handle our differences," he said.

"You were right to leave, Hayden. You tried to tell me, so many times, but I just didn't listen." She felt tears prick her eyes. "I don't want to be like Mom."

He reached across the table and took her hand in both of his. "But there's only one thing."

She sniffed and looked up at him. "What's that?"

"We can't live together anymore. I won't move back in unless we're married."

Rain felt stunned. "But why not?"

He shook his head. "It's not right, Rain. I already talked it over with the pastor. If we're serious enough to live together, we're serious enough to commit to each other and do it right this time."

This was so totally unexpected, yet she sensed their relationship hanging in the balance, and resisted the urge to pull her hand from his grasp. She studied the dark hairs on his wrist and the small white scars from the scrapes he'd gotten on the back of his hand while building the church. She pushed aside her mother's voice in her head telling her that marriage was a trap and remembered what Bebe had said about trusting God for the answers. She and Neil had been happily married for many years, and Bebe didn't appear to be trapped in any way. On the contrary, it was her mother who had been bound by fear and Bebe who had enjoyed a fulfilled life.

Rain had released her mother that day, and she knew it was time to release some of the baggage that she had lived with for so many years.

Hayden gently caressed the back of her hand with his thumb. "After all, a baby should have a father." His eyes glistened. "What do you think?"

Rain knew their chances were slim for having a baby, but not impossible. And even if they didn't have a child, they could be happy.

"I think you'll make a wonderful father," she answered, smiling through her tears. "But it would be okay if it turned out to be just the two of us, wouldn't it?"

He brought her hand to his lips and planted a kiss squarely in the center of her palm.

❖ ❖ ❖ ❖

Bebe greeted Mare and Toni as she sat down at the small table across from them and plugged in her laptop. Toni jumped up when she heard the barista call, "I have a grande berry chai infusion for Toni."

She retrieved her drink from the counter. "Thank you, Mitchell," she said sweetly.

Mare glanced at her and said under her breath, "She never stops."

"Sit down, Toni, and quit flirting with the employees." Bebe pulled up an Internet site that Lawrence had suggested they check out as an example for their endowment fund.

Toni handed Bebe the paperwork she'd brought. "Here, Lawrence sent this 501(c)(3) information."

"Good. Rain said she would take care of this to make sure we were legal," Bebe said. "In the meantime, we can work on a website."

"I know a reasonable web design company. They did mine for about twelve hundred dollars," Mare offered.

"That's more than we've got," Bebe said. "I played around with a free website last night, just to see what I could do. We may have to create our own until we get some money coming in."

Toni said, "Oh, don't worry. Lawrence has decided to donate a little seed money to help us get started."

"That's great, Toni," Mare said. "Make sure you thank him for us."

She smiled devilishly. "Oh, I already have."

Mare waved to Rain, who was coming in the door. "Rain, over here."

She smiled at them and gave a little wave as she put in her order at the counter.

"My, doesn't our girl look happy these days," Toni observed.

Bebe said, confidentially, "Yes, very."

Toni cocked her head as though listening to music. "Do I hear wedding bells?"

Bebe lifted her eyebrows and raised her finger to her lips for secrecy.

Rain joined them with her drink and waited expectantly by the empty chair.

"Sit down, sweet—" Toni's eyes grew large, and she jumped to her feet and grabbed Rain. By that time, Mare had also noticed the diamond on Rain's left hand and jumped up to hug her. After the commotion died down, Rain pulled out the chair beside Bebe and kissed her on the cheek as she sat down.

"So I assume you already knew," Toni said, chastising Bebe playfully.

"Of course, I did. She and Hayden came straight from the jewelry store and we celebrated last night."

"No fair, holding out on us like that," Mare said.

"So when's the wedding? I have to go shopping," Toni said.

Mare began, "I just got in a shipment of—oh, never mind."

"It's in eight weeks. We were lucky to find a place for the reception that had a cancellation available. The wedding's going to be at his brother's church in Davis. It's a pretty building for a wedding. His pastor is going to marry us."

"So you've met the pastor?" Mare asked.

"Yes. Hayden started going there after he moved out, and I've started going with him, you know, just to check things out."

Bebe and Mare exchanged discreet, meaningful glances.

"Okay, enough wedding talk for now. Let's get started." Bebe turned the laptop so they could all get a glimpse of the screen. The words "Jude Rasmussen Memorial Endowment" ran in the banner and their names were listed in a block to the right.

Toni reached behind her to an empty table and dragged a chair over. "Here," she said. "This is for Jude."

Acknowledgments

My heartfelt gratitude goes to:

Writing mentors and friends Jan Coleman, Susan Gregory, Marty Reeves, and Laura Jensen Walker who first encouraged me to attend the Mount Hermon Writer's Conference. Also to my Novel Matters family Patti Hill, Bonnie Grove, Kathleen Popa, Sharon Souza, and Latayne Scott.

To Barbara Curtis, Julie Brockman, DVM, Tracie Vaillant, Stanley and Teresa Williams, Annette Smith, and Kristan Shabanov for generously sharing their experiences and professional expertise.

My agent Wendy Lawton of Books and Such Literary Agency, and to the wonderful staff at Moody Publishers who made creating this book a joy.

We hope you enjoyed *Raising Rain*. For discussion questions from this book, please visit debbiefullerthomas.com.

Tuesday Night at the Blue Moon

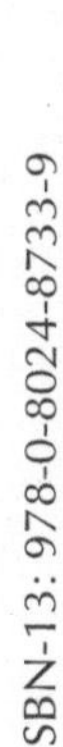

When Marty Winslow's daughter dies of a devastating genetic disease, she discovers the truth: her child had been switched at birth. Her actual biological daughter was recently orphaned and is being raised by grandparents in in an undesirable environment. Marty is awarded custody, but Andie refuses to fit into the family, adding one more challenge for this grieving single mom that pushes her toward the edge, and into the arms of a loving God.

For Andie, being forced to live with strangers is just one more reason not to trust God. Her soul is as tattered as the rundown Blue Moon movie drive-in the family owns. But Tuesday night is Family Night at the Blue Moon, and as her hopes grow dim, healing comes from an unexpected source—the hurting family and nurturing birth mom she fights so hard to resist.

1-800-678-8812 • MOODYPUBLISHERS.COM

THE MISSIONARY

David Eller is an American missionary in Venezuela, married to missionary nurse Christie. Together they rescue homeless children in Caracas. But for David, that isn't enough. The supply of homeless children is endless because of massive poverty and the oppressive policies of the Venezuelan government, led by the Hugo Chavez-like Armando Guzman.

In a moment of anger, David publicly rails against the government, unaware that someone dangerous might be listening—a revolutionary looking for recruits. David falls into an unimaginable nightmare of espionage, ending in a desperate, life-or-death gamble to flee the country with his wife and son, with all the resources of a corrupt dictatorship at their heels.

1-800-678-8812 • MOODYPUBLISHERS.COM